THE DEFENDER

THE PEACOCK THRONE

THE
DEFENDER'S
THRONE

by

Alessandra Woodward

RENAISSANCE
CREATIVE BOOKS

Edited by Jaquelin Cangro

Copyedited and Proofread by Iulia Marin
Map Illustration by Alessandra Woodward
Cover art by Alessandra Woodward
Cover Design by Lena Yang

A Renaissance Creative Book

www.alessandrawoodward.ca

ISBN: 978-1-7775979-0-0 (Paperback)
ISBN: 978-1-7775979-1-7 (Ebook)

First Edition August 2021, Canada

To the ha-mazaans in my life—friends, sisters, mothers.

You have shown me what courage is,

what sisterhood is,

what love is.

The World of
Ancient Ha-mazaans
Circa 1210 BCE

Dniester R.

Southern Bug R.

Dnieper R.

Gelonia

Tanais R.

Maeotian Swamp

Danube R.

Thrace

Zalapa Sea

Sinope

Themiscyra

Lygos

Galatae

Chadesia

Lykastia

Paphlagonia

Terme R.

Wilusa
(Troy)

Hattusa

Tigris R.

Aegean Sea
&
Achaean Lands

Euphrates R.

GLOSSARY OF NAMES

Aello (Aye-YEL-low)

Aife (EYE-fee)

Alkippe (AL-ki-pay)

Antiope (An-TIE-o-pay)

Anva (AN-va)

Arpoxais / Arpo (Ar-POX-ays / ARE-poe)

Asteria (Ah-STAIR-ia)

Camilla (Kam-ILLA)

Colaxais /Col (Coal-AXE-ays) / (Coal)

Cyra (SEE-ra)

Eri/ Erioboea (AIR-ee/ AIR-ee-oh-BOW-a)

Essri (ESS-ree)

Esten (ESS-ten)

Glaukia (GLOW-ki-a)

Heracles (HAIR-a-klees)

Hippolyta (Hipp-ALL-it-a)

Hipponike (Hip-PON-i-kay)

Ifito (Ih-FEE-tow)

Lampedo (Lam-PAY-doe)

Leandra (Lee-AND-ra)

Leya (LAY-ya)

Liopoxais / Lio (Leo-POX-ays / LEE-o)

Marpesa (Mar-PAY-sa)

Melanippe (Mel-AN-i-pay)

Mura (MUR-ah)

Otrera (Oh-TRAY-ra)

Phillipisa (Fill-i-PEES-a)

Pisto (PEES-tow)

Prothoe (PRO-thow)

Sagitta (Sag-EET-a)

Scoti (SCOTT-ee)

Sylviu (SILL-vee-oo)

Targitaos (TARG-i-ta-ows)

Tekmessa (Tek-MESS-a)

Thraso (THRAY-so)

*

PROLOGUE

My bow and arrows and the small blade I had been given for my tenth summer were farther away from me than they had ever been, lonely in the cave at the base of the mountain. I had slept there on the first two nights of my moon-blood, as was custom. In this way, my mother said, I would step into the wilderness as a girl, but when I emerged, like a she-bear from a winter's sleep, it would be as a woman, ready to face the world with courage and wisdom. As ha-mazaan. The Great Mother would protect me, my mother said. I should not need my weapons.

I was fairly sure she had been wrong.

Heat waves danced and obscured my vision when I looked up the steep steps to the dark cleft in the rock. The Womb of the Mountain. The opening appeared to fade in and out of existence, blinking closed like a sideways eye, luring me forward with its secretive wink. I hesitated far below it, the hairs on the back of my neck straining to stand on end, but they were firmly plastered to my skin with sweat and dust. My fingers twitched at my sides, itching for a spear or a knife. Anything would have been welcome to clutch other than the small sack of bird body and fistful of trepidation.

Squaring my shoulders and gripping the felted sack tighter, I shoved one foot in front of another up each narrow stone step, the centers of each so worn by the ravages of time that there were barely any edges to them, barely enough room for my feet to find purchase. The stone burned under my bare feet, forcing my reluctant steps to be quicker. If I had the choice, I would not be visiting the Oracle at high noon in the middle of the hottest summer anyone in Themiscyra could remember. But I did not have that choice. Every ha-mazaan must appear before the Oracle during her first moon-blood, as they had since the days of my grandmother's many-times grandmother. Today marked the end of twelve summers since my mother had whelped me under the old sycamore and three days since I had received the Great Mother's blood-mark as one of Her own. I was ready to serve Her. Eager—and also terrified—to hear of Her destiny for my life.

I was at the top before I felt ready, standing inside the shadow of the great cleft in the rock. Cool, honey-scented air wafted a gentle caress across my sweaty cheeks and throat. I cast one last glance over my shoulder. There was no sign of Themiscyra beyond the edge of the mountain, nestled on the banks of the great Terme. No signs of normal daily life going on as usual, while mine was inevitably, irrevocably altering with every step I took.

The thought excited me but also sent a frisson of fear down my spine. Today, I would learn the shape of my destiny as sister queen of the ha-mazaans, beside my cousin Penthesilea. It was what I had been born to do, but I was here to learn how the Great Mother would call me to fulfill that role. And now that I was here, I was anxious and more than a little sick to my stomach. But I was also ha-mazaan; courage flowed undiluted in my blood. I had been born to do glorious things.

I stepped over the stone threshold. A shaft of sunlight filtered down through the dome's fissures, acting as skylights high overhead, and though the sun was still bright at my back, it was very dark ahead of me. I was debating if I should blindly continue on into darkness when the shadows moved. A lithe, slender form, barely visible, slunk toward me. There was no mistaking what it was, even in the murky blackness.

A lioness.

I took an involuntary step back, the lumpen bag held in front of my chest like a flimsy shield, my breath hissing inwards through clenched teeth. The cat stopped. I wasn't sure if I could actually see the glimmering yellow of its eyes or if I was just imagining they were fixed on me, sizing me up for a meal. Fed to the Great Mother's lionesses was not how I had imagined dying.

The big cat turned on silent paws, her sleek, muscled flank rippling with power as she strolled away with all the aloofness befitting a queen. The breath I had been holding squeaked out of my lungs. There was barely time to draw in another when the cat stopped moving again. There, against the lightness of the stone walls, my eyes adjusted enough in the darkness to see the lioness looking at me over her shoulder. Looking...expectant. I took a tentative step forward, and the cat immediately padded forward again. I followed.

All I could see for a moment was the gently gliding tail, rounded at the tip and streaked to shimmering red gold with the bars of light falling from high overhead. Yet as we went deeper into the Womb, it did not seem as dark as it had moments before, when we were closer to the entrance. As though the walls were lit by flames set within, or the pink-white stone itself glowed and reflected its own light back to me again. Soon, my eyes adjusted enough, or the light increased, so that I could easily make out the svelte, tawny coat of the lioness ahead. Eventually, I could see beyond the rounded ears of the big cat to where the passage widened, stretching open into a cave-like room so bright that my eyes squinted at the sharpness.

We emerged into a cavern of light. It reflected everywhere, from walls that no human hand had carved but which stuck out sharp-edged and pointed in long spears of white and clear quartz. Cylinders of crystal and rock hung from the ceiling, and high above, great discs of hammered silver, more silver than I had seen in my whole lifetime, were suspended from the walls, positioned just so to capture the light from above and reflect it into a dizzying display of brilliance below. In the center of the cavern, a great fire burned. It glowed inside the bowl of a gold-rimmed stone cauldron, the flames leaping high and frenzied, the heat reaching me even from far away. I slowed as I emerged into the room, until I stopped completely, my mouth dropping open in awe.

The big cat stalked past the burning cauldron to fling her sleek body down onto a rug at the base of a stone chair, where a second lioness was already lying. The chair was more of a throne, made of the same quartz as the walls, though the sharp edges had been molded into softer curves. At the end of each armrest, two perfect replicas of the lionesses sat proudly, chins high and tails curled upward at the ribs. The seat and back of the stone chair were draped with the furs of snow leopards and antelope and a strangely striped black and white fur of an animal I had never seen.

On the throne sat a woman, and she was completely bare. Her hair twisted down in long black ropes, fixed at the ends with tiny bone beads, and falling over skin as red-black as the earth at the banks of a river. Her skin was marked darker still by tattoos on her cheeks, stomach, thighs, and arms. The roundness of her breasts was fecund and plentiful, bigger than I had ever seen on any ha-mazaan, her nipples round and thick and the color of the pomegranate seeds my mother was so fond of eating. Her shoulders were broad and strong, her belly round, and her hips settled over her thighs as honey might spill the edges of a jar. Her limbs seemed impossibly long; even seated as she was between the two stone lionesses, I could tell the woman was taller than any person I had ever seen. Taller even than the Hittite men who sometimes visited from the south. The amber of her eyes shone bright, matching well the stare of the lionesses, both of whom now watched me with half-lidded eyes from their cushioned resting place.

"Cyra, Daughter of Melanippe."

I nearly jumped clear of my own skin. The woman's voice was deep, powerful, alarming in its resonance within the cavern of crystal.

"Y-yes," I stammered, though it had not been a question. My mouth was too dry for anything more.

"Come forward."

I went, my steps small. I stood near the cauldron of fire, but not too near, lest the leaping flames singe my unbound hair. The heat was comforting against my skin of sudden gooseflesh.

"Matar Kubileya welcomes you," the woman intoned. Her voice was deep and smooth and firm as the stone at the bottom of a swiftly flowing river. "We, the Kebat Oracle, welcome you."

"Thank you," I managed, unsure if more, or any response at all, was expected.

Any of the bravado and excitement I had felt moments before leaked away as awareness of the moment set in. This woman was a First Daughter of the Great Mother. Mouthpiece of Matar Kubileya. Moon Mother, and Keeper of the Old Ways. Embodiment of Old Magic. She had already known me, known my name, before I came. There was nothing hidden from her sight.

The Oracle rose, gliding toward me as gracefully as the lioness, so tall that I had to crane my neck to meet her eyes when she came near. She brought with her a squat cup of silver in the same shape as the cauldron, plain and unadorned other than three small lion's feet at the bottom. She cupped it in both hands, dwarfing it with her massive fingers, and extended it to me with a smile that was neither friendly nor false. It was... knowing. I took the cup, the small sack forgotten in my other hand.

"Drink, Cyra."

I drank. It was neither *kimiz* nor water; the heady sweetness of honey and the sharp tang of fermented fruit blossomed on my tongue, filling my senses. Mead, but also more than mead. There was an aftertaste of something green and almost swampy. With one sip, the parched feeling was gone from my mouth, and I smiled tremulously back at the woman.

"All." Yellow eyes glinted down at me.

I drank the rest, not ungratefully, wiping my chin when I finished. The midnight-colored woman took the silver chalice again, turning away without another word and returning to the furs nestled on the quartz chair. I began to feel slightly light-headed, whether from the drink or the room or the occasion, I did not know.

"Cyra, Daughter of Melanippe," the Oracle repeated. "What is it you wish?"

"I—"

I was struck dumb for a moment. I had not expected to be asked what I wished. I had only ever heard the stories of those who were told the pattern their life would follow, the destiny set out for them by Matar Kubileya. The destiny that had been patterned for them by the Three Weaving Fates since the Weaving of the World had begun in the lap of the Great Mother.

I remembered the bag I held.

"I have brought a dove," I blurted. "Should I...would you like me to sacrifice it?"

The Oracle smiled again and shook her head, bone beads rattling.

"No, child. The dove shall whisper all in time. But first, you must tell me what it is you wish."

I stared, and the Oracle stared back. It seemed as though her eyes were pools of hardened sunlight, lit from within as the stone walls appeared to be, burning through my eyes and deep into my soul. I did my best not to shrink under the stare. My chin lifted. I was ha-mazaan.

"I wish to bring glory to the ha-mazaans when I am the Defending Queen." My words were strong, sure, unfettered by doubt. I felt proud and full of conviction.

The flames to the right of me leaped, high and almost exultant, and I flinched away with a gasp, arm half-raised to protect myself from sparks. None spilled from the cauldron. In fact, nothing came from the deep stone bowl at all—not even the crackling sound of fire eating away at wood. The blaze, big as it was, emitted no sound, gave no scent of charred oak or cedar or apple. And yet, the flames cavorted upward and licked at the pointed quartz columns of the ceiling, strong as a bonfire in the Moon Hall of Themiscyra's palace.

I lowered my arm, the frisson of cold fear I had felt earlier settling into my bones and chilling me to the very core.

"You speak your desire truly," intoned the Oracle. Her voice was expressionless, impartial. "Come, Cyra, Daughter of the mighty Melanippe. Release your offering, and I shall tell you the destiny of that which you desire."

My shaking fingers fumbled at the knotted cord of the sack. Stretching the opening wide, I reached in and then turned the woolen bag upside down, gently lifting it from the white dove. She sat frozen in the palm of my hand, her head tucked under her wing as though to shut out the glare of the fire. I felt a pang of sorrow, but this was what I had come to do. Unsure of what to do with the bird, I raised my arm and extended her away from me, toward the seated Oracle. The eyes of the lionesses glinted, no longer feigning sleep, but neither made a move toward the dove.

All at once, the dove realized the constraints had been lifted, and with a tiny prickle of toes against my palm, she launched from my hand into the air, flying directly toward the fire. Into the flames. She was incinerated the moment her wings touched the magic of the fire, without smoke or smell or feather or any trace that she had ever existed. It happened before I could even cry out, but I must have made a sound after all, as the call seemed to echo back to me from every part of the cavern. The towering shroud of the Oracle came into view on the other side of the cauldron. I had not seen her move from her throne.

"Step closer to the flames, child." Her voice was gentle, caressing. I sidled closer, fully fearful now. My thoughts were like the toys the *matars* carved for the small children in the palace, spinning and spinning on a sharp point. There was one revolving feeling in me, spinning tight around my thoughts. Dread. The way the bird had died felt wrong. Portentous, even, though I had not known what to expect. More blood and breaking of necks, perhaps?

The fire, hotter and more frenzied now that it had consumed blood, sent eerily quiet fingers of flame to kiss at my flesh until my cheeks became taut and painful and the black hairs of my lashes and brows curled with the heat. I did not flinch back. The Oracle, towering on the other side of the flames so that she appeared to stand among them, raised her arms high into the air and began to speak with a voice so loud and booming that it shuddered from the walls of the cavern. The lioness that had come to fetch me left her spot at the base of the throne and began to pace with listless intensity, trying to escape the sound.

"Cyra, First of her Name, but not the last.

"Never shall you rule in Themiscyra.

"Never will you share Themiscyra's throne with the seed of your mother's sister. The role of the Sister Queens shall die with Hippolyta and will not be reborn before your grandchildren's grandchildren have traveled back to the Great Mother's womb many times over.

"Never will your mother see you rule over any living ha-mazaan.

"You will be made queen after you bind yourself to a man. This man will sit by your side and be a king in his own right. His voice shall speak beside yours, over the ones you rule, and together you shall form a new path and a new Way. Many shall the children of your children be, daughters and sons spreading wide like the herds of horses they shall ride. For this legacy shall you be remembered.

"Cyra, beloved Daughter of Kubileya. The day comes when the Sisters are feared by all. They will be killed like the wild beasts and even forgotten. A time approaches when the ways of the Moon Mothers must go beneath the ground, with only the sacred life-blood that flows from the thighs of one generation to the next sustaining her secrets. You, Cyra, shall bear witness to a new way which no ha-mazaan has ever known. By your choice shall the Great Mother's Ways be kept, when otherwise they would be lost.

"Find, now, all that your soul truly longs for. See it before you," the Oracle swept her arms toward the flames, and I stared, terrified and transfixed.

There, the face and torso of a man, broad of jaw and shoulder. His hair was golden-red like a lion's mane, falling in waves to the edge of his collarbone, the stubble on his face tinged with dark rust. He smiled, his green eyes twinkling through the red of the flame, staring into mine as boldly and as piercingly as though he was not simply a phantom of the flames. His chest was bare, and in the center of it, the mark of a twisted beast in the style of the ha-mazaan's *rhu-tasiyas*. A mark forbidden to any man.

In a flash of bright flame, his face was replaced by the sun over a great sea of waving grass, the ends undulating to and fro with the breath of an eastern wind. I almost thought I could smell their seeds and the richness of the earth underneath. Upon the fields of green grazed a hundred, maybe even a hundred hundred horses, as many as the stables of Themiscyra had seen in three generations. Their hides shone black, white, chestnut, and golden under a rising sun, and their manes lifted as a wave with the wind. One chestnut with long white socks on each leg raised its head from the grass and pricked its ears as though seeing me. Recognizing me. In the sky, an eagle circled higher and higher toward the burning sun. I heard it scream and thought it was the sound of my name I heard in its cry.

Again the image wavered, shimmering like the steps had on my way into the shrine. Where every horse had been stood a woman, sometimes two. Each of them wore a belted tunic like the one I wore, but with strangely colored trousers underneath and leather boots over top. They wore the leather armor of ha-mazaans, as well as swords and bows, and some carried the traditional crescent moon axe of our people. But when I peered closer, I saw that not all were women. Men stood amongst them, dressed identically in all ways so that you could barely tell one from another. Could not tell man from woman.

"Hail, Grandmother," a voice echoed from the cauldron, but it was the voice of many, not just one. I jerked back in surprise. Then the people were gone, swallowed by the flames as the man's face had been. When the images disintegrated, the flames shrank into themselves, diminishing in height and brightness until they barely licked the top of the cauldron. I stared dumbly at the small, feeble fire, and then at the Oracle.

"Cyra, Daughter of Melanippe. Have you seen what is before you?"

The Oracle's voice was flat, no longer booming, but the double meaning was there.

"I..." my tongue was swollen, and something seemed to be gripping the inside of my throat, constricting it. Hot tears boiled from that tightened place and erupted out of my eyes, scalding my cheeks and my pride. The heavy weight of the Oracle's message settled over me. Confusion and grief warred in my breast.

"I don't understand!" My thoughts jumbled, and I struggled to bring any sense to them, but the words began to tumble out of me.

"Why will I not rule in Themiscyra? I am to be *Ishassara.*" A terrible thought struck me. Anger sparked, then flared. "I will not abandon

Themiscyra and the Ways of my people to be married to a cretin in some other land! We bind ourselves to no man. It is Law. And I don't *want* children." I heard a tinge of hysteria in my voice, but it was all pouring out too quickly to change my tone. "It is my *right* not to enlist with the *matars*. It is Penthesilea who will be Hearth Queen. It is supposed to be *her* duty to whelp children for the throne. And now you are saying I must be a *matar* and a *wife* in order to be queen? Are you saying that I will...that I will..." the words were too much. My hand waved frantically at the flames, now shrunken and unimposing, where the vision of the green-eyed man had been seared into my inner eye. I could not accept what I was hearing. Even if I didn't understand the whole vision, I understood enough to know it was not what I wanted.

"You shall bind your fate with a man and bear children together, and they shall spread across the seas of water and grass. Your daughters shall be priestesses with no fixed altars, but through them, the flame of the Great Mother will be kept burning. But you shall never reign beside Penthesilea. This is your destiny, and Great it shall be."

Great? I almost laughed, a bubble of hysteria rising. I would abandon Themiscyra? I would rule as queen only if I tied myself to a man who was already king? I would be forced to bind myself to some brute and whelp his children? Ha-mazaan queens did not take husbands. It had not been done for generations, for the good of our people. To take one as queen... to claim one would be king... it would be treason and a betrayal of the very foundation our lives were built upon.

"No." The word was a snarl as much as a cry. "*No!*"

I turned and raced from where I had come, past the startled lioness and into the darkness of the passageway. Somehow, I found my way, the great oval of the entrance flashing into view in just seconds, and I was across the cavernous entry and out into the searing heat, down the steps two, three at a time, almost stumbling after one hasty jump, but I didn't care if I broke an ankle. I didn't care if I tumbled head over heels into the canyon or if the bracken along the rock walls scraped the bare flesh from my running legs. I didn't care.

I only cared that I, Cyra, the daughter of mighty Melanippe, was destined to betray the sacred identity of my people.

I ran down the mountain path without care or thought for anything other than leaving this knowledge behind. Rocks turned to loam, and shrubs to pine trees, and the sharp dry needles from the trees stabbed at my bare feet. I barely noticed. I simply ran. I ran until I could not breathe, and then I ran slower, but I did not stop running. The farther I ran, the less the prophecy settled on my shoulders. Or so I felt.

By the time I reached the cave, all of my tears had been cried. I wrenched the bow over my shoulders and forced the quiver's belt buckle into place with an overzealous tug. I was not about to let some dusty Oracle in some dusty shrine tell me what my destiny would be. I *would* be queen in Themiscyra, as I had been born to be. Not a *matar*. I would be a warrior, like my mother and her mother. Not a wife. I would be the greatest warrior Themiscyra had ever known. I would be the Defending Queen.

I slid my dagger into its sheath on my arm and set off toward home.

I would make my own destiny; prophecies be damned. And if any man tried to take the throne from me, or even with me, he would feel the cold edge of my blade in his belly.

PART I

THEMISCYRA

CHAPTER 1

THE ARRIVAL

___

The ships came on the eve of my twenty-first birthday. Sluggish and limping upriver from the bay, they gave the scouts ample time to sound the horns and the Savaran more than enough time to prepare a welcoming host of archers and mounted warriors. I watched the ranks of riders and infantry gather along the riverbank from the shadowed safety of my chambers, fuming.

Tomorrow, I would graduate into the Savaran. Tomorrow, I could have ridden with them, proud and ready. Today, I was simply a Xanharaspa, youth cavalry, and as my mother had gratuitously reminded me before heading out to lead the army, about to be sworn in as heir to the Defender's throne. Too risky when we did not know their purpose, she had assured me.

I had been disqualified from defending my own city, my own inheritance, by the measure of one day, and also an entire lifetime. A lifetime of rules, protocol, and my mother's strict adherence to the Way.

I peered down from my window and found my mother's muscled, tall frame in the crowd. It gave me someone to focus the weight of my scowl upon. Melanippe was at the front of the host, conferring with the queens. Anyone might have thought it was me riding the horse, at least from a distance, though her skin was sun-darkened more than mine could ever be, and more heavily tattooed. But we had the same silver eyes and raven hair, and our shoulders were often set in the same proud square against the sky. Sometimes, I felt we were towering over other ha-mazaans, though we were only a few inches taller than most. Many times had visiting ha-mazaans from our sister cities, or traders from east and south, remarked at how we looked like two shadows of the same self.

I wondered if they actually saw me like I saw her. Sometimes, when she moved, I felt like I was watching a panther prowl in the night, and I saw it now, though the evening sun blazed full on her dark skin. The long black rope of her hair was a shaft of midnight between the sunset of Hippolyta's braid and the golden dawn of Antiope's. Her skin was like an acorn, where theirs was fair and aureate. A black horse between palominos. Three sisters, each from different fathers, and who could not have been more opposite in appearance or personality, and yet all of them had been immediate and resolute in their decision forbidding me to be on the beach for the arrival of the ships. One was a general, two were queens. All were formidable in their own way. What say had I against such forces?

I fumed harder at the window, my bow and quiver slumbering in the corner, taunting me. I flipped my star-forged dagger carelessly in the air, spinning it higher and higher and catching it by the handle as it fell. I found myself almost willing my fingers to catch it by the blade and move some of the sharpness my soul felt into something tangible. Something treatable. But my skin never felt the blade, and I soon grew bored of that game. I sheathed the knife in the pocket of my arm guard and pressed my hands on the warm pink rock of the window ledge, leaning my face into the slanted evening sunlight. I breathed in the warmth of it, letting it soothe some of the frustration as it warmed my tight throat and heavy chest. A knock sounded.

"Who is it?" I said curtly.

"Eri."

She swung the heavy wooden door open before I could welcome or deny her, and I turned to watch her stroll into the room. Her long legs were still dusty from our earlier training with the horses, and her red hair was darker still at the tip of her braid, where some of the blood from our fight had crusted into the folds of the plait. I bit my lip and met her blue eyes with an apologetic grimace.

"How's the arm?"

"Only a few stitches," she shrugged. "Marpe is not gentle with a needle, though. Next time, I will visit a *zizenti*. They probably scold less."

"Probably," I said and looked again at the thin line that ran down her left bicep, six painful-looking stitches intersecting the length in a neat ladder of knots. Now that it was clean and tended, it did not appear as bad as when I had seen it blossom under the tip of my careless sword, splitting apart as easily as a ripe strawberry.

She joined me at the window, leaning her hip against the edge and pushing her fair skin into the same beam of light I had been enjoying. The evening sun highlighted the blue veins that spidered under her translucent skin. She looked delicate, almost, but I knew it was a complete illusion.

"Sorry," I repeated, though training injuries were a daily occurrence.

"We both know you would never have touched me if Aunty Nightmare had allowed me to use my axe rather than a spear."

"True," I nodded. "But my mother is not one to listen to what she considers excuses. I also wouldn't have cut you if Risa had not shied at the last minute." I chewed at my lip as I thought of the upcoming Trials and the trouble I was having with the horse. "I am less and less sure the mare is the one I wish to complete my Savaran Trials with. I would almost—"

"Look," Eri interrupted, drawing my attention to the river below. "I can see the dark sails. Prothoe said their ships were all black, but I hardly believed her."

We looked to the inky water sparkling with diamonds of light as the last of the sun reflected on the surface. Three dark ships inched toward the docks like bloated beetles, their legs crawling forward in eerie unison. Their flanks were scaled with round shields of bronze hung from the ship rails, flashing brightly against the dull, bitumen-coated hulls. Their wings of black hung slack and lifeless in the still summer air, and from this distance, silhouetted against the lines of armored ha-mazaans on the bank, they appeared as unthreatening as any bug, ready to be squashed if they dared show their fangs.

An expectant hush had fallen over the gathered host, even though there were upward of two hundred women gathered along the shoreline. The buzz of preparation, the clatter of spears and swords, the shouts of instruction and stamping of impatient horses had faded into a focused calm. Even those still within the palace, whether they were Crafters or Xanharaspa or ha-mazaans whose joints ached with age and no longer wished to fight, waited for the newcomers with a heightened vigilance that smothered the normal sounds of life into an eerie, expectant silence. All attention was given to the arrivals to determine whether they were friend or foe.

My mother sat astride Zanas at the front of the Savaran, like a centaur made from different shades of black. Hippolyta, as Themiscyra's Defending Queen, stood on the mound of rock that formed the docks with her palomino mare at her back, her half-moon axe still secured to the belt between her shoulder blades, and her fingers slack at her sides. She stood above the small reed boats and the larger wooden skiffs the ha-mazaans used for fishing, though none of those were big enough to venture further than the wide bay where the Terme emptied itself into the sea. As the ships came closer to the queen and our own fleet, their dark bug-bodies no longer seemed so small, or perhaps Hippolyta did not appear as formidable.

Antiope, Hearth Queen, stood near my mother's horse. Her axe was also sheathed, but she held her bow and a notched arrow loosely before her body, ready to draw. Most of what I had learned of helping an arrow find its mark had come from her wise council. Between the three sisters, I did not doubt they could take on any intruder to our city, but the fact that I was disqualified from being at their side right now was more galling than I could say. I crossed my arms, trying to keep my clenching fingers from betraying my frustration.

"There are a lot of them," Eri said. She was still looking at the ships, but she meant what was inside of them.

Every oar was manned. I counted at least fifteen oars on one side of the first ship, making thirty rowers. Ninety or more possible enemies. *I should be on that beach*, I fretted and shifted against the window again. Two men stood on the prow of the first ship, on either side of the carved wooden wings of the griffin figurehead, whose feathered chest cut through the water with each plunge of the black oars. I shivered, the hackles on my neck rising to see their grimacing smiles.

"Look at their arms," Eri said.

I glanced at her and curled my lip.

"Nothing wrong with appreciating a well-made man," she said lightly, not taking her eyes from the men. "The tall one looks as though he was sculpted by Ares himself. He is huge."

"Are you also noticing he wears the head of a lion as a hat, Erioboea? And a sword on his hip? That both of them have weapons?"

"Fetching."

I scoffed in disgust. The oars had stopped, and the first galley rocked gently against the current as it turned into the dock. Hippolyta gestured, but she was too far away to hear any words. There were no arrows spearing the air from ship to land. No flash of bronze swords, to be met with our army's star-forged iron. I did not know whether to be disappointed or gratified that they seemed to be coming in peace rather than war. I had been almost energized by the possibility of a real fight, even if I was forced to watch it from the safety of my tower like some feeble, pathetic grandfather.

One of the men swung himself by the beak of the griffin to land on the rock in front of Hippolyta. His golden hair shone in the bronze sunlight, like the mane of a lion, though it was the other who wore an actual lion skin. Eri gasped softly, and I slanted another irritated look at her. She stared at the man in front of our queen, her lips parted in astonishment and her eyes round as the shields lining the edge of the ship.

"Seriously?" I said with scathing disapproval.

Eri ignored me. The first man knelt in front of Hippolyta as the second man jumped down from the ship. The lion pelt caught the wind of his leap and flung its legs out, wrapping around him as he landed so that it looked like he was being swallowed in the embrace of a still-hungry beast. Antiope appeared beside Hippolyta, stepping up onto the stone platform, and both men knelt before our queens with their heads bowed and their swords safely sheathed. When they stood, the four of them gripped each other's forearms in welcome, golden cuffs meeting golden cuffs in a gesture of peace.

"I suppose your initiation to Ishassara is going to go ahead after all," Eri said, crossing her arms.

I raised my eyebrows at her. "Was there talk of it not?"

"If that had turned ugly," she uncrossed one arm to point down to the shore again, "I don't think anyone would have been focused on your birthday, Cyra."

I frowned in indignation, a bit hurt by her tone. The second and third ships docked, and hewn logs were slid to the shore as walking planks. Men dressed in short, once-white tunics, some with their chests gleaming bare and wet with sweat, began to clamber slowly and carefully onto the shore, tying ropes from their railings to the hooks drilled into the rocks. My mother approached them on horseback, her axe laid casually across Zanas' withers. She spoke to them briefly, most likely giving commands for where to unload whatever trade goods they brought, although they did not look like any of the regular traders who came to our shores.

"It's not about my birthday," I said after we had watched in a silence that began to feel uncomfortable. "It's about finally being Savaran."

"And proving you deserve to be Ishassara."

"That is only a formality," I said dismissively, but my stomach clenched. I pushed away an intruding memory of a soundless fire and the Oracle's booming voice cursing me.

"Yes," Eri agreed, after a short pause.

"Are you not excited about our Trials tomorrow?" I asked, curious. Both of us, along with four other Xanharaspa, were scheduled to compete in the Trials of initiation to prove ourselves ready as Savaran. We had worked toward this day for years, since entering the youth cavalry at fifteen. Now, we could finally prove ourselves as ha-mazaans. I had thought Eri would be just as excited as I was. I knew for certain she had been just as irritated at not being allowed to join the Savaran on the beach. Then again, we would end the Trials by testing our skills against each other, and even though we had fought each other in the practice yard since we were old enough to heft a long stick, the idea of possibly blocking my closest friend's path to Savaran did not bring me any pleasure. Perhaps she felt the same apprehension.

"I am going to find Anva and make sure she keeps away from these visitors," she said, avoiding my question and spinning away from the window. She strode to the door and cast a quick look over her shoulder, more in my general direction than directly at me. "See you at the Trials tomorrow?"

"Yes," I said, watching her go. When the door shut behind her, I turned back to the scene along the river. The banks were crawling with men now. They were milling with the infantry and foot archers, while the Savaran rode between them, bows and weapons holstered once more. The queens walked toward the palace with the two men, already appearing to be on agreeable terms. My mother rode Zanas along the shoreline, her head turned to the water and the ships, but they were empty and lifeless, bobbing in the gentle sway of the current.

My eyes were pulled back to the figurehead on the first ship. The griffin's chest slapped against the water, its forelegs extended in hungry, grasping talons as they dipped in and out of the small waves. Its beak was wide with a silent scream, as though it saw the exposed back of a horse running beneath it and was ready to rip at its spine. My hackles rose further in an almost painful prickling, and I turned away from the window, not sure what to do with the feeling.

)(

"Achaeans. A king and a hero of their lands, so they say, though what they are doing here in Themiscyra is yet to be determined," Sagitta said. "Antiope has invited them to the celebration dinner tomorrow night since it was too late this evening to prepare a proper welcome for them." She twisted a stream of water from her long blonde hair back into the steaming pool and began to comb her fingers through the long strands. "They will camp on the beach while they stay, apparently. But you will be glad to know Melanippe decided against them attending the Trials."

I scowled at her through the steam. The water was hotter than usual, especially where it was bubbling up through the cracks in the stone beneath our feet.

"The Trials? Why would that have even been a discussion? Surely it was not a consideration?"

Sagitta shrugged and then stood to wade through the waist-deep pool toward the linen towels at the far end. She climbed up the steps and began to briskly dry her skin, removing the last of the day's grime. I followed her and did the same.

"Are you ready?" she asked, glancing at me. Her dark blue eyes showed more curiosity than concern. "For your Trials?"

"I think so," I said, tipping my head from side to side. "For the weapons portion. And my own skills portion."

"But?"

I hesitated, scrubbing at the skin on my arms where the tattoos of my moon-marks swirled in black bands against the olive tones of my skin. I looked at Sagitta's fresh tattoo of her *rhu-tasiya*, high on her left hip and only visible when she was naked, unlike many of the other ha-mazaans, who placed their *rhu-tasiya* in prominent, visible places. But then again, Sagitta was often naked, so the tattoo was often visible exactly where it was.

"But I don't think Risa is the right horse for me," I said finally.

"You do not need your *rhu-tasiya* for the Trials, Cyra," Sagitta said, following the direction of my gaze. She put a hand over the mark affectionately before reaching for her clothes.

"I know. But I don't trust her. And she doesn't trust me. She looks for apples from my hand, and that's all she seems interested in from me. Or anyone. She prefers little girls and treats to cavalry games."

"Then you will be deducted points for your training abilities and perhaps a few missteps. I am sure it will not be bad enough to disqualify you from the Savaran. I have seen you train with her, Cyra, and it is not so dire as you believe. The mare is good enough. It is yourself you must trust."

I shrugged into my tunic, wishing I had brought a fresh one for the walk back to the central palace. Both of us would have walked back naked from the bath house on a warm night like this if not for the ninety men directly on the other side of the city wall. It would be far too uncomfortable to buckle a sword belt on a naked waist, and I wasn't about to walk by them unarmed.

"I would rather not be deducted any points. Ha-mazaans, and the queens, and *especially* my mother, are going to be judging me a lot more critically than they will be any of the other women."

"Yes, they will be," Sagitta said, not offering me any apology for the truth. Taking up her silver-tipped axe like a walking stick, she followed me out of the narrow stone doorway, ducking her head as I did to not crack it against the lintel.

I raised my eyes to the ripening moon, full in two day's time. The night air felt cool against my still-hot skin, but the sounds of men around their fires on the other side of the low stone wall interrupted any peace the night might bring. The cacophony of male chatter set my teeth on edge.

"You should not worry overmuch about what any of the ha-mazaans think or why they will be more critical of you," Sagitta said. "You are one of the best, Cyra. Show them that, and you will have nothing to worry about."

I smiled at her. "Thank you, Sagitta. It will be an honor to compete against you tomorrow."

"It will be I who have the honor, Ishassara," Sagitta said, clapping a hand against my shoulder.

I huffed a short laugh at her. "Careful. If Risa lands me in the dirt and I cut someone's arm off by accident, there will be no swearing-in ceremony on the full moon, and then I will not be your Ishassara."

Her chuckle was low and amused. "I can't imagine an Ishassara being dis-inherited from the throne on such a technicality," she said. "But I hope it is not my arm you cut off if that is how you plan on abdicating your destiny."

Her grin was white with reflected moonlight in the darkness as she teased me, but I could not return her smile.

You will never be Queen in Themiscyra...

I shook my head. I could not think of the Oracle's curse. My supposed destiny. Not now.

"I will see you tomorrow," Sagitta said as we came to her small adobe hut outside the palace. "Rest well."

"Thank you. You too."

I made my way to the inner palace and up to my chamber, next to my mother's rooms. Outside the window, the fires of the men camping along the riverbank lit up the night like stars fallen from their places. I went to sleep with their light burning in my mind far brighter than it should have.

My sleep was filled with strange smells of bitumen and black earth reddened by blood. Green eyes flashed into my view and disappeared again in the way of dreams, and though the sight of them brought my soul peace while I slept, when I awoke, the memory of them made me feel disjointed and angry.

Today was my Trials. There would be no room for Oracular curses or mistakes of focus. Today, I would become Savaran, and tomorrow, I would be crowned as worthy to be Ishassara.

CHAPTER 2

THE TRIALS

"Your last drink as Xanharaspa, Cyra. May the Great Mother bless your Trials with the strength of a lioness, the speed of a mare, and the cunning of a serpent."

Tekmessa handed me a waterskin, and I took it gratefully, downing the cool, slightly musty water in a few long swallows. The *zizenti* wiped the sheen of sweat on her bald head while she waited for me to finish, smearing it across the blue-lined tattoo pointing down her forehead. I almost envied her lack of hair on a day like today. I smiled my thanks at her before she moved to Eri's side of the pavilion, the priestess' long red linen robes trailing in the dust. She offered my friend the same waterskin with the same words of ritual.

The pavilion was mostly here to offer the horses shade, but I was thankful Eri and I could wait for our starting times away from the heat of the sun. Only Asteria and Phillipisa had completed their Trials so far. The second pair, Prothoe and Leya, were in the forest now, working together to complete their tasks before they would race each other to the finish line and ultimately test their weapon skills against one another. If both managed to keep their weapons and remain standing by the time the sand-clock drained and the horn sounded, both would graduate into the Savaran. Then it would be my turn, together with Eri. I grinned at my friend as Tekmessa moved on, and she returned her own sideways smile.

"Waiting is the worst part," she said, shading her eyes to see the hill where the ha-mazaans would appear.

"I would rather fight my own mother in the practice yard every morning than have been picked to compete last," I agreed.

My stiff leather vest creaked as I bent down to adjust the long straps of my sandals, tightening them around my calves. I thought one last time about removing them. I preferred to feel the earth under my feet, especially when fighting hand-to-hand combat. To plant my toes in the dust and know the Great Mother's Hand cupped my arches and would spring me into the air when I needed it. Even the thin leather of the sandals felt like they hindered my steps. Constrained me. But the rules were clear; all armor must be worn, including helmet, trousers, and footwear. Sandals at minimum, though boots were preferred and strongly suggested.

I would not put boots on when the sweat was already running in narrow rivulets down my back, under my breasts, and along the inside of my thighs. The trousers were standard chevron-marked linen and stuck to my skin with the heat, but it would have been much worse if I had chosen the thicker protection of wool and leather. Even Sagitta had raised her eyebrows when I refused the thicker pair, but I would rather feel unbound and supple than protected and suffocated. The point of the Trials was not to be maimed before we had even gone to war, Sagitta had reminded me. It was simply to test our skills in combat and horsemanship and prove we were ready to face any battle ahead of us. But I had chosen the lighter sandals anyway, despite Sagitta rolling her eyes at me.

Risa snorted and shoved her head against my back until I gave in and scratched her along her braided mane. Her eyes closed to half-mast, reveling in the pleasure. I moved to scratch along her black withers when the pounding of hooves echoed over the brow of the hill. Eri and I both stepped forward to see more clearly, and my pulse began to race with the excitement of it. Eri's breath whooshed out when the horse and rider came into view, the horse sweating on the chest but still running hard.

Leya, long lance held low at the horse's shoulder and her teeth bared in a grimace of determination to reach the final battlefield before the sand-clock disqualified her. We were given two turns of the sand clock to leave the battlefield after our first fight, complete our tasks, and return to face our partner, hence her breakneck speed. Leya whipped her head around to look for the other rider. Prothoe appeared over the hill, her horse eating at the ground with furious hooves.

Leya and the mare flew past the posts and into the oval battlefield. She circled the mare in a wide arc around the shields on the ground and leaned far over the side of her horse, scooping a wicker shield from the dirt just as the second rider crossed the line. Prothoe, her short sword gripped in her right hand and her nearly white braid dirty with grime and sweat under her helmet, grinned at dark-eyed Leya and then whooped as she leaped from her horse to land next to the remaining shield. She grabbed it, shoving her arm through the straps. Leya slid down the side of her mare, and both ha-mazaans slapped the flanks of their horses to start them trotting in a wide circle. Once the horses were cantering in their well-trained pattern, the two women met in the center of the field.

Prothoe raised her sword, and Leya twirled the spear above her head like it was a slender twig, making the shaft almost disappear in a whirl of wind. When she brought it down, Prothoe's shield was there to block it. Prothoe stabbed with her blade, but Leya was not where she had been, and the blade met air. They fought back and forth, just as in rehearsal, but with far more fatigue, I could tell. Whatever Trials they had encountered had already taken much out of them. Still, they were well-matched, though Prothoe was much taller and broad of shoulder than delicate Leya. That was why Leya had chosen the spear over sword, to give added reach. And what Leya lacked in brute strength, she made up for in lithe speed, so Prothoe was wise to not count her own height as any advantage. The two women parried and thrust, danced forward and pirouetted back, while their horses circled around the perimeter, watching and listening for their imminent summons, and the sand-clock emptied itself on its high stand. By the time the horn sounded in a long blast, signaling the end, both of the women were caked with sweat and dust, but both of them were also standing, weapons in hand, and their horses ready to command. They had both completed their Trials successfully and were no longer Xanharaspa. More importantly, they would not have to wait another two years to compete in the Trials, had they been disqualified, which was my own fear. If either Eri or I were disqualified, whether by technicality or outright failure, one would go on to Savaran, while one would remain an apprentice in the youth cavalry, and our days would be spent in completely different worlds. And if I did not graduate today, my Initiation as Ishassara would be postponed, and the Oracle's curse would have even more room to gain a foothold.

I cheered along with the rest of the watching ha-mazaans as the last

of the horn faded into the midday air, and my mother led the tired ha-
mazaans, now officially Savaran, off the field. My mouth was suddenly
dry, either from cheering or nervousness. I looked over at Eri. She was
tightening the belt against her ribs, shifting the golden-etched axe, a
recent gift from her mother, between her shoulder blades so that it
rested there more comfortably. I twitched a finger against my own
sword at my hip, feeling the ivory handle of it with my thumb.

The bugle of the ram's horn shuddered through me, and Risa startled
at my shoulder.

It was time.

I put a soothing hand on the mare's neck and took a deep breath.
With a click for her to follow, I walked forward into the heat of the sun,
my helmet underneath my arm and the stiff horsehair crest tickling me
through the armpit of my tunic. Eri walked out at the same time, and
both our horses, black hides glistening, followed close behind without
us needing to touch their leads. Toward us came Alkippe and Ifito on
foot, one with a sword and one with an axe. Another trill of nervous
apprehension snaked down my spine. Alkippe was my mother's captain.
Ifito was head of the infantry. Both of these women were among the
best fighters in the city and had not fought yet today.

As I walked, I scanned the far pavilion where my mother had
returned to stand with the queens. The sisters watched in solemn
silence, dressed in their finest armor for the occasion. Hippolyta wore
her thick studded belt, gifted to her by my grandmother, Otrera, and
Antiope stood with her bow slanted across her back. Melanippe's axe
glinted behind her head. I thought perhaps my mother smiled at me,
but I could not be sure it wasn't a trick of the heat. I raised my arm in
her direction anyway and tried to swallow the feeling of dread that had
begun to push bile into my throat. If there was any time I could not let
my mother down, it was today. This meant as much to her as it did to
me, I knew.

When the four of us met in the center of the field, I nodded formally
to each of them, Alkippe first, then Ifito, then Eri. They returned the
gesture with solemn respect, and we all donned our helmets. As one,
we turned and bowed to the queens and to our general. Another ha-
mazaan stepped forward from the edge of the arena and took Risa's thin
rein, trotting away with her. Another took Eri's horse, until both were
led away out of sight.

I drew my sword as Eri's back pressed against mine. In this test, we would defend each other and prove our ability to fight as a team. We circled back to back, Alkippe and Ifito circling with low, sideways steps around us. Ifito blocked out the sun; her body was so big. Her arms were almost the size of my legs, and I was not dainty by any measure. Alkippe's axe was double-bladed, like Eri's, and my short sword felt paltry and thin in comparison. The helmet pressed stiflingly hot against my head, and sweat dripped down the back of my neck.

"Ready?" Eri said from my back, her voice tight but eager.

"As—"

The horn blared.

Ifito's sword swung for my head before the sound had even registered, but my body reacted before my mind. My sword flashed over my head to block the blade, pushing it away. Then Ifito was moving from my sight, and it was Alkippe's axe lashing out at my waist. I parried, grunting, and made a strike of my own toward her thigh. She blocked it easily, but the circle turned, and now Ifito lunged so that I had to bring my sword between her blade and Eri's shoulder. I felt the wind of Eri's axe and registered her grunt as she blocked Alkippe's thick blade from hacking into my exposed neck.

Their moves were snake-like and unpredictable. Unfamiliar. This did not feel like practice. Actual practice was drills and repetition and choreography, with a heavy emphasis on where to put your feet and where the other might put their weapon next. There was no real danger in practice other than the odd flesh wound. This fight had a looming shadow to it, as though the Gate of the Otherworld had swung open and was waiting for a new guest to arrive.

I grunted again as Ifito's sword reached for my calf, then Eri's knee, but I parried both and feinted a blow at Ifito's hip. Metal grated on metal next to my ear, but I needed to trust that Eri would have my back, the same as she would need to trust that I would defend her. The sweat began to bead in earnest, and I grew short of breath far earlier than I expected. Still, we turned and parried, our weapons flashing, and my back never strayed from Eri's, nor hers from mine. Alkippe's axe lunged toward my leather vest just as the horn sounded two quick bursts. She withdrew the strike in an unbroken motion and stepped back to let me pass, her dark face, many shades darker still than Melanippe's, inscrutable in the depths of her helmet.

My relief at the reprieve made the air suck into my lungs in a desperate gasp. I ran in the direction they had taken Risa and saw Eri loping beside me out of the corner of my eye, beyond the glinting bronze of my cheek piece. Her long strides quickly overtook mine, but I did not want to use all of my energy at once. Our paths split apart soon enough at the edge of the forest, where a red ribbon fluttered on a low-hanging pine branch, signaling for her to take the left-hand trail. We would rejoin soon enough, after we found our horses again. A black ribbon hung from the sycamore tree, and as I jogged past it, I glanced down at the spot my mother always pointed out to me when she would recount my birth. Thinking of my mother added some power to my legs and steadied my breathing. I gripped my sword in front of me, ready for the next challenge, and loped on.

Inside the forest, the shadows were a blessed reprieve from the heat of the sun, but they also hid anything that wanted to stay hidden. My helmet thudded against my skull with every step, and the curved metal pressed into my cheeks as my eyes scoured for enemies. Or rather, mentors and friends who had taken the role of enemies today. I wished I could rip the helmet off and be free of it. I wished to cut the sandals from my feet and feel the loam springing under them. Even as I contemplated stopping to do just that, a shadow fell from the tree in front of me. I met the spear handle with my blade, but not before it cracked into my forehead.

I landed with a grunt of forced air and the sound of a bell ringing in my ears, but it was only my helmet striking a rock. The wooden pike came at me again, and I brought my sword up, flinging the shaft aside as Thraso's grim face came into view above me. Ifito's sister was the bigger of the two, her shoulders as wide as any man's, and I had never seen her normally stoic face so unfriendly. When she brought the shaft up over her head with both hands and swung it down, like an axe chopping wood, I rolled rather than try to meet it with my sword. It cracked into the ground where my chest had been, and as I rolled once more and scrambled to my feet, an unfamiliar tightness took hold in my stomach.

I had not expected today to feel easy. But I had perhaps been foolish in expecting it to feel safe.

Thraso spun the spear above her head, just as Leya had done earlier, until it whirled almost invisibly with its speed. I crouched with my sword, ready to intercept it. That was when I glimpsed my bow, slung in the tree behind Thraso's right shoulder. I did not wait for her to strike. I lunged at her, a fierce cry lending force to my swing, and she brought her spear down to block it. Her spear's wooden handle splintered with a deafening crack between her hands, and I was already running forward.

I wrenched my bow from the branch, then blocked Thraso's shortened spear just before it entered my ribs. The stiff leather of my vest would not have offered much protection if I had not seen it coming. The knot in my stomach twisted further, and the sweat ran cold between my breasts, but Thraso thrust again. I parried, noticing the huge ha-mazaan was more careful now that she did not have the same reach, but she was still blocking the path draped with the black ribbon, and I only had one hand to swing the sword until I could get the bow slung over my shoulders. As we crouched in a tight circle around each other, my eyes darted to every branch and shadow, looking for the quiver and arrows.

But of course, they would not offer all three together. The rest would surely be a part of my next trial. Even as I realized this, Thraso threw her spear at my face.

I snapped my head down and to the side at the last instant, and the bristles of the horse-hair crest parted as the tip of the spear rushed through it. My eyes wide, I met Thraso's grin with a sickly "Oh" of shock before I lunged past her toward the black ribbon. I ducked my head through the bowstring as I ran and tried not to think of that spearhead flying toward my eye. These women were my friends. I did not want to think of how it might be to face them as my enemies.

Again I ran, faster now as I wondered how Eri fared. How far ahead of me she might be, because she had always been better on foot than me, and I had no idea where my horse had been taken. If either of us ended up waiting for longer than two turns of the sand clock at the race's finish line, the other would automatically be disqualified. Picturing those sands run out, I willed my legs to go faster and nearly missed my quiver lying against the trunk of a tree. I skidded to a stop and raised my sword, immediately on the defensive. I looked up into the branches, and past the tree, and then behind me, my black braid swinging from one shoulder to the next with the frenzied motion. Nothing. I bent and scooped the quiver with my free hand. It was empty, of course. I clipped it to my belt and ran again but was soon brought up short by an arrow whistling past my chest and into the trunk of an old beech tree.

I crouched, looking to my left where the arrow had flown from, and flattened myself to the ground as another arrow followed the first. The sound of its black fletching so close to my heart made the sweat on my back creep with icy fingers. I crawled, which was very difficult with a sword in one hand and a quiver that tried to hide under my thighs with every shimmy forward. Another arrow hit the tree in front of me.

The arrows.

I paused in my shuffling, my breath panting so hard that it puffed small clouds of dust into the air under my chin. I couldn't turn my head on the ground to see above me properly without the metal of the helmet poking into my cheeks. I dropped my sword, wrenched the thing off my head, and threw it, along with a vulgar curse, as violently as I could in the direction of the arrows. I heard a laugh in the distance.

Ossy.

I took a deep breath. My goddess-mother would not shoot me with an arrow. This I was sure of. I grabbed the sword and stood, wrenching both arrows from the trunk. I started running again as another arrow planted itself just behind me. I thrust the first arrows I had taken into the quiver and kept running, ignoring the ones that landed behind me. Another arrow landed in front of me, and this one I did not hesitate to grab as I ran, wrenching it from the poor pine as my legs carried me past. Ossy gifted me three more arrows this way, and my quiver rattled with their ash shafts as I finally sprinted out of shooting range.

My lungs heaved. I had spent too long using a horse's legs to carry me over long distances rather than my own. When I stumbled into the bright sunlight of the city's apple orchard, I stopped and gasped deep breaths into my burning chest, hoping Ossy or some other bloodthirsty ha-mazaan was not currently aiming another arrow at my prone back.

A tall, leanly muscled ha-mazaan lounged against an apple tree, a young girl with a bright cloud of yellow curls perched in the cleft of its lower branches. Sagitta. Her daughter, Leandra, barely more than a toddler, was feeding ripe apples to Risa, whose lips were foaming with the sweetness of pulverized fruit. The horse was completely tackless, with not even a bridle left on her head. Sagitta smiled when she saw me, but it was a smile of wicked delight. Holding an apple in one hand, she pulled her helmet off a low branch and ducked her head into it. Leandra giggled and said with unabashed cheer,

"Get her, mama!"

I groaned softly in anticipation, bringing my sword up even as Sagitta flicked her toes in the grass and flipped her own sword into her hand. I felt a small measure of relief. She was not using her axe, which was her preferred weapon, and the one I likely could not match her with. I would have a better chance against her sword. As she came toward me, however, casually throwing the uneaten apple over her shoulder to the mare, I felt my bubble of relief evaporate along with her smile.

Her blue eyes appeared hard as agates when she swung her sword, and though I parried and matched her thrust with another, and then another, the bow across my chest and the quiver at my hip were hindrances to my movements. Not to mention I had already fought twice and run a considerable distance, whereas Sagitta was fresh as a new colt in the morning. The seasoned ha-mazaan gave me no quarter, though, and soon I began to grunt as the effort to meet Sagitta's blade made my shoulders weary and my wrists ache. Each blow jolted into my bones until my teeth pulsed with the shock of every hit. When had she become so good with the sword? When had I grown so weak? So slow? I shoved away another blow to my chest with an indelicate shout, but she came at me again from overhead, forcing me to leap back. Leandra shrieked with delight from the apple tree. I stepped back again, far enough away that I could circle and take some breaths, and Sagitta twirled the sword at her hip just to hear it sing in the air.

"Time's running out, Cyra," Sagitta said casually, making the sword sing again. "You'd better take your horse and get going."

My eyes darted to the mare, who was pulling another apple from Leandra's chubby fingers. I wondered how many she had already eaten from the girl's hands. Probably enough to give her a stomachache. Not enough to make her disinterested in her favorite treat, I was sure. But I knew I would not get past Sagitta to collect the mare—the mare would need to come to me, as I had trained her to do. And I had conveniently given Sagitta the mare's weaknesses only last night, in the baths. Girls and apples.

Fool, I thought and swung my sword to meet Sagitta's thrust. I pushed back against her, slashing my sword carelessly at her legs, her arms, her hip, trying not to imagine the blade actually sinking into the tattoo under her leather tunic. I could not wound this woman in front of her own daughter, but I knew my hesitancy to hurt my friends was making me weak and causing me to hold back too much. To lose, now that I faced Sagitta. Possibly lose my place in the Savaran. But I could not find it in myself to switch from defensive to offensive when it was her familiar face under the helmet, even though she seemed to not be suffering the same qualm.

I glanced back at the mare, and a dollop of foamed apple slid from her lips to the grass. Her eyes were closed in ecstasy as Leandra's hands smoothed over her face. I whistled, shrill and loud. Risa's languid eyes opened and turned to me. Her lips chewed. Her feet remained still, her hip cocked lazily. She reached for another apple in Leandra's lap, and I screamed in frustration.

Sagitta laughed at me. It was the same low, husky laugh I had always loved. That her lovers must love. But right now, it was at my own expense, and it made me angry. I felt the rage build in my chest, born of frustration and fear. I pictured the sand clock turning and my time running out. I whistled again for Risa to come to me. She chewed like a dumb cow.

The hilt of Sagitta's sword smacked into my fingers, and I yelped with pain and shock. Her next blow caught the blade with such force that it spun from my hands, landing in the grass far beyond my reach. Sagitta sliced her blade at my chest, and I was forced to leap backward again, and then again, farther away from Risa and my sword. This time when I shrieked her name, the mare turned to look at me with a startled expression.

"Risa!"

I whistled again, but as Sagitta came at me with a determined lunge, I turned my back to the horse and ran toward the black ribbon. One more whistle, and as my chest burned and my legs felt like they might give way, I heard the thunder of hooves behind me. I glanced over my shoulder, tripping over an exposed tree root when I did, but I had enough momentum that my feet caught me again in an ungainly lurch. Risa galloped toward me, but Sagitta was close on my heels, sword glinting dangerously. Leandra shrieked with glee. The mare overtook the running ha-mazaan behind me, and I reached for the horse's mane as she ran past me. My bruised fingers almost lost their hold as the mare sprinted on and I ran beside her, but I clung with a desperation I didn't know was in me and used her momentum to spring my feet off the ground and over her back. My thighs gripped black ribs just as the trees whizzed past, and I heard Sagitta's voice call after us with a good-natured cheer.

"Good luck, Ishassara!"

Leandra's delighted screeching was the last sound to reach me from the grove.

CHAPTER 3

SAVARAN

---

guided Risa at a gallop through oak and hornbeam, hazelnut and pine. It was a long, looping trail from where I was back to the battlefield, so there was no time to ease our speed. I knew the cliffs would be ahead of us soon, with a half-league drop onto the rocks and sea below, but we did not slow, even though all I had were my knees, my seat, and the sound of my voice to keep the mare on track. A log appeared on the trail ahead, and I had only a split second to adjust my seat before Risa was flying over it.

A person appeared on the side of the path as we landed. I braced myself, and then, when I saw the multiple arrows sticking from its belly, realized it was one of the pinecone and straw-stuffed replicas we used as archery and spear targets. I glimpsed the yellow fletching of Leya's arrow in its chest, but Risa was past the dummy before I could even unsling my bow. I fumbled at the bowstring caught in a buckle on my vest. Cursing furiously, I leaned back so that Risa slowed, and when she finally reared to a halt, I reefed the bow over my head. I pressed my knee into the mare's side, and she spun back up the trail as I pulled an arrow from the quiver and nocked it.

Risa nearly collided with Eri's mare as they burst from a different path in the forest. Both horses reared as I loosed my arrow, and the raven fletching swung wide into the trees. Eri sunk her arrow deep into the target before her horse's front hooves were back on the ground. The look she shot me when she screamed her horse forward again was as fierce as I had ever seen on her narrow face, and her red braid flew like a pennant behind her. I turned Risa again and shouted as I kicked at her sides. The mare flattened her ears in fury at such treatment, but she lunged after Eri's horse, and we soon overtook them. I grinned fiercely at my friend as we raced beside her, but the ground began to slope downward, and I set my eyes back on the path.

The hill angled gently at first, then more sharply as the trail narrowed. Risa did not slow, and I did not make her. Eri followed less recklessly, though her horse was older, and bridled besides. By the time the cliff edge was straight ahead and valley bottom to the left came into view, the hill was steep and covered in crumbling shale. I pressed my right knee into Risa's side, and she veered from the cliff's edge as the ground turned to shale. I leaned back lest I pitch forward over her neck with the steepness of the slope, but the mare did not slow. She simply tucked her legs underneath, and we slid that way on the scree until the ground leveled once more. Risa was galloping again as soon as the ground smoothed, and the rocks were behind us, and within moments, I heard the hooves of Eri's mare pounding behind.

Another target peeked from the bushes. I loosed my second arrow, watching with satisfaction as it sank deep into the dummy's chest. Eri's red-fletched arrow quivered beside it at almost the same time. I shouted at Risa again, urging her to greater speed, and as she obeyed, it felt as though her hooves did not touch the ground. The next target flew through the air across the path in front of us, suspended from a line stretched between two trees, and I nocked and loosed my arrow into its shoulder before it reached the middle of the path. A second stuffed target appeared, and Eri's arrow took that one.

For the first time since the trial began, I felt a surge of exaltation. This is what I had been born to do. This is where my strength lay. With a horse between my thighs and a bow between my fingers, there was nothing that could stop me. I let the thrill of the race and the satisfaction of the last arrow quivering in the chest of a straw man lend much-needed succor to my tired body. Risa fairly flew ahead of Eri's mare now that the targets were behind us, and as I crested the hill to see the pavilions ahead, I let out a whoop of victory.

My exhilaration was short-lived as the crowd came into view. White tunics were scattered everywhere amongst the ha-mazaans. Men. I caught a glimpse of the lion skin on the man next to Hippolyta. Beside him stood the shorter man, next to Antiope. My mother was off to the side, her hands on her hips, but more men were standing behind her, and all of them were watching. Anger flooded through me.

It was only when I saw the swords hanging at their hips that I remembered. My sword lay in the apple orchard. I did not have a weapon to fight Eri other than my bow. I needed sword, spear, or axe, and I had only my star-forged blade the length of my own hand.

Risa thundered past the goal posts, past the middle of the field where two wicker shields sat on the ground, ready for me to scoop up. I attempted to grab one, but the mare galloped so swiftly toward the rope barrier on the far side that I was forced to right myself. I thought she might try to jump the rope and land in the crowd. I leaned back and tried to relax my buttocks, the signal for her to slow, but she galloped forward, out of control. Women's and men's eyes widened in the crowd as they flung themselves out of the way, and I clenched every muscle again to prepare for the mare to leap the rope. She turned at the last second, nearly unseating me. My bow flung into the dust as my hands gripped her neck. My calf clung to her withers, and I hauled myself upright onto her back again as she continued to canter around the ring. My face burned with embarrassment, and I was certain a man's mocking laughter followed me.

As I circled the mare in a trot back to the center of the ring, Eri galloped through the finish line and reined her horse to an easy stop next to the shields. I was about to dismount as well when I saw my sword. It dangled high overhead, even mounted as I was on the tall mare, from a black ribbon on the flagpole next to the queen's pavilion. I pressed my knees to Risa's sides and moved across the ring toward it. Eri was already sliding her arm into the wicker shield and un-slinging her golden axe, her horse moving in a steady canter around the ring as it was supposed to. Then, to my surprise, Eri ran toward the flagpole as well. I kicked Risa to run faster, then put my hands against her withers and pushed, bringing my body under me in a smooth motion.

As soon as I felt the rhythm of her cantering body echoed in mine, I stood up straight, just as Risa's nose came even with the base of the pole. I reached up so high that I was forced to arch my feet and lose the rhythm of her moving back, but my fingers found the sword pommel. I pulled. The sword came free, but my balance was off. My toes no longer felt the rhythm of Risa's back. I felt myself falling, and I glimpsed Eri underneath me with her axe. So many thoughts flashed through my mind at once.

Do not fall on your sword.

Do not embarrass yourself in front of your mother. In front of the queens.

In front of these men, who should not even be here.
Eri is not your friend right now. Her task is to disarm you.

I tucked my shoulder into my hip and rolled on the ground with a much heavier landing than normal. I used the momentum to roll up and onto the balls of my feet, crouched and ready, but my hand was empty. I had thrown my sword aside in a moment of self-preservation, and Eri's foot now pinioned the blade firmly to the ground. The frustration swirling in my breast took hold of my lungs, and I hissed a curse at her.

She swung her axe at me, though I had neither weapon nor shield. I leaped back. I moved even further back before she could swing again and circled with low, long steps to the side, luring her away from the sword. She still wore her helmet and had the crescent moon of her shield firmly over her heart. I considered pulling the star-forged dagger from its sheath on my arm, but it would do me no good against her axe unless I threw it, and I did not actually want to harm her. I took another long step in a circle. Eri's blade reached out to bite my throat, but I leaned back, and it whistled over my head. Another step, then two. Eri's mouth was fierce, almost a grimace. She lunged, but I moved toward her, catching her by surprise. I rolled under the axe blade and under her feet, and my hand caught the handle of the sword just as she swung the axe. Blade met blade with a sharp clang of metal above my chest. I pushed against it and rolled away, flinging myself to my feet, but I did not wait for Eri to come at me again.

I swung the sword with all my remaining strength, catching my friend slightly off guard with the furious scream that came with it. My blade caught in her shield, shearing clean through the woven willow and stiff leather backing. I wrenched the sword away, and the shield dangled uselessly from her arm so that she was forced to try and rip it off. I did not give her the chance. I stepped in and swung at her exposed waist, then at her knee. She blocked the first and had to leap away from the second, but all I could see was an angry white haze before my eyes, and I kept coming at her.

She shouted something in my face as my sword caught under the curved edge of her axe, but I did not understand any of her words. The horn blared. She tugged, hard. My sword spun through the air just as the sound ended, pulled from my grip by Eri's axe.

It was over.

Sweat dripped into my eyes, and I gulped air again as I wiped the loosened strands of hair from my face. Risa lounged, hip cocked, next to the queen's pavilion, while Eri's horse still cantered obediently in a circle. I did not know what it might mean, that my horse was not in position, and my sword was not in my hands.

But then my mother was beside me, her silver eyes flashing into mine. She took my empty hand and held it high into the air, and Eri stood the same on her other side, the golden glow of her axe glinting mockingly at me against the blue of the sky. The crowd cheered. I looked to the pavilion, where I could hear the queens cheering. Even the men beside them were clapping their meaty hands, their faces openly displaying their astonishment.

"Welcome to the Savaran, Daughter," Melanippe said, and her eyes glowed at me.

"Let us rest in the pools and then complete your tattoos. Tonight, we will feast." She led us from the field, her hand gripping my sore arm like a vice, and I went with her in a numb haze of exhaustion.

I had done it. I was Savaran, senior cavalry of the ha-mazaans, sworn to protect and defend Themiscyra, or any ha-mazaan city that needed our help.

Relief crashed through me like a tidal wave against a small reed skiff, pulling me off-center so that I could barely walk straight. I had tried not to think of what it might mean to actually fail on my trial day, but the threat had been there for more than eight summers, looming in the back of my mind in the shape of a stone cauldron and a cruel curse. But now, it was done. Tomorrow night at moonrise, I would be crowned as future Ishassara, and then everything would be as it should.

There was nothing that could stop me from becoming Themiscyra's Defending Queen. Not even my destiny.

CHAPTER 4

THE MOON HALL

The Moon Hall was crowded as I had never seen it before, even during the mid-summer fire festival. Perhaps what made it seem so stiflingly devoid of air were the hundred men smelling of sea and sweat, turning the air salty with their stench. I was glad to be near one of the windows.

I sat at the opposite end of the table from Penthesilea. My cousin, daughter of Antiope and one day Hearth Queen beside me, huddled head to head with her best friend, both of them somehow ignoring the goings-on. My mother sat next to me, leaving space for the queens in between herself and Penthesilea. We all drank freshly fermented *kimiz* while we waited for the sister-Queens to arrive with the guests. Alkippe lounged indelicately on my other side, watching the men in the room and the ha-mazaans talking indiscriminately with them, with half-lidded eyes. One might have thought her a sleeping seal, with her dark skin glistening in the light of the torches, her tattoos dancing across her face in the firelight, but her eyes all shadows and quiet. I knew her flat stare for what it was. She was as thrilled with the intrusion of these men as I was, and I was glad for a companion in my glowering.

I was even more glad when Eri threaded her way through the crowd and swung a long leg over the bench next to me, forcing Alkippe to shift down a bit. There had not been a chance to talk after the Trials, as the ritual tattoo was done in silence, save for the *zizenti's* prayers, and the baths had been so crowded I had not been able to get close to her. I felt awkward and a little ashamed when I thought of how I had let my anger overcome me during our fight. She slid closer to me and helped herself to a long swig of *kimiz* from my goblet.

"Those were some fancy acrobatics you pulled off, getting your sword down," she said. I smiled at her, and a knot of worry I had not known was inside my chest loosened when she smiled back. Eri seemed to have already put it behind her, if she had been upset about our fight. Everything was changing in my life, with so many new milestones at once, and I counted on Eri to be the sister I never had. I couldn't afford to let my temper get in the way of that, although I knew well enough she had one too.

"You weren't so bad with that axe, either. I'm lucky to have my hands still attached." She grinned and drank my *kimiz*. "I wish we could just get this over with," I said, leaning in closer to her so my mother would not overhear. "This is not how I envisioned our Savaran feast."

"You have to admit they do lend a certain appeal to the Moon Hall," Eri said, and I flashed a startled glance at her sparkling eyes.

"Don't tell me you think welcoming a hundred armed men inside the gates was a good idea. And to our *Trials*. I don't know what the queens are thinking."

"They are probably thinking what most of us are thinking. In fact, that's probably why they are so late." She smirked suggestively, raising the goblet to the room full of men as though to toast the idea, and then downed the last of my drink. I gaped at her.

"They would never."

"Why not?" She shrugged, her eyes meeting mine in a level stare. "Most of the *matars* have already welcomed a sailor or two into their bed by now. These men would sire wonderful ha-mazaans. I have to admit; I wish I already had First Blood." She looked away again, ignoring my growing incredulity. "The one who is apparently a king showed off his skills earlier in the armory...I must say I'm a bit jealous of whichever queen picked him." She laughed when she said it, but there was raw desire in her words, and I couldn't help the surge of disgust inside of me. I smiled tightly at a younger Xanharaspa as they refilled my goblet with fresh *kimiz*, but as soon as they moved on to my mother's cup, I leaned toward Eri and hissed at her,

"You can't be serious, Eri. They are so..." I waved a hand at the throng of men, their voices a constant jangling in my ears. I fumbled for the right word to express my loathing. "Uncivilized."

"You make them sound as though griffin feathers grow on their backs," Eri slanted a disapproving look at me and then returned her gaze to the Achaeans nearby. "You might be the only new Savaran who hasn't fantasized about conscripting with the *matars* early, or at least breaking their vows of First Blood to be with one or two of them."

I choked slightly on my *kimiz* and wiped the spittle off my chin as I stared at her. She grinned wickedly. I curled my lip.

"Nothing is stopping you from First Blood. Especially not me. By all means, complete the ritual," I challenged, raising an eyebrow at her. "You can stick your pike in as many of their throats as you want and then drag the last living Achaean to your chambers, for all I care. But I know for a fact you don't want to be a *matar* yet."

"No," she agreed, still staring out at the Achaeans. A faint pinkness colored her otherwise *kimiz*-toned cheekbones. "I wouldn't want to be saddled with a babe when I've only just made it to Savaran. But the *zizentis* have potions for that. I also don't think I should have to kill such a fine specimen before I—"

A stirring near the doorway drew our attention, cutting off the rest of Eri's appalling thought, and a hush fell over the room. I saw the lion head first, its intact fangs pressing into the tall man's forehead. He could be considered handsome, if one liked a man to appear as a bull aurochs in mating season. The man beside Hippolyta laughed. I frowned. Antiope appeared next to the second man. His hair was much darker than hers, but in the way bronze was darker than gold, and less precious for it. Though he was short, he was thick and bullish around the chest. His bulging jaw was spread wide in a grin similar to Hippolyta's, an easy intimacy already apparent between them. My frown deepened to a scowl, even as they all approached the dais, and Antiope stepped up onto it, turning to the crowd so that her back was to me.

"Told you he was handsome. And that's my cue," Eri whispered, and I wanted to protest both her taste in men and her leaving me at the high table alone, but she was gone too quickly, back to her own table where her mother, Hipponike, and younger sister, Anva, were seated.

"Ha-mazaans!" Antiope called, and all the women turned their attention to her. It took a few more moments for the deeper voices of the men to settle into full quiet, and I shifted on the bench with irritation at the disrespect. After several moments of muttering and male laughter, all eyes were finally on the queen.

"Let us welcome our guests and offer them the hospitality of

Kubileya, that they may know the welcome of the Great Mother's arms." She turned and gestured to the man in the lion skin. "I present to you the mighty Heracles, Hero of the Achaeans, journeying far from the Aegean Sea to be among us. Heracles, as a guest of the Ha-mazaans, please accept this milk from the breast of the Great Mother and be welcomed among us as brother."

Antiope handed him a golden cup filled with *kimiz*. Heracles took it and swallowed it readily as an encouraging cheer erupted from men and women. Antiope turned to the second man.

"And Theseus, King of the Athenians, honors us with his presence as he aids in the quest of Heracles. Honorable Theseus, as a guest of the Ha-mazaans, please accept this drink from the breast of the Great Mother and be welcomed among us as brother."

Theseus took the cup and drank, some of the thick, creamy mare's milk running from the corner of his mouth to drip onto his white tunic. He swallowed the last with a resounding sigh of relish and returned the cup to the queen. Antiope gestured to the table in front of our own.

"Please, sit," she said.

Hippolyta stepped up, then, and I noticed she had left her axe aside for the easier, more dinner-suited sword belted at her waist.

"Ha-mazaans, and welcome guests!" she called across the room. "I hope my sister queen has made you feel welcome. We have much to celebrate. I ask that the Savarans who successfully completed their Trials this day stand and be recognized!"

Alkippe shoved her fist against my thigh when I paused as the rest rose to their feet. I stood reluctantly, feeling many of the men's eyes turn to me because of my raised position at the high table. Another cheer went up from the crowd, the women's voices loud and exultant this time, and it took some of the heat from my face. My newly poked tattoo burned against the inside of my wrist, a mark of pride and pain, but I held my arms still and my chin high.

"And Cyra, Daughter of our sister Melanippe," Antiope said. Every eye turned to me. "An extra special day for you. May the twenty-first anniversary of your birth be forever remembered as the day you earned your Savaran title, having proven yourself against the best fighters in all of Themiscyra!"

Another cheer went up, and I nodded my thanks. When I met Eri's eyes across the Hall, her smile was tight and a little bit mocking. She knew as well as I did that if the horn had sounded only a breath later, I would have been disqualified for not having my weapon in hand.

"Let us eat!" Antiope called.

I sat again as both queens finally took their places next to my mother, in front of Heracles and Theseus. All were still within speaking distance of one another, but I could tell by the slightly awkward glances that the king and his friend gave one another, and then to the high table, that they were unaccustomed to women being positioned above them.

Xanharaspas entered the hall with great platters of sizzling meat and herbed vegetables held between them. More followed with baskets of freshly baked bread, bowls of nuts, and platters of cheeses and olives, their steps swift and nimble over the tiled mosaic hunting scene that covered the entire floor of the round Hall. When they served a platter of shelled and roasted hazelnuts, dried apples, figs, fat olives, and soft cheese made from mare's milk to our table, my stomach let out a loud growl of hunger. I, and everyone else in the Moon Hall, watched until the Hearth Queen took food before we took food for ourselves. Ravenous, I stuffed ripe cheese into my mouth. I had not eaten since the meal of thick porridge at dawn.

Alkippe watched me spear a hunk of roasted mutton and stuff it in after the cheese, and her full lips pulled sideways in her particular version of a smile as I ate it like a starving dog.

"You did well today," she said. I glanced at her, raising an eyebrow as I chewed.

"It did not feel like it."

She grinned, her white teeth almost glowing against the blackness of her skin. "It never does, while you're in it. But the amount of handicaps they threw at you today should let you know you are as good as any and better than most."

I ducked my head. "Thank you," I said, and I meant it.

"I did not expect young Erioboea to give you such a hard time," she said, slowly eating a piece of soft cheese.

"Nor I," I agreed. I looked over the sea of faces to find Eri, but her eyes were fixed on the table where Heracles and Theseus sat. She had not even touched her food.

Alkippe followed my eyes and looked like she was about to comment when Theseus spoke. His voice was loud enough for everyone in the hall to hear, although he did not seem to make an effort to make it so.

"Tell me, Queen Antiope. How is it that the Amazons built such a fine city and such a marvel of construction as this?" His eyes swept over the great arches overhead and around the circumference of the hall, to the enormous round window that was behind Antiope's chair. "It is as fine as any Achaean palace, or those in Ilia and Minos. The stonework is so precise. Do you keep men as slaves to do your building, then, as the stories say?"

For a moment, Antiope was taken aback by the question. Even Hippolyta frowned slightly as her sister answered, but the Hearth Queen's voice was surprisingly even. "We keep no slaves in Themiscyra, King Theseus. Although," she conceded, waving her goblet toward the eastern wall of the hall, "the Sister-Queens in Chadesia and those in Lykastia have, at times, kept prisoners of war to perform the more menial tasks they do not have time for, amongst matters of state and such. And to father their children, if they are so inclined."

"Ah," Theseus nodded, chewing a hazelnut. His blue eyes glinted from the Hearth Queen's creamy face to my mother's dark one, then over to me. I skewered an olive with my dagger and ate it pointedly, not looking away from his eyes.

"As for this palace," Antiope continued, "the Cyclopes tribes were paid fairly for their labors by the architect—my mother, Otrera." She smiled. "It was her passion, and it took much of her attention in life, as this was not the only great building she commissioned. There are several temples, and even the palace at Wilusa, which you call Ilia, all from her imaginings and instruction. I am happy to hear this one stands in favor of one who has surely seen many marvels in the world beyond our lands."

"Indeed, it is as grand as any palace I have seen," Theseus agreed, sounding sincere.

Heracles, who looked ridiculous with the lion's teeth puckering the dark skin of his forehead, looked up at Antiope questioningly. "I am surprised to hear you say Cyclopes had a hand in constructing it," he said, and his voice was markedly rich. Deep and reserved, as though he was afraid to speak too loudly, lest his voice break something delicate. I felt myself leaning forward to hear his words. "They are such brutes, as I am sure you know."

"Are they?" Hippolyta said. Their eyes turned to her. "The ha-mazaans have only ever known them to be peaceful men in all of our cities."

Both Heracles and Theseus looked skeptical, and a few of their men in the crowd let out unrestrained huffs of laughter.

"I trust you would know best, Queen Hippolyta," Heracles said.

"Tell me, Heracles, when shall we know the secret quest which brings you to our city?" Antiope said, ignoring their rudeness.

"Ah," Heracles said and chewed another olive with thoughtful contemplation. His eyes slid to Theseus, who shrugged. "It is a long story, Your Majesties, and one which involves many tales of fantastic beasts and many more of our trials and tribulations across the seas. It begins in tragedy and ends many years from today, I fear. We would not bore you with the matter at such a special occasion as this."

He raised a cup of *kimiz* to the queens and smiled. Theseus' blue eyes gleamed with a curious light.

He is more wolf than lion, I thought.

"I am sure you would honor us with the telling, my lord," Antiope said politely.

"Yes, we would be most interested to hear of your journey, Heracles," Hippolyta said, smiling down at him.

"As you wish, my Queens," Heracles said easily, as though he had been waiting for the opportunity but had not wanted to appear too eager. He took a long drink from his cup and then began. I no longer needed to strain to hear his voice, as it carried through the Hall without effort.

"As I said, my journey begins in tragedy. I hate to think you might feel pity for me, so let me only say that I lost that which was dear to me, my wife and children, and it was the fault of my own hands, though not of my will. For this fate, I have been sentenced by the Oracle to serve King Eurystheus and to complete the ten tasks he has set before me in order to keep my life. The first task was this."

He put a hand to the fangs against his forehead and pushed his fingers back through the mane of the lion's neck. My ears had perked at the mention of the Oracle. Men did not enter the Womb of the Mountain. It was forbidden. Was there another Oracle in the lands of the Achaeans?

"The mighty lion of Nemea," he continued, "whose hide was too thick for arrows and could not be stopped as he decimated the town's livestock, and soon, its villagers. I set upon it in a cave and strangled it. Now, it protects me as I go about the rest of my tasks."

"You must be very strong to strangle a lion," Hippolyta said, and I was sure I detected admiration in her voice. "Strong and brave." I glanced over at her with ill-concealed surprise. Then I glanced at Eri, wondering if she was right after all in surmising the queens might consort with these brutes, but she was not looking in my direction.

"Such words from a mighty warrior queen are generous, Your Majesty. However, my second task did not go as well as the first, and I fear my uncle Eurystheus was not as gracious. Though I slayed the mighty water snake and now use the poison from its gall on my arrows and blades, my nephew lent me aid in the fight when the viper overpowered me. For this reason, my uncle disqualified me and set me on a new task."

He then went on to tell the most fantastical tales I had ever heard, from hunting the same hind for a year to chasing a giant bull across one kingdom to the next. Every story was more ridiculous than the next, but to my astonishment, Hippolyta appeared engrossed with his tales. At one point in his crowing, I slanted an irritated look at Alkippe, unable to conceal my disgust, and she met my eyes with a resigned shrug.

"This talk is something I do not miss from the men in my former city," Alkippe said, her breath warm on my neck as she leaned close to keep her words hidden. "Always boasting. Always bigger than reality. They think we will see them as strong. Capable. I see children hungry for their mother's teat."

I huffed in response.

"For my seventh task with the bull, Theseus helped me tie up some loose ends." Heracles clapped a hand on Theseus' back, and the smaller man ducked his head in a futile attempt to appear humble.

"A small help for a friend," Theseus demurred.

"And your help I would have welcomed against my eighth task, those gruesome horses which ate the flesh of men," Heracles said. "But it was finished without you, though with much grief to my companions. But now you are with me once more, good friend."

They clasped their arms in tight affection, and I crunched down hard on a hazelnut, wishing for the evening to be over.

"You mentioned ten tasks, mighty Heracles," Hippolyta said, cocking her head at him. "Yet you have only spoken of eight, and two of those were disqualified. What other feats does your uncle bid of you?"

"Ah," Heracles said, in the same evasive tone as before. Again, the sly look between the men.

"S'truth, we have come to your shores for more than simple respite, my Queen," Heracles continued, his words more hesitant than before. He shifted in his seat.

Hippolyta raised a strawberry-golden eyebrow at him. "Oh?"

Melanippe moved her hand on the bench next to me as though feeling for something—her axe, perhaps—and the atmosphere in the room shifted from amused boredom to attentive concentration between breaths.

Heracles smiled and darted a glance around the room at the ha-mazaans, and the men scattered among them. "I must confess, we brought three ships of men to your shores expecting a great battle. But now that we have met you, and seen the fine display of fighting, and mastery of the horse," his eyes flicked over me briefly, so quickly I wondered if he was mocking me, before they moved on again, "I realize we may not have succeeded even if we had brought a thousand of my best men."

There was a tense pause. Alkippe shifted beside me, and I glanced to the wall behind us where our weapons stood within easy reach.

"You sought war with us?" Hippolyta asked finally, more wary than confused.

"We did not, Your Majesty," Heracles said gravely. "But we did expect to be attacked when we reached your shores. The reputation of the Amazons precedes you, even across the seas."

This did nothing to mollify her. Using the epithet for us, the insult of being breastless and therefore without feminine nature, rather than our real name of ha-mazaan, which meant simply "warriors," did not endear him to any woman in the room. The queen frowned down at him, the easy smile I had seen on her face since their arrival gone completely from her handsome features. "Speak plainly, Heracles," she said, and there was much of the Defending Queen in her voice once more.

Heracles sighed as though his own words pained him. Theseus put a hand on his shoulder, quieting him before he could speak, and looked to the queen himself.

"Eurystheus has set the ninth task to be one he considered impossible for my friend, Queen Hippolyta. The king is boorish in his ways, and uncultured. Quick to anger and slow to understand, and what he believes of the world outside of his own gates is small and superstitious. I am sure you know the type." He smiled ingratiatingly at her. She did not smile back. His blue eyes moved to Antiope, who was regarding him with equal wariness, and there was some form of pathetic apology in his expression as he continued.

"Heracles has been tasked with bringing back the belt which girds the waist of the mighty Defender of Themiscyra," he said. "Eurystheus assured us we would only take it by force, and that is certainly what we expected, though we were loath to set our swords against women. I think we can see now that if we had tried, we would have been sorely tested."

I tried not to gape at their table. The faces of the queens turned stony, and my mother was so tense next to me I thought her skin might crack if she moved too quickly.

"Why did you not attack when your ships docked, then?" Hippolyta asked tightly. "I was wearing my belt then."

"The moment I saw you, my Queen, I knew I could not raise a hand against something so magnificent," Heracles said. "It would be like setting my blade to the finest cattle in Macedonia, or your prized mares from Paphlagonia. To attack such a sacred beauty would surely curse me with every Goddess we know."

"It surely would," Hippolyta agreed, and her voice remained cool. Composed. Unalarmed that these men had just confessed to coming here with violent intentions and now sat in our midst, drinking *kimiz* and eating salted lamb.

"Once a guest has drunk the milk from the Great Mother's breasts, by our own offering, we are sworn to do them no harm. Surely you have a similar code of honor where you are from?" Antiope asked, her eyes moving from Heracles to Theseus.

"We do, great Queen," Theseus nodded.

"And now that you have made your truth known, how may we know you will not betray the gift of brotherhood that has been granted to you?"

They hesitated, looking at each queen and then at each other. Theseus was the one who finally answered.

"You have my word as a King of Athens, my Queen, that unless we are required to defend ourselves, no blades or arrows from our men will be set against Themiscyra. If I break this vow, my kingdom is yours. May every warrior here be my witness."

Heracles looked aghast at his friend, but Theseus simply held Antiope's eyes for a long moment. She nodded after a while, accepting his sworn vow. Heracles sat back, his face concerned.

"I have long wished to journey south to your lands, Theseus," Antiope said. "Do not give me reason to make the journey so close to our sea's storm season."

"And what happens if you fail in this ninth task?" Hippolyta asked, bringing everyone's attention back to Heracles. "If you return to your uncle without my belt?"

"Then I fail once more, and every time I fail, my tasks grow more difficult and more deadly, my Queen."

She nodded thoughtfully but did not say more. An awkward quiet settled over the hall as every ha-mazaan seated next to a man found it difficult to resume the light-hearted conversation from before. Antiope called for the desserts to be brought in, and Xanharaspas arrived with bowls of pomegranate seeds, my mother's favorite, though she did not touch them, and oat cakes dripping with honey and dipped in pistachios. A low chatter resumed as the majority of us picked at the food.

"Don't rub at it, or it will not heal," my mother said. I looked down and pulled my hand away from where the new tattoo burned on my wrist. Even my older marks, the moons and the chevrons of triangles wrapping around my forearm, were itching and burning despite having healed months and even years ago.

"You should get some rest, daughter," she said, a curious light in her eye. "Tomorrow is another big day."

I nodded, more tired than I cared to admit. Especially to my mother, who never seemed weary, though she spent much of her day in the saddle or training with the Savaran.

"Come, let us go to your chambers, and I will show you your gift," she said, standing abruptly. She turned toward the queens and the men seated in front. "You will excuse us, sisters, and honored guests," she nodded politely to Heracles and Theseus, who watched us with unguarded curiosity. "I must tend to my daughter's special night and prepare her for the ceremony tomorrow."

We left the hall under more scrutiny than I liked, but when we were finally away from the heat and the crowd, I breathed a sigh of relief. When we reached the door to my chambers, she went in ahead of me and went to stand beside my bed, waving a sun-darkened hand toward the cover.

"I hope you like it," she said.

A vest of scales and leather, much finer than the thick leather I had worn for the Trials, lay on the bed. I brushed my hand over the delicate mounds of the scales before picking it up, marveling at how light it was and how flexible. Where the scales were sewn with fine sinew, the vest moved and bent in supple folds, and where it was made of hardened leather for extra reinforcement, the tooling was ornate and precise. The buckles were silver, and the rivets at shoulders and joints were so delicately set I wondered that such a craft could exist. I had never seen anything like it. I looked up at my mother, speechless.

"From an animal in the far east," she said and put a finger to one of the scales. "Farther even than Camilla's mother's home in the Indus Valley. Not even your star-forged dagger will go through this without considerable force."

"It is beautiful," I said, and I meant it. I shrugged it over my head, and she helped me with the straps at each hip.

"Your belt will go over it, here," she said, pressing strong fingers into my waist.

I turned and raised my arms, testing it. It fit over my tunic like a second skin, as though it had been molded for my body. It held my breasts firm, but not uncomfortably so, which would help for riding and running. There was no creaking or groaning of leather when I moved, and it felt as light as one of my woolen tunics. *What I would have given for this armor only a few hours ago*, I thought wryly.

"It will serve you well, daughter. And it is well deserved. You made your general and your queens proud today." She met my eyes with a grave pride, and I felt a peculiar lump in the back of my throat. Praise from my mother was as rare as it was unexpected.

"Thank you," I said. "Although...I did not feel like it went well," I admitted, glancing at her and moving to sit on the edge of my bed. "I fumbled at every Trial. I barely made it past Alkippe and Ifito, if I am honest."

"You are wise to recognize it," Melanippe said. She leaned her tall frame against the bedpost and tipped her head at me. "Did you think it would be easy to defeat them?"

"No," I said. "But they have never been so..."

"Determined to see you fail?"

"Yes."

She grinned tightly, and her silver eyes flashed with humor. "You did not see it, but they were not so hard on your friend at your back."

I frowned. "Then why—"

"Because you are to be Ishassara, Cyra. And eventually, the Defending Queen. You will never be only a Savaran, and your Trials needed to prove that. You met our best fighters, with many years of solid battle experience, and you prevailed. None of the other riders had the same handicaps as you. All were allowed to keep their weapons and their bridles, and most of them fought the most average of the other hamazaans. Yet still, you prevailed. This is not something to take lightly. You should be proud."

I considered for a moment, then nodded, grateful for the perspective. I had assumed we all went through the same routine and the same level of difficulty. I felt a small stirring of pride that I had not failed my mother or my queens.

"I am glad no one told me beforehand, to have even more to be anxious about," I said.

"We are not complete fools, or that cruel," Melanippe said.

"But still, you let me go into it with that damn mare," I said, a spark of anger flaring in me. My mother grinned at my indignant tone.

"She is a trial of her own, that one. I am glad you are not considering her for *rhu-tasiya*. Binding your soul to such a mare could mean wandering forever in the Otherworld while she searches endlessly for apple trees. Can you imagine?" She shook her head, pushing herself off the post. "Get some rest. Tomorrow, we will see you crowned as Ishassara. A day I have waited for since I knew you were to be born."

There was a strange hint of nostalgia in her words, an unfamiliar emotion coming from my normally stoic mother. Stoic when she was not in a rage, that is. Our tempers had been known to try to burn each other down many times in the past.

"Thank you again, mother," I said, smoothing my hands down the scales over my chest and ribs. "It is truly the most wonderful gift."

"You wear it well, daughter," she said, and then she was gone, the door closing softly behind her.

When I dreamed, it was a recurring feeling of falling. I was falling off Risa's back, and there was a golden-bladed axe beneath me, but I never hit the ground. I was riding again, unable to turn Risa as we ran, and then I was falling from the edge of the cliff and into the churning waters of the sea, but water never touched my face. I was fighting Eri in the ring, but I had no weapon, no shield, and, I eventually realized, no tunic. The men were laughing and jeering, and the queens did nothing to stop them. Then, I was falling into blackness, and the scream of a griffin was following me into the dark abyss. There was nothing to hit in the blackness. Nothing to stop my falling.

Chapter 5

HIPPOLYTA'S BELT

The swearing-in ceremony would take place at moonrise. That meant I had all day to occupy myself with minor tasks, but after training day in and day out for the Savaran Trials, to switch pace so suddenly was not an easy adjustment. I ate a small breakfast of leftover honeyed oat cakes, then went back to my chambers, unwilling to mingle with the excess of men wandering freely in the city. Men were often in our city, visiting the *matars* or bringing their wares from the Indus Valley or Colchis, but there were never so many at once. That they were still welcome here, and especially that they were allowed to keep their pathetic bronze swords after admitting they had come to steal Hippolyta's belt, was galling in the extreme.

I paced my room with long strides. Something in my soul felt itchy. I flipped my dagger in the air as I moved and resisted scratching at the burning tattoo on my wrist. When the knock came at my door, I was both relieved at the interruption and frustrated that I could not pin down why I felt so irritable.

"Cyra?" Ossy's voice followed the knock.

When I pulled the door open, my goddess-mother beamed at me, her arms filled with folds of grey cloth draped over something round and lumpy. Her dun-brown hair fell in a neatly plaited, somewhat thin rope over her shoulder, and eyes of slowly tarnishing bronze twinkled at me.

"What's that?" I asked, eyeing the mound.

"Let me in, and I will show you."

I stepped back, and she went to the bed, dumping the items unceremoniously on the linen cover.

"You did well yesterday, Cyra. I'm sorry I didn't have a chance to speak with you after." Ossy turned to give me a kind smile, and I shrugged as some of my tension leaked away with her comforting presence.

"There was much that needed your attention, goddess-mother. I didn't expect to be able to see you." I paused, slanting an accusing glance at her. "I suppose I should thank you for not hitting me with your arrows."

"Your arrows," she corrected and gave me a sly smile. "Thank you for missing me with your terrible aim when you tried to throw your helmet. You never were very good with that arm." She brought out the lumpy item from under the folds of grey. My helmet. She hung it on the bedpost, grinning.

I scowled at her, but it took too much effort, so I put my energy back into pacing the floor. Ossy went to work unfolding the lump of material she had dumped on the bed. When I passed by her for a third time, she turned to watch me.

"Care to share what is troubling our newest Savaran, the Ishassara?"

"I am not yet Ishassara."

"You were born Ishassara," she replied matter-of-factly. "Today is only a ritual of recognition, just like the Alsanti will be a year and a day after the Defending Queen dies. A formality."

"It is not just a formality, though, is it?" I said. This beast had been eating at me as I studied beside Penthesilea all these years, wondering why the Oracle insisted I would never sit beside her on a sister-throne. It had been eating at me as I practiced and trained for the Savaran Trials, wondering if it was all a waste of time, and I was destined to fail. But I had prevailed, as my mother said. There was no longer any kind of technicality that could prevent me from becoming Ishassara this very day.

You will never be queen in Themiscyra...

"Why would the Initiation be required if it is only a formality?" I continued. "There are still ways I could fail at this whole thing."

"What's this, now?" Ossy frowned and grasped my arm as I made another pass by the bed. She tugged, drawing me down onto it, on top of the grey folds, and sat next to me. Unable to move my feet, I twisted the silver rings on my fingers instead, round and round, to keep my hands from itching at the tattoo. I entertained the thought of sharing my prophecy with her, but I threw the notion far from me as soon as it entered my mind. It was not customary to share our words from the

Oracle, anyway. Perhaps if it had been like my mother's prophecy, full of glory and hope for the ha-mazaans, I would have dared. But it was a curse, and a burden, and it would be mine alone to bear for as long as I managed to avoid it.

"Nothing," I hedged, not meeting her eyes.

"Are you worried about your speech in the ceremony?" she asked gently.

I shook my head. "To be completely honest, I have no idea what I'm worried about. I'm..." I let my words trail off, unsure of what I needed to say. What I *could* say.

"Ah," she said enigmatically and brushed away a loose strand of hair that had escaped my braid. She tucked it behind my ear, then pulled the end of my braid in a sharp but painless tug, just as she had when I was a young child. It made me smile, as she had intended. Where my mother lacked in tender affection toward her only daughter, Melanippe's dearest friend had been christened my goddess-mother for exactly these more delicate moments.

"You will make a good queen, Cyra," she said. "You have much to learn, but already you have had the best teachers, in your mother, and the queens, and the ha-mazaans who helped you win Savaran yesterday."

"And you."

"Yes, and me," she said. "And when Hippolyta dies, or transfers her rule by choice, these people who love you will still be by your side, or in your heart. You have nothing to worry about. You have no reason to fail at what you have been born to do. Your destiny began with your mother."

Your mother will never see you rule over any living ha-mazaan...

My throat tightened, and I did not trust myself to speak, so I nodded instead. She hugged me, and for a moment, I felt safe. Protected. I frowned anyway.

"I still can't believe you shot at me with my own arrows."

She chuckled, and it sounded just as it had from inside the forest after I threw my helmet at her.

"Alkippe wanted to make you re-fletch them in the middle of the Trials before they could be used. You have me to thank for fending off that cruel torture."

I leaned back, my mouth falling open. "How in the Goddess's fiery armpit would I have had the time to re-fletch an arrow in the middle of my Trials? I barely made it back in time as it was because of that damned mare!"

"But it did not happen, and you have already completed your Trials, so you have nothing to worry about."

"I have an argument with Alkippe in my future, is what I have," I muttered, standing again. I began to pace but only took one step before I caught myself and turned to the window instead. The beach was littered with cold campfires, black scars on the formerly pristine riverbank. I wondered if they would leave the mess for us to clean up when they left. If they ever left.

As I looked down at the stone houses close to the outer wall, I saw Sagitta's door open, and a white tunic emerged from the doorway. A man. An Achaean man. Not one of her lovers from Galatae, or Hattusa from the south, or a horse lord from Paphlagonia. I frowned in concern, but Sagitta looked satisfied enough as she adjusted her sword belt and tucked her hair back into its braid before shutting the door behind her and making her way toward the stables. Beyond the wall, my eyes caught a flash of sun in bright red hair. Eri and Theseus walked together along the riverbank, their heads turned toward each other. I could not see their faces, but I knew her long legs, bare under her tunic, and the way she folded her arms across her ribs to hide their length. What was she doing with Theseus?

"Cyra, you are going to break something with that frown," Ossy said beside me. "You really are in a bother today, when you should be celebrating. Come, let's go to the baths and relax, and when we come back, I will show you your present."

"I will have a bath at the ceremony," I said absently, watching as Eri unfolded her arms to place a hand on Theseus' elbow. He turned and took her hand in his. My frown deepened.

"Did you hear me?" Ossy said, and I realized I had missed her reply. "What is it you are trying to impale with your eyes out there?"

"Eri is with the man they call Theseus," I said slowly. "There," I pointed to the bank close to the harbor. Ossy came to peer out the window and soon raised her eyebrows.

"They seem friendly."

"Too friendly."

Ossy made to reply but then paused, watching as the pair continued walking. "I cannot think talking is too friendly," she eventually said. "And I am sure young Erioboea would not be foolish enough to break the Law of First Blood."

I looked at Ossy in consternation, worried that this was the second time I was confronted with the idea that a ha-mazaan might break the Law to be with one of these uncouth barbarians. She watched my mouth try to make words and smiled slyly at me.

"They are fine-looking men, Cyra. You could not blame her for wanting it. But since they're the only men around and she has not completed First Blood, she would have to kill one of them first, and I don't think they would respond well. She is not so foolish."

"I can't believe you would even suggest that," I managed.

"You cannot tell me you do not find them attractive," she said, looking down at one of them walking under my window. His shoulders were massive from months spent at the oar, and his hair gleamed black like mine in the sunlight.

"I do not prefer great dumb aurochs, no," I ground out. She laughed merrily.

"They do look like bulls, to be sure." But then her eyes pierced me with an intent expression. "But perhaps it is not men you prefer?"

I darted a look at her, irritated. Then I spun away from the window. "I don't prefer only women, like Alkippe, if that is what you mean. Or even in the way Sagitta does. I don't think. But I have no intention of taking a man to my bed if I don't have to," I said in a clipped tone. "Penthesilea will be the *matar*, as it is her duty to bear a child, not mine, and there is no other reason for me to lie with a man. I will choose not to, as is my right."

Ossy regarded me curiously for a long moment before saying, "Yes. As is your right."

"What is this?" I quickly changed the subject, pointing to the now crumpled grey fabric covering the bed.

"It is your gift, goddess-daughter."

She moved to the bed and grasped the fabric, pulling it up in front of her. As it draped down, the silver embroidery along the edge gleamed in the soft light of the room. Swirls and moon marks, as on my left arm, gilded the entire edge.

"A cloak for you. For winter's chill," she said softly and stepped forward to swing it around my shoulders, fastening the silver chain across my collarbone. I was warm already and could feel the heat gather underneath the folds, hugging the warm air against my flesh. The cloak was finely woven wool, but the inside was lined with the softest of silks, and it caressed my skin with a luxurious rustle as Ossy adjusted the folds. The hood draped over my shoulders and back, and she pulled it up over my head before turning me to face the polished silver mirror beside my wash basin.

"A cloak fit for a queen," she said, meeting my eyes in the mirror.

I touched a finger to the embroidery along the hem, marveling at the workmanship. "It is beautiful, Ossy. I shall treasure it forever."

Her hands squeezed my shoulders, then she unbuckled the chain and tossed the cloak over the helmet on the bedpost as though it was a dusty blanket. She grinned at me.

"Let's go get you that bath, even if you are having another one later," she said and pushed me out the door.

$$) ($$

We spent the rest of the day preparing for the evening ceremony. I bathed with Ossy, and Sagitta, who always seemed to be in the baths, but also Leya and Phillipisa, who chattered about their Trials as we sluiced water and the sweat of summer from our skin. In their stories, I heard none of the handicaps I had been given, and I realized my experience of the Trials had been much different after all. For this reason, I did not share my stories, but praised their success instead, truly happy for my friends, and grateful they had not experienced the same anxiety.

The evening meal in the Moon Hall was small and more intimate than the previous night. The men had taken dinner around their own fires, after asking permission from the queens to hunt deer on our lands and supply their own food. Supposedly, Antiope had gone with them on the hunt, since her duties as Hearth Queen meant she was responsible for all provisions in the city, and by dinner time, there was much talk and laughter at how she had brought down the hind that Theseus could not catch with his own arrow. Neither queen had come to the Hall yet, but we could imagine the scenario well without Antiope's retelling. I laughed along with the rest of the women, and drank my *kimiz* and tried to ignore the gnawing pit in my stomach that grew bigger as moonrise grew closer.

I left the Moon Hall with Sagitta and Ossy at my side, as all of us had grown weary from the heat, and the night was still long ahead of us. The emotions from the past few weeks piled up so that they weighed my eyelids down, as though my body wished to sleep and forget the evening ceremony was upon me. I was just about to tell them I would take some time alone before the ritual when Eri burst through the palace entrance, her blue eyes wild and her red hair tangled with wind.

"He has the queen!" she shouted to the room. We stopped as one and stared at her. "Heracles! He has taken Hippolyta to the ship! He means to take her. Not just the belt! I didn't—Theseus said just the belt—"

She stopped, gulping air as the ha-mazaans surrounded her.

"What are you saying, Erioboea?" Ossy demanded. A steely authority had replaced the gentleness I was accustomed to hearing in her tone. More ha-mazaans filtered from the Moon Hall into the foyer, curious at the commotion. Even as Eri answered between ragged breaths, my mother strode from the Hall behind us.

"Heracles has taken Hippolyta onto the ship," Eri repeated, and her eyes were still wild in her deathly pale face. "The men have made preparations to leave. They are taking her to the Achaean lands!"

All eyes stared at her. The gnawing in my belly intensified, and the itching in my tattoos overwhelmed my thoughts, so that I could barely concentrate on my mother's brisk commands. I should have been more alarmed, but I felt weary and tired.

"Sagitta, fetch Alkippe," Melanippe ordered. "Ifito, you know what to do. Savarans, prepare yourselves for battle, but you will wait for me at the gates, and you will wait for my command. There will be no time for horses. We will meet them on foot."

Then she was gone, loping away with her hand on the sword at her hip, no doubt looking for the queens and her favorite axe. Eri turned and ran out of the hall before I could speak to her, and I was left standing for a moment in stunned silence as everyone else rushed to follow their general's orders.

I was Savaran now. The orders were mine as well. I shook the stupor off and bolted for my rooms. I sprinted through the winding corridors of the palace and back to the stairs that led to my chamber, long legs taking the stone steps two, three at a time, my blood pumping loud in my ears. I slung my bow and a quiver of freshly fletched arrows across my chest before sweeping up my sword and turning to run out. My eyes went to the closet in the corner, and I stopped. I unslung the bow again, unbuckled my belt, and tossed them both to the bed as I strode to the tall armoire. I pulled out the new vest of scales and quickly shrugged into it, pulling the side buckles tight over my tunic with careless haste. It left my arms bare still, but the scales protected the heart well enough, and I did not want to take the time to change entirely. I didn't even stop to don my trousers, as the day still felt hot and I would not be riding Risa. Besides, there was no time. I re-fastened my thick leather belt over top of the vest, buckling my sword to it, slung the bow and quiver over my shoulder once more, and checked to make sure the small dagger was safely hidden in the pocket of my arm guard. Satisfied, I left my chamber at a run. It wasn't until I was bounding back down the stairs and out into the frenzy of swarming ha-mazaans that I realized I had not thought to put my sandals on. My mother would surely give me extra laps on the training field for such an oversight, but I was not about to go all the way back now.

My mother, already at the gate with Alkippe and Ifito, stood atop the wall and looked toward the ships, her axe glinting between her shoulder blades and her hand on the handle of her short sword as she paced. When she jumped down from the tall height, landing with the grace and ease of a panther among the milling Savarans, her face was grim with fury.

"The girl spoke truly. Hippolyta is on the ship with Heracles, though she appears unharmed. I have not yet found Antiope."

"If we attack, the oath of breast and blood is undone, Melanippe," Ifito warned. Melanippe looked over our faces, pausing only slightly on mine before her cool silver eyes moved on. She nodded.

"I know."

More ha-mazaans flowed into the courtyard, some still buckling their weapons to belts, and I looked around for Eri. I did not see her, though her mother Hipponike was there, her own red hair a flame in the setting sun. Ossy smiled at me when our eyes met, but her golden eyes wrinkled at the edges with concern. Sagitta grinned at me and raised her eyebrows in quick succession, clearly relishing an oncoming fight. I quirked my lips at her expression, wondering if it would be so easy for her to go from being their lover to their executioner. Knowing Sagitta, it probably would be.

"Bows ready, ha-mazaans!" my mother called, and as the gate swung open, she moved to the front of the line. I unslung my bow and nocked an arrow, and there was a *shushing* as every other soldier did the same. We marched forward, spreading out into a wide line of swiftly moving legs and pointed arrows. I found myself next to Alkippe. Her tattooed face was set in grim lines of focus as she stared at the black ships and the men standing in uneven groups in front of them.

I noticed Hippolyta first. She sat on the railing of the ship, inside the wings of the griffin. Heracles stood in front of her, his massive arms crossed over his chest and the lion skin hanging limp along his back. He saw our advancing army of arrows and stood straighter. Hippolyta looked over her shoulder. She stood and began to draw her sword, but when she moved forward toward the plank leading to the dock, Heracles caught her arm and dragged her back in front of him. I could see the gleam of bronze against her throat.

My mother held a fist in the air to halt our steps as a voice rang out over the field.

"Amazons! Hold!"

Theseus. My eyes darted for the source of his voice and found him on the bank of the river next to the second ship. Men had scattered and found their swords and shields, though it seemed like they might have been better prepared to fight us if they were going to steal our queen. Both of our queens. Theseus held Antiope just as Heracles held Hippolyta, by twisting her arms behind her back and holding a blade to her throat.

"You cannot win this, fair Amazons, though you are fierce and lack no courage." Theseus sounded almost conciliatory as he called out to us. Antiope struggled in his embrace, but his knife pushed harder against her throat as he pressed his lips close to her ear. Even from a distance, I could see her teeth bare and her chest heave with fury. My breath came harsh in my lungs, yet somehow the pumping blood in my veins made me feel drained and exhausted before the fight had even begun. Alkippe shook her head like a dog next to me and grunted.

"Let them go," Melanippe commanded, her great axe ready and threatening beside her. Her voice carried across the distance with ease, and the firmness of it straightened my spine.

"If you fight us, your queens die," Thesus called. "It does not have to be this way."

The sounds of a struggle made us look back to see Hippolyta locked in a wrestling match with Heracles. It was difficult to tell if she wrestled with a lion or a man, but she slipped from his embrace and rounded on him with sword flashing. I do not know how it happened. Her sword flashed toward his chest and pushed his blade aside, but then she cried out, and red dripped from the point of Heracles' blade as it pierced her heart and broke through her back.

My mother screamed her sister's name as Hippolyta fell to her knees. Heracles ripped the blade from her breast, his free hand reaching for her body even as it fell, grasping her by the belt he had come for. There was shouting and then chaos as the men ran toward us, swords high.

"Ha-mazaans!" Antiope screamed over the blade against her throat. "*Fight!*"

I had already raised my bow and aimed it at Heracles. My arrow sank into the skin of the lion around his neck, but he was still dragging the Defending Queen's body and did not even feel it. I ran forward, nocking another arrow and loosing it as I moved, but the cat's skin was like an impenetrable shield, and I was too far away to pierce it. More arrows landed around him, but he stood unharmed, Hippolyta's belt in hand. I skidded to a halt and breathed a deep, grating breath, then aimed my arrow at his heart, where there was no lion skin. I loosed it as Alkippe stumbled into me. The arrow went wide into the side of the ship, and then Alkippe pitched forward onto her knees, her axe skidding into the gravel in front of her.

"Alkippe!"

Kneeling next to her, I pulled her body over, looking for an arrow, but there was no visible wound. Her eyes were heavy and closed completely even as I shook her and called her name.

"*Matar*," I cursed. I bolted to my feet again and nocked another arrow, but the time for that had gone. Ha-mazaans and Achaeans were locked together along the riverbank, making it impossible to use my bow without killing one of our own. I ducked my head through the bowstring and ran forward into the setting sun, drawing my sword.

An Achaean appeared before me, teeth flashing between tight lips, and I raised my sword to my shoulder and brought it down with a scream of fury. Sword met sword, the impact shuddering up my hands into my arms. I swung again, lower this time, slashing at his knees, but he blocked the move easily. I felt slow and weak, as though all my energy had been used up in my Trials. But I refused to die at the hands of an Achaean coward.

Again I swung, trying to keep my form as I had been taught, thinking somewhere in the back of my mind, "He does not swing first," but again, his bronze sword was blocking the sharper blade of my iron, almost easily though he did not seem a better fighter, pushing my sword aside as though it was a fly and he was annoyed with its buzzing.

I lurched backward, putting space between us. I held my sword low in front of me with both hands, knees bent, and moving with low, cat-like steps in a wide circle. I watched the man through slit eyes against the lowering sun, my thoughts racing to find my next move. The sounds of battle were all around me, almost as it sounded in daily drills, with the clang of metal against metal and the grunts of soldiers lunging or shouting, but different also from anything I had ever known, for there were men's voices in this fray, and the shouting from the ha-mazaans penetrated the air with a frenzied anger I had never heard.

Beyond the Achaean's shoulder, I caught sight of the tattooed arms of my mother as she swung her axe high overhead. She staggered. She went down to one knee, and her arms went slack for a moment, and a new terror gripped my guts, but then she finished the swing. The Achaean before her screamed and gripped his waist where the blade buried deep. Then my mother was falling forward, and I could not see more as the crush of ha-mazaans and men hid her from my vision once again.

The man in front of me lunged, and I was distracted enough by my mother's fall that he caught me unawares. I was sluggish in raising my blade, and he caught the handle in such a way that when he pulled, I was carried forward with it. I used the momentum, letting the sword fly from my hands, my hand moving to my arm instead. He was wide open, surprised at my rush toward him, and in a flash, my knife slid between his ribs. The entire weight of my body pushed it forward, all the way to the hilt, before I saw his eyes widen and felt the hot, wet blood gush over us both. He stumbled backward, and I pulled, the knife jerking loose and more blood gushing with it, spreading across his gut and onto the ground, and then he was falling, the sword tipping from his fingers into the dirt. I sheathed my bloody knife and crouched to pick up my sword.

Turning, I watched in horror as Prothoe fell to an invisible foe, her axe spilling from her hands into the dirt though no Achaean fought against her. The beach was covered with more ha-mazaans than I would have ever thought possible, lying prone against the gravel, their weapons still or gone. I stumbled forward into a run, leaping over a red braid that may have been Hipponike's, or Eri's; I couldn't tell. Another Achaean turned to meet my swinging sword, but again, my arms were weak and uncooperative, the sword unwieldy. He knocked it from my hands like it was a toy in the grip of a helpless babe. The edge of his blade swung faster than my torpid limbs could move and caught me just above my wide leather belt, under the armpit, ringing off the scales of my armored vest. Fire burned through my chest, and I wondered if the blade had sheared into me. His sword swung again, hilt first. I tried to step back, but there was something tangling my feet, another dead ha-mazaan perhaps, and I landed heavily, my breath sharp in my chest and everything in my mind tumbling together in confusion. I fumbled for the dagger at my elbow, trying to draw the still dripping knife from its sheath, but I was not fast enough.

The hilt of his sword swung downward, and all was blackness.

CHAPTER 6

ABDUCTED

W aves of nausea rolled through my body. My stomach pinched to the base of my spine one moment, and then the next, it was trying to climb out of my throat, leaving fingerprints of bile on my tongue. My head felt as it had on the day Alkippe used the butt of her axe to ring my helmet like a bell and knock me unconscious, to remind me what losing focus would mean in a proper battle. That had been when I was fourteen. I had not made the same mistake again, nor had my head felt like a boiled quail's egg since then. My eyes were crusty and swollen, and the skin pulled as I tried and failed to open them.

The wave rolled through me again, and I bolted upright, headed for the latrine to empty the contents of my stomach there rather than on the bed. I made it into a slightly curled fetal position before at least one of three things stopped me. The screaming pain in the ribs along my side that made me cry out and fall back again. The fact that my hands were pinned behind me, immobile, and my ankles stuck together as tightly as my eyelids. Last, what felt like a sandaled foot, heavy and forceful against the side of my throat as soon as I struggled to move. It shoved my cheekbone firmly back against what should have been the soft mound of my pillow but was unmistakably a piece of rough, damp wood.

This time when the rolling came, I knew it did not begin in my stomach. I was on the sea. Waves heaved the ship up into the heavens and down again, while the foot on my throat pressed me down into the wet plank, keeping me tight against the deck. The creaking of oars, the stench of men straining at them, and the pungent *slap, slap, slap* of salty water against the hull filled my senses.

Hippolyta.

The image of a sword erupting through her back, reddened with her own blood, flooded my mind, and after it came the sounds of ha-mazaans screaming, ha-mazaans swinging their swords and axes and loosing their spears or arrows. Ha-mazaans lying dead on the beach in impossible numbers. My mother falling.

I tried to swallow it down, but the bile, encouraged by both the waves and the memories, made its way forcefully out of my throat. The man with his toes curled into my neck cried out in alarm as the warm fluid splashed over us both. His foot moved away, but I did not try to sit up again.

The retching had set fire to my ribs once more. *Broken, or badly bruised*, I thought and fought to control my stomach and my mind. I needed to clear my thoughts of everything, pain included, and think as I had been trained to. As ha-mazaan.

"Cyra?"

"Sagitta," I cried in relief, but it was no better than a croak.

"I am also here," Melanippe's voice came from far away, sounding worn and tired. I almost cried to hear my mother's voice.

More voices came to me from the darkness beyond my eyelids, several at once, and I could picture each of their faces clearly in my mind's eye, but I could not reconcile the twinges of fear and uncertainty I heard with the undaunted ha-mazaans I knew of Themiscyra.

"Leya," a voice called, even further away than Melanippe.

"Ifito."

"Phillipisa."

"Prothoe."

"Tekmessa."

"Asteria."

"Silence!" a man's voice shouted over them. I heard flesh hitting flesh, and someone grunted heavily. Then one more voice said, defiantly,

"Aello."

Another dull thud, and I could only assume it was Aello who grunted in pain.

They had filled the ship with some of the finest warriors in the city. The thought brought me both courage as well as grief. Some of the best of us still lived and were together in this trouble. That brought me hope. But how they had taken so many of our best...and to think of what had become of those they had not taken alive...

Abruptly, the foot that had been on my throat planted between my shoulder blades and shoved my body forward through my own vomit. I slid along the planks and came to a stop against another warm body, but then his foot was gone. I heard an oar being wrenched with a wet squeak over wood and then feet shifting around my body before moving away. The person in front of me did not move or speak, despite my face being pressed into their shoulder. I rubbed my face against the folds of their tunic to remove the dried blood. The hold of the galley was dimly lit by only narrow oar slots at each side, and what sky I could see through them was dark and ominous. But it was daylight. The sun had been setting when we fought on the beach, and I knew I had been unconscious for longer than an hour. We had been on the water all night.

It was Alkippe I lay behind, and she was still unconscious. Raising my head, I peered over her shoulder. I could see the outlines of ten, maybe twelve rowers ahead, with their backs facing us, and at their feet, the tangled bodies of other ha-mazaans, similarly bound. I recognized the distinct swirled tattoo on my mother's calf lying across the aisle about halfway down. At the far end of the hold, there was a short ladder leading to the upper deck. The man who had shoved me must have gone above. I could hear voices murmuring through the hatch, low and indistinct between the sound of waves slapping the hull.

The men were shouting orders from above deck to the rowers below. The sky through the oar slots changed from slate to pewter to blackened charcoal as the clouds changed. The ship was turning.

"Hold steady!"

A man clambered down the ladder again, and even from a distance in the shadowed light, I could make out the bronze that gleamed between his teeth when he reached the bottom deck and turned.

In a quick movement, he took the knife from his teeth, bent, and slashed at the ha-mazaan's legs nearest to him. There were several gasps from women lying nearby, but he reached with the other hand and grasped the woman's arm, hauling her to her feet, and I could see he had only cut the bindings around her ankles. It was Eri. Roughly, the man shoved her to the bottom of the ladder and pointed upward. She could not mount the steps with her hands tied behind her back, though she tried as he prodded her cruelly in the ribs with the hilt of his knife. Muttering a curse, the man called to his shipmate above.

"I'm cutting them loose to climb, Heracles! Tell them to have ropes ready once they are moved."

Heracles.

I pictured him with his arm around Hippolyta's throat, the lion's teeth gouging his forehead. His face as his sword sliced through her. He had looked almost...bewildered. Everything within me wanted to see the look on his face once more, as my own blade slid through his heart. But I was bound and had no weapon, and this time it was Eri they were manhandling.

Eri's hands were free now, but the Achaean held the knife firmly pressed to her ribs. "No chances," he warned and pointed up the ladder once more. She cast a final glance over her shoulder, and her terrified eyes met mine for the briefest of seconds before she began to climb. As soon as her head disappeared through the hatch, a hand gripped her arm and practically hauled her the rest of the way. There was some talk above, and Heracles' voice called down,

"Another. We will move them two at a time."

The man bent and slashed at the ropes binding another ha-mazaan, dragging her to her feet and shoving her unceremoniously toward the ladder. Short brown hair and powerful shoulders. Ifito. They hauled her onto the deck when those above could reach her arms, and this time the man climbed up after her.

"Starboard ship oars! We're closing the gap."

Each of the men on my side of the aisle pulled their oars in unison out of the water, through the narrow slots and into the hold with a squeak of wet wood. I saw the sky darken and change, and what seemed to be the bitumen-blackened keel of another ship blocked out most of the light from my side of the galley. They were moving us to a different ship.

Loud thumps echoed through the galley, then Theseus was climbing down the ladder. His eyes swept over the hold, viewing the cargo with unconcealed delight. The first man followed him down and, sweeping his hand wide as though showing a guest an amazing view, said,

"Is it not glorious, Theseus? Enough Amazon women to fill every room in Eurystheus' palace."

"It will not be as idyllic as you make it sound, Pirithous," Theseus warned, hands on hips. "One from our ship has just killed two of the men, though they were not as careful as they could have been. The sooner our bounty is stored in the merchant hold, the better."

Another wave rocked the ship, and there was a grinding shudder as the hulls of the two vessels met. Gesturing to a woman lying on the planks, Theseus spoke to the oarsman seated above her.

"Cut them free and send them up." He climbed the ladder again and was gone.

One by one, the oarsmen dragged the women to their feet and shoved them to the galley ladder. When they hauled my mother to her feet, she staggered, and I gasped to see her face covered in blood that looked wet and fresh. When they turned her with rough hands and shoved her toward the stairs, Melanippe let out a soft moan and began to fall, so that the oarsman had to catch her roughly by the arm and drag her upright again. He shoved her mercilessly toward the ladder, but I had already seen that her right leg was smeared dark with blood. Slowly, she climbed upward, moving with pained stiffness and using only her left leg to pull her body up the steps.

Icy fear twisted my guts. I had never seen my mother so unsteady. But perhaps the blood was not all her own, and it was only a head wound that made her dizzy? Somehow, I knew the hope was false.

Myself and the still-unconscious Alkippe were the last two they came for. They prodded at Alkippe, then hoisted her over their shoulder with an audible grunt at the weight of her. They slashed the ropes around my wrists and ankles with quick precision. I rolled to my knees and tried to climb to my feet but had forgotten about my ribs and clasped my arm against my side, grunting. Pirithous reached for me as though he would throw me over his shoulder as the other man had with Alkippe, but I put up my other hand to block him and clambered painfully to my feet before he could touch me. They shoved me down the aisle and up the ladder, hands grabbing at my arms and pulling me up so that I cried out, despite trying to bite my tongue against the pain. They did not let go of my arms as my feet found the deck but held me close between two of them as they dragged me forward, stumbling on numb legs to the bow of the ship.

The second ship's deck loomed far above my head; it was double the size of the galley I stood on, with a mast taller than any I had ever seen and an enormous sail that crackled in the gusting wind with the sound of a breaking tree. A second black Achaean galley like the one I stood on was docked against its far side. More ha-mazaan women stood on the deck of that ship, and as I watched, an Achaean shoved the point of his spear into a ha-mazaan's thigh and prodded her forward toward a rope ladder which dangled from the enormous ship.

I recognized the girl's face, brown and dusky like an autumn evening, as the daughter of the blacksmith in Themiscyra. Camilla. An apprentice silversmith in her own right, but not one of our fighters. A Crafter. How had they taken her? She would not have been part of the fight. It made no sense.

"Now you."

Pirithous shoved me toward a rope ladder that trailed down onto the wet deck. I looked up to where it attached to the deck above, and two bronzed Achaean faces leered down at me, black clouds billowing dense and ominous behind them. Thunder rumbled in the distance.

Then Theseus himself was at my side, and before I could react or step away, his fingers clasped my jaw, squeezing into my flesh and turning my head to face his. My flint grey eyes met his blue ones, and I hoped he saw all the hatred I felt for him.

He turned my face the other way as though studying my profile from all angles. "Niece of the beautiful queens, if I am not mistaken." He nodded as if pleased with what he saw, despite my attempts to sear the flesh from his face with my eyes. "You'll make a fine mother to an Achaean warrior, girl. I saw how you performed in the ring. Perhaps I will even make you a fighter in the pits. I wonder if you will prove as good against the lions." His hand released my face abruptly, and I turned my head slowly to look into his eyes. I did not look away as my spit landed with a satisfying splatter across his left eye and cheekbone, which was already showing a swelling bruise from the fight against us.

There was a moment of shock on his face before his hand wiped away my spittle, the gloating smile disappearing along with it. Teeth bared, he yanked my arm from Pirithous and marched me to the rope ladder. If I had not instinctively reached to grab it when he shoved me forward, I would have fallen headfirst into the cold, seething blackness of the water below. Then his hand gripped my hair at the base of my skull, pulling my head backward as I scrambled to keep my feet under me on the wet deck.

"For that, you will be one of the first to know what it feels like to have an Achaean between your thighs. I promise you will not like that half so much as being in the Pit."

He shoved a hand against my backside, hard, forcing my feet off the deck, and I scrambled to keep hold of the sagging, pendulous rope ladder. The rough hemp buckled and swayed underneath me, my ribs a band of fire as I tried to find purchase with my bare toes. When it stopped trying to twist me off, I looked down at the black water between the ships. A part of me wondered whether I should let go and take my chances with the waves. I looked around, toward the horizon, but saw nothing but wine-dark water for as far as the eyes could see.

Somehow, I made it up one unsteady rung, then two, and when I was high enough, the men leaning down from the deck grasped me under the arms and hauled me over the railing, my ribs and hip bone dragging painfully against the wood even through the thick scaled vest and leather belt. There were more ha-mazaans crowded on this deck, being brought up from the ship on the other side. Their faces registered in my mind with numb astonishment. So many women. How? The question would not stop repeating in my mind.

"Move along, little bitch."

A soldier pushed me forward, and another prodded me down a set of stairs to the rowing deck. The men at the oars were far greater in number on this ship, with at least thirty low seats on each side of the aisle, and almost all of them occupied. Yet another Achaean prodded me forward with the tip of his sword, and I moved slowly toward another set of stairs leading down to a third level of the ship. I had never imagined a ship with three levels could exist. Cautiously, I stepped down into the lower space, which was dimly lit by a single flickering torch in the hands of a short, pimply-faced youth who could not have been over twelve or thirteen summers. A soldier busied himself tying ropes around Aello's wrists, and behind her, against the hull and all around the hold, sat maybe fifty more ha-mazaans.

I scanned their faces in dismay. So many women. I searched until I found the white, drawn face of my mother. Melanippe gave me a weak nod before closing her eyes, as though she had been waiting for me but was now too tired to remain awake. My hands were wrenched behind me, and a rough length of rope wound once, twice, before the man tied a knot, giving it a jerk to test its strength when he finished.

"Sit."

He shoved me down next to Tekmessa and Aello, both of them sitting with their legs drawn to their chest, as there was little room in the cramped space. The hold was filled with everything a normal merchant might travel to Themiscyra to offer or accept in trade. Enormous urns, likely filled with smaller jars of olives, olive oil, pomegranates, figs, or perhaps hazelnuts, which was a major crop we exported to the south. We sat on a layer of bronze and copper ingots, laid out in a herringbone pattern so as not to shift in the unstable conditions at sea. Traders often brought the oxhide ingots to our shores so they might trade for our higher quality metals, like star-forged metal. The glint of glass ingots reflected beside my left arm, richly dyed with cobalt and malachite. A wealthy merchant ship, to have so many precious wares, and now there were a good number of ha-mazaan captives to add to their bounty.

"That's the lot, Denys," Pirithous said as he came down the stairs. "Fifty-six plus the one who jumped into the sea, and the one that Theseus has kept. Their lady queen." Several ha-mazaans exclaimed angrily at this, but he paid them no attention. A yawning despair inside the pit of my belly grew deeper as his words crept through the fog in my brain. Antiope being kept as Theseus' captive. There could be no greater humiliation.

Pirithous took the torch from the young boy's hand and replaced it with a large waterskin.

"Ambers, have them drink this," he instructed. "Denys, please instruct them on their stay. Ladies," he nodded to us casually, handed the torch to Denys, and was gone again.

Denys turned to face the rows of ha-mazaans seated haphazardly between the shiphold goods.

"You will drink twice a day, and eat once, until we reach Theseus' lands. You use that bucket to relieve yourselves." He pointed toward a squat wooden bucket, barely visible in the corner, with bales of linen and elaborately carved wooden boxes stacked on each side. Denys stood directly in front of me, so close I could see the golden hairs on his bronze legs and the long dagger carelessly tucked through the leather of his belt. If my hands were not tied so tightly...

"If one of you causes trouble, none of you eat for a full day. Trouble includes talking back, or talking at all. Or attempting to prove how great of a warrior you are." His teeth flashed in the dim light, but his eyes held no humor. "You are no longer what you call ha-mazaans.

You are captives. If you refuse to follow direction, or if you make life difficult, you will be tossed to the waves."

He held the torch aloft, observing as the boy, Ambers, doled drinks out one at a time as the women tipped their heads back, eager for fresh water. The youth tipped the waterskin over Aello's face beside me, and she gulped a few mouthfuls before he moved to stand over me. I swallowed as much as I was able, much of it splashing onto my cheeks to mingle with the dried blood before he moved to Tekmessa.

It took the boy a long while to make his way through all of us. Fifty-six, the man had said. Plus one in the sea. And Antiope. And of the hundreds left in Themiscyra, how many still lived? How many were wounded? Wounded and free was still better than this, though. I wondered which of the women had jumped into the frigid waters rather than be bound in the belly of an Achaean galley. I almost wished I had been so brave. I turned to see the faces of the other ha-mazaans, their features pinched and weary in the flickering of the flame.

Melanippe sat behind me with her back against the ship's hull, her head bowed to her chest and her black hair, much of it freed from the tight braids by the effort of battle, obscuring most of her face. I could not tell if she was awake or asleep. The knot of worry tightened in my stomach.

Ifito and Prothoe sat to either side of their general, the first one rugged and grim-looking, as she always was, and Prothoe pale in hair and features, like the moonlight, her ice-blue eyes almost glowing in the dim hold. Witty, always teasing, light-hearted Leya was nearby as well, and Camilla, with her enormous almond eyes wide and darkly shining in the firelight. Camilla would have stood little chance against the Achaeans, who had clearly been undiscerning in who they claimed as spoils. To see her and Tekmessa, a *zizenti* priestess, here amongst the warriors was as puzzling as it was unsettling.

Ambers held the waterskin above Melanippe, and I bit my lip as he reached with one hand to push her forehead back, gently tipping her face into view. It was covered in blood, her eyes closed, her mouth slack. The boy tipped water carefully between her lips, and she spluttered, coughing it back up again. Her eyes opened blearily before closing again. Ifito and Prothoe each sidled closer to her, propping her body between them as my mother lost consciousness once more.

"We must tend her," Ifito said urgently, looking first at the boy who was about to serve her water and then at Denys. "Her wound is deep. She will bleed to death or become infected without it being stitched."

The knot pulled so tight in my stomach that I thought I would vomit once more. Denys shrugged, unfazed.

"Fifty-five of you is as good as fifty-six," he said dismissively.

Aello spat at him, and it splattered on his leg. He slapped her casually, though still with considerable force, with the back of his fist, and she toppled sideways from the force of it. I struggled to my knees to shield her from another blow, but he put his knee into my collarbone and shoved me hard. I sprawled against Tekmessa, my ribs clawing at my chest.

"That's enough water for today," Denys motioned sharply to Ambers to step away, though many had not had their share.

"Captain warned there was to be no trouble," Denys said, and raised an eyebrow first at Aello, who glared furiously back, then at me as I struggled into a sitting position, my ribs and tied hands making any movement difficult to accomplish with any dignity.

"You can thank this little bitch and your queer-eyed raven here," he said, pointing a thick finger at Aello and then me, "for not having your thirst quenched today." He pointed a meaty finger at me again in warning. "Think twice in the morning if you want to cause more trouble because this trip will be long if you choose mischief over water. Or perhaps, not as long as you would like."

With those words, he turned and made his way up the steps. Ambers darted fretful looks at the angry faces staring up at him, his long, pimpled face uncertain and apologetic as he clutched the nearly empty waterskin to his narrow chest. Stepping carefully between the tangle of legs to find a path out, he scurried up the steps and out of sight.

Like the snuffing of a candle, the light was gone with them. The cramped space was thrown into darkness as the trap door thumped closed, echoing with dreadful finality when the latch clicked into place.

CHAPTER 7

THE BELLY OF A SHIP

"*Matar!*" someone cursed in the darkness.

"Matar Kubileya on a spit," another agreed.

"Cyra, your mother—" Ifito's normally gruff voice, taut with worry, cut through my helpless anger. "I cannot wake her. She has lost much blood from her leg."

"I will come."

Bodies shifted to clear a path for me. I wiggled over the cold metal ingots, blindly inching backward until my fingers touched flesh. My mother's bare calf felt cold, as though she had swum too long in the sea and was not yet warm again from the sun.

Prothoe wriggled aside, and I shoved myself all the way back to the wall, bracing my body against Melanippe's sagging shoulder. I felt my mother's head loll forward, but there was nothing I could do with my hands behind my back. Sagitta's voice came from the darkness, low with anger.

"How are we here? *How?*"

"There were more than enough of us to overpower them," Ifito said nearby. I turned my head toward her voice in the darkness.

"But we did not, and yet most of us are barely wounded. Other than my mother," I said. There was a long pause; the only sounds were our harsh breathing and the drums pounding above to keep the rowers on a steady rhythm in the stormy sea.

"There were many wounded. They did not bother to bring the dead," a voice I did not know said in the darkness.

"I—I could not keep my feet or focus my eyes when the fighting started..." Leya whispered the words as a confession, and her voice trailed off in shame, but another voice continued.

"Yes, it was the same for me." It was Ossy. Dear, beloved Ossy. I did not know whether to despair or delight in the fact that her wise and steady presence was here with me. "I felt as though I could have lain down and slept," she said.

"Poisoned," Ifito said flatly.

I nodded slowly in the darkness. It had to be.

"But how?" Sagitta said. "They had no access to our stores. They were not with us when we took our evening meal. And yet, I felt the same. I thought I had grown weak and cowardly. I would not have admitted it unless you had said it aloud, Leya."

A chorus of voices added their own fears to the room, and though the truth of it was dark and worrying, it was less of a horror than thinking we had not been strong or brave enough to overcome their pitiful host. There had been at least two hundred skilled warriors against their ninety men with dull swords. Poison was the only answer.

"I heard them shouting from one ship to another once we were away," Ifito said. Her voice became quieter. "They boasted of having taken Antiope and their luck in capturing so many of us. Good mothers of future warriors, they said. Though Heracles spoke of regretting what happened with Hippolyta."

"Murdering her, you mean," Sagitta said harshly.

"Achaean scum," Thraso's deep voice came from far back. "We should have heeded Otrera and never let another enter our lands."

The bitterness in her words echoed in my own heart. Heracles would no doubt return to his homeland and gloat of his exploits, as he had gloated of his tall tales in our Moon Hall. It galled me to think our queen's name would ever be on his lips, other than to weep for mercy at what he had done.

We sat silently for a long while, our breaths at once harsh and faint in the blackness and mingling together with the sound of creaking oars coming from the hold above. We were so deep in the belly of the ship that we must have been below water level. The thought left me feeling queasy and suffocated, as though the water was not outside but pressing into my mouth and fighting to fill my lungs so that I could not draw a breath without pain. Ha-mazaans did not belong on the sea, in the belly of a ship. We belonged on the back of a horse or running free on bare feet across sand and rock. I tried to breathe deeply, to fend off the panic, but my ribs burned anew.

"Who is lost to us? To the sea?" Tekmessa asked softly. The *zizenti* delivered souls from woman's womb to woman's arms, and again from this world to the Otherworld, back to the Womb of the Great Mother. She offered light when it was a warrior's time to pass through the Gate to the Otherworld, and to undergo a journey such as birth or death without the aid of a *zizenti* was arduous and difficult. No doubt she had already said many prayers for the lost ha-mazaan's journey.

"It was my mother." It was Eri who finally spoke, and soon her stifled sobs echoed in the dark hold.

The shock of her words slowly seeped through my consciousness. I thought of Eri and me braiding each other's hair while Hipponike hummed softly over her household chores. I remembered her strong voice, lilting and musical, teaching us the songs of her mother's grandmother. How round and taut her belly had been when she carried her second daughter, Anva. How I had laid my head next to Eri's on the mound of Hippoinke's womb and listened to the mystery of two heartbeats echoing inside a woman's body, giggling with my friend over the strangeness of it. That had been well before either of us had received our moon-blood prophecy. Hipponike had been a good mother. Her daughters should not have to suffer like this. My heart ached for my friend as it never had before.

"She stabbed one of them in the ribs when we were being moved from the other ship," Eri continued. "She must have still had her knife somehow. Or grabbed his. I don't know." She sobbed again. "But then when he fell toward the water, he grabbed her hair and...she hit another one in the throat with the blade. But they fell..." her words became gulps of air as her sobs took over. I wished I could comfort her, but I was too far away. There were inaudible murmurs as the surrounding women attempted to soothe her pain.

So, no ha-mazaan had jumped after all. I felt ashamed for believing one had. Hipponike had died bravely, but her last daughter was all alone now in Themiscyra, with no mother or sister and not even old enough for her first moon-blood. Eri cried harshly from somewhere against the far wall, perhaps thinking the same thoughts.

"And Antiope?" Tekmessa said.

"She is unharmed," Thraso's voice was heavy in the darkness. "When I saw her last, anyway. I don't know why they did not move her along with the rest of us."

But we did know, and the thought sent a shiver over my cold flesh.

Another heavy silence penetrated the hold as we each thought of the fate that awaited us. There was little doubt what it would entail. We spent our lives preparing to avoid the threat of it. Ha-mazaans did not make good slaves, though, for long ago, our Ways had sworn us to be subject to no man, and none in this hold would consent to bear a life of drudgery, rape, or domesticity under the thumb of an Achaean man.

The ha-mazaans in this hold had either been born into freedom, as I had, or had fought for and won it, as Alkippe had, far to the South in her homeland of Punt. Women like Alkippe, young and old, free or former slaves, traveled from all corners of the world to join our cities and become ha-mazaan. Many left their homes after being forced to bear children for brutish men or even marry those who raped them. This had been Alkippe's story, although I did not know the whole of it. Some left their homelands because their brothers, less capable or adept, inherited land and the coins from their fathers, while they, because they were women, were asked to bind themselves to a man five times their age and bear his children in trade for shelter and food. The thought was unconscionable to me. If the Achaeans imagined we would willingly be sold into such a life, becoming docile and meek for the exchange of gold or silver, they would learn soon enough that every one of us would rather die than be captive broodmares.

I thought of Antiope again. She was beautiful, and Theseus would no doubt be unable to quell his own urges. Nor would he consider why he should, for he was a man accustomed to having what he wanted when he wanted it. I smiled grimly. His end would not be swift or painless if he violated her. I relished the thought.

There was a moan from somewhere to my right, beyond my mother and Ifito.

"Alkippe wakes," Ossy said. "They must have hit her hard, to put her out for so long."

"She was not hit at all," I said. "She was down before the fighting even started. Whatever poison they gave us worked well."

"What is…" Alkippe began, her voice thin and reedy.

"Many are with you, Alkippe, do not struggle," Ossy said gently. "We are in an Achaean galley. Prisoners."

Alkippe's breath whooshed out in a rough cough. "I cannot feel my hands."

"They are tied, for a full night and half a day now. Try to move your wrists and let the blood flow," Ossy said.

Had it been so long? We must already be past the port of Sinope. The smaller ha-mazaan city lay a day's journey on horse west of Themiscyra, but I had never traveled farther than our own bay by ship and had no idea where we might be. How long would we be at sea before reaching Theseus' lands? How long in this dark hold, with no fresh air, no light other than the torch they would bring twice a day? How long did they expect us to shit in a bucket like sick animals in a stall?

"Water?" Alkippe asked weakly.

"None until the Achaean returns. I am sorry."

There was a grunt, then the sounds of more shifting bodies.

"I knew those bastards meant trouble. I should have chopped Theseus' feet from his ankles when he jumped off that ship."

"We should have burned their blackened ships with flaming arrows the moment they entered the bay," someone else said, and there were angry murmurs of agreement.

"No use for what-ifs about the past, ha-mazaans," Ifito said briskly. "What we need is a plan for the present so that we have a future other than serving the Achaeans—or any other cursed man—as whores and chambermaids."

A grim silence met her words. Finally, Ossy said, "Does anyone still have a knife? I was struck in the head and dizzied with poison, but I know they had little time to gather us onto the ships. They took our weapons as they tied us, but it's possible they were careless and missed a blade."

I thought of my dagger, slick with blood when I shoved it into its hidden sheath on my forearm. Hope sprang in my chest for the first time since I had felt the waves of the sea rocking my body.

"Prothoe, turn your back to me and feel for the dagger under my arm guard."

She did, and our tied hands met awkwardly in the dark before we found a position that worked. Her fingers groped around the top edges of the leather against my forearm.

"I think it's stuck to my skin with dried blood," I said and felt the hope expand. It was possible they had missed the small blade, crusted over as it would be with the blood that had flooded from the man's stomach. The memory brought a roaring of blood to my ears.

I had made my first kill. First Blood.

Prothoe's fingers were peeling away the leather stuck to my skin, pulling my arm hairs out by the roots. I barely noticed the pain.

First Blood was a sacred rite. The Law required at least one kill to be completed before a ha-mazaan could lie with a man. Further, any ha-mazaan who wished to bind herself to a man for life must complete three kills in battle, but this was rarely practiced, as only those who enlisted permanently with the *matars* ever chose the binding.

"I feel it," Prothoe interrupted my thoughts, her fingers finally slipping under the tight gauntlet and digging against my flesh where the hidden sheath was. I felt the knife, warm from being pressed near my skin, slide free. "I have it," she said.

There was an exhalation from every set of lungs into the darkness. It felt as though the wind of the sea outside rushed through and cleared away all the hopelessness and fear in a single sweep.

Her fingers felt carefully down my wrists and across my palms, looking for the edges of the rough hemp rope. Then she slowly began sawing the short blade back and forth. The action required the movement of her whole body, tied as she was, and she made a few incoherent grunts as she struggled to keep the knife steady.

"And what happens when each of us is unbound?" Sagitta asked.

"We kill them," Thraso answered.

"We kill the pimple-faced boy, and the man who denies us water if he visits again, yes," Ifito agreed, but her voice was harsh and contemptuous. "And then? Do we storm the rest with our fists and Cyra's tiny blade? We are strong, and our courage outweighs theirs tenfold. But we must see reality, ha-mazaans. Even all of us cannot overpower fifty, sixty men bred from bulls in hand-to-hand combat. Not without our weapons."

The fresh breeze of hope quickly became a stagnant, heavy cloud of frustration. I could not keep my mind from tracing back over her words to the "fifty-five" when the fifty-sixth was my wounded mother, still unconscious next to me and in no condition to fight or lead us as general.

"There will be a way," Ossy said firmly. Ifito answered with only a grunt of disbelief.

Prothoe made a small exclamation of success. The ropes fell away, allowing my arms to drop to my sides. My shoulders ached, and my hands were tingling, but they were free. I ignored the burning and turned, feeling in the dark for Prothoe's hands and the sharp blade. Taking the knife, I quickly sawed through her bindings. She let out a sigh of relief as her own hands came free, and I turned back to my mother, who I could feel was sagging lower without my body there to support her weight.

"Ifito, I am going to lay my mother on her side," I said so that she was not alarmed when my mother's body began falling away from her in the dark. I crouched with the knife between my teeth, trying to ease Melanippe's slack frame to the floor as gently as I could, but she was not a small woman, and the best I could do was keep her head from knocking against the cold copper. I then pulled her body forward so that her tied hands were within reach, felt along her arm for the ropes, and sliced through the hemp with two quick jerks.

"Let me cut yours, Ifito."

Carefully, I shimmied over my mother's legs in a low crouch, feeling my way against the wall of the galley and reaching blindly for Ifito. My hand found her shoulder, then her wrists, and soon Ifito was free.

"Take the dagger to free the one next to you," I said and flipped the blade into my palm so that she could grip the wooden hilt. I felt my way down her arm and pressed the hilt into her hand. She squeezed my fingers before I could move them away.

"Cyra, we must close Melanippe's wound. It is too deep. She has lost too much blood already."

My throat constricted, and bile threatened to rise once more as I turned back to my mother. I had seen the amount of blood when they moved her. And now she was unconscious, cold to the touch, her breathing so silent it felt as though I crouched next to a tiny bird, delicate and fragile. I was afraid to move too swiftly, or speak too loudly, lest her fragility be damaged. I had never seen or thought of my mother as anything but powerful, untouchable, invincible, like the mighty griffin she had killed when she was my own age. The only person I had ever seen best her in weapons training was Alkippe, who had the stamina of three horses when it came to fighting. But my mother never showed weakness because she had never been weak. An awful knowing rose up within me, unbidden and unwelcome.

I shook my head fiercely as though to shake the thought out of my mind and then nodded just as quickly, though the others could not see it, as I managed to say, "I will try to bind it for now with my tunic."

The sound of the dagger sawing through ropes was loud in the hold. I leaned back against the hull and laid my hand on my mother's brow. Her skin was cold and clammy, and when my fingers found her lips, dry and cracked and too long without water, her breath moved across the ends of my fingers in short, shallow bursts.

"We must devise a plan," Ossy said. "At least one of them will be back soon to fetch food from the stores or simply check on us. I think it would be best if we did not yet reveal our advantage."

"Yes," Alkippe said. She sounded stronger, though still hoarse from lack of water. "We need a proper plan before they know we cut the ropes."

"We could cut their throats one at a time as they come down the stairs," Thraso said. "At most, only two of them can come at once."

"No. The lot of them would be upon us in seconds," Ifito disagreed. "Or, no more would come at all until we reach the shores of Athens. They could simply lock us here and stop in ports for food and water for themselves on the way. It is three weeks to their land, if the winds favor them. I do not relish the thought of starving to death in this darkness because we could not think of a better plan."

More silence. Three weeks in the dark belly of a ship. I did not know if I could survive such a terror, though I felt ashamed to admit it out loud. There would be no ha-mazaans with sharp axes coming to our rescue and killing the men above. We were on our own, with nothing more than my small knife and our bare hands, and nearly sixty men with shoulders as thick as an ox's neck above us.

"How many more remain tied?" Ifito asked. Ten or twelve women named themselves.

"The rest of you, hide the pieces of rope under yourselves, or tuck them in your boots if you are wearing them, in case they enter," Ossy said.

I reached over my mother's shoulder, sweeping the floor with my hand until I felt the frayed edges of my cut bindings. I had no boots or trousers, but the stiff leather belt at my waist was thick and wide and would hide the pieces well enough. I had just sat upright and was about to push them between the belt and my scaled vest when the thump of the latch being flipped sounded overhead.

CHAPTER 8

PRIESTESS OF LIFE AND DEATH

The room was a mass of quick scuffling, as though a thousand mice ran from a grain-filled storeroom at the scent of a cat. When Pirithous descended, holding a fresh torch low in front of his steps and regarding us with suspicious curiosity, we appeared to adjust our seats out of discomfort. Ha-mazaans met his gaze with grim-faced resolve.

"Ambers tells me you did not all receive water?" His tone was gentle, almost apologetic, but he received no reply and did not seem to be expecting one.

"The boy will come once more with the waterskin, but I beg you, do not attempt to harm him or seduce him with your wily mischief. It is in your best interest to realize we will not hurt you. We do not *want* to hurt you, unless you make it necessary." He shook his head as though speaking to small children. "You cannot reach your weapons, and there is nothing but water for leagues and leagues, so there is no point in making this harder for yourselves." Beside me, Ifito tensed and caught her breath in a quick gasp. "Here, Ambers, make sure they all have their fill, would you?"

The young boy lurked at the entrance to the hold and scurried downward as Pirithous beckoned. The waterskin bulged with water, and he carried it awkwardly, as though it was a squirming pup that might jump from his hands if he squeezed it too tightly.

"I'm afraid we will wait for the evening before taking a meal. You will forgive the lack of hospitality, I hope." Pirithous smiled.

"My mother is badly injured," I said loudly, hands clenched behind my back. They were still clutching the bits of rope I had not had time to tuck away. "She must be treated, and her wound stitched, or she may die. She is our mightiest warrior. I am sure Theseus does not want her to die before reaching his fighting pits."

Pirithous considered me from his place on the steps, the firelight making his features dance and writhe. I gambled, now, for if they chose to help, they would quickly discover her hands were untied, although I planned to say Denys had simply overlooked binding her during the onboarding. As for the rest of us, I could only hope they would not realize our deception, but it was a gamble I needed to make. As I looked down at my mother in the dim light, the greyness in her skin made it clear I had no other choice.

"Please," I said, meeting Pirithous' hesitant gaze once more. Whether he, too, saw the unhealthy tinge to her face, or something of the desperate child in mine, I am not sure, but he nodded curtly. He was about to say something when Tekmessa spoke.

"Sir, I am good with medicine," she interjected softly. "If you would free my hands, I could do the work quickly and well and be tied once more when I finish. Besides," she smiled up at him, "I am simply a midwife and no real ha-mazaan. I do not even know how to fight."

I barely kept my face composed. The meekness of her voice was so disarming that I am sure a raging bull in full charge might have thought twice before spearing her. Pirithous' eyes wandered dubiously over her shaved skull and the blue lines of tattoos across her forehead, but he seemed to find no threat in her. He nodded.

"You will have water and bandages. Stitching will need to wait." His voice changed from compliant to firm, and his eyes met mine again. "If you cause any trouble, I shall slit the woman's throat and feed her to the fish myself, along with any who stir up nonsense. Is this understood?" He did not wait for a reply. "Ambers, when all have finished drinking, cut the bald one loose and fetch what she needs." He stepped down another two steps and stretched the torch out over Asteria's head, fixing it to the brace on the wall above her. "You will have until this torch burns out to finish the job."

Ambers flitted from woman to woman, making his way from the far side of the room over to Ifito and me, and I noticed as he moved through us, carefully stepping over leather-strapped ankles, trousered legs or bare ones, that all squirmed to face him, careful to keep their hands behind them and their backs away from his view at all times. He splashed water into Ifito's mouth and was about to tip it for me when I shook my head.

"I have already had water," I said. "Please...my mother."

His eyes darted to her body on the floor and then to the few of us seated around her. He nodded jerkily before scurrying to the stairs, where he laid the water skin down on the steps and turned toward Tekmessa, nervously picking at the small dagger at his hip. But she smiled at him, sweetly, like a mother smiles at an upset baby, and his lips could not help but echo the smile back at her, shy and tentative.

He stepped toward the priestess and used his knife to cut the ropes around her wrists in two quick swipes. In a voice that cracked in the way of young boys, he said, "I will fetch..." his words trailed off as he struggled to recall the allowed supplies.

"Linen, and a bowl of water," she prodded helpfully, and his head jerked up and down in a nod.

"Would you help me rise first, Ambers? My legs...they feel so weak, like pins and needles." Tekmessa's limpid brown eyes were as wide as a doe's. I was glad our roles were not reversed. I could never manage sounding so helpless. Ambers fairly lept to grasp her arm, putting a steadying hand under her elbow and helping the delicate *zizenti* to her feet. The boy could not take his eyes from her face as he helped her back toward where Melanippe lay. He was so enraptured by her sweet smile and shining eyes, and perhaps the markings on her face, that he definitely did not see the untied hands clearly visible at my mother's hip.

"Thank you," Tekmessa said breathlessly, touching the boy's hand on her arm with a brief caress before saying, eyebrows puckered with innocent entreaty, "The supplies...?"

"Um. Yes." The boy whirled and darted away to the far end of the hold, where piles of wooden boxes were stacked around the small bucket we were meant to use to relieve ourselves. As his back was turned and his hands sorted through what sounded like heavy pieces of metal and wood in the trunk, Tekmessa's movements changed from slow and pained to quick and purposeful. She knelt and tucked Melanippe's hand under her hip with swift precision, turning my mother's heavy body so that she lay on her own hands, hiding them completely. With a quick glance at the busily searching Ambers,

Tekmessa slid the pieces of rope I had cut from my mother's hands toward me. I shifted so that she could slide them under my thigh.

When Ambers returned, carrying a small bundle of undyed linen and a wooden bowl, the *zizenti* had already begun to inspect the wound on my mother's leg. The cut ran from the top of her thigh to the side of her knee. It was longer than my forearm, and even in the dim light, I could see the meat of muscle gleaming wetly between the edges of the skin where her thigh was roundest.

I had seen wounds before, of course. I had tended to foals and horses that had caught themselves on stones or fences or injured each other while fighting in the stables. But I had only done small chores in the infirmary and never as part of the medical team for ha-mazaans returning from battle. I had never seen a wound so fresh or so bad on a person. To see it on my mother made the despair lurking at the edges of my heart stand and grow large and formidable until I felt the shadow of it darkening every corner of my body.

"We must stay strong, for her." Tekmessa's hand was on my shoulder, her deer-like eyes soft and empathetic as she met my gaze. I nodded numbly. She turned back to Ambers. "Would you bring the light closer to me? And the water?"

He darted to fetch the waterskin and the torch, eager to do the bidding of the beautiful priestess. She took up the linen and shook it out, her movements brisk and practiced as though she was home in Themiscyra's birthing lodge rather than a cold, foreign Achaean merchant ship. She pulled the cloth tight in each hand, and it parted with a loud rip, tearing along its length so that she had a workable piece to bind the wound. Ambers returned with the light and helpfully poured water into the bowl for her, blushing hotly when she beamed her thanks up at him. Soaking the linen in the water first, Tekmessa dabbed gently around the wound. The linen came away dark after only a few touches.

"Is all well, boy?" Denys' voice boomed into the hold as he bent from the waist to peer down at us rather than coming down the steps.

"Yessir!" Ambers answered quickly, and with a quick glance around the hold, Denys' face disappeared, his retreating steps nearly silent on the deck above.

Tekmessa repeated the process of soaking the cloth and dabbing at the edges of the cut until the water in the bowl was black and inky. She had to tear away another strip of linen to finish the cleaning. She tucked my mother's tunic high on her thigh so that Ambers looked away as though it embarrassed him. Finally, she sat back, biting her lip.

"I wish I had my herbs," she said, almost to herself.

Ambers looked as I felt—sick to the stomach at the sight of gaping flesh on my mother's thigh. It was still oozing blood, but slowly, as though her heart tired from sending the blood to her legs. I saw the gleaming white hardness of pearlescent bone flickering under the torch, and the shadow in me grew darker.

Tekmessa turned her face up to the boy and asked, "Do you have any mead?"

Ambers gaped at her, and she gestured to the wound. "To keep it from festering before I bandage," she explained.

"Er….the captain…" I could tell the desire to please her was warring with his strict instructions from Pirithous.

"I am sure the captain will not mind, for it is her best hope of keeping her leg, and her life," Tekmessa assured him. When Ambers still looked undecided, shifting from one foot to another and teeth chewing painfully at his already fat bottom lip, she continued in an off-hand manner, not looking at him. "I am not sure your captain realizes, but this woman is sister to the queens, and general of our army. She will be very important for whatever is planned when we reach your home. You would not want to lose such an important prize, simply for a cup of mead…?"

Again, Ambers was no match for Tekmessa's innocent brown eyes that she turned back on him. She continued to smile sweetly up at him and said, "Here, I shall hold the torch for you if you would like?"

Without thinking, the boy handed her the torch as she stood. With one more glance down at my mother's leg, he scurried toward the barrels at the other end of the hold. The *zizenti* followed him carefully, holding the torch high so that he could see his steps and not crush any toes, which the ha-mazaans were careful to tuck out of their way. When he reached a small, brass-bound barrel, the oak of the staves still bright and clean as though the cask had been made only yesterday, he stopped and considered it before glancing back uncertainly at Tekmessa. Though her back was to me, I imagined from the blush on his beardless cheeks that she aimed her most winning smile at him as encouragement. On top of a nearby barrel was a small leather cup, and he took it up and opened the spigot at the bottom of the small cask. The sound of liquid trickling into a cup was loud in my ears as I watched what was happening.

As he filled the stiff leather, his back to the hold, Sagitta quickly raised her hand and gripped Tekmessa's. Tekmessa glanced down at her, and the woman's gaze darted to the far end of the hold and back again, her expression intent. Sagitta pulled her hand away just as Ambers turned. I held my breath, as did many others, for if he had seen even one of us free, he would sound the alarm. We would surely be tied again and likely severely punished. Worse, I was sure my mother's wound would not be tended.

But Ambers merely gazed at Tekmessa with the hopeful eyes of a puppy desperately seeking love, both hands gripping the cup in front of his chest as an offering to a goddess. He saw only the pleased and gentle thanks in that goddess's face and not the hands being swiftly tucked out of sight near his legs. He motioned with the cup for Tekmessa to go before him with the light, and as she turned, I saw the flash of my blade as she deftly tucked it into her belt. Her glittering eyes met Ossy's, then Ifito's, then mine.

When both reached my mother's side, the torch was traded for the cup of mead, and Tekmessa once again crouched down, carefully arranging the long red skirts that identified her as *zizenti*. The priestesses were robed in the blood of the Great Mother, just as we entered this life. Just as we spent our many moons of womanhood in the world. And just as we had committed to leave it.

Tekmessa tipped the mead onto the deep gash in Melanippe's thigh, and the golden liquid disappeared into the wound as though it was a gentle waterfall into a deep canyon. She poured half the mug before stopping to sop up the fresh blood mixed with honey-wine with a fresh piece of cloth. She repeated the process once more. I watched in fascination and some disgust, but the priestess did not seem to mind the gore of it. Ambers did. He was very deliberate in where he put his gaze—he would not look at Melanippe's leg, nor would he look at any ha-mazaan other than Tekmessa. Instead, he studied the hull of the ship so intently that it may as well have been the elaborate mosaic back in our Moon Hall.

Finally, she set down the empty leather cup and took up a new length of linen. She ripped it once more so that it was two long strips and set to work winding it around my mother's leg. Her fingers were swift but gentle as she tried to pinch the wound together and wrap the bandage tight, but blood seeped through before she had wound it more than twice.

It took all of my discipline to not pull my hands from behind my back and help her, for the work of holding up Melanippe's leg while winding the bandage underneath, all while keeping the wrapping tight, was obviously a frustrating struggle. I dug my fingernails into my palms and resisted, letting her finish alone, though sweat gleamed on her brow. When she had reached the end of the wound and was about to tuck the end of the bandage behind my mother's knee, she glanced up at me, her face not visible to Ambers, and mouthed two words.

Be ready.

Then she twitched her head to the side, motioning toward the boy, who was still staring fixedly at the wall above us.

"Ambers?" she said suddenly, her sweet voice discordant with the fierceness in her eyes. "Could you help me tie this? I know you only have one hand free, but…"

The boy glanced down at her in alarm. The torch was burning low, and the flame spluttered. My entire body tensed as I tried to guess at Tekmessa's plan. She sidled closer to my mother and left a gap between her body and mine. "If you could crouch here, Ambers, and hold your finger on the bandage while I tie it?"

Ambers glanced at me uneasily, but I gazed steadily at Tekmessa's hands, keeping worry for my mother plain on my face. He crouched next to me, cautiously, the flame from the torch burning hotly against my face as it drew nearer. He moved his left arm behind him at an awkward angle to keep the fire from burning me and reached a shaking hand toward my mother's thigh, tentatively placing a thin finger where Tekmessa motioned. Slowly, methodically, the *zizenti* pulled the ends of the two strips and tied them with a deliberately slow tug.

"And again, like this," she said softly, using one of her soft hands to gently pull the boy's finger from the first knot and place it on top again so that the tension held tight. She smiled into his eyes, her mouth so close to his face she would barely have to lean to kiss it. He nodded and gulped, thoroughly captivated.

More swiftly than I knew she was capable of, the knife was in her hand and at his throat, and she used her whole body to shove him backward against the wall. My own hands tangled with Tekmessa's as they covered the boy's mouth, shoving hard into his shocked face as his head met the wall. Ifito scrambled for the torch, tearing it from his hands before it could clatter to the floor.

Ambers' eyes widened with terror, and he began a high-pitched, muffled scream, but Tekmessa shoved the blade harder against his throat until blood dripped down his neck and onto his chest. He stopped his noises, but his eyes were frenzied with panic as both of us crushed him against the hull with the full weight of our bodies. I put my knee into his groin until he stilled completely. His eyes were wild, trying to see past our faces and up the stairs for his only help.

If there had been time, I might have felt sorry for the boy. For his confused fear. The woman he had been so sure only moments before was an angel or nymph, or even a goddess herself, was now every inch the ha-mazaan she was trained to be. Priestess of life, and of death. She would say a prayer to help his soul find its way in the Otherworld, to be sure, but she would have no problem initiating the process.

"Silence," Tekmessa hissed, her face only inches from his and her breath moving hot against my fingers smothering his mouth.

The tense quiet in the hold felt dangerously conspicuous, and I expected Pirithous or Denys to appear again to check why it was suddenly so deafeningly quiet. Prothoe stood, moving with quick, stealthy strides to the chest Ambers had rummaged through earlier. My ribs screamed with the effort of holding the boy still, but Prothoe's movements transfixed me. All of us stared—except for Tekmessa, who did not take her eyes or my blade from the boy's terrified face—as Prothoe opened the lid. She reached inside, and when she pulled her hand out again, it held a long wooden handle, bound with hammered brass on the end and in strips along its length. And at its head, shining in the quickly dimming torchlight, the crescent-moon-shaped blade of a star-forged axe.

Our weapons.

Our triumphant gasps of relief were terrifyingly loud.

Tekmessa smiled tenderly and then drew my blade across the boy's throat, swift and sharp and deep enough that we did not need to worry whether he would ever scream again.

CHAPTER 9

THE INHOSPITABLE SEA

T here would be no turning back.

Ha-mazaans sprang into action in a frenzied shuffle of feet and arms and hoarse whispers. It was impossible to be as quiet as was wise, but speed mattered more now. Ifito, Prothoe, and Ossy lifted weapons from the enormous trunk—ha-mazaan axes and swords as well as several spears and a few short Achaean blades—and hurriedly passed them on. Alkippe and Sagitta moved with the light feet of dancers to either side of the steep stairs, axes ready. Those who still had hands bound behind them stood to attention and waited for their bonds to be cut with swift, military efficiency. A fierce pride in our sisterhood smothered out much of the fear that had stifled my lungs since waking as captive.

By the time Ambers bled out, his blood pooling and mixing with my mother's before dripping away through the cracks between the metal ingots, every ha-mazaan was free, and most were armed. There were not enough weapons for all, but the best warriors among us held at least a sword or axe or spear. The familiar, beautiful weight of a star-forged sword in my own hand was comforting, like the kiss of a familiar friend.

The torch sputtered out, casting us back into a darkness so fraught with excited tension it felt as though I could reach out and touch it. It had only been a few moments since Tekmessa had slit the Achaean boy's throat when footsteps, quick and heavy, sounded above us. The ship rocked from side to side, and I steadied my legs against the rolling while breathing deep, dank air into my squeezing lungs.

"Ambers! What in Hades is going on down here?" Denys thumped impatiently down the first few steps, ducking his head under the lintel of the narrow entrance to the hold. "The torch—"

He screamed. The shriek echoed from one end of the hold to the other as his leg was separated from his foot in one clean motion. The axe sheared through flesh and bone as though his leg were a mound of soft mud, with Alkippe's axe burying itself into the wooden stair on the other side of his ankle. He screamed even louder as he fell, tumbling down the stairs in a thunder of flesh against wood, while Alkippe pulled her axe free and Ifito leaped over his body, charging up the stairs. She used the burnt-out torch handle to brace open the trapdoor before any of the Achaeans could think to shut it on us. The men at the oars did not react with the haste the situation demanded, however. They likely never imagined the women in their hold would be free and armed again so quickly.

Denys rolled to a stop at Aello's feet, clutching his severed leg, as Sagitta and other women bounded over him and rushed the stairs. Aello paused in front of him, and her eyes caught his with grim fury before she slapped him with the back of her hand across his blubbering face.

"Now we will show you trouble," she promised tightly, and her sword ended the sound of his screeching with a gurgle of blood.

With a brief thought for my mother, who lay still at our feet, I rushed the stairs behind Aello, lunging upward two at a time with Ossy pressed close to my side. Most of the men were still trying to ship their oars and pull their short swords or belt knives when we set upon them. When I emerged onto the rowing deck, ha-mazaans had already killed the two men nearest the trap with an axe, severing their spines at the neck so their blood made the deck slick under my bare feet. An Achaean jumped clear of an axe swing and leaped toward me, over a fallen comrade and the low-backed seats, sword swinging. My blade met him in the throat, and when I pulled it free with a vicious yank, I marveled calmly how different a man's puckering flesh felt under my blade from pine cones and dried grass.

We advanced that way through the entire galley, some ha-mazaans falling back to dispatch a man and make sure he would not rise again, and another warrior taking their place to push forward, as a battering ram does at a flimsy, poorly defended city gate. Some Achaeans scrambled onto the upper deck, eager to be away from our hungry blades and into an open space, making it all that much easier to bring down the ones who were left behind.

We were a revolving path of deadly weapons, fresh muscles eager to swing or jab, and hearts elated to be not only free but finally killing those who had thought to enslave us. I found it easier to swing my sword to sever a hand or still a heart than it had been to complete my Savaran Trials. Those had been my friends, and I had been defending myself without intending to harm. These were not my friends. These were men who had killed my Defending Queen, kidnapped my aunt, and wounded my mother. They deserved justice, and I was happy to deliver it. I felt euphoric with the rush of it. I did not feel my ribs or register their screams of pain and fury.

It was only when I saw Ifito charging the steep stairs to the upper deck, axe in one hand and a sword she had snatched from an Achaean in another, that some of the fear came back to me. She held the two weapons crossed above her, somehow managing all the steep steps without needing to brace herself, but the weapons were not enough to shield her. A knife appeared in her collarbone as she charged, though no hand placed it there. It simply flashed in the air and sunk itself with a sickening thud deep into the bare flesh just above her leather vest, piercing downward into her heart. She paused, but she did not cry out. She finished the climb, and her axe swung wildly in one hand as the sword flew from her other. But the knife had found its mark. She fell to her knees.

"Ifito!" I cried, but Aello pushed me backward, wrenching the sword from my hand.

"Stay back," she growled to my stricken face, and then she and Prothoe were climbing together. Another ha-mazaan pushed me aside, rushing past me to the step, and as I looked around with an almost frenzied frustration for another weapon in order to join them, Ossy's grim head shake stopped me.

"No, Cyra. Stay in the hold and let us finish this."

Then she was gone, and more after her, Alkippe and Asteria and Sagitta and another, each one pushing me farther back into the hold before disappearing up into the grey light. I heard shouting, and cursing of father gods and mothers, and thumps of flesh against the hollow deck.

I pulled at the arms and shoulders of dead men in desperation until I found an Achaean knife. Ignoring the warning cry of the ha-mazaan I pushed past, I lunged toward the stairs and up the steps behind the rest, despite their unwarranted attempts to try to keep me safe. Now was not the time to be thinking of politics and keeping heirs to the throne out of the fray. This was the very thing I was meant to be, as Defender of Themiscyra, whether or not the position was mine yet.

There were no Achaeans to slow my ascent, as they were all occupied with the ha-mazaans already on deck. The wood was slippery with fresh rain and blood and the smell of salt and death mixed into a heady perfume that tempered my frustration with the ha-mazaans and restored some of the previous euphoria. The sky was darker gray than it had been earlier, like star-iron freshly beaten on the anvil. A curtain of water rolled across the waves from the southeast in a dense storm front, headed directly toward our rolling ship. Over the stern, a black ship crawled over the water, and far off the port-side, another ship. Their sails stretched taut as men struggled to haul them closed on the ship closest to us. Our own sail snapped high overhead as gusts of wind caught the expanse of canvas and stretched it almost to the point of ripping.

Ifito lay at my feet, motionless. Her weapons were gone, most likely snatched up by a desperate Achaean. There was chaos on all sides, with determined ha-mazaans matched against frantic Achaeans, some men using just their knives to pathetically slash away much larger swords or axe blades. Several of the men were naked now, their short tunics wrapped around their arms as makeshift shields.

As I attempted to dart in and help Aello against two men, a naked Achaean leaped at me, mouth open in a grimace of hate and a growl of fury pouring through it. I swung my stolen knife, but his arm, swathed in the thick cloth of his tunic, absorbed the blade, and my jab did nothing to stop his forward movement. His thick body hit mine and sent me sprawling onto the deck. I landed on my hip and shoulder, and the back of my head hit the wood with such force that stars filled my vision. Stunned, I vaguely registered him wrenching the knife from the bindings on his arm and then swinging it down at my stomach.

An axe also swung. It severed his arm at the elbow, and his thick-fingered hand, still clutching the knife, fell with a thud onto my bruised ribs, though the blade did no harm against the scales I wore. The man screamed at his severed stump, but then the other side of the axe, long and pointed like a pick, buried itself in his throat before tearing loose again. Even as he fell to his knees, eyes round with shock at his own death, Ossy reached down a hand to pull me up.

"I told you to stay below, Cyra!" she yelled, but as soon as I was on my feet, she was leaping away again, axe held low with both hands.

I retrieved the knife from the severed fist that still held it, peeling the man's clenched fingers from the handle as I scanned the deck. The Achaeans had no chance. About fifteen of them remained, and they were being pressed closer to the outer railings one forced step at a time. Sagitta had backed an Achaean against the railing, his makeshift armor of cloth a poor match for her sharp axe. His tunic hung in tatters off his arm, and bloody lines crisscrossed his torso and arms. She was toying with him. She arced the curved blade toward his throat after he tried to defend his legs from a feinted jab, and when he leaned back to duck under it, his center of balance shifted. He tumbled backward off the deck and disappeared with a scream and a splash. Sagitta's lip protruded in a disappointed pout as he went over; it was an expression her daughter Leandra often wore when the sweets had all disappeared after an evening meal, and it brought a smirk to my face to see it on Sagitta as she watched her ghoulish entertainment swallowed by the black waves.

Nearby, Pirithous was still fighting. His face grim and intent, the Achaean captain raised his sword to beat aside a spear thrust from Leya. She twirled the spear in her hand, under and over her arm and then her head as though it was light as a feather and each move had been choreographed ahead of time, even the sword swing he aimed at her left hip. Her spear whirled and flashed, and bronze blade met bronze-wrapped handle with a sharp clang before the butt of Leya's spear poked sharp and quick into his throat. His head snapped back, and his sword arm swung wildly as he tried to keep his feet planted. Leya wasted no time. She leaped into the air, and one long leg, calf wrapped in leather strapped sandals, reached high in a swift, powerful kick to the center of his chest. Pirithous was comical in his astonishment as his knees buckled against the railing and he felt himself falling backward. The sword fell to the water with him. Leya was already spinning, spear in hand, ready for the next fight.

I heard other splashes as more men followed their captain to the frigid sea rather than suffer certain death at the hands of ha-mazaans. The men who were left on deck cursed and shouted obscenities at us and our mothers, their eyes wild with desperation, but they knew that the fight was lost to them.

A horn cut through the din, long and thin as it echoed across the water.

I spun toward the sound. It came from one of the smaller ships, some distance behind, the sail puffed forward like the throat of a croaking frog. Theseus clung to the prow, leaning past the great carved head of the griffin, one foot braced on the railing. The sound of a drum matched the steady to and fro of their oars, but his ship fell behind ours ever so slightly. The oars had been stilled on this galley, but the mast of our ship was almost twice the height, the sail bigger than theirs by a half, and the wind strong at our backs.

Theseus raised the horn and sounded it again. Almost as one, every Achaean pressed against the railing by a ha-mazaan weapon dove or fell backward from the ship into the roiling blackness of the sea. The last two men who struggled against our ha-mazaans fought with furious, hopeless desperation. One lunged at Asteria bravely, and died the same, with an axe pike erupting from the front of his throat, having never seen it coming as Sagitta thrust it through the back of his neck. The other dropped his sword and fell to his knees, his arms crossed above his head in surrender. He died like a coward, with his head separated from his shoulders and Thraso's roar of vengeful fury echoing in his ears. She had watched her sister die by their hands. There was no room for mercy.

For a moment, the silence was all-consuming. Our breaths panted raggedly into the rising wind, and rain splattered with increasing force and frequency against the deck. The sail clapped alongside ominous thunder, but there was still a silence. It was a silence I would eventually come to realize was only ever heard after a battle had ceased, and the fight was won, or lost. The silence did not care.

"Antiope," Alkippe said, and the silence was broken.

As one, we turned to face the ship crawling like a monstrous caterpillar across the rising waves toward us, the oars thin insect legs on ground that shifted and moved beneath each tiny footstep. Our remaining queen was on that ship. Theseus stood boldly at the prow, but he had traded the horn for a length of rope, and as we watched, he tossed it into the writhing black water. Arms stretched up to catch it, and Theseus dragged the rope hand over hand and brought the Achaean soldier up and over the railing as though he were pulling a fish from the waves. The drums ceased, and they towed another man onto the deck, then another. More lines were cast, and they dragged more fish in the shape of defeated Achaeans out of the hungry waves and onto the deck.

But there was no sign of Antiope.

"We will take their ship," Prothoe declared.

"They will kill her before we even board," Ossy said, her voice heavy with sorrow.

"Better dead than captive," Aello retorted, still breathing hard.

"That will be her decision, if she chooses to make it," Alkippe said in sharp reproach.

Another silence, heavier this time. The wind roared in my ears, and I fought to keep my legs steady beneath me as the ship bucked under our feet. The rocking motion, or the thought of my aunt and the fate we discussed for her, made my stomach heave and my head spin. I gripped the handle of the knife until the metal dug into my palm, and the pain distracted me from the sick knot of my stomach.

"They do not pursue," Thraso said. "They are drawing sail."

"They will gather their men from the sea first," Ossy said.

"The wind rises," Alkippe's words were punctuated with a thunderclap of sail as it filled with wind in a single heartbeat, rocking the whole boat. I feared the canvas might rip at the seams from the pressure.

"I have never steered such a craft," Thraso said, her neck craning to see to the top of the mast and then scanning the width of it.

"Nor I," Sagitta said grimly.

The words had barely left her mouth when a deafening boom of thunder roared above our heads. Lightning forked into the water several leagues away, and the rain began to fall around us in earnest, smacking into my bare skin. I turned my face to the sky for a moment to let the rain pelt against it, the feeling of it a relief after the terror of the ship's hold, but soon I was forced to duck away from the sting of it.

"We must drop the sail!" someone shouted above the wind.

The deck pitched under my feet again, and I stumbled, falling to my knees on the slippery wood. I still clutched the knife, and I stabbed the point of it into the wood as a grip while I knelt on one knee and peered through the driving rain. Other ha-mazaans had fallen as well. Our legs were meant for wrapping around a horse's ribs and were unfamiliar with the unsteady sea. A few women clambered below to the sheltered decks. Thraso slung her sister's body over her shoulder, running for the hold, her mighty thighs straining. A few who had kept their feet under them shouted directions to each other as they gathered around the base of the mast and felt along the ropes that tied the sail into place.

I stood to help them just as the ship rolled, and it seemed as though I was climbing a roiling mountain. The deck rose to meet my foot before I could place it down, and I thudded into it with a painful smack. Just as quickly, it sloped away again, and I fell on all fours, the knife skidding from my grasp. I crawled forward to where Sagitta wrestled with a rope, the taut line helping her stay on her feet as the deck shifted and swayed.

"It's like vaulting, Cyra!" she cried as I gripped the rope to haul myself to my feet and stay there. Her voice was almost exultant with the thrill of danger. I wished for my earlier euphoria to blanket me again, but fear was creeping like water seeping from a spring, pooling into the heavy earth of my body. Sagitta shouted again through the rain. "Like when we stand on the back of a horse and fly! Just think of the ship as Risa, and she is trying to be rid of you!" She laughed, a mad creature in a torrent of rain and wind.

I imagined the wet, hard wood as Risa's warm body, undulating with perfect rhythm under my feet as I balanced high on her back. But the ship did not have the perfect rhythm of a cantering horse. If Risa bucked while I stood upon her, which she certainly had many times, I would tuck my shoulder and roll when I hit the ground. But if the ship bucked hard enough, there would be no ground to welcome me. Only the cold, ruthless water of the Zalapa Sea if I slipped from the heaving deck of this ship, or a wave scooped me from the edge.

With no guiding hand at the oars, the ship careened in the waves. A rising wall of sea water hit the starboard side, sending us all flailing sideways. I fell hard against the rope, barely keeping my grip. Sagitta wrapped her elbow around the line and grunted as her feet were swept from underneath her. A shrill scream pierced the air. Through the sheets of rain, beside the railing, a flash of light skin against the dark sky, and then the ha-mazaan was lost to the waves. I could not even scream for her in my terror.

We had traded one foe for another, for a storm at sea would be just as deadly as a ship full of Achaean captors. Many called the sea The Inhospitable One, and it was because of storms such as this as much as the dense, threatening blackness of the waters. None of us knew how to direct or manage a vessel so big or waves so large. Our skiffs and fishing boats could be handled by a single ha-mazaan, and had room for no more than three, because we never ventured beyond where the Terme river flowed into the sea when we fished.

A hand latched itself around my arm, and I turned my face to see Ossy. She shouted at me through the furious wind, her brown hair plastered against her forehead with the rain.

"Go below, Cyra!" she shouted, and I was about to shake my head when she yelled again. "Your mother needs you!"

She was simply trying to get me to safety, for we both knew Tekmessa would be tending my mother. I did not want to seem like a coward, even though the last place I wanted to be was above deck, where the wind or waves or the deck itself could sweep me into the salty sea forever. I looked down the rope to where Sagitta and Thraso were struggling to haul the sail inward. It was a battle they were not winning.

"Go!" Ossy yelled again. "We will do what we can here and then join you. You must take care of your mother!"

I nodded, and she squeezed my arm before letting go. I looked toward the hold's entrance and knew I could not make it all the way there on my feet. I dropped to the wet deck just as another wave buffeted against the hull. My lips sent a prayer to the Great Mother as I scurried forward, fingers grabbing for purchase but finding none on the slick wood. The deck careened sideways, and I screamed as it felt like I was about to be thrown into the air. I would have given anything in that moment to be in the throes of battle, or facing a griffin in the forest. Nothing in my life had ever terrified me as much as the sea did right now.

A streak of lightning lit the sky, much closer than before. I could feel the sting of it on my arms and neck. I flung myself down the stairs and into the dim aisle between the oar seats, where several ha-mazaans strained futilely at the oars. Alkippe and Sagitta followed, but everyone pitched sideways as another wave pummeled the side of the ship. Water sprayed through the oar slots, washing across the lower deck, and a rising panic choked my throat as I envisioned the lower hold filling with water, drowning everything—and everyone—within it.

I raced forward and was at the edge of the hold when a crack of thunder deafened me. The sky lit up as though the bright summer sun had risen within the ship itself. Light filled the galley for a half a breath, along with the explosive sound of splitting wood. Screams tore through the wind from above, and the entrance to the hold darkened as more bodies poured through it with reckless, terrified speed. Ossy had not bothered to use the steps, diving as though she plunged into the depths of our summer swimming hole, and she rolled hard when she hit the second deck. Above, another crack as though a tree was being felled, and everyone grabbed for purchase as the entire ship shuddered and groaned, listing to one side. I gripped the back of a seat, stunned and breathing heavily, watching as several more ha-mazaans hurled themselves down the stairs.

"Lightning has taken down the mast!" one of them shouted.

"Ship the oars!" Ossy yelled, struggling to her feet as another wave smacked against the ship, though it was not full into the side as the last one had been.

Each of us took an oar and hauled it into the ship. Some lengths of smooth oak had already been sucked into the waves or snapped with the strength of the water cracking them into the hull. With a loud grunt, I shoved the final oar into its bracket and turned back to the cargo hold. The opening was Stygian and ominous, and once more, I pictured the waves rolling over us, pouring into the depths of the galley and suffocating everything under its immense power. But it was no better here, on the mid-deck, for if we were to be lost to the Great Mother's bosom, it would happen whether I was trapped in the dark belly with the rest of the ha-mazaans or not.

"We are at the mercy of the Great Mother, now," Ossy said behind me, and with one more frightened glance through the narrow oar slots at the lightning-streaked sky, I stepped down into the blackness.

CHAPTER 10

THE SUN SETS IN THE WEST

I dreamed of an unfamiliar mare carrying me at full gallop over an ocean of sand. Above us, a griffin screamed, and the smell of sulphur and rotting carrion gagged me as the monster's breath washed hot over the back of my neck. The horse under me screamed back at it. The griffin was its greatest enemy, even more so than the leopard, and the mare knew it would soon be torn to shreds by talons and claws and beak. Thick strands of black mane wound around my fingers and cut my skin with the fierceness of my grip, but I would not let go. I spurred the horse again with bare heels against ribs, and we flew faster over the sand.

The wind of the griffin's wings beat fetid air against my back, and another terrifying shriek shredded the darkness of the evening sky. I ducked forward, lying flat against the flying mane of the horse, just as long talons skimmed my back. Then the griffin was past us, its great wingspan carrying it forward past the galloping horse like an arrow flying wide of its target while its claws and feet clutched at empty air.

I unslung my bow as the griffin beat its wings to change course, nocking an arrow and aiming and letting it fly all in the same smooth, practiced motion. The arrow flew true, burying itself deep in the shoulder of the monstrous beast, just under the place where the wing attached to its great leonine body. The beast screamed, this time with anger and pain, and the mare reared to a halt. My legs pinched tight to its sides as I drew another arrow and nocked it. I shouted at the horse to be still, and she danced under me, quivering.

The griffin turned in the air awkwardly, every wingbeat a painful spear in its side as the arrow buried itself deeper. I drew my bow, the muscles in my arms straining against the tension of the heavy string and every ounce of strength in me working to keep the point of the arrow focused. I sighted as the griffin turned, the feathers mixed with fur on its chest coming in to sharp relief. The beast's bellowing and the rush of air from the wings became quiet, as everything condensed into one point of focus; the length of my arrow and the curve of the space between it and where I needed it to be.

I let it fly.

The griffin screamed with ear-shattering fury, the second arrow sticking from its chest where its heart lay. It tried to scratch the arrow away with great eagle talons and bite at it with its deadly beak, but the point was too deep. Wings beat out of rhythm, and the griffin shrieked again, falling from the sky.

But Melanippe landed on the ground in front of me, not the griffin. She shrieked the same terrifying, wordless shriek as the monster, but it was her silver eyes staring up into mine from the dust. I had killed her. I leaped from the horse and raced to where she lay. My knees did not feel the skid of gravel as I fell to her side. The ground felt like it swayed under both of us, bucking her bloody chest toward me. I clutched her and cried out, but I had no voice.

"*Mother!*" I tried to say, but no sound came from my lips, and she simply shrieked at me. The arrow sticking from her chest beat once, twice, before it stilled. Another arrow was in her thigh, though that made little sense, for I had shot her...no, shot the *griffin* in the side. Blood soaked the ground, and I screamed again, but still, there was no sound except in my head.

The horse had followed me, and as it hung its grey head to sniff at my mother's lifeless body, it said urgently into my silently screaming face,

"Cyra."

I looked at it in numb astonishment, the screams quieting themselves inside my head. It looked at me and said again with black eyes intent on mine,

"*Cyra!*"

I awoke with a violent jerk, my own name echoing inside of my skull. Eri crouched next to me, her face barely visible in a faint ray of light. I stared at her in dumb confusion for a moment before I bolted upright.

"Mother!" I said urgently, reaching my hand out in the panicked and disoriented way only night terrors could elicit.

"She sleeps," Tekmessa's gentle voice came to me, and the tense anxiety left my body. It was quickly replaced by a weary fatigue and the sticky, thick residue left in the mind after a night terror.

"It was only a night terror," Eri reassured me softly, but she would not meet my eyes before moving back into the far corner of the hold, where she had stayed for the entire storm. I wondered if what had been silent in my dream was not so silent for those who were awake. I looked around the dim hold, but most of the women lay motionless. Ossy leaned against the hull nearby, her eyes closed.

I looked back again at the soft light filtering through the open trapdoor of the hold and scrambled to my feet.

"The storm is over?" I asked, the words tight with both hope and fear as I looked up the stairs to where light peeked through the oar slots.

Ossy shrugged and opened her eyes. Her face was drawn with exhaustion when she spoke again. "The thunder and lightning have gone, but the wind and the waves remain. Though not as bad as they were," she conceded.

Footsteps echoed overhead, moving swiftly through the upper hold.

"Ha-mazaans, wake!" It was Thraso. Her shout brought a great rustling as the ha-mazaans who slept from pure exhaustion were shocked from their fitful slumber. "Land in sight! We need the oars!"

There was a frantic scramble as women untangled their sleepy limbs and dashed for the stairs. Even tiny Camilla raced for the oar deck, eager to help steer the ship to shore though she was barely more than a girl. The end of being at sea was a fire under tired feet and a flame of hope in hearts that had almost extinguished much of that feeling many hours ago. The storm had raged for over two days, as the sun had darkened and risen again twice since our uprising. The sky had been black and thunder had still been sounding when I had fallen to sleep, but I was not sure how long I had slept before the dream about the griffin and my mother woke me. I looked at my mother now, uncertain. Tekmessa had not moved and sat calmly next to my mother's head.

"I will stay with her," she said in her soft voice. The ship rocked under my unsteady feet, but the priestess held my mother's shoulders to keep her still.

I nodded and moved toward the stairs, but as I set my foot to the first stair, still muddied with Denys' blood, I noticed Eri's hunched form in the edge of the hold, barely visible in the thin light. The flame of her hair was unmistakable.

"Eri?"

Long limbs twitched, but the head between her arms barely lifted at my voice. I went to her and crouched down, but I was unsure what to say. I had only thought of my mother through the storm; whether she had enough water, whether her fever was higher, whether she would wake and speak to me, whether I would hear her laugh again. By the time I had helped the other ha-mazaans remove the dead men from our hold and toss them into the sea, and search the stores for food and fresh water, Eri had retreated into her own world and wanted to speak to no one, including me, so I had let her be. Still, I should have been more persistent and more attentive. A pang of intense guilt pierced through me for my thoughtlessness. She had already faced my greatest fear in losing her mother. The least I could have done was support her, but I had been too absorbed in my own fears to be a good friend.

"Starboard oars, forward!" Thraso's voice cut through my self-recriminations, and I glanced up the stairs. Eri stirred at the sound and looked up at me. Her grief was etched into her face, and it was heartbreaking. I reached my fingers to brush her arm gently, near the stitches I had caused.

"Eri, I am so sorry about your mother," I said lamely, my tongue thick and awkward around the words. They felt useless and trite. Eri stared at me dully.

"This is a nightmare that shouldn't be happening," she whispered, her voice hoarse and anguished, and then she bowed her head onto her folded arms once more.

"She must grieve properly to be with us again," Tekmessa said to me from the shadows. "Leave her with me. When we reach land, and the Great Mother holds us in her palm once again, I will speak to her of Hipponike's travels in the Otherworld."

I looked over my shoulder at the *zizenti* as she spoke, then back at Eri. But Thraso's voice echoed again, urgent and demanding.

"We must turn, ha-mazaans! Starboard oars, forward! Portside, reverse!"

I squeezed Eri's arm and then left her, hastening up the stairs. The women's arms bulged with the strain of holding the enormous oars steady. Some, like Camilla and Leya, were doubled up on a single oar so that they could better manage the huge lengths of oak, but still, they struggled. The lifeless bodies of Ifito and another ha-mazaan I had not known took up two seats. I felt a pang of guilt that I could not think of the woman's name as I rushed by her frozen, blue-tinged face.

I found an empty row behind Sagitta and sat on the hard, polished wood of the bench. Being port-side, I would have to match the forward thrusting rhythm of the other rowers without breaking their movements. I gripped my palms around the smooth wood and counted one, two, three forward rows before quickly heaving the heavy handle up, dipping it into the water for the fourth rowing motion, and pushing it down and away from me. The impossibly long oar dipped wildly in my hands and never struck water at all. I heard and felt the loud crack of my oar against the one behind me as I failed to move fast enough, and I grunted an apology, but it was already time to be pushing again, and I did.

This time, my oar dipped into the sea, and there was tremendous pressure on my arms to push it through the water. My ribs screamed where they were bruised or broken, but I pushed on. I felt the length of the oar catch in the waves, and the tug of the water on the wood almost made me lose my grip. Again, I pushed forward, watching Sagitta's shoulders ripple with strength in front of me, and this time, I was ready for the force of the current against my oar. I completed the full motion of an oar stroke without breaking anyone's rhythm and grimaced a fierce smile of triumph at Sagitta's back.

"Row... Row...!... Row... Row...!" Thraso screamed the words in rhythmic intervals from the top deck. Seven, eight times, I pushed against the water as her voice punctuated the end of the wood dipping into the waves, and by the ninth, I was grunting with the effort, my ribs a band of pure fire. I focused on Sagitta's bronzed shoulders hunched into the oar, spine shining with sweat beneath the long flaxen braid still coiled with the copper wire she favored as decoration. I noticed a crusted red cut high on her arm, earned in our battle with the Achaeans, but she did not seem to pay it any mind.

"Port-side, hold!" Thraso yelled. I gasped air into my lungs with the brief respite. For the first time, I looked out through the small window. The clouds were parting, and I marveled at how brilliant the blue of the sky seemed after two long days in the darkness and all the time spent wondering if any of us would see sunlight again.

"All rowers, forward!" Thraso called, and as one, my side of the ship reversed our earlier movements. It took a few rotations for the rhythm to come again and for us to match it with the other side of the galley, but it was much easier to row now. Perhaps the waves helped carry us forward. My ribs felt as though a horse was kicking them over and over again, but my breathing had not become troubled, so I simply ground my teeth and used the pain as fuel for each stroke.

The entire deck was awash with the sounds of women grunting, heaving their backs against the oars, and shouting their breaths out, as though it added strength to our muscles. It felt much the same as weapons practice, with the smell of sweat and the rhythm of the body and mind working to keep a set pace and the grunts of exertion adding force behind a spear or axe thrust. The crisp salty air, the sound of the water below, and the labor of it made my head rush, much the same as a race on the back of a swift horse, or at the end of a fast footrace through the mountain trails.

I could not wait to be in Themiscyra again. To breathe the wet air of the coast and smell the beech and ash and pine of the forest around the palace. To see my mother under the care of Marpe in the infirmary. I wanted to see my cousin Penthesilea again, if she still lived. Any of the ha-mazaans, the Crafters, the Xanharaspas, the children. I missed our city, teeming with life the fresh air of the coastal mountains. And the horses. I wanted the sweet, musky scents of horse sweat and leather. I missed the way Risa's eyes sparkled with mischief and her ears flicked before she bucked. I swore to feed her extra apples and give her another chance at being my *rhu-tasiya*. As soon as I was home. Every pull on the oar brought me closer to what I had taken for granted my entire life, and I vowed I would not make the same mistake again.

"Ha-mazaans!" Thraso cried triumphantly, her sandaled feet clattering down the steps behind me. "We are close! Do not falter! The sea is shallow, and if we have enough speed, we may beach the ship." She fairly threw herself into an empty seat and took up an oar as she spoke. My heart trilled like a songbird at her words.

"Row!" she called.

"Row! Row! Row!" We chanted, faster than before and with more energy, though our muscles were exhausted to the point of trembling. I noticed Eri move through the galley and take up an available oar and grinned at her as she tried to get into the rhythm of it, but she paid me no attention as she concentrated on matching our strokes.

I pulled against the oar and felt the water push against it. The waves pushed us also, propelling the great ship forward, and when the strange sound echoed up from the keel and reverberated through the decks before the ship ground to a halt, there was a moment of confused silence before every ha-mazaan leaped to their feet and screamed with pure, unadulterated joy.

The boat listed to one side with a grinding shudder and creak before stilling itself in the rocking waves. I joined the others as they raced toward the stair and the upper deck for our first sight of land. When the cool air blew across my face and the thin sun glinted into my eyes, I laughed in sheer delight. Sagitta swept me into a hug that could have crushed a lion.

We had indeed beached the ship, though the water stretched ahead of us for quite a way before I could see dry sand. We had hit a sandbar or rock, but it did not matter. Beyond the edge of the water was a long beach, stretching far in each direction I looked, and beyond the beach stood tall, imposing white cliffs of sand or limestone that were topped with a grassy, treeless plateau. I had never seen a shore like it and wondered how far west from Themiscyra we actually were. Perhaps these were the grasslands of Paphlagonia, where Risa's sire and dam had once grazed.

A wave rocked the boat, which still sat precariously on the edge of its keel. It brought everyone on the crowded deck out of their personal reverie.

"We must drop anchor," someone said. As Thraso and a few others moved to shove the enormous stone into the water, Tekmessa appeared from the deck below.

"The hull is cracked," she said. "Only enough for a leak right now, but we must bring Melanippe from the hold."

I was already moving to the stairs when Alkippe's urgent voice stopped me.

"The sun!"

We all peered into the sky, shielding our hold-dimmed eyes against the light. With the way our luck had been the last few days, I would have believed it if she told me it was cracking into pieces and falling into the sea, but I did not see any cause for the alarm in her tone.

"What of it?" Sagitta asked.

"The sun sets in the west. And we face those cliffs to the north, if it sets as it always has."

An icy chill swept through me. I lowered my hand from the sun and turned again to the distant shoreline, serene and beautiful in the late afternoon light. Alkippe was right. To face the shore, we had the sun on our left shoulders. But if we had been looking at our own coastline, toward Themiscyra or Sinope, or even as far west as the Thracian city of Lygos, which lay at the entrance to the Aegean Sea, we should have been facing south, watching that sun set to our right.

"We have landed on the northern coast of the Zalapa," someone said.

"No," Ossy shook her head, staring down into the water. "Even farther. We have landed on the edge of the northern Maeotian Swamp. This water is not that of our blackened sea. It is too shallow."

"It's not possible!" someone said, a tinge of panic in their voice. "It would take days to sail that far from Themiscyra—"

"Five days, maybe six," Ossy agreed. "In normal weather. But this was a powerful storm, and the waves were strong. The sun does not lie."

We stared in numb silence toward the unfamiliar shore until another wave rocked us.

"An island?" Leya suggested with weak hopefulness, but Ossy shook her head again.

"Neither the Maeotian Swamp nor the Zalapa holds an island, other than the one which contains Matar Kubileya's Heartstone at Chadesia. This is not our land. We are more than a thousand leagues from Themiscyra, with an entire world of water between us and home."

PART II

ISHASSARA

CHAPTER 11

THE PROMISE

We took Melanippe to shore first. Tekmessa worried about moving her before we had built a fire or shelter, even though water was seeping through the crack in the hull and slowly filling the hold, permanently grounding the ship in shallow waters. When I felt my mother's fevered brow, I worried it would not matter whether she was on a beached and sunken ship or a barren, sand-filled stretch of nowhere. I remembered my dream and the way she had shrieked at me. The way the arrow had stilled her beating heart.

Thraso carried her to the top deck. We used some linen to wrap around the lengths of two spears and tried as gently as possible, with six women lifting at various un-injured places on her body, to slide her onto the makeshift stretcher. As careful as we were, blood seeped faster through the bandages Tekmessa had wound. We lowered her from the deck with ropes tied to the spear handles to the women waiting in the water below. They held her above their shoulders to keep her free of the water, though it came to their chests and rose higher when the waves rolled in. Tekmessa climbed down the rope after them and waded through the water, her red robes pooling around her like blood flowing in a river. I wanted to follow, but there was much work to be done before we abandoned the ship, and every available hand was needed.

The galley's heavy ballast of metal ingots, food, and trade wares helped moor the ship in place as the waves shifted restlessly against its side. The sun arced downward in a long, lazy trail as we worked to offload the injured and dead ha-mazaans, and then the cargo. Though the autumn air was still damp and humid the way it is after a violent storm, and we were hot and sweating and sore with grief and exhaustion by the time the sun was touching the ocean to the west.

We took everything we could carry that was not already swallowed in water. Some goods, like the copper and tin, we dropped from the deck to the shallow water below at Camilla's urging, as they could be used to make more bronze for weapons. Nowhere near as good as our star-forged iron, but it would be better than nothing if we needed something to trade for passage home. Ha-mazaans dove into the shallow water two at a time to lift them out of the sea again, carrying the handles on their shoulders and wading through breast-deep water to shore.

We took all the rope and the leather belts and sandals the women had stripped from the dead Achaeans before tossing their stiff bodies into the sea. We took the smaller casks of mead and skins of fresh water, and the bundles of animal hides—spotted leopard, snow cat, antelope, red deer, moose, lion. There were jars of oils that smelled, even corked and sealed with beeswax, like frankincense and cedarwood. We took all of it. As Ossy said, what we could not carry with us could be hidden away or buried, to be retrieved later, but whatever we did not take would be left to the sea and lost forever.

In the third chest we carried out, we found my bow. I did not think it was possible to feel joy on such a dark and foreboding day, though the quiver and freshly made arrows were not with it, and its string had been cut when they took it off my back. When Sagitta solemnly handed the precious weapon to me, tears of happiness swelled in my eyes. As soon as I held the smooth curve of wood, felt the horn and sinew under my fingers, my mother's strong hands rose in my mind.

Melanippe had taken me deep into the forest shortly after my second moon-blood, far behind the orchards in Themiscyra, where the trees grew dense and dark in their groves, on a hunt, though not for a hind this time. A tree.

"You must ask the tree before you cut it," my mother cautioned. "If you do not ask, the bow you fashion will not bend for you. And if you ask and do not heed the answer, the bow will break when you need it most."

I had not known what she meant about heeding an answer, for surely trees did not speak. I followed her deeper into the forest regardless, approaching beech and ash at my mother's beckoning, hesitantly asking first the rough trunk of one and the rustling leaves of another, again and again, feeling utterly foolish as the wind sighed and I understood nothing of the speech of leaves. I had thought my mother might be playing a trick on me every time she shook her head and moved on again, until finally, on the outer edge of a small grove thick with lichen and ferns, a maple stretched its limbs down to me. The tree was not so old as to be past its prime but not so young as to be filled with sap. My mother watched as I approached, and as I laid my hand on its trunk, craning my neck to see into the canopy over my head, she urged softly,

"Ask."

I asked, and this time when the leaves rustled, I imagined a bright sound, as though Eri's baby sister giggled nearby. I glanced at my mother. She nodded and then handed me her axe.

I took a thick branch from that maple for the core of the bow, and my mother's strong hands guided mine as she showed me how to peel it and plane it down into many layers, which we fastened together with rabbit skin glue. My mother gifted me the horns for the bow's ends, telling me she had brought them back from the lands of my father in Wilusa. The sinew had belonged to the first horse I had sacrificed with my own hands, the animal old and suffering as it walked, so that its death was both a mercy and a service to the ha-mazaans. My mother's hands had shown me how to stretch the sinews over the bow, lending it both strength and flexibility. Now, my mother's hands may never have the strength to hold a bow again.

Sagitta's concerned blue eyes penetrated my reverie, and I managed to smile at her.

"Small mercies," I murmured, and she nodded. Then, we went back to work.

The ship was more useful to us as firewood, so that is what it became. We took every piece of wood that could be burnt, including the oars, and Thraso used her axe to chop pieces of the seats and the railing to carry to shore. It seemed to give her some mental relief, swinging the magnificent weapon into the wood and hearing the resounding crack as it splintered to pieces. I wondered if she thought of Ifito. If the splintering wood was Achaean bones in her mind's eye. If her grief was now compounded by knowing her sister's body would be buried in a foreign land, so far from home.

Eventually, we had taken everything we could. With one final glance at the ship's deck, at the splintered, charred remains of the mast and the stains of blood clinging to the deck even after all the rain, I swung my leg over the railing and found the first rung of the rope ladder with my toes, happy to leave the cursed Achaean galley behind.

The others had carried my mother to the place where we planned to shelter for the night, close to the base of the dense white cliffs that towered above the water. The scouts had reported only long stretches of summer-dried grass blowing in the wind above us, with low hills to the north and coastline stretching as far as the eye could see to the east and west. We made the decision to stay on the beach until we could get our bearings and become familiar with our surroundings. The cliffs would act not only as a shield for our fires in the night, in case the scouts had overlooked any signs of people nearby, but also from winds blowing from the north. Ha-mazaans were busy building those fires now that the twilight would hide the smoke, and others were stacking the barrels of mead and bundles of linen as a breakwind on either side of the camp. Others were breaking open the sealed amphorae to find what food lay within.

I made my way to where Camilla had already built a large, crackling fire from bits of dried driftwood and pieces of ship railing. The sparks spat and popped as I came near to Melanippe in the circle of golden light. I stumbled down to the sand next to her, all the strength pouring from my body now that the manual labor was finished. Others sat wearily in a circle around us. Ossy and Thraso and Alkippe and Sagitta, all of them looking at my mother's face, once swarthy and vibrant, now ashen. Tekmessa, her long tunic dirty with blood and sand, knelt on the ground next to my mother's wounded leg, setting the jar she cradled into the rough sand, and began to cut the bandage away.

Moving mechanically, I helped the *zizenti* peel the edges of the linen away from the wound. When they stuck, Tekmessa lifted the jar and hovered it over the wound. "Seawater," she said simply at my questioning glance.

It wet the dried blood enough that we did not tear the wound more when the bandages pulled away. But we had not finished cutting all the blackened cloth away before my mother moaned, her hands that had been limp for days suddenly twitching.

"Cyra," she said then, her voice wispy and hoarse, completely unrecognizable from my mother's usual strident tones of command.

"I am here, mother," I said quickly and grasped the hand that was reaching feebly into the twilight darkness.

"Cyra," she said again, almost a sigh. I squeezed her hand.

"Don't talk. I am here. We are here," I said, and though I tried to sound calm and authoritative, my voice wavered as my throat tightened.

Alkippe knelt at her head, a small piece of wet linen in her hand. She shush-shushed her general as she raised my mother's head and held the soaked cloth to cracked lips. Melanippe sucked at it a bit and then smiled weakly at her captain, but shook her head feebly when Alkippe offered her more.

"I must clean the wound," Tekmessa said quietly.

Melanippe did not speak. She simply squeezed my hand. I nodded at Tekmessa, and the *zizenti* gave instructions for more bandages to be prepared. Camilla moved to help, and their small hands made quick work of the cloth bandages. My eyes scoured my mother's feverish face, noticing the glint in her grey eyes that seemed to burn on its own, separate from the reflected light of the fire.

"Cyra, gather the women." The words were a command, even though her voice was thin.

"Mother—"

"All of them, Cyra. I will tell all the promise that was given to me. They must know."

"Promise?" I repeated dumbly.

She nodded once. Then her free hand lifted, and one finger spun in a circle. She whispered hoarsely, "All must listen."

I looked up. The few who could hear edged closer, not wanting to miss a word. My confused eyes met Ossy's, but she was already standing and calling for the other women to gather. They heard the tone of command from my mother's closest friend and obeyed. Everyone gathered around the fire, surrounding us in dark shadows. I could not make out all their faces in the dancing light of the flames, but I knew they all respected my mother. Not just respected. They loved her. She was a mother to all of them, though I was the only child she had born in her body. She had tended to them and trained them, pushed and protected them, laughed with them, and made them weep with frustration and accomplishment. She had taught them how to be brave when they felt fear, as she had tried to teach me, although I no longer felt I had learned that part well. And she had gifted them with the strength of a warrior's heart because it was her gift to pass on to them. They loved her for these things, I knew. As much as they had loved their queens, now lost to us. One by one, we were losing each one of the sisters to some terrible fate that I could not accept.

I gripped my mother's hand tight as Ossy stepped back into the ring of light, nodding her head at me.

"All are listening, Nightmare," she said fondly and knelt next to Alkippe at my mother's head, her hand gently stroking my mother's hair. Only Ossy and Eri ever called her Nightmare, a play on the meaning of her name, which meant "black horse."

Melanippe kept her eyes closed, and I would have thought she slept again if not for the faint twinges of a grimace before she began to speak. Tekmessa tended the wound, and I knew it must be excruciatingly painful. I wanted to put my finger to her lips and tell her to save her breath, but I knew my mother well. I would not steer her off course once she had the bit between her teeth.

"The Oracle's promises to me were many," she began, but she had to stop and lick her lips, and Alkippe held the soaked cloth to her mouth. Bodies shifted around the fire as women leaned in to hear her low voice, and I could sense their surprise at her chosen words. The prophecies of the Oracle were sacred, private, intimate things.

"Promises that I would be the greatest warrior Themiscyra would ever know, which is for you to decide the truth of. She promised all men would tremble at my feet, and this they have done, except for one." Her hand squeezed mine, and I swallowed uncomfortably. She rarely spoke of my father, but I knew that was who she meant.

"She promised my followers would be many, though I could not be queen as I...as..." her words faded into another grimace. Ossy glanced around with a concerned frown as Alkippe held a different cloth to Melanippe's lips. This one was soaked with mead, and my mother's parched mouth sucked on it for a few moments before she turned her head away and continued speaking.

"She promised me a daughter. A daughter to be my mirror image, born to fight and to lead. A daughter born from a man who would love me, and I him, though we must part ways." She swallowed heavily but still turned her face from the offer of more drink. Alkippe frowned in frustration.

"Named as one throned on the rising sun, for a new dawn would be upon her. The Oracle promised that my daughter's choices would carry our people to the ends of the earth in the ages to come, spreading the Great Mother's glory." She paused again, much of the strength leaking from her body and from the fingers that held mine. I bit the inside of my lip, but she gave another faint squeeze on my hand, longer this time, and continued. "A daughter who would be the founder of new nations. Whose destiny it would be to keep the old ways and discover the new. She would do this as Defending Queen, though her mother would never be called by that name."

The ha-mazaans were silent, and when I could stand it no more, I glanced up at them. Ossy and Sagitta had fire-bright eyes wet with tears, and even stoic Alkippe looked as though she might cry for perhaps the first time since arriving in Themiscyra before my first moon-blood. Eri, far on the edge of the firelight, stood with her face shadowed in grief. I did not want to imagine what she must be feeling about her own mother. I did not want to feel it myself, but I knew with foreboding that the Gate of the Otherworld creaked slowly open, ready to claim my mother with each faltering breath. I gripped her hand tightly, willing my own strength into her body.

She opened her eyes then and smiled.

"Your destiny begins, daughter."

Breathless panic overwhelmed me when her eyes closed, but Alkippe's hand was already on her face, feeling for breath. Her eyes met mine with solemn assurance. "She only sleeps."

When I looked up again, over the wavering features around the firelight, I saw them looking at us, at me, with thoughtful, perhaps fearful expressions. As they realized no more words would be forthcoming, they melted back into the night, back to their own fires and beds, and perhaps thoughts of their own promises from the Oracle. I wondered if they felt as confused and lost as I did. If they wondered why my mother told such a story now, in this place. If they wondered why she spoke with so much hope even in her weakened state. If they thought the Oracle was a fraud, and me along with her. I would not blame them. I felt the same, but I would not let my mother know.

I bathed her face with a cool cloth as she slept, though the action felt trite and useless. Ossy rose to leave the circle of light, but I barely noticed. When she had finished the bandaging and cleaned the blood from her hands, Tekmessa lay down next to Melanippe, pulling a moose skin over her hips, and closed her eyes with a sigh. But I was too full of trepidation and foreboding to sleep, even though I was exhausted in every way possible.

Quietly, I got up from my place near the fire and went in search of Eri. I needed the comfort of a friend, the understanding of a sister in life if not in blood. I found her sitting cross-legged by her own fire, with Santo and Melo, and Hipponike's closest friend, Glaukia, and a few other tired ha-mazaans already rolled in furs for the night.

"Eri," I began as I crouched down beside her, but when I saw how sunken and shadowed her eyes were, my words fumbled into silence. She had been crying.

"I hope Aunty Nightmare is okay," she offered and then looked back into the flames. "I'm tired, Cyra. I'd rather not talk tonight. Please."

Her rebuff stung, even though I knew she suffered. Unsure what else to say, I nodded stiffly and stood again, making my way out of the light of her fire and away from the glittering stares of the women who were only pretending to sleep.

I moved restlessly about the camp. I thought about eating something, as it had been a long time since I had tasted food, but I could not. I continued to pace until my feet carried me past the other campfires and down the beach, away from camp. The sand grit against my feet and between my toes, and I felt more conscious of the earth under my soles than I ever had in my life, for the time spent on the ship had made me very aware of how much I appreciated solid ground. If the sea was our fastest route home, I did not know if I could choose to set foot in another ship. My body tingled with fear to remember how frightening it had been to be tossed upon the hollow water that could swallow me at any moment. Yet even that terror had been better than the surety growing within me that my mother would not be with me for much longer.

I walked to the far end of the beach, where it curved into a point on the water and great grey rocks jutted from the sea, rising up to kiss the starry sky. The fires on the beach behind me were small and distant flickerings. Looking up into the night sky, the stars shining overhead in comfortably familiar patterns, I wondered, not for the first time, if the Oracle ever spoke falsely. If she did, I did not know whether to be relieved or terrified. I had spent my entire life living according to one prophecy—the promise given to my mother—and in denial of another—the one given to me. I did not feel the hope of my mother's prophecy around me now. I felt the terrible inevitability of my own curse falling into place, piece by jagged piece.

Never shall you rule in Themiscyra.

Never will you share Themiscyra's throne with the seed of your mother's sister. The role of the Sister Queens shall die with Hippolyta and will not be reborn before your grandchildren's grandchildren have traveled back to the Great Mother's womb many times over.

Never will your mother see you rule over any living ha-mazaan.

I had never understood, since my first moon-blood, how my prophecy could ever align with the one my mother had fed to me like *kimiz* and honeyed figs, since before I was old enough to understand her words. And now, I wondered if either were true, or if the entire process was simply an archaic, foolish tradition that held no meaning, no truth, and served only the infantile dreams of those naïve enough to believe them. I hoped it was so. I hoped the Oracle knew nothing and spoke of something she did not understand. I hoped she was wrong about all of it because then my mother would not die.

"Ishassara," a voice said in the darkness behind me. "Come back to the fires, where it is safe."

I started and spun to face Sagitta.

"Why must you call me that?" I said with a harshness I did not intend. There was a battle between anger and panic warring inside of me.

"Because it is who you are."

I stared at the shadow of her against the white sandstone of the cliffs in the darkness, then shook my head in sharp denial.

"No," I said flatly. "Hippolyta—"

"Is lost to us," Sagitta interrupted calmly. "Antiope as well. You are what we have."

"No," I said again, stubbornly, even though moments before I had wondered whether it would ever be my destiny. But I had never stopped to think of what it would mean for that reality to materialize, and I certainly did not want to think of it now.

"Cyra, you are Ishassara, Heir to the Defender's Throne. And in a year and a day, after the Alsanti, you will be Defending Queen."

I shook my head again, but weakly. "I did not even complete the Initiation. And I have no city to be queen *of*. Look at us!" I swung my arm in a wide arc that encompassed the shallow sea shining under the stars, the waves now deceptively gentle. Almost soothing. I finished by pointing to the barren, towering cliffs hemming us in from the other side. "Fifty-three of us stranded at the top of the world, with a broken Achaean galley and a horde of animal skins and perfume. Of what am I to be Ishassara or queen? There *is* nothing. There is not even a horse to be my *rhu-tasiya*. And my mother—" The last words choked from my throat as it tightened into a knot.

"You do not rule over piled stones and rose gardens, Cyra," Sagitta rebutted, more sharply than I had ever heard her speak to me. "As Ishassara, you are Heir to the responsibility of defending and protecting the ha-mazaans and our sacred Ways. Our choices as women and as free people. And as Ishassara first, and then as queen, you will lead those ha-mazaans, the women, *me*, through the old ways and into the new. Did you not listen to what Melanippe spoke? Do you think your mother wanted to hear her own story as a night-tale to sleep better?"

I frowned at her in angry silence. Finally, I spoke with a tight voice.

"What if I don't want those things anymore? I want my mother to live, and I want us to be home. The rest I will trade to the Great Mother in exchange for those two things."

"We will not find our way home with no one to lead us there, Cyra," Sagitta said more gently. "You will be Ishassara, just as Penthesilea now is, for a year and a day until Alsanti."

In Themiscyra and the other ha-mazaan cities, there were always two queens, sister-rulers, to fairly and proportionately represent the people. One to defend the city and declare war when necessary, and one to keep the Hearth, the sacred mysteries of home and Ways of our people, and to birth new daughters to inherit the throne. I thought of the task Penthesilea now faced and shuddered. I had been born into the role of Defending Ishassara as my mother's daughter, as niece of the queens. I had proven my right to hold the title with the Trials. But Alsanti was also ancient law, giving the people the right to pledge their allegiance to the new Ishassara as their queen, but only if that Ishassara proved themselves worthy after one year of leadership following the previous queen's death. For Penthesilea, this would mean she would bear a daughter within one year of her mother's death to ensure the line continued. For me, it would mean keeping the ha-mazaans safe from all harm.

Perhaps this is why I argued against Sagitta. I was not ready to lead anyone. I should have had many more years of mentorship before I was truly ready to take on the role. I now had the coming year to prove myself either worthy or wholly incapable. Doing so beside my cousin, with the familiarity of our court and people and landscape, hopefully with my *rhu-tasiya,* was one thing. But doing so here, in a foreign land amongst foreign people, while trying to navigate the vast distance between where we stood and home...and possibly without my mother to guide me?

I was destined to fail.

With that realization, the weight of the Oracle's prophecy settled its heavy mantle across my shoulders once more, and I felt the clasp of it tighten as a torc of lead around my throat. It was all beginning to make perfect sense. Either we never made it home, and being Ishassara meant nothing, or we did, and I had spent the year leading up to Alsanti failing at what the ha-mazaans needed from me: wise decision-making and keeping them safe. How could I possibly keep them safe when I didn't even know the way home?

Sagitta waited expectantly. Wordlessly, I brushed past her, heading toward the dimming light of the fires. Her feet were quiet in the sand behind me as I made my way to my mother. I found a lion skin as a barrier from the wind before settling myself next to her and Tekmessa. I lay for a long while looking at the stars, so familiar in their patterns of centaur and ox, swan and lion. And yet, from this unfamiliar shore, I felt as close to those twinkling diamonds as I did to my home, and for this reason, I believed in the deepest part of me that the Oracle, for all her promises to the generations of women before me, was truly a liar, and a fraud.

CHAPTER 12

ISHASSARA

W e stayed on the beach for two days and three nights. We spent the first day recovering from our ordeal. We ate and slept, and in the evening, after we had built makeshift steps into the cliff's edge, we buried the dead on the high plateau, where the wind from the Great Mother's sighs could blow over their bodies. Thraso dug the graves herself, whatever tears she cried for her sister mingling with the sweat that beaded on her brow and mixing with the dust that would forever hold Ifito's temple. I did not fail to notice she made enough room for a third body to lie next to her sister, and beside the ha-mazaan who I had learned too late was named Pisto.

But my mother did not die, as I, and the rest of the ha-mazaans, feared she would. When we gathered on the top of the cliff as the waning moon rose in the eastern sky, and as Tekmessa spoke her incantations over Ifito and Pisto's bodies, smoothing her hands over their *rhu-tasiya* tattoos and calling the spirits of their horses to find them in the Otherworld, my mother lay alone on the beach below us, her breathing shallow, but steady. When Thraso threw the first handful of dirt over Ifito's chest, I threw my own handful over Pisto, as her Ishassara. I prayed with every ounce of faith left in me that her journey had been swift and merciful to the Otherworld and would remain so in her search for rebirth. And when we returned to the beach, Melanippe still breathed.

I dreamed that night of the grey mare from the griffin dream. She stood on a sea of jade grass, and her eyes were somehow the same color.

Cyra, she called. Her voice echoed like a crystal bell across the landscape. *Welcome, Cyra.*

How do you know my name?

Because I named you. Called you.
Who are you?
Inara.

Her strange green eyes, too familiar from another face, blinked at me, but when they opened again, they were black and fathomless. I thought I could see the constellations twirling inside of them.

It is time, Cyra. You must find me.

And then she was gone, running over the swirling waters of jade grass, and I was alone. So very alone.

On the second day, the ha-mazaans crowned me as their Ishassara.

When I awoke in the morning, it was to the smell of smoke from long-dead campfires and the tang of salt on my lips from the sea and from the sweat of the previous day. The sky was light, though the sun had not yet risen, and the air was brittle with autumn. I checked my mother. She lay in a deep, fevered sleep, her cheeks grey and chalky rather than brown, and her brow knit with an unaccustomed expression of pain.

As Tekmessa still slept, I crept away softly, finding a place farther down the beach to relieve my bladder at the edge of the water, and splashed my face in the cool waves to wipe the last of my dream away. I wrapped the lion skin around my shoulders and headed for the stacks of barrels and food stores, my bare feet crunching in the sand. I had just found a round of hardened cheese, smelly and striped with strange yellow veins, and a loaf of hard, dry seed bread wrapped in a beeswax cloth when Alkippe approached.

"What does the *zizenti* say about the general?"

"She doesn't. But she doesn't let me see the wound, either." I carved a piece of cheese with my small dagger and held it to her.

Alkippe grunted her thanks, chewing the sweet cheese thoughtfully, and then accepted a crumbly piece of seed bread. I swallowed another mouthful. "I suppose, until my mother is better...you will take on the duties of general?"

She glanced at me, her black eyes sharp with understanding. "I will do what is needed," she nodded. "Ishassara."

I swallowed another piece of nut bread, suddenly dry as dust in my mouth, and smiled ruefully.

"Yes," I answered, acknowledging the term she used and also her promise of support. "I never thought it would happen this way. I never really thought of how it would happen at all, I guess," I shrugged. Alkippe simply raised her eyebrows, pointing her dimpled chin at me in the way so particular to her speech.

"Few who live by the axe die in their beds, surrounded by great-grandchildren and guzzling *kimiz*. Not even queens," she said matter-of-factly.

"What's this? Eating all the food without sharing?" Ossy's voice was disturbingly bright and chipper for the sun not having breached the horizon yet. We turned to watch her trudge through the deep sand. I held out another piece of cheese and hard bread to her with a far less cheerful smile, though it was genuine.

"A fine morning to do some exploring, wouldn't you say?" she asked lightly before biting into the food.

I eyed her skeptically.

"Looking to find some locals to fight?" Alkippe asked dryly.

The sun-kissed skin of Ossy's cheeks wrinkled into a familiar, wide grin. Despite her morning cheerfulness, there was something in her face that made her look older. Worn. I saw streaks of wisdom in the hair at her temples. I had not noticed those before.

She was around my mother's age, perhaps a few years older, and had conscripted into the *matars* at the same time as Melanippe. Her son, Silviu, had spent much time with Eri and me, riding horses and sneaking honeyed figs from the kitchens, before he was of an age to live with his father in Galatae as all of the sons of Themiscyra did. Her second child had been stillborn, when I was barely six, and she had devoted the rest of her life to the Savaran rather than continue living as a *matar*.

I looked from my goddess-mother's face to Alkippe's stoic one. Both were wise beyond their years, and their years were well beyond mine, though Alkippe's true age I did not know. It did not seem possible that I could suddenly be their Ishassara. These people were my teachers. My friends. I had nothing to offer them for leadership other than my name.

Ossy looked at me, seeing something of my doubt. "Ishassara, will you join us to scout the lay of the land as the sun rises? We must find fresh water." She took another small piece of cheese from my blade. "Otherwise, some ha-mazaans will stay here, diving for fish, and sea-sponges for our moon-blood. I am sure they would also welcome your help."

I glanced over my shoulder to where my mother lay. Tekmessa had awakened and knelt next to her, and Camilla was preparing more linen strips for bandages.

"There is nothing you can do for her that the *zizenti* or blacksmith's daughter cannot," Alkippe said as she followed the direction of my gaze. "Moving your body will heal your mind. You should join us on the scout."

I had no desire to be back in the terrifying waters of the sea, and I was already feeling hemmed in by the narrow beach and tall cliffs. I nodded, hitching the lion skin higher on my shoulders. "I will come."

"And when we return," Ossy said in the same light tone, "we will finish what should have been done on our last eve in Themiscyra."

My eyes snapped to hers. "I don't—"

"Yes," Alkippe nodded at Ossy. "That is a good plan, Oistrophe."

"What plan?" Sagitta asked, pushing through the sand on bare feet and helping herself to the cheese on my knife.

"We will complete the ceremony for Ishassara," Ossy said. "Tonight."

Sagitta chewed, considering me. "Good," she said and filled her mouth again.

"It is not even a full moon," I protested.

"Kubileya will not mind," Ossy said.

They nodded in agreement while I chewed the inside of my lip. I could not protest, and had no real reason to, other than a sense of lostness. The feeling of still being in the ship at sea, adrift and directionless, had not left me, and completing the Ishassara ceremony would do nothing to change how obscured our future had become.

"Shall we set off? The sun rises," Alkippe said.

) (

Seven of us scouted the land, as far to the north as we could walk before the sun was at its midpoint in the sky. I walked with Sagitta and Ossy, Thraso and Alkippe, and Prothoe, as well as the *zizenti*, who had joined us in search of healing herbs for my mother's wound. We needed yarrow and clay for the bleeding, wild garlic and oregano for infection. And maggots, though Tekmessa decided those would need to be cultivated rather than found.

When we tried to move west, the ground boiled like stew in a cauldron over a low fire. Great bubbles of mud ballooned from the ground and burst with a hiss of steam before lying flat again, sitting a while before the entire process started over. Some bubbles were small and quick, and others were bigger than my head, the steam erupting from them in a hot hiss when it met the cool morning air. It smelled of swamp and rotting duck eggs. The land was treacherous, forcing us to keep north on the sandy soil woven with summer-dried grass, so we moved toward the low-lying hills covered in green. There were trees there, and more likely fresh water. At one point, Alkippe stopped, putting her nose to the air like a dog on a boar hunt.

"I smell water."

Thraso looked down at her skeptically from her great height, but Alkippe shook her head and made a tsk-tsking sound. "You spend enough time in desert, surrounded by burning sun and sand, you learn to find water with more than just your eyes and ears," she said. "I tell you I smell water. And it does not have salt. Or boiling mud."

We found the source of the scent close by. A small lake, with cattails and marsh grass around its outer edges. When we crested a slight rise to see the shining surface of it, a flock of swans lifted from the water with indelicate honking sounds, startled by our sudden presence. They did not go far, though, landing near the far bank, their great white bodies sending ripples across the smooth blue surface of the water. When they flew again, I brought two of them down with my re-strung bow and the poorly fletched arrows from the Achaean stores. Prothoe clapped me on the shoulder for a job well done, and I felt a twinge of pride. Never before had my skills meant anything other than a boost to my ego. I had hunted with Antiope, of course. Deer and elk and the occasional boar, but always with the knowledge that our people were well fed with *kimiz* and fruit from the orchards, fish from the Terme, and in no dire need of sustenance. But being able to feed the ha-mazaans here in an unfamiliar land brought me a sense of purpose and buoyed my spirits. We had a large supply of food stores from the ship, enough to feed all of us for many weeks, but finding fresh food and saving what could be preserved was now a priority.

As Thraso and Prothoe waded into the marshy water to fetch the bobbing white bodies, I looked toward the hills and the green line of trees sprouting from the land in the distance.

"I think we should search there for a stream that feeds this," I said, feeling somewhat foolish for offering suggestions to seasoned women like Ossy and Alkippe, but both of them nodded and began walking before the others had cleared the lake.

It was not long before we found the running water feeding into the lake, though it was barely more than a stream, which I leaped easily without so much as wetting my bare feet. The water ran clear and burbling in the morning light, the sound almost playful to my ears still traumatized from the sea storm.

We each knelt and cupped the cool water in our hands, slurping it noisily. It was sweet and fresh, better than the stale water in the skins by far, and I gulped several cupped handfuls of it before I was satisfied. The others were doing the same, making loud sighs of satisfaction while water dripped from our chins. When everyone had drunk to their satisfaction, and the waterskins were filled, Thraso said,

"Freshwater and these meadows could work well for a more permanent camp."

"They would," Prothoe said slowly. "But it would be very easy to see our fires from every direction."

"True," Thraso grunted, looking around speculatively.

I was still kneeling at the water's edge, cleaning the salt and grime from my face. When I reached down to pick up my bow, my hand froze in the air above it.

"Look." I pointed to the mud along the bank of the narrow stream.

Cyra. Come find me. The voice tinkled like the brook, clear and bright.

Ossy stepped forward to peer over my shoulder, startling me into reality again after hearing the disembodied voice in my head.

"What is it?" Sagitta asked, jumping across to my side of the bank. Her eyes found the mark as I stood, shouldering my bow.

"Horses," I said.

Sagitta and I stared at the prints and then at each other for several long moments before she let out a resounding laugh and shook me roughly by the shoulders. "Kubileya's tits!" she laughed jubilantly. *"Horses!"*

)(

Our return to the camp was much quicker than our morning meander away from it, and on the way, Sagitta found a freshly killed rabbit in the mouth of a too-eager snake, also dead, both corpses ripe for breeding maggots. Sagitta tossed them over the edge of the cliff when we approached, eliciting screams of consternation from below. Sagitta merely grinned.

I went with Tekmessa to check on my mother, but I was waved away by the *zizenti* after Camilla assured us my mother had slept the whole time. I wanted to stay and help, and offered to crush herbs or cut bandages, but the priestess was adamant. I pressed a kiss to my mother's fevered face and left, knowing I would not win this battle, Ishassara or not.

I made my way to where Alkippe and the others were helping themselves to more cheese and bread and dried figs from the jars. Several more women had gathered to ask questions about the morning scout.

"...as fresh as this morning. An entire herd of them, judging by the tracks. Marvelous!" Ossy finished. The women exclaimed with delight at our good fortune as I approached. I cut some cheese for myself, suddenly ravenous, though I noticed the wheel was considerably smaller than it had been this morning. I was glad for the swans we had found for dinner and for the fish that a few of the other women had caught with their quick spears during the day.

"So there must be a settlement nearby, for horses to be roaming?" Aello asked.

Alkippe shrugged. "We saw no sign of people. Not even a track in the sand. If they are here, they may be closer to the hills and forest or farther down the shore where access to the sea is not so difficult."

Aello nodded, her face thoughtful. "If we can take the horses, it will not matter much who we meet. We will take what we need for supplies and not worry about being overtaken, as we would be on foot."

"If we can take the horses, we can simply go home," Glaukia said. She was a handsome woman, several years older than my mother, with muscular hands and a long scar across her face from an old battle. Her suggestion was greeted with exclamations of agreement, but Thraso shook her head.

"It is a long route around the Maeotian Swamp and the Zalapa Sea to Themiscyra, or even Paphlagonia," the bigger woman argued. "And whether we have horses or not, to the east and the west, there will be impassable mountains flanked by equally impassable tribes of savage men. Horses mean we can flee danger quickly, but they do not mean home is within easy reach."

"My mother needs more time," I said. Many pairs of eyes turned to me, and I met their gaze steadily. "It will take time for us to capture those horses, and more time to train them to ride as we do, even if they are used to the hands of another. We will find the horses, but we must wait for my mother to..." I did not know whether to say *to heal* or *to die*, so I left it unfinished. "After, we can find the way home."

"The weather will make such a trek hard, this close to winter," Ossy said. "You are right about the time it will take for the horses. And by then, the light will be growing short and the days colder. If I remember the tales of the merchants, before we could enter Colchis to the east, there stretches a wide range of mountains that will be filled with ice and cold, not to mention snow cats and griffins."

"And to the west?" someone asked. Ossy shrugged.

"West lies the mountains Thraso spoke of, and Thrace, and the Aegean lands to the south, and that's all before we could move along the southern edge of the Zalapa toward home. I know nothing of what savages we would meet along the way. But I don't relish making that trip under freezing rain and no shelter."

I couldn't agree more, though I wanted to be safe in my chambers at Themiscyra as much as anyone. "We will risk moving my mother only to find the horses. Then, we will re-evaluate, but home is not in our immediate future." The firmness of my voice surprised even me.

There were some hushed murmurs among the gathered ha-mazaans, although of agreement or dissent, I could not tell. Eri's voice cut through the crowd.

"So we are just going to let everyone in Themiscyra think we are captive, or dead?" I turned to watch her shoulder her way past Sagitta and Thraso. "What about my sister, who has no one left?" Eri's blue eyes flashed in her pale skin, and her red hair was like a brand of fire in the afternoon light. There was a wildness in her eyes I had never seen before. The loss of her mother had surely scalded her spirit.

"Who is going to perform Anva's first moon-blood ritual?" she demanded. Everyone could hear the pain in her voice. I moved to offer her comfort, but she turned away from me.

"And what of you, Sagitta?" she whirled on the blonde ha-mazaan, who raised her eyebrows in surprise at being singled out. "Your daughter is still home, wondering what has happened. Leandra is not even four summers! She will want—"

"I know what my daughter wants, Erioboea," Sagitta said sharply, cutting Eri short. "I do not need lessons from someone who is barely graduated from Xanharaspa, and is years away from qualifying as *matar*, to tell me about how my daughter must feel." Sagitta's eyes were hard. There was fury in her voice, but also grief, and my chest ached for her. All the *matars* in our stranded group must be haunted by the same loss. At least when their sons were sent to Galatae, they were still within a few day's ride for visiting.

Sagitta's eyes softened, and she laid a gentle hand on my friend's shoulder. "I am sorry about your mother, Eri," she said. "We all are. She died bravely, which is what every ha-mazaan hopes for. But neither you nor I want to die from exposure or see savage armies in numbers we cannot survive by hurrying our steps home before it is wise. No matter how much we want to see our families again."

Eri wrenched her shoulder out of Sagitta's hands.

"You will take direction from her, though." Eri's long arm pointed stiffly in my direction, though she did not actually look at me. The resentment in her voice shocked a hot flush into my cheeks as everyone's eyes followed her gesture. "Even though *she* was still Xanharaspa just a few days ago, yet you won't let me speak what is true when I am only trying to think of our families? You're just going to do what she says?"

There was incredulity in her tone, but also a sharp, cold fury. I stood in shocked silence, blindsided by Eri's animosity. Sagitta stepped forward and faced Eri, close enough that the younger girl almost stepped back, but she squared her chin and stood her ground. They were of a height, and blue eyes met darker blue eyes in unswayed anger.

"We will take direction from the *Ishassara*, just as you will," Sagitta said calmly, but flint hardened her voice. "And if you feel differently about it in a year, you may cast your stone at the Alsanti, just like the rest of the ha-mazaans. But here, now," she poked a sharp finger down to the ground we stood on, "we answer to Cyra. *You* answer to Cyra." The finger stabbed into Eri's chest. "So if she tells you to patch that ship," the same finger stabbed out at the black mound half-submerged in the water, "with your own dried blood, and to begin rowing us back across the black waters of the sea with only your hands at the oars, that is what you will do. What we will *all* do," Sagitta emphasized, looking away from Eri's flushed face to the eyes of the other women.

"We will hold the ceremony at moonrise," Ossy stepped forward and looked around at the same faces. Most met her eyes with thoughtful curiosity, but I noticed a few looked uncertain, even upset, and their glances in my direction did nothing to quell the thundering of my heart.

"We have neither queen to complete that ritual," Glaukia said. Her scar pulled as she frowned at my goddess-mother.

"Nor would we if we still stood on the banks of Themiscyra's river this moment," Ossy countered, her normally soft eyes firm and fixed on the other woman's doubtful expression. "Yet I do not think you would quibble if we were there. If we abandon our Ways now, there is no point in thinking of home at all. Cyra will be the Ishassara for a year and a day from Hippolyta's death, as she was sworn to be at her birth. You were there," she reminded Glaukia, but the older woman merely pursed her lips as Ossy continued.

"We will bless her—Matar Kubileya will bless her—in the ritual with the strength and wisdom she needs to lead us well. If anyone objects to her leadership in that year, it will be their right to cast their stone at the Alsanti, just as Sagitta says."

Eri left the gathering with swift, jerky strides before Ossy finished speaking. I watched her go, a desperate loneliness taking hold of my heart. What would have been a celebration between friends, had everything been as it should and we were still in Themiscyra, had instead become a thorn in the tender flesh of our sisterhood at the worst possible time. I was no longer the same as Eri, with the same freedoms or the same needs. A wedge in the shape of all the responsibilities of the Defender's Throne had been shoved between us.

The horrible feeling of still being adrift at sea made my head swim until I thought I might be sick. Glaukia and a few others followed Eri, and the rest of the crowd gradually dispersed to continue their chores of dressing the swans and chopping more driftwood and oars for the fires.

Alkippe clapped me briskly on the arm. "Don't worry," she said in her clipped tone, but she smiled a rare smile into my troubled face. "Erioboea will come around. They all will. Until then, I am your general, and Sagitta is my captain." Sagitta nodded her acceptance of the position with no hint that it came as any surprise. Perhaps they had already discussed it.

"And I am your advisor, as always, goddess-daughter." Ossy held my eyes with calm assurance. We both knew the term she used was no longer just one of affection. There was weight to it now, and purpose.

"Thank you," I said thickly.

When they finally went their own ways, I was forced to find new distractions for my thoughts. I thought about going after Eri, but now did not seem like the time. I would let her anger, wherever it had come from, cool first, and then we would talk. I returned to my own fire.

"The bleeding is less," Tekmessa said to my questioning look as I checked on my mother. It was all I could get from her, and it did nothing to ease my mind.

I spent the afternoon washing my tunic in the sea, scrubbing it under the gentle waves, the water growing murky where I rubbed the linen between my palms. I could not remove the stains of blood from the men I had killed, but the worst of the filth came away. I washed my hair in the salty water as well, wishing I had done it in the fresh stream earlier that day. But I did not want to arrive at my own ceremony like an old hag fresh from the mountains, come to sell her pigs at market.

I donned the wet tunic and left my scaled vest beside my bedding, and spent the rest of the afternoon wandering the beach, helping the ha-mazaans with various minor tasks. When darkness fell, we lit the fires and roasted swan and fresh fish for dinner. The mood was somber as every woman thought of what lay beyond the water. Children and aunts, sisters and sons in Themiscyra, lovers and brothers and grandfathers in Galatae.

When the moon finally glowed over the eastern edge of the sea, the mood in the camp was more morose than celebratory, and I sat next to my mother in silence, listening to her shallow breaths and wishing I had her strong words and wisdom to guide me forward.

Ossy came and helped me strip from my clothes, folding them in a neat pile that was most unlike her before she led the way to where the ha-mazaans had gathered on the shoreline. I couldn't help but wonder what shocking interruption would derail the ritual this time around, but we arrived undeterred, my bare skin prickling into gooseflesh in the night's chill. Every face turned to watch me step forward to the lion skin laid across the ground. When I knelt on it, facing them, the faces of the women were lit by moon and starlight and the flickering torches Ossy and Alkippe held on each side of me. I felt small in front of the women, and vulnerable, though not from my nakedness. I heard the rustle of Tekmessa's red robes as she stepped up behind me.

"Cyra, Daughter of the Mighty Melanippe," Tekmessa intoned. There was no hint of the gentle doe-eyed woman in her now. She embodied a Priestess of the Moon, and her voice rang with the echo of the Ancient Ones.

"We gather here to witness your initiation as Ishassara, who will one day take the Throne of the Defending Queen a year and a day after that sister queen's death. This sad day has already come to pass. We would know, Cyra, will you take up her cause?"

"I will."

"Then hear the wisdom of the Great Mother. For if you adhere to these Ways, Matar Kubileya will surely bless your day of Alsanti."

I resisted shifting my knees on the lion's skin as the sand underneath became as hard and unyielding as stone. A breeze ran thin fingers over my bare breasts, and I shivered. Ossy stepped forward, her bronze eyes gleaming down into mine.

"To lead, you must also follow, both the old ways and the new," she said, loud enough for all to hear. "You will learn the old ways from the milk and the blood of your Great Mother and from the stories and wounds of the ha-mazaans. You will create the new from the light that is in your heart, from the old place within you where the Great Mother speaks. Cyra, will you swear to do this as Ishassara?"

"I will."

Sagitta stepped forward, taking the torch from Ossy, and now it was her blue eyes that I looked into as she spoke the traditional words.

"To lead, you must have a path to lead others forward upon," she said. "If there is no path, you must create one and make sure it leads to where there is good for all, not only yourself. Cyra, will you swear to do this as Ishassara?"

I swallowed. "I will," I said hoarsely, afraid that I was lying. How could I create a path in an unknown land?

Alkippe replaced Sagitta, and the torch did little to light her dark face in the night. Her dark eyes glinted down at me like black agates.

"To lead, you must be fierce enough to defeat the griffins of our great enemies and gentle enough to suckle a babe. Both have risk. You must know which risk to choose when the time is right. You must protect, and defend, and know when each is needed. Cyra, will you swear to do this as Ishassara?"

"I will."

"To lead, you must know in your heart what is wrong from what is right, not what others tell you is one or the other," Thraso said. Her huge shoulders blocked out the stars, and I craned my neck to meet her eyes. "When you know right from wrong, you must pursue without delay. Cyra, will you swear to do this as Ishassara?"

"I will."

Tekmessa spoke again, coming around me in a rustle of red robe until her dark eyes were looking into mine. She held a knife in one hand.

"You must serve those who follow you, and in so doing, you lead. You must walk in their footsteps, cry their tears, and bleed from their wounds. If you cannot do this, you cannot lead others, only force them. Leading the ha-mazaans means life, or death. If it lands somewhere in between the two, it is not leading at all, but merely following. We do not follow the Way of another. To protect our Ways, you must know life from death. And for all these things, you must be willing to lay down your life for the Way of the ha-mazaans. Cyra, will you swear to do this as Ishassara?"

"I will."

She held out her hand, and I offered my left palm. The cut she made was quick and deep enough to let the blood flow freely. I clenched my hand, squeezing until the blood welled through my fingers, feeling the sting of it blossom all the way past my wrist. When I opened it again, bloody and dark, she placed a stone there, round and smooth from the bottom of the sea.

"By your own blood, you bind yourself to what you have promised this day. Your blood sets into stone what we have all heard, and if, at the Alsanti, you have failed to keep these promises to any ha-mazaan, they will cast their stone aside, breaking the bonds of your rule over them. Step forward, ha-mazaans, and seal the promises of your Ishassara."

One by one, each ha-mazaan brought their own stone, dropping it onto my bloody palm so that the blood marked it with my solemn vow to defend and protect them and our Ways. When Eri's turn came, her eyes were as hard as the rock she pressed into my cut, but I did not look away. When the last stone had been marked, Tekmessa raised me to my feet and led me to the edge of the water. She waded in beside me until we were chest deep, where we turned again to face the shadowed mass of women along the shoreline.

"Cyra, Daughter of Melanippe. You enter the waters of Kubileya's Womb as ha-mazaan. When you emerge, may you be reborn as Ishassara, Heir to the Defender's Throne."

The water was cold when she pushed me down, and for a moment, my body tensed with the panic of drowning that had so recently filled my mind. But when she pulled me out of the water, the coldness of it ran between my breasts and down my thighs, and I stood proudly for the first time since my Savaran Trials. I thought, for a moment, that I heard my name once more on the breeze, calling me from high atop the cliffs.

Cyra. Welcome. It is time.

CHAPTER 13

MANY NAMES, ONE MOTHER

We brought only what we could carry and buried the rest at the beach, in case we needed to come back for more later. Still, our loads were heavy and our bodies were tired when we made it to the stream where we had seen the signs of horses. When I lowered the spear handle in tandem with the others who helped to carry my mother's stretcher, I felt the ache of where it had pressed into my shoulder for several hours. I was glad for a respite, and for food. But we did not tarry for long, and as the sun crept through the sky between racing clouds, we continued on the path to the hills, following the marks of our salvation.

There were plenty of signs that the horses had been about, even as early as that day. Their manure was fresh, and the tracks were round and clear in the mud the closer we came to the low mountain. I felt a thrill at the evidence we were on the right track, but also a frisson of anxiety, as we still did not know if the horses meant people, and if people meant danger. Not that we were unable or unwilling to fight. The axes and spears were freshly sharpened, and every ha-mazaan was armed. It was just that we were so tired. Bone tired, as my mother used to say when she would return from weapons practice with Alkippe, and now I knew firsthand exactly what she had meant.

There were still no signs of people when the forest began, so we took the chance to set up camp and light fires, eating the last of our fish and cheese close to the warmth of the flames. There was little conversation, and as soon as it grew dark, most of the camp was silent with sleep. I offered to post as sentry but was waved away by several women who had already settled themselves around the edges of the forest, spears and swords ready. I thanked them, feeling guilty relief, and then settled myself under the lion's skin near my mother.

My dreams were strange and provoking. In one, Risa threw me to the ground as we ran, and then turned on me with sharp, flashing hooves, while Leandra, Sagitta's daughter, urged the mare on with shrieking giggles from her back. I screamed and rolled from under her feet, but she came after me with bared teeth, and they were pointed and long like a wolf's, ready to tear at my flesh. The dream switched even as I covered my face from her gnashing.

I lay in long waving grass, staring up at a wide blue sky and fluffy, lazy clouds drifting overhead. I chewed a stalk of grass, the seeded end of it bobbing gently in the air above my head. It was so peaceful. Harmonious, though there was no sound. I could feel the peace of it in my soul. How dense and tangible the perfectly warm air felt on my bare skin, naked to the waist. A hand stretched toward the sky next to me, pointing at one cloud that looked like a jackal. The arm, corded with muscles, was banded on the wrist with a gold cuff etched with eagles and deer and a tree with twining roots. A man's hand. That man's hand settled with palpable warmth on my thigh, and the weight of it stilled everything inside of me that felt shaken loose from being cast away from my home.

Just before dawn, I dreamed of the dappled mare. Her nose pressed into my side as she nuzzled the seams of my tunic for dried apples, and I pulled the last one out to give it to her. She took it from my palm with careful lips, her muzzle both soft and prickly against my skin, and then she butted me with her forehead against my chest so that I stumbled and fell, only I was falling from a great height, as though from the palace walls in Themiscyra, and when I hit the water of the river, my body jolted awake with a delirious urgency, the first shadows of dawn just reaching through the treetops overhead.

When it was time to leave, the mare's eyes still shone in my mind, and I wondered at the strangeness of my dream. Ossy took up the pole next to me at my mother's shoulder, smiling with her usual morning cheerfulness. We hefted the stretcher, with Alkippe and Sagitta at the foot, and turned to follow the rest who were already winding their way through the small thicket of trees toward the low, densely forested hills that lay another half day's walk ahead of us.

"I have been dreaming about a mare," I said casually, but Ossy immediately glanced over at me with an intent look that I pretended to not see. "A few times now, she has appeared to me, but she is not a horse I know." I hesitated. "Is it strange that I think she told me her name?"

"What are the dreams?"

I told her a few of them, in which the mare had spoken to me. But not the one with the griffin who turned into my mother. That one still felt raw and terrifying. Premonitory. Ossy considered what I told her for a moment, then said matter-of-factly, "I suppose it should be expected if she is your rhu-tasiya."

"Do they always give their names?"

"If a person pays attention, everything gives its name one way or another. Through dreams, or the wind, or a simple knowing that a name is not right until you stumble upon the one that finally fits. Your name came from the Oracle, for instance. Cyra, Throned Upon the Sun." She said it with a grand sweep of her free arm. "To call something by the wrong name is a grievous insult," Ossy continued. "It is the only proper way we can know something or someone. It would not surprise me that your rhu-tasiya needs you to know who she is."

"I don't know that she is my rhu-tasiya."

Ossy gave me a sideways glance that was as loud as the laugh that followed it. "I can't fathom what more you need to finally know it, goddess-daughter. She has come to you in a dream and called you to her by name. What more do you want?"

"I used to dream of Risa and Otho before her."

"And did they tell you their name in those dreams?"

"No," I admitted grudgingly.

"And did those dreams feel like Spirit dreams?"

I eyed her sideways. Once, when I was young, I had dreamed of a great boar with deadly tusks tearing through the halls of the palace. I had awoken in a sweat and immediately ran to tell my mother. She comforted me absentmindedly, for her attention had been elsewhere. The next week, a wild boar, its tusks the size of my arm, had killed a dog at the gates and somehow made its way into the courtyard and then all the way into the Moon Hall, despite many attempts to corral it. It destroyed several tables and much pottery before a few brave ha-mazaans speared the beast. Later, my mother apologized to me, saying she should have asked if it was a Spirit dream, and assured me I would come to learn the signs. Yet here I was, still oblivious.

"What name did the mare give?" Ossy asked curiously.

"Inara," I offered finally, after pondering whether I should say it aloud. Ossy looked at me intently.

"Inara!" she repeated, sounding both bewildered and surprised.

"Have you heard it before? I never have. So I don't think I could have named her even in my dream."

"I have," Ossy nodded. "Though not for a long time. As long as you are old, in fact." She said this wistfully. Her eyes had become far away, as though she was seeing something else in front of her rather than the grassy, rock-stubbled ground we walked over. "The father of my first son would often tell us stories of Inara. He called her the Mistress of all Wild Things. He said I and our 'peculiar ha-mazaan ways' did her proud," Ossy smiled fondly as she remembered. "His mother's people called her Cybele." She looked at me then, her eyes returning to this place. "Our name for Cybele is Kubileya."

"Matar Kubileya?" I said, an uncomfortable prickling erupting on my skin.

"Aye, some call her Matar, for she carries all in her womb and suckles us at her breasts, gifting us with wisdom and nourishment and bleeding from her thighs to cover and protect us from harm. Kubileya, Great Mother, Cybele, Moon Mother...Inara...it does not matter. She is known by many names and many faces. Our city shares the name your grandfather knew her by, which was Themis. Themiscyra, 'Where Themis is Supreme.' The Achaeans call her Artemisa, as did your great-grandmother's people in Mycenae."

"My mother's people called her Zat-Badar, or 'She of the Wild Goats,'" Alkippe interjected from behind us. "And my father's mother—who was evil with breasts, may her soul forever be trapped in a bog of mud—" she said this with an easy hatred that might have been shocking if I had not heard it a hundred times before, "that hag called her Asase Ya, who is Wife of the Sky."

"I often wondered if Leandra's father was telling me tall tales when he spoke of their goddess," Sagitta put in from my mother's ankles. "He said their poems in the temple claimed 'beauty ran after her like a puppy,' and he would embarrass me with the comparison without end. Sauska, I think he called her."

After a few steps of thoughtful silence, Alkippe said, "Zat-Badar gives prophetic dreams to her priestesses, the khalimah. You would do well to listen to this Spirit dream, Ishassara. Zat-Badar, who has called herself

Inara to you, comes to you for a purpose."

I pondered their words. "I thought you said the correct name was important for a thing to be known. How can Matar Kubileya go by so many names? Only one of them can be right."

"She is all things to all people. Therefore, all of them are right, and all of them wrong," she said, confusing me further. "Kubileya is different to all who see Her, and for those differences, and from what is known, they call Her by that name. But She is also unknowable, and therefore Unnamable. To have the name of something is to bring it into your realm of understanding, and in some way, under your control. This will never be fully possible for the One we know as Kubileya. So we call Her as we know Her, but She will always be outside of our control, as all truly wild things should be. Life does not flourish once the spirit has been tamed. This, the ha-mazaans know."

"We know," Alkippe agreed grimly.

We walked silently for a while, and I mused over all they had said. What it would mean for the spirit of Matar Kubileya to come to me in the body of a mare in my own dreams, I could not imagine. I could not make sense of it. And what would it mean to find Her if She was indeed the Great Mother? She was everywhere. I walked on Her, breathed Her, lived inside of Her and because of Her. There was nowhere to go to find Her. I scowled in new frustration and shifted my shoulder under the spear, my thoughts more jumbled than they had been before I asked the question.

) (

When we finally reached the gently undulating hills, the forest was thick with beech, aspen, oak, fir, and spruce, their dense trunks encrusted with the passage of time. We wound carefully through the trees, the late afternoon sunlight falling in gentle streams through the branches high overhead. Thraso, leading our caravan of weary walkers, put her hand in the air as a signal to halt. The entire troupe became quiet as a lone hare when it feels itself in the sights of a dog. Barely even a breath moved from our tired lungs, and I watched attentively as Thraso turned her head to stare up at the tall tree, and then around, as though expecting to see something. We were about to lower Melanippe to the ground in order to be ready with our weapons when Thraso waved her hand, indicating there was no danger, and made her way forward again.

It was a small grove that we moved into, a fine place to shelter for a while. The massive branches of the trees ringing the grove offered good shelter from possible rains and the heat of the midday sun, and the creek ran nearby, cool and deep and wider than where it trickled as a stream further out on the plain. There were tall boulders placed around the far outer edge as well, like sentinels. We set my mother down where others were busy building a fire with sticks and deadwood from the forest. Tekmessa, though tired and wan from our long journey, immediately came to her side. I stretched my sore back and shoulder muscles and looked on while the zizenti removed the furs from my mother's legs. Camilla was busy building the fire, so when Tekmessa moved to cut away the bandages, I knelt to help her.

"No, Ishassara, Camilla will aid me soon enough," she tried to wave me away again, but I resisted.

"You do not need to hide it from me," I said quietly, and her eyes met mine. "I already know."

She hesitated for a long moment, then gave a small, reluctant nod. Carefully, I pulled back the edges of the bandage as she cut the cloth, and almost immediately, I regretted my insistence that I not be sheltered from the reality of my mother's wound. The flesh of her entire thigh was red and angry with streaks of even darker red, running to black. They radiated out from the edges of the cut, where it ran deepest through the front of her thigh. The inside had crusted over with black, which seemed to be better than constantly bleeding, but I knew the signs of infection well enough in the green pus that oozed. My eyes met Tekmessa's again, and her face was as grave as I had ever seen it.

"There has not been time for the maggots to form on the carcasses," she said, waving a hand toward the basket, woven from cattail reeds, which held the remains of the snake and its half-eaten meal. "I need them now if we are going to turn the tide. As it is, her blood slowly poisons. I collected some burdock at the edge of the forest and some nettle and rosehips. But they will not be enough to keep the poison at bay."

I stared down at my mother's leg, nodding mutely. I was about to ask her what I could do to help when my mother stirred, her eyes fluttering open. The furs were bunched up around her throat. I gently pulled them away so that she could breathe easier and smiled at her as her eyes, feverish and glinting in the shadowed light of the grove, found my face. "Good morning, sleepyhead," I said, echoing her oft-repeated greeting to me at morning weapons practice, though hers had usually been delivered with acerbic disapproval. "Although, it is evening now," I clarified, feeling awkward. "But there won't be any more jostling on our clumsy shoulders. We have found a place to rest for a while. How do you feel?"

Camilla approached with a cup of fresh water from the stream, and I lifted my mother's head and shoulders so that she could drink. She managed a few tiny, weak swallows before she turned her head away, and I laid her back on the cloth of the stretcher as gently as possible.

"I am cold," she said then, her voice thin and transparent. I still had my hand on her shoulder and felt the heat of her skin under my calloused fingers. I looked at Tekmessa with worry plain on my face, but the priestess only smiled and said,

"We will have you warm again soon, Akka." She used the ha-mazaan term of respect for an older sister. "The fires will burn bright, and you will sing with us under the stars tonight."

"I heard your dream, Daughter," Melanippe said then, as though the priestess had not spoken. "You must listen to the others and to the mare. It is a Spirit dream."

Her eyes, bright silver mirrors of my own, fixed firmly on mine. I nodded, not knowing what to say.

Melanippe grimaced as Tekmessa wound a fresh bandage around her thigh. I tried to distract her from the pain by telling her of the landscape of this land, so different than ours with its rolling grasslands and mounded hills. Eventually, she drifted into sleep, and I left her near the crackling fire to make my way over to the stream. The water gleamed rich and smooth beneath the darkening sky, and it was chilly here on its shaded path through the forest. I splashed it over my face and neck after I drank and then found a rock I could sit on and do the same with my dirty feet. I washed the mud of the last two days from my legs and my arms, noticing as I did that the first tattoo I had received for my moon-blood initiation had become dark and blurred on the inside of my wrist, opposite to the fresh, barely healed tattoo marking me as Savaran.

I felt along the edges of my moon-blood mark, tracing around the upside-down triangle and into the open top. It was the same that every ha-mazaan received to honor their first moon-blood. Two lines encircled my wrist above and below it, thin and blue-black. One was for the unbroken line of my mother, and one for my father's mother, for both their mother's mothers, as far back as it took to reach the Great Mother. I thought of what Ossy and Alkippe had told me today, about the names of Matar Kubileya known to all the mothers across the earth. For some reason, it brought me comfort to think that there were many ways to know the Great Mother. The way I thought about Her was probably not the way my mother did, and even less so the way my grandmother had, though I had barely known Otrera before her death. And what we knew was different again from Alkippe, or her mother-in-law, and Ossy and her mother, although Ossy had been born and raised in Themiscyra alongside my mother. It seemed that what we knew of the Great Mother beyond her body, the very ground we stood on, was open to interpretation.

And perhaps, I mused, it was possible to assume the prophecies given at our first moon-blood could also be open to interpretation. I wanted to think so, but so far, nothing that had happened in the last few days made me think it was anything but words written in stone. I wondered, not for the first time, if I should share my prophecy from the Oracle with my mother. To see what wisdom she had for me. To beg her forgiveness for something I had not yet done.

She had always respected my choice to keep the prophecy a secret, believing I held it as sacred, intimate, between me and Matar Kubileya. But it had never been for that reason. I had been ashamed, and confused, and did not consider it a prophecy at all. Only a curse. Every part of the prophecy had been confusing and terrifying. To admit to my mother that I might bind myself to a man and force his rule upon the ha-mazaans as my equal was unthinkable. I had refused to speak it aloud for fear it would help the curse become reality, and yet...

Never shall you rule in Themiscyra...

The role of the Sister Queens shall die with Hippolyta...

Never will your mother see you rule over any living ha-mazaan.

The realization that I might finally know what those words meant was no comfort. Hippolyta was dead. And my mother...

My mother would not see me rule because she would be dead as well.

I felt a tightening on my neck, like a noose. I had always known the prophecy was a curse, but I had done my best to escape it. Seeing my mother's leg made me realize it did not matter what I chose. Destiny would find me, and I would live out my fate as it had been woven. There was nothing I could do but let it happen.

Even if it meant betraying the Way of the ha-mazaans.

CHAPTER 14

INARA

W
e had been in the grove for three days, my mother slowly, inexorably slipping from fevered dreams to a heavy, unconscious sleep that I feared she would not wake from. Tekmessa had finally harvested enough maggots to clean the wound; each morning, she placed new ones inside the cut, so that they could eat the dead and poisoned flesh, while removing the older ones before they could hatch. Each morning, I offered to help with the task, my hands sweating just at the thought of it, and each time, Tekmessa waved me away, calling poor Camilla to her aid instead.

And thus, each day, I left my mother's side with a knot of fear in my stomach, needing a task that took my mind from her pain and an inevitability I felt we were simply prolonging. I fletched new arrows for my bow and hunted for deer and other game in the forest. But mostly, I ventured to the edge of the trees, where they met the undulating land to the northeast, giving way to a vast expanse of grass and sky spreading south to the sea. I was pulled there every morning by the promise of horses and my dreams of the grey mare.

For two mornings, my tunic stuffed with dried figs as bait, I found hoofprints, manure, and the short, perfectly-leveled tufts of grass where the horses had eaten to the nub. But no horses. The same report was given by the others scouting west and south when we met back at the camp. The herd, or perhaps herds, covered a lot of ground, and always as shadows under the cover of night. The third day, I followed the same easterly path, my steps light lest I come upon them unawares and startle them into fleeing.

Above me, a hawk circled with slow, still wings, higher and higher into the sky. Its shadow whirled on the ground in front of me, and I tried to make my steps as light as its imprint on the ground, my body as insubstantial, but in the end, I need not have worried. The moment I stepped from the edge of the forest into the undiluted sunlight, she was there, head high and tail swishing to one side, then the other, in the casual rhythm of a horse at ease, but still watchful. I halted, my breath catching at the unexpectedness of her presence, but she blinked languid dark eyes and put her head down to tear another mouthful of dry grass.

She was beautiful. Even my dreams had not done her justice. I knew it was the same horse as my dream from her eyes and from the way the dark charcoal of her face and legs spread upward into a dappled dark and light that would one day grow to pure white. Her black mane was long and untangled, hanging from her neck in waves but flipped undecided over both sides of her poll and between her ears, and her tail brushed the grasses behind her when it was not removing flies from her ribs. The nose that searched with precise twitching along the ground for the sweetest morsels of grass was finely sculpted and black as a jet carving, as were her face and legs.

She was magnificent.

Slowly, barely daring to breathe, I dug a hand into a pocket and pulled out the dried fruit, holding it in my palm as though it were a cup of honeyed wine in a silver goblet. An offering to a goddess. I was about to take another cautious step toward her when she lifted her head, ears pricked, and came with quick, sure steps to me. I tried to keep my breathing light though my heart raced, afraid that even the slightest movement would startle her, but within seconds, her nose was stretched out, upper lip reaching eagerly for the sweet morsels. Her lips curled around them, and I felt the soft prickle of her whiskers against my hand. She chewed, bobbing her head when the dried, sticky pieces clung to her teeth. She was not even finished before her nose was reaching for my hand again and, finding it empty, pushing insistently into my sides, searching for more. I laughed aloud, forgetting myself, and was instantly afraid she would disappear as a wisp of smoke or a dream at the sound. Her ears only twitched, and her eyes blinked, asking for more sweets. I fed her another fig, though I saved a few for the other horses behind her, which were now sidling forward, curious and hopeful.

I peered around in search of a stallion, a potentially dangerous obstacle I had not yet figured out how we would overcome, but most of the horses appeared to be mares and geldings—a clear sign of people—and a few yearlings alongside mares farther out in the grass. The smaller foals had been born just a few months prior, in spring. That meant a stallion for sure, but he was not in sight.

The grey mare's ears lay flat against her neck, and my heart thumped a beat, thinking that I had misread the docility of a truly wild creature, but she snaked her head toward an approaching bay in the unmistakable language of a horse saying *"Mine."* The bay shied backward, and the mare was calm again. She was clearly the head mare, used to eating before the others and having her way, and the rest were respectful of her position.

Her head turned toward me, ears forward and eyes soft once more, with only my arm's length between us. I marveled at the beauty of her and the simple, quiet energy that seemed to exude from every muscle, even as she stood still and calm in front of me. Pure, unadulterated power. Hesitantly, I said out loud, feeling more than a little foolish,

"Inara?"

Her tail swished. She blinked lazily, and then her nose stretched out toward my other pocket, searching for more treats. I raised my hand slowly, holding the back of it to her nostrils that were busily searching every inch of my torso for more figs. She sniffed around my hand as though it was impeding her process, up my ribs, and lipped at the edge of my leather belt, trying to peek underneath. Her curious lips began feeling at the raised triangles of the animal scales on my vest, tickling her lips on them in curious fascination. I took the chance and laid the back of my fingers across the bridge of her nose, stroking her gently. She ignored it, switching her head to my other side, where the few treats still sat next to my thigh.

"Not another Risa when it comes to food, are you?" I bemoaned, but with a smile. She replied by shaking a fly from her neck with a twist of her head and snorting a long, drawn-out sigh, effectively covering the front of my tunic and my arm with dusty, moist horse snot. "Hmm," I said, pleased.

We eyed each other for a moment, and finally, I took half a step forward. I smoothed my hand down the side of her neck. Her eyes blinked lazily, with no sign of fear or discomfort. I stroked her under her mane, where her flesh was hot, and scratched her where I knew she would be itchy from bugs and loose hair. Her eyes watched me idly, and her left ear flicked in my direction, but I sensed no tenseness in the muscles under my hands. I smoothed my hand high on her flank toward her tail, careful to keep my body close to hers in case she tried to surprise me with a hoof to the leg. Then I made my slow way back to her head, moving to the other side with careful steps. Her eyes followed me, although she did not move her head. I spoke to her, and her ears followed the sound of my voice, which was what I wanted.

"If Inara is your name, and you came to me in a Spirit dream, it seems possible you are my *rhu-tasiya*. What do you have to say about that? Are you my *rhu-tasiya*?"

I stood at her other hip now, my hand resting lightly on her dappled rump as she cocked a leg and went into a resting position, unconcerned by my presence. She was clearly used to human contact. The thought brought a crease of worry to my brows as I made my way back to the mare's head. Her nose stretched out to sniff at the bow slung across my chest and the horned tip peeking up over my shoulder, nuzzling the taut string curiously.

I felt a pang of guilt at the thought of appropriating someone else's horse, as I had every intention of doing. It would not matter if I thought this mare was to be my *rhu-tasiya* or not. We would make the herd our own either way because these horses were our best chance of survival, for hunting and defending ourselves if need be, and of returning home. But if someone else thought of her, or any of the herd, in the sacred way we held our horses, it would be one of the most heinous crimes imaginable.

I looked to the increasingly large group of horses that had cautiously gathered a few lengths away, smelling the figs and hopeful for a share. They were eyeing my movements with slightly more trepidation than their lead mare, but only because I was strange to them, and not because they were wild. I approached the closest horse, a thick-boned black mare with curious eyes, and reached into my pocket for another piece of dried fig. Soon, my dried fruit was gone, and most of the horses had warmed to me. Satisfied, I returned my attention to the mare.

I spent some more time brushing her everywhere with my hands and picking the sweetest grass I could find, though that was in short supply this late in the fall. I spoke to her, at first to make her accustomed to the sound of my voice, but soon to share what was on my mind and relieve the weight I had been holding in my heart for so long now. I spoke to her about the ship and the terror of the sea. About the men, and the blood, and the feel of their lives fleeing from my sword. I cried, and then I wept, as I could not have in front of my people. She listened, and sometimes her nose brushed across the scales on my vest, and the scent of her warm body comforted me. I told her of my mother and my heartbreak over her, and the curse, and losing Themiscyra, and the pressure of being Ishassara so suddenly and unexpectedly. The animosity between me and Eri, now that we were not children playing at ha-mazaan games anymore. The confusion of it all. I told her of my strange dreams and my fear of betraying my own people. She swished her tail and watched me with languid eyes.

When I left her to return and tell the rest of our good fortune, I felt lighter. Freer. Stronger.

I had found my *rhu-tasiya*.

)(

I was stepping carefully over the fresh deadfall of a beech tree, likely felled by the windstorm that had brought our ship to this land, and keeping a close eye on the ground for stray blackberry vines when Sagitta sucked in her breath with a sharp hiss.

"Down!"

Immediately, all twelve of us crouched, eyes scanning the terrain and hands going to our weapons.

A man with hair as white as frost walked toward the herd of horses from the edge of a sparsely treed hill that protruded into the grassland. Our first proof of people nearby, and I was more than a little relieved that he appeared a decrepit grandfather. He moved with a limp, as though his leg was too heavy to lift. The herd, which we had tracked to the base of this low mountain from the place I had come upon them the day before, was a fair distance into an open field, and it seemed to take forever for the man's slow, creaking steps to finally reach them. My legs grew numb from being crouched so long. I shifted my position carefully, letting some blood flow into my calves, and the others did the same, trying to be as quiet as possible. We were not quiet enough, though. Someone rustled leaves underfoot, and one of the horses swung its head in our direction. Black ears pricked directly toward where I was hidden. Inara.

We froze, but the man noticed nothing untoward. He approached a white horse, the same color as his hair, and took a coil of rope from his shoulder, looping it around the horse's neck before slowly, agonizingly slowly, leading it away with his shuffling gait. When the old grandfather and horse had disappeared from sight, we crept as quickly as possible into the thick trees at the edge of the forest, where we would have more cover.

"Matar," Sagitta swore softly, and someone else added their own low-voiced curse.

Ten of our best riders besides Sagitta had come with me today, including Leya, and even Eri, in hopes we would find the horses. We had even brought the last of our stores of dried fruit as bait, though I did not think we would need it. The previous afternoon, after I had relayed my encounter with the horses and made it known they were habituated to people and likely even trained, we had crafted new bridles using scraps of leather from the Achaean belts and sandals and bones from the hunted deer for cheek pieces and bits. It had been easy to track them to this place once we knew where to start. But now, we faced the reality that the horses did indeed come with their own set of problems. Problems in the form of people.

"He looks harmless enough," Leya said, her voice low.

"Aye, he looks like a strong breeze would flatten him on his back," Sagitta agreed. "But he's not likely to be the only one around."

"We need to go back and warn the others," Asteria said.

"No," I shook my head decisively. "We need to know what to tell the rest, other than 'there's an old man who lives in the hills.' We have to know how many people are nearby. What we can expect from them. If they will hinder us in taking the horses."

"Maybe we don't need to take the horses," Leya offered. "We could offer something in trade."

"Like what? Deer hides?" Phillipisa asked with open skepticism.

"What about the ingots we buried at the beach," Leya said. "It would be only another couple of days to return with a few ha-mazaans and gather enough copper and tin. We could pay for the horses."

"If they even have any use for copper and tin," Asteria said.

"Even tiny villages have a blacksmith for making bronze," Sagitta said. "It could be our best plan."

"And then we do what?" Eri's voice was stern. All eyes turned to her. "Return to our tiny grove with fifty horses, while at least one village—filled with who knows how many people, who will by then know we are a small group of strange women, lost and possibly carrying more precious wares—decides to round up the rest of the locals to come and take what they want from us?"

I nodded slowly, considering her words carefully. Though we had not spoken more than a few curt words to each other since the Initiation ceremony, the tension had mellowed to a sullen withdrawal on her part. I had been glad when she had put forth her name for today's venture because at least she was not avoiding me entirely, although I still did not know how to approach her and erase the tension completely. It felt like something she would do when she was ready and not for me to force. Even choosing to come today had been a step in the right direction. And now, we were in agreement on one thing, at least. I smiled at her, feeling a renewed sense of camaraderie between us that I had been sorely missing.

"Eri is right. Revealing who we are will make us vulnerable to future attacks, whether from greedy men seeking bronze or barbarian men seeking pleasure, and there are not enough of us to constantly defend against unknown numbers. Too risky," I said, noticing Eri's eyes flash with an unfamiliar light as I spoke. "It will be better to scout this settlement and make our plans accordingly, but we should keep the truth of our situation as secret as possible. No trading or making alliances with strangers in a land that offers us only danger."

"As you say, Ishassara," Sagitta agreed, after a long silence. "Best to know what we're dealing with, I guess." She looked over her shoulder in the direction we had come from. "I suppose they have not seen our fires because of the way the forest angles back to the north in our direction. We've been lucky. Then again, we have not seen smoke from their fires, either."

"Matar Kubileya guides us," Leya said easily. I hoped she was right.

The blackberries were even thicker as we moved east, and the undergrowth more dense. Though we had been careful and relatively quiet on every venture since our feet first touched the land at the edge of the sea, finally seeing our first human had refreshed the need to be inconspicuous and ready with our weapons. I held my bow and an arrow in front of me, ready to nock it if needed. I had spent the last three afternoons stripping bark from thin branches of oak, trimming the ends, and carefully fletching the heel of the arrow with the feathers we had taken from the swans. I had taken apart some poorer quality Achaean arrows and used the bronze arrowheads and sinew from those, and fashioned fifteen more from bone and flint. Twenty-five in all. It would not be enough if we came upon trouble, but it was better than nothing.

Sagitta and Eri held their axes, and Leya her spear. The rest were carrying swords or axes, or very green bows, newly made since being in the grove. We were well prepared to fight, but twelve of us would be easily outnumbered if we stumbled into a settlement full of people.

When we came to the base of the hill that jutted into the pastureland, we stopped, debating the best way to move forward. The man had disappeared around the far side of the embankment, and it was impossible to see beyond the edge without exposing ourselves. Wordlessly, Sagitta pointed up the hill, using her hands to mimic us walking to the top and looking down on whatever was below. I turned to the rest of the women and motioned for them to stay behind and keep watch while Sagitta and I scouted ahead.

The hill was easy to climb, as it was less dense with shrubs and blackberries, but it took some time since we placed every step so carefully, lest even a rock be dislodged. Even if they thought it was only a wild animal traipsing through the woods, if there were people down the other side, the last thing we needed was for them to be readying their spears and arrows before we even arrived. When we neared the top, we sank to our hands and knees, and then our bellies, crawling awkwardly with our weapons in hand and the sharp rocks scraping our skin. As soon as my head breached the top and I could see the ground below, I was glad for our caution.

A village, built into three terraced levels along the hillside, which curved around in a half-bowl shape. The houses, six of which were visible from our viewpoint, were squat, low to the ground, with steps that went down at the entrance as though part of the house were underground. A few rows of roughly hewn timber were visible underneath the eaves of well-thatched roofs. Below, on the level ground, were pens of white and black sheep, a few enormous pigs, and at least fifty head of fat, stubby looking cattle. Scattered here and there among the pens were small wattle-and-daub huts, one of which looked like it could be a smithy with the amount of smoke billowing from the round hole in the open center of its thatched roof. A small wagon sat outside the hut, its yoke empty, filled with what looked like rocks and dirt. Beyond the pens, farther to the east and north where the forest turned back to the west again, perfectly symmetrical fields of golden emmer and einkorn waving in the gentle breeze. Between the grain fields and the pens ran a thin stream of water, perhaps the width of two horses standing nose to tail, running south. A road of sorts ran beside it, dusty and rutted with heavy use during rain.

People milled about the huts and pens. A young boy poked at one of the pigs with a long stick from a safe spot behind the crude wooden fence, and they squealed and moved away from his prodding. He upended a clay pot of something wet that, even from a distance, I could see splattered everywhere when it hit the ground in the midst of the animals. They scrambled to eat it, and the boy turned away, swinging the stick in one hand and the empty pot in another.

On the other side of the pigpen, close to the stream, a woman worked on her knees, using a scraper to peel the flesh away from a skin that was stretched between four stakes in the ground. She pulled her hands down the skin in a steady, sure rhythm, and it was obvious she had done the backbreaking labor many times before. We had been doing it in our own camp with the deer hides, and my back ached just watching her. Nearby, another woman with grey hair, unkempt and knotted looking as though it had never met a comb in all its years, wound a length of what was probably sheep's wool onto a long spindle, her hands moving back and forth with deft precision.

More people appeared from directly beneath us. A younger-looking woman wearing a long robe of dark cloth, her hair covered with a kerchief as she carried a fat-bellied jar in each hand and made her way toward the cattle pen. We heard the faint sound of voices, then. Men's voices, which began as an indistinct murmur and increased steadily until a small group of them became visible, following the same path that the young woman with the jars had taken. Each held a scythe or longer, narrower sickle. I saw the glint of bronze at their hips as well. Knives, although none wore a sword that I could see. That did not mean much. These people were not likely to expect invaders on an average day, as they appeared to be farmers, not fighters. Still, we could not be sure how many of them were here or what their attitudes to strangers might be. And though I felt a twinge of guilt for the plans we made to steal the horses from them, I still felt that Eri and I were wise in concealing our true situation from any group of people, whether they appeared as harmless farmers or not.

Sagitta and I watched for a while longer before slowly inching our way backward until we were well enough below the ridge that we could stand again, and we made our way down the hill with swift, silent steps. When we finally came within sight of the others, they were startled by our stealthy approach, readying their swords and spears before relaxing again at the sight of us.

Eri was about to ask what we had seen when Sagitta motioned for silence and pointed back the way we had come. We made our way west, deeper inside the forest this time, where fewer blackberry thickets caught at our feet and legs and no open spaces could give us away. It was some time before we were back at the place where I had first come upon the horses.

"Well?" Eri demanded as soon as we were on the track leading back to the grove. I waved a hand at Sagitta to relate what we had seen, but she did not start with an explanation.

"Matar Kubileya smiles upon us," Sagitta said grandly and turned to face the women, her smile wide. "Ha-mazaans, soon we will be dressed in new clothes, without these bloodstains and slashes." She plucked at the front of her once white linen chiton, now dingy and grey and stained black-brown with Achaean blood in the places where it peaked out from the leather vest. "And, if Kubileya aids us, we will have all the grain and mutton we could want. Along with horses, of course. We need to gather the others. It's time to plan a raid!" And with a jaunty spin on her heel, she set off toward the grove.

When my eyes met Eri's, she smiled, but the unfamiliar glint was still there in her eye. I smiled back, while inside, my stomach flipped nervously, and I couldn't help but wonder—had I agreed with Eri's advice because it was best for the ha-mazaans and our future safety, or because I wanted to mend our friendship?

CHAPTER 15

RHU-TASIYA

W e discussed the village on the walk back to the grove—how many people there might be, how many amongst them who could fight, the probability of us being able to take what we needed and return to the grove undetected. This last was the sticking point. If we managed to take enough horses for everyone, and hopefully even a wagon, coming back to the grove would not be an option. Not only was there no room nor grazing enough for all those horses, but it was also simply too dangerous to remain so close to the village after raiding it. Unless, of course, we killed all or most of their able-bodied people, but that was not something we relished the thought of. It was not our way to kill without regard for life. If we took the horses or raided for more supplies while we were at it, we would need to move on, and quickly. North, following the road we had seen.

However, there was my mother.

Back in the grove, the branches of the trees interlaced like fingers overhead, barely letting in any of the afternoon sun. The first thing I noticed was the way Melanippe tossed and turned on her furs, her brow unnaturally ashen and dry, and when I went to her and felt it, burning to the touch. Tekmessa knelt beside her, but Camilla, distressed and weary, moved away when I approached, unwilling to meet my eyes.

My mother found my face with glazed eyes when I touched her, and she breathed my name through clenched teeth. "Cy...ra," she managed.

"Don't talk, mother, just drink." I held a cup of water to her lips, but she turned her head to the side.

"Zanas."

I felt the increasingly familiar sensation of a hand gripping my throat from the inside, squeezing until I thought I might choke, while the knot in my stomach spread outwards until every muscle felt stiff. I tried not to let the fear show on my face, though she probably felt the tension in my arms as I eased her head up for a drink from the mead-soaked cloth.

"I am sure she is well, mother," I answered thinly, pretending to not understand. "Someone is likely feeding her apples and grain as we speak. Later, when the air is cool, they will run her with the others in the field, and she will stretch her legs and gallop like she loves to do and eat fresh grass for a while."

I tried to keep my tone light, but I know I failed. She shook her head and said, so softly I could barely hear, "*Rhu-tasiya.*"

She slipped into unconsciousness once more. Above us, a hawk's scream pierced the air with such ferocity that the hair on my arms stood to attention.

My throat choked tighter until I could not get any breath in or out of my heavy chest. My eyes met Tekmessa's as she returned her gaze from the hawk high above the treetops. The *zizenti* did not look away, nor did she offer any words of consolation.

"Her time is close, Ishassara. For this life, there is no more I can do." Her eyes were full of sorrow. My own brimmed with hot tears. "For the next life, I will perform the rites that will guide her soul. It is all we can do."

"And Zanas? We are so far away. Will she be there, at the Gate?"

Tekmessa considered me, tipping her head from one side to another. "I cannot say for sure," she finally said. "The spirits are bound together when the rite is completed with the tattoo. Even over such a great distance, once the ha-mazaan has died, the spirit of their horse will eventually be pulled into the Otherworld with them. But I cannot say when." She shook her head. "I spoke the incantations for Ifito and Pisto, and Palla and Hipponike, but their spirits had long left them. I could not see the Gate." She hesitated, looking up at the hawk once more. It circled lazily now. I wondered if it was a messenger from Kubileya.

"There are many instances in which our people have traveled through the gates of the Otherworld without their *rhu-tasiya*, sometimes never having found one in life. As I have not found one, so far." Tekmessa frowned thoughtfully, her fingers absentmindedly smoothing the golden lion pelt over my mother's lap.

"What about another horse, even if it's not her *rhu-tasiya*? Another will be able to meet her, perhaps? Protect her for a time?" I asked.

But it would not be what my mother deserved. She should have her *rhu-tasiya* to guide her in the next life. To be buried under the dirt without the protector and carrier of one's soul meant my mother could wander aimlessly, searching fruitlessly for the Womb of Matar Kubileya. Fighting Shadows alone. Only when she reached the Womb across vast distances and times would she once again be reborn.

"Again, I do not know for sure, Ishassara. A *rhu-tasiya* in life is perhaps more important than in death. Here, they absorb the blows from the Shadow world, which is oft hidden from us. Their spirit protects us from harm even when we do not see it. This was the gift of Matar Kubileya when she set our steps on this sacred path. For all they do for us in life, we owe the companions of our souls much honor. But in death," the priestess shook her head and looked up from her hands, meeting my eyes again. "In death, I have seen the *rhu-tasiya* come to the Gate as the incantations are spoken, and the Shadow spirits who sometimes lurk there cannot come close because of their presence. Beyond that, I am not permitted to see. Only the dead can go beyond that threshold. It is simply what our mothers and mother's mothers have always believed, that the *rhu-tasiya* carry our souls to the Great Mother's womb, protecting us from the Shadows along the way." An actual shadow flickered across her face, and both of us looked up through the branches overhead to the circling hawk.

"And what are the Shadow spirits?" I asked. These were all things I had heard before, but I had never paid them much attention. But the stories mattered now, as they had not before.

"Those who fell away from the Great Mother long ago and chose to oppress all who are made in Her image," Tekmessa replied. "It is said that those who have met great opposition in life shall meet the same in the Otherworld, for those which seek to malign our purpose here will do the same there, especially for the daughters of Matar Kubileya."

"Can they do that? Hinder my mother's path to the Womb?"

Tekmessa shrugged again, splaying her hands in a gesture of apology. "I can only know what has been taught, Ishassara. And what we believe is but a piece of that which is True, for none alive know all. But yes, it is thought that the Shadows do all they can to hinder the soul from reaching the Womb of the Mother. The birth of a fierce spirit in this world is a threat to the Shadow in all worlds. That is why the horse protects our spirit here, as well as there. It is why we gift the departed with the finest of weapons and the most precious of our companions, so that they may find their way back to this world and continue their work on behalf of Matar Kubileya. It is why we say the prayers that we do to help the *rhu-tasiya*, to aid their battles and lend them strength for the journey, in this life and the next."

"So how long can my mother wait for her *rhu-tasiya* once she has passed through the Gate?" I pictured my mother's spirit, surely one of the greatest in our world, set upon by a host of evil Shadows, without Zanas to aid her. The knot in my stomach tightened.

"I do not know, Cyra," Tekmessa said, her voice thick with sorrow. "Time in the Otherworld is not the same as time here. She will need to protect herself as best she can until her *rhu-tasiya's* spirit is pulled to her. Or," the *zizenti* offered, spreading her hands and her voice taking on a tinge of wry amusement, "it is possible that, because she is Melanippe, she can ride even a strange and wild horse in the Otherworld and make its spirit do her bidding, until Zanas joins her. This would not surprise me."

I stared down at my mother's face and smoothed a hand over her feverish brow. I laid her shoulders down gently, resting her head on the rolled linen, and stood.

"If there is a chance, it is what we will do," I vowed. "My mother will not travel alone through the Otherworld."

)(

The excitement of the morning's discovery of the village was all but forgotten as the entire grove became shrouded in the quiet introspection of busyness that comes before both birth and death. In this case, taking the horses and what we needed from the villagers would be a rebirth of our strength, for without horses, we remained vulnerable. But all within the grove sensed the Gate of the Otherworld opening to welcome Melanippe in death. For this reason, talk became hushed and reserved, as though speaking too loudly would open the Gate wider or entice the Shadow closer.

Alkippe approached me as I washed the morning's dust from my face and arms at the edge of the creek.

"Sagitta has told me of the village," she said quietly, her hand gripping the handle of the axe in her belt. She once again wore the short-handled weapon at her side, like a sword, after making new covers for the blade from the deer antlers. "Is it your wish to raid them, as well as take the horses?"

I looked up at her, cool water dripping from my chin, and felt the responsibility of Ishassara push heavily on my shoulders, pressing me down into the soft sand at the edge of the stream. I stood, pushing back against the weight of it.

"Yes. I do not know how many days she has left," I said, gesturing toward my mother. "But I don't know whether it is better to…wait…or take her with us and hope we can secure a wagon."

Alkippe kept her grim gaze focused on my face, her dark eyes unreadable.

"I think it would be best if we did not wait more than one night," she said finally. "Sagitta and I can go there tonight and scout their activity. Get a better idea of who is there and what we can expect. How many weapons they have."

I nodded, and she looked toward my mother.

"She deserves all the honor of a queen," Alkippe said. Her voice was a peculiar mix of sadness and determination. My throat clenched again, and I simply nodded, but her dark eyes turned back to me again. "It may be best to take our chances by tomorrow night, Ishassara. If we can secure a wagon and travel north, it is more likely we will find a place for her to…rest. For us to honor her." Her eyes were intent on mine to make sure that I understood. "We cannot risk that here. We have been lucky that they have not seen our fires already. To shout and sing and dance as we must to properly honor her would be to call them straight to us."

Again I nodded, not trusting myself to speak, and we stood that way for some time. Alkippe still clutched the wooden shaft of her axe at her hip, but my hands hung uselessly at my sides, the weight of grief and my responsibility curving my shoulders toward the ground. I felt older by twenty years, just within the span of a week. These were the kinds of decisions I had never fathomed, for all my hopes of escaping the curse and being Defending Queen. Eventually, I said, "We will carry her with us as we brought her here, and hope for the best. Tomorrow night."

Alkippe nodded. She reached out a hand and laid it gently on my shoulder. Somehow, it eased the weight I felt there.

"She will be remembered as the best of us," the ha-mazaan promised. "We will make sure of it." She turned and made her way back to a group of the others to share the news and to instruct on preparations.

Every ha-mazaan went about their chosen tasks as though we were simply preparing a hunt in our own mountains of Themiscyra. All knew their part. Prothoe and Aello skinned and dressed the deer they had tracked deep in the forest, the sharp-tanged smell of the blood thick in the grove. Asteria, Phillipisa, and several more wove thin willow wands into crescent-shaped shields, which we would line with the hide of the deer, and use to protect ourselves from arrows and blades. Others sharpened their axes and spears or made new arrows from elm, ash, and willow, and more arrowheads from the bones of the deer or from flint. Others continued their work on new bows, carved from thin branches of fallen trees already seasoned by time. They would not be the bows we preferred, made of layers of curved sinew and horn and wood that would send an arrow farther than the eye could see or through the metal armor of the enemy with ease. Bows like mine took years to make due to the curing process between each layer. Still, these simple bows would work well enough for our purpose.

I chose the task of making sinew from the deer's tendons, as it was meditative and kept my hands busy. Already some freshly made ropes were drying on the sun-drenched rocks from the first deer we had taken some days ago. We would use the sinew for bowstrings and anything that required wrapping, such as new arrowheads and fletching. It was gruesome work, but every Xanharaspa learned how to process the pieces of bear or griffin, deer or elk, and even our beloved cavalry horses upon their deaths, into materials for weapons, armor, and survival.

By nightfall, most of what we could do had been done, and all that was left was waiting. Waiting for tendons to dry, for venison to cook, for the moon to rise, for my mother to die. It was excruciating, and I grew almost angry with the pressure inside of me that came from waiting and not being able to do anything meaningful about what I was waiting for. The Gate was opening, and I could feel the coldness of it on my heart. I was helpless, and nothing I could do or say or prepare would change what was happening. I made my way over to Alkippe and Sagitta, who were preparing to leave the grove and scout the village.

"I am coming with you," I announced, but Alkippe was already shaking her head and making dismissive motions with her hands.

"No. You must stay with the general."

"There is nothing I can do for her here." I sounded a little frantic even to my own ears. I made my tone more forceful. "I am coming with you."

"No, Ishassara," Sagitta said, but tenderly. "If your mother's spirit leaves her body and you are not here to bless her journey, it is something you will regret for the rest of your life. I know this." She stared earnestly into my eyes, and I thought of how her own sister had died many years ago, killed by a boar in the mountains while Sagitta had been safe in the palace bathhouse. Still, I shook my head and was about to argue further when Alkippe said,

"There is something you can do for her, Ishassara."

I stared at her dumbly.

"Where I am from, we tell the greatest stories of those who have lived them so that they may be fresh in their memory before they begin their next journey. This way, they remember who they are. They remember why they are loved and respected. They know how they will be remembered." Her dark eyes were luminous as she looked at me.

"She sleeps," I said thinly, looking over my shoulder. "She will not hear anything I or anyone else says."

"She hears everything, Cyra." Alkippe placed a long-fingered hand on the center of her chest. "She hears it here."

I shifted from one leg to another, staring at them. I wanted to take my mind off of my mother, not delve further into the grief of what I would lose. But something in me told me they were right, no matter how much I wanted to deny it. If my mother died while I was far away, I would regret not being at her side, and everything in me knew her time to pass through that Gate drew near. They saw the acceptance of it on my face, and this time, Sagitta stepped forward and placed a strong, gentle hand on my shoulder.

"You are a good daughter, Cyra. And you will be a good queen. She will be blessed to hear her stories told and know that her legacy lives on in you. Remind her of why she is loved and of why she should be proud. Of why she will be remembered as one of our greatest."

With that, they shouldered their weapons and waterskins and made their way out of the grove into the soft light of the waning moon.

CHAPTER 16

GRIFFINS AND MEN

O ssy sharpened her axe in the firelight, her tawny head bowed over the blade in concentration. She looked up at me as I approached, a kind smile warming her tired features. I sat cross-legged next to her, across from my mother, watching hands strong and calloused from many years of hard use glide the sharpening stone down the curved edge of the axe blade. The sound rang out crisp and tinkling in the night. It reminded me of home.

"Ossy," I said, my eyes mesmerized by the movement of her hands. She made a noise of questioning acknowledgment. "Would you tell the story of my mother and the griffin?" I asked, finally looking away from the shining metal to where my mother lay on the other side of Ossy. She lay so still it was easy to imagine she simply slept peacefully next to the heat of the fire, but I knew peace was far from this place. The six or seven others who sat around the fire fell silent, looking on expectantly.

Ossy gave me a considering look, turning the axe over in her hands to begin working the other side of the blade. The engravings etched along the surface caught the light of the fire, and for a moment. I thought they moved on their own accord, the swirls twisting in and out on themselves, the leaves of the vines rustling in a breeze, and the horse opening its nostrils to suck at the wind. *Just a trick of the firelight,* I thought.

"Alkippe and Sagitta suggested that my mother should hear her stories," I said, feeling the need to explain.

"I think I need a cup of mead if I'm to tell that one properly."

"I will fetch you some," Leya said quickly. She disappeared from the ring of light toward the food stores lifted high in the trees, in case we attracted bears with our butchered kills. Two women holding hands approached the fire, Phillipisa and Ariadnai, followed by Eri, and then another ha-mazaan came forward, and soon, most or perhaps all were there, although I could not be sure as the light did not extend far enough to reach all of their faces. As soon as Leya had offered the leather cup of mead to Ossy, a hush of expectation fell over the camp.

"It started with a Spirit Dream," Ossy began, her voice round and clear with the stentorian tones of a practiced teller of tales. I was glad Ossy had agreed, since she spent many a night in the Moon Hall telling stories passed from her nan and *matar*. This was what my mother needed right now. What we all needed.

"When Melanippe, Black Horse and Nightmare of the Foe, was sixteen summers, and two years a bleeding woman, she slept under the sycamore tree that sits high on the hill of Themiscyra. It was to be the same sycamore she would whelp her daughter under, alone in the light of the full moon, bringing censure on her head from the *zizentis*."

I smiled, having heard it all a hundred times before.

"Whenever she slept under that sycamore, she had the most fantastic dreams. Sometimes she dreamed of a black horse to match her name. It was a mare which came to her in the moonlight and showed her the way to a great cavern, filled with pieces of the stars that had fallen to earth as a gift from the Great Mother. Kubileya had shown us long ago how to use these starstones to add strength to our weapons and sharpness to our blades, and they were as highly prized to the ha-mazaans as the mares from Paphlagonia. Melanippe searched for this cavern for many moons after that first dream, but she did not yet have the black mare to guide her and could not find the secret to where the cave was hidden.

"In yet another dream beside the roots of the sycamore, Melanippe saw again the black mare, but in this dream, there was also the great enemy of our people, and of our *rhu-tasiyas*."

She paused here, her arm sliding with perfect precision to ring the stone along the edge of that star-iron blade. The sound pealed out with a sharper tone than before, emphasizing the words of her story, and I felt the hairs on the back of my neck stand to attention.

"Melanippe dreamed of that monstrous and terrible fabrication, made by Shadow and men—men who sought to gain power and dominion over all of creation and over the Great Mother Herself. These men cast aside the governance of Kubileya and the Ways She had set in place for all the beasts of the field and of the sea and of the air. They schemed against the Order of the World and that which is right for all wild creatures, who are our sisters and brothers. Unsatisfied with their place in Her holy order, they sought to make themselves prominent over Her children. Dominant and undefeatable.

"In their quest for dominion, they corrupted the ways of the children and brought together all kinds of animals, or women and animals, or men and animals. From these unions, they brought forth monsters with the heads of humans and the body of beasts, or the body of humans and the heads of beasts, though most of these creatures have long gone from this world. Even so, they worshipped their own creations as gods, and they worshipped themselves as gods, because of the terrible power they had discovered in their dominion.

"Eventually, they brought together the Queen of the Land and the King of the Air. A lion and an eagle they forged together, and through help from the evil forces of Shadow, they produced an offspring that was neither of those, yet both. They brought into being a Griffin." Another peal from the axe and stone in Ossy's hands. She drank from her cup of mead before continuing with the ancient tale.

"The beast had the body and hindquarters of a lioness, who was Queen of the Land, and the forequarters and head of an eagle, who was King of the Air. The beast was as great in size as three stallions, and the span of its wings could block out the sun on a summer's day. Terrible it was, and mighty. Its beak was curved and glistening black, like dragonstone, and it sharpened the edge of that beak on starstones high in the mountains where it lived. The greed of the men and the evil of the Shadow caused them to breed the monster so that it hoarded pieces of the stars and gold as well. In this way, the men might grow rich and more powerful with little work from their own hands.

"They bred it also to feed on the flesh of a horse. But because it was an unnatural monster born of Shadow, it ate not just a horse's flesh, but its spirit, too. Its talons could lift a full-grown mare from the ground and tear her to pieces, to be devoured wholly and completely, never to be Reborn through the Womb of the Mother. Never to assist to ha-mazaans on their journey in the Otherworld. Now, all the days of their lives, our *rhu-tasiyas* would have a foe that could destroy not only their bodies, but their spirits. In this way, the men sought to destroy all women, all ha-mazaans, for without the *rhu-tasiya* to protect us in life, and later in death, they knew our chances of survival here and in the

Otherworld grew fragile. They created the griffin to destroy us when they realized how powerful we were.

"But just as some men had forgotten who they were, which caused them to do evil things, so they had forgotten who *women* were. Created in Her image, and powerful beyond measure. Beloved Daughters of the First One. Matar Kubileya saw what the men had done and grew angry, for the King of the Air and the Queen of the Land had been beloved to her also, and now the corruption of their flesh had created a monster. To aid our fight against such a monster, and indeed against the machinations of Shadow and the men who had fallen into its shade, She gifted women with the Old Magic. And with this Old Magic came the gift of Second Sight."

Ossy took another long swallow of mead and set her axe aside. Around the fire, women's faces shone with rapt attention.

"It is with this Sight that all women may look, and when they look, they may See, so that they can choose a path that is right for their spirit. Sometimes this Sight comes to women as a whisper of the Great Mother. Sometimes the Sight is a knowing, deep in the womb. Sometimes it is borne in the blood of their own bodies or those of a sacrifice. And sometimes, it comes as a Spirit Dream.

"This is the kind of dream Melanippe dreamed under the old sycamore, high on the hill behind the palace, when she was only sixteen summers. She dreamed that she rode the black mare over a mountain pass, deep in the forests of our home country. There was another by her side, a ha-mazaan with hair the color of field mice and eyes the color of stones under the Terme." Ossy looked from one woman's face to another, until her eyes, the color of stones in the Terme, met mine. "She dreamed how they rode, and passed through forests of pine and ancient oak, and stopped for water next to the spring that is said to give wisdom and strength to all who taste it. She dreamed how they came closer to the canyon, and when they had found the narrow entrance to its hiding place, how they heard the shrill scream of a monster echo from rock to rock and inside of their very skulls. She heard the scream of a griffin, and she awoke.

"Several years on, Melanippe completed her Trials and became a Savaran, at the age of only nineteen. She practiced daily with her axe and spear, and her bow and arrows, which she fletched with the feathers of the deadly strixes, whose females were the same color as her hair, and whose males matched her silver eyes. In this way, she made sure that all would know who felled either boar or man, deer or leopard. Melanippe became skilled with every weapon and was admired and feared by all. Yet, her *rhu-tasiya* had not found her."

Ossy took another long drink. I was becoming anxious with impatience, even though I had heard this story many times before. I glanced over at my mother and thought I saw her lips move in a smile, but her eyes were still closed.

"Three fillies she raised from the womb to the stable, but though each grew to be fine mares, none chose her. And then one day, a man came." Ossy smiled, and this time I was positive my mother's lips moved as well.

"A man from the south, from the City of the Ilusians. All the way from Wilusa he came, over the mountains in the spring when the moon was full and bright, leading a caravan of wagons and camels, horses and people. The man, who was a Prince in his own land, a grandson of their people's Oracle. He came seeking guest-rite from the ha-mazaans, from Queen Otrera and her fair daughters, whom he had heard were the most intelligent and powerful women in the land. And he came with a request for their help, for he had also heard that to have the ha-mazaans as allies was to assure victory in war, and he assured them they shared the same values and the same goal. Though at first she had no interest in the affairs of men, when Melanippe caught sight of the man's horse, a young black mare barely three years old, she knew he must be offered the guest-rite.

"Now the man saw Melanippe, and saw that her eyes shone with the light of the moon even on the brightest day, and her hair was black as the underside of a raven. Her skin was like chicory mixed with mare's milk. He loved her at first as men love women—with their eyes. But after he spent time with her, seeing her prowess with an axe and the way her feet danced light as a cloud over the ground, the way she walked straight and proud among the people she cared for, he loved her in the way some people can. With their hearts and their souls. He asked for her hand in marriage, but she refused. She believed, as her mother and grandmother did, that marriage to a man would only cause a woman's heart to be split in two when it came time to fight, and this was a dangerous thing for a ha-mazaan.

Instead, she offered to give him the alliance he sought, and led an army of ha-mazaans to his home near Mount Ida, the Right Breast of the Great Mother. There, she and her ha-mazaans gave aid to his mother and father, who is still King of Wilusa because of the intervention from the ha-mazaans. She gave the man her axe and her loyalty, for though she would not give him herself in marriage, she did love him. In exchange for her aid in the battles of his homeland, he granted her the mare, for the horse was her *rhu-tasiya*, and had brought him all this way so that they could finally be together. Still, he wanted to make her his wife and asked her to stay with him in Wilusa, but she refused.

"Saddened by her rejection, the man nevertheless loved her as he could, and they shared many nights together under the light of the stars and under the fire of the sun. In this way, her *rhu-tasiya* had found her and also brought to her the love of her heart.

"When Melanippe returned to Themiscyra, the Prince of Wilusa, which he called Ilia, did not return with her. However, she and her ha-mazaans did not return alone, for the mighty Black Horse was with child, despite the laws of her people which forbid swelling with a man's seed before a woman's twenty-fifth summer, or five years of service as Savaran or Crafter had been completed, while Melanippe had only completed three."

Ossy's eyes slid to me and away again. I nodded for her to continue, though I was familiar with this story. There were many who still frowned upon my mother's decision to become a *matar* so early, I knew, but she had proven herself tenfold in service to the queens, as General of the Savaran and as the best warrior Themiscyra had ever known.

"Melanippe spoke secretly with a *zizenti*, who told her what herbs she could drink to be rid of the swelling. Melanippe thought many thoughts and prayed to the Great Mother. The night of her return from Wilusa, she journeyed high into the orchard to sleep under the Old Sycamore.

"While she slept, she dreamed again. And when she awoke, she set about bringing the dream to life, for she knew in her heart it was the only way forward. She took the black mare and her mouse-colored friend and rode into the mountains. She told her friend not to help her in any way, no matter how dangerous it became, or her prophecy from the Oracle could not be fulfilled. She had seen the truth of this in her dream under the old sycamore and in her visions of the cauldron's fire.

"It was there in the mountains they came upon the griffin, mighty and fierce as ten lions. Her friend feared she had sworn Melanippe to certain death by accepting to keep her axe and bow sheathed, but she watched as the two of them fought and refrained from helping no matter how ominous it appeared for Melanippe. The black mare screamed and used her teeth and her hooves, and Melanippe used her bow and her axe. The horse and rider were like one being, and it was a miracle to behold.

"Melanippe fought the griffin until the sweat ran in rivers and the scratches ran deep on her shoulder and arms, but finally, she killed it, and the screech of its dying was a sound none could ever forget. And so part of the dream had been fulfilled."

Ossy took another long drink.

"The two women entered the cavern. There, in the darkness of the great cave, they collected rocks that were pieces of the stars and chunks of gold the size of their fists. Together, Melanippe and her friend carried them back to the palace, dragging behind their horses the body of the griffin, which clearly showed strix-fletched arrows in its heart.

"There was a great celebration to honor Melanippe. It was the biggest bounty ever seen within the walls of the city, and not even Queen Otrera could believe her eyes. They listened with awe and fear to the story the mouse-colored friend recounted. Only after she had been praised for her courage and her cleverness did Melanippe make her confession to the queen."

Ossy paused then and looked at me, then glanced at my mother. I thought I saw uncertainty and something like guilt flash across her face. She was silent for so long I thought she might not finish the story. When she went on, finally, her rhythm had slowed, and I could tell she was carefully considering what words to say next.

"The Nightmare faced the queens in the Moon Hall. 'I carry a child by the man from Ilia,' Melanippe declared. Her hand went to her flat stomach as she tilted her head proudly before them.

"Her mother and sisters stared. Ha-mazaans who were there, Ifito and Hipponike, Thraso and Vesta, Aello and Glaukia, and her mouse-colored friend, all stared. All who had gathered in the Moon Hall listened with shock. She kept her head high and proud.

"'This child was shown to me by the Oracle of Matar Kubileya. She will be a Daughter that Rides a New Dawn and carry the strength and wisdom of our people into new lands. For this reason, though I am not of age or within the Laws of Themis, I will not drink the potion of the *zizenti*. This is my decision.'

"There was shock and dismay among all who were gathered, but Melanippe knew this would be so. Her sisters were upset, but her mother was furious, for to disregard the Way of the Ha-mazaans was unwise, unsafe, and untenable. And," Ossy's eyes slid to me again and back to my mother. "And Melanippe was first-born daughter, Heir to the Defender's Throne."

I gasped aloud this time, and my head spun. My mother was Otrera's third daughter. Antiope was the oldest, and Hippolyta the second. The rulership had gone to the two eldest, as was custom. I didn't understand what Ossy was saying.

"Otrera was firm when she spoke to her eldest. 'If this is your decision, daughter, you will never be Ishassara, or Queen of the Defender's Throne beside Antiope as Hearth Queen. Hippolyta will proceed to *Alsanti* in your place, uncontested. Decide carefully, for to have this child, you forfeit your right to the Defender's Throne forever.'

"Melanippe and Otrera stared at each other, and Melanippe saw both sorrow and understanding beneath the anger in her mother's words. The choice would be hers, but the law would not be changed. She nodded and said simply, 'I accept the consequences. I will bear the child.'

"'I ask you truly,'" Otrera said again, shaking her head in warning, "is it because of this man from the land of the Ilusians that you decide to bear the child?'

"Melanippe thought about the man that her heart loved. She smiled. Then she shook her head.

"'I choose freely.'

"And so it was decided.

"In this way, Hippolyta's path became that of Ishassara, and eventually Defending Queen. But because of her love for her older sister, and for Melanippe's great courage and skill, Hippolyta made her general of the ha-mazaan army. All who would have cast their stone for Melanippe in the *Alsanti* asked that the child she bore, if it were a daughter, be allowed to follow the path of Ishassara. And all ha-mazaans were sworn to uphold the new order and to never speak of what had once been. And so it was done."

When Ossy finished speaking, she turned her head toward my

mother and said, so softly I almost couldn't hear the words, "It was time, *Akka*. She must know."

My breathing had grown shallow, and my body flashed between hot and clammy and shivering cold. This was not the story I knew. If this were true, my mother had not only broken the Laws of Themis to whelp me but also given up her birthright. Her place as queen. I was too dazed to speak.

Ossy looked at me and smiled wanly. "There were many who would have followed her as queen and pledged their loyalty. This, Cyra, is why you are with us as Ishassara. As One who will Ride a New Dawn."

"And these are the new lands."

A voice like dry parchment that I could barely hear. My mother's voice.

Startled, everyone looked to where she lay. Her eyes were still closed, but there was a furrow of concentration between her brows. I crawled to her, sitting carefully next to her head and smoothing my hand along her brow.

"Mother?" My voice sounded like a young child. The confusion I felt was immense. Overpowering. "I don't understand. Is this true?"

But because I felt deep down that it was, I said, "You *kept* this from me." I did not mean to sound so harsh. Why had she not told me these things? What else had she lied about? Hidden? As though she heard my thoughts, her eyes opened, silver and bright under the waning moon.

"There is more you must know, daughter." Her voice sounded far away and hollow like a broken reed. It caught at the ragged edges of my heart, tearing me apart. Everyone was still watching, wordless, and when I looked up, I saw Thraso's face, and Aello, and Glaukia, who scowled into the night. All of them who had been there. Had they really kept this truth from me my entire life?

"The Oracle..." my mother's voice ended in a harsh rasp, and I looked around urgently for her cup of water. Ossy wordlessly handed me what was left of her mead, and I took it, holding my mother up and pouring some through her lips. She swallowed, then closed her lips so I could not pour more. "The Oracle told me...things I have told no one, not even you, daughter," Melanippe said, still looking up at me.

"What do you mean?" I asked warily, thinking of my own prophecy with some guilt and more than a little trepidation.

"In the fires of the cauldron..." Her voice regained some strength as she went on, the memory stirring something within her. "In the flames, I saw a black ship, darker than the blackened sea. I saw a great white bank of clay rising from the water. I saw myself, standing next to a grey mare. Only when the vision of me turned to stare out of the flames did I realize it was not me. It was you," she said, eyes identical to my own staring up at me. Even through the haze of fever and pain, her stare was intent on my face. "It was you, daughter," she breathed, and again the gooseflesh rose on my arms and over my entire body.

"I saw you ride across this very land, and eventually you came to a hill, with a tree that was carved with the Tree of Life. There was a horse, a deer, an eagle, and the sun and moon. You said to me through the flames, 'Safe journey to the Womb of the Mother, Mother of my Heart.' And then you rode again and left me. To find your destiny." Melanippe coughed, and her face grimaced in pain. I tried to shush her, to give her more mead, but it was no use. She brought a weak hand to my wrist, and her fingers circled it, following the tattooed line of the maternal mother all the way around.

"You rode to your destiny, Cyra. And the ha-mazaans rode with you. Your destiny is tied to this land," she said, her voice becoming more urgent. "I have never asked your message from the Oracle be spoken aloud, but please, tell me now if I am wrong."

I looked down at her, thoughts swirling, throat tightening. Then I looked up at the other faces of the ha-mazaans. They looked curious and expectant. Wary. I did not know what to say.

"I will go within the bosom of the Great Mother in this place, daughter," Melanippe said softly so that I had to lean close to hear her. "I would know that, like me, you will follow your heart, no matter the cost. Even if it goes against the Laws. What I chose long ago was for you, and the future of our people. I have never regretted it."

Tears welled in my eyes, and I felt my face screw into a grimace I could not hide. I wept, then, and could not seem to untwist my mouth to speak. Finally, through my tears, I managed to say,

"It never made sense! The Oracle...she told me I would be Defending Queen, but..." I hesitated to say it, even now. "But never beside Penthesilea. And never in Themiscyra." I heard a gasp from one of the women, or maybe several. I shook my head, remembering my time in the cave, the towering Oracle next to the strange burning cauldron. The lioness' eyes glowed in my memories.

"She told me that you and my aunts would never see me rule. That the sister queens would die with Hippolyta. I didn't understand. I still don't!" I cried, looking up at the rest of them, almost pleading. "I still don't understand. I didn't think it would be…this," I managed, my voice thick. "But—" I bit my lip, not managing to keep the guilty fear from my face. I did not want my mother to know the part which brought me shame. I did not want her to die thinking poorly of me.

"But?" Ossy said softly from behind, and I looked back at her with a tear-streaked face. I looked back down at my mother, who waited, eyes focused on me. I swallowed what felt like a dagger and went on.

"She said…I would only be queen once a man sat at my side, who would be king in his own right." As soon as I said the words aloud, I regretted it. This was treason. All the ha-mazaans would turn their backs on me, I knew it. I heard their murmuring and could not look at them. I could not look my mother in the eye for fear of what I might see there. I stared away from them, out into the night, the darkness blurry with my tears. "She said I would have many children and grandchildren who would protect the ways of the Great Mother, which was being threatened after I bound myself to this man."

"Ah," my mother said, and she sounded only curious and thoughtful.

I gulped and swiped at the tears on my face. I chanced a look at her, and she simply stared at me with calm, quiet love. I looked up at the rest of them, fearing what I would see. Eri glared at me with unconcealed anger, perhaps because I had kept such a secret from her for so long, and Glaukia's face was as white as her scar. They both turned away when my eyes implored them to understand, and Glaukia left the circle of firelight. The other ha-mazaans shifted and frowned when my eyes met theirs. I could hardly blame them. But even as I revealed a part of my terrible truth, I felt lighter, more free.

I told them everything, then, every word from the Oracle burned into my heart that day. From the promise to be queen to the threat of losing my family in order to become one. From the king I would bind myself to, to the crumbling of the old ways of the sisterhood, and Matar Kubileya's priestesses going into hiding, never to have a fixed altar. I told them all of it, and when I had finished, my tears had stopped flowing, and a chill had taken over me, as though all the heat was leaching from my bones. My mother was smiling. She had closed her eyes to listen, but she opened them again and looked at me.

"It is only by following your own heart that your true destiny will ever find you, daughter," she murmured. "You must listen for my love on the wind and in the rustling of the leaves while you follow after it."

And then she closed her eyes, and even as my hand held hers, tight against the horse tattooed on her chest, her breath stilled, and the light of the moon went out of her eyes, back into the waning crescent hanging above us in the sky.

CHAPTER 17

THE TREE OF LIFE

I crouched under the branches of an enormous oak, the leaves rustling and pattering as heavy drops of rain fell from the night sky. I waited for the rest of the group with eight or ten others, all of us breathing heavily from exertion, though the hard part was yet to come. We had carried all that we could take with us, including my mother's body. Her stiff form lay wrapped in the lion's skin on the stretcher. I felt a part of my heart wrapped up with her, tight and suffocated, but the rest of me was numb with grief.

We were near the base of the mountain, the villagers hopefully asleep on the far side. More women crept up behind us, their arms laden with furs and skins of mead and clay jars of food. When everyone had caught up, I nodded to Alkippe and Sagitta, who signed for their assigned women to follow close behind. I motioned the same to the ones who would help me take the horses, and slowly, carefully, under the cover of night and hidden by the sound of autumn rain, we crept closer to the base of the mountain's outcropping, and to the village. Alkippe stopped and laid down her burden of food and wares in the place she and Sagitta had prepared the night before. Everyone else did the same, and Ossy, Prothoe, and Aello helped me lower my mother's body to the ground, carefully sheltering her under a small beech tree. Hopefully, once we secured a wagon, we could come back for all of this and load it for travel. If not, my mother would suffer more indignity, but I tried not to think on it. We would succeed. For her.

Sagitta had confirmed from the previous night's scouting that the village seemed partially deserted and that it was modest to begin with. She had counted only two wagons, one of which was still half-filled with copper ore and one which sat nearly empty near the edge of the grain fields. They had watched the white mare, the one the grandfather had led away, being released from the traces, so we knew which horse we needed to pull the wagon. Alkippe had counted seventy-nine people when the early dawn sun had risen, and the village began to stir. Seventy-nine people against fifty-four. The odds would be well in our favor, even with the skewed number. We had the elements of darkness, rain, and surprise, and several generations of battle training. Soon, we would have the horses as well.

Alkippe confirmed a small grove of trees, spread in an almost perfect ring on the far side of the hill, was the place the horses appeared to shelter often. It was our hope they would be there now, hidden under the branches from the driving rain, and that is where I led the twenty women who would each take at least two horses, three if they could manage. Once we had done that, by friend or by force, Ossy would help Tekmessa hitch the white mare to the empty wagon. We would return to the stores and my mother's body to load them while the rest of the women raided what they could from the village.

Alkippe remained optimistic the ha-mazaans could keep the village's fighters occupied for long enough that my group could be safely away upriver with the horses and wagon, too far gone for any to follow on foot, while the rest of the women infiltrated the camp and stole what supplies they could. It would still be dangerous, especially at night, but it was our best plan.

When we breached the edge of the mountain, the looming shapes of the trees against the dark sky marked the copse where the horses should be. I could see almost nothing in the darkness and rain. The inky blackness was good for our cover, but I was pessimistic how ha-mazaans might find their way in or out of the village again without a torch to light their way.

A horse knickered, startlingly loud through the rain.

I motioned for the others to stay back, then crept toward the sound of it, praying the horse would not whinny again and rouse the villagers' suspicions. Ossy grabbed at my arm, slick with rain, and I stopped. A shadow moved toward us. I nocked an arrow to the bowstring, ready to draw, and the sharp, night-darkened blade of Ossy's axe was next to me. Another soft whicker. Inara stepped forward out of the night, eyes shining like polished onyx and mane dripping.

Heart in my throat from the heightened tension, I laid my bow in the wet grass and made a soft shushing noise, stepping forward to meet her and raising my hand to her nose in greeting. I grasped her dripping mane and held the sodden leather bridle up to her nose, which she sniffed curiously. Carefully, rubbing my hands soothingly on her neck the entire time, I looped a length of leather over her neck and drew it down the other side. Holding it in one hand like a lasso in case she resisted and tried to run, I slowly slid the bridle up over the mare's nose. She started, holding her head high, and I had to stand on my toes to reach. I stopped moving the bridle upward and pet her neck with my right hand, making soft murmuring noises of reassurance. She brought her head down when I pressed my fingers into her poll, nuzzling the scales of my vest for more treats. I moved my hand back to her muzzle and pressed the bit against her lips. Then I stuck my thumb in the side of her mouth. Her lips opened in surprise, and before she knew what was happening, I had slipped the bone bit between the gap in her teeth and the top of the bridle over her ears.

Inara squealed with fury and reared into the air, her black hooves flashing past my face. I jumped backward, but I did not let go of the leather loop around her neck. She settled again with a toss of her head, her angry mouth chewing at the bit, trying to get it between her teeth.

"Sorry, girl," I apologized softly, wishing it did not have to be this way. "It's just for a while, but right now, I need your help in getting all of us out of here."

The mare blew air through her nostrils, loud enough to wake the dead, pulling backward a bit at the tension against her head. I kept it tight until she relaxed, praying she would quiet, and then I quickly tied the looped rein and the bridle together with a knot under her chin.

"Are you sure about this?" Ossy's dubious voice came from the darkness.

"We have no choice. Give me your hands. I don't want to startle her more by jumping."

Ossy stepped close, tossing her axe in the grass, and lacing her hands together, and cupped low to the ground. Drawing a deep breath, I steeled myself and placed one shaking hand full of the reins on Inara's tall withers and twisted the other in the base of her mane. Ossy boosted me so hard that I thought I might fly right over Inara to the mud on the other side, but I landed perfectly astride.

Inara neither bucked nor reared. She...twisted. One moment I was gripping wet ribs with my thighs, and the next, I was on the ground. Instinctively, my fingers clutched tighter to the reins, even as I was falling. I tried to land on my feet, but the way Inara threw me pitched me too far forward, and I went down on my knees. I scrambled back to my feet, expecting the mare to pull away and try to run, but she simply stared at me through the rain with an implacable expression.

"Perhaps you should have asked," Ossy supplied unhelpfully.

I approached the mare again, and this time noticed the way her ear flicked when I laid a hand on her withers. I took a deep breath, which was mostly rain water, and let it back out again.

"Inara," I said, rather curtly, feeling foolish. Another ear twitch. "It would be an honor to ride you and to have your help tonight. Especially," I added, somewhat acerbically because I didn't have time for this, "if you are going to be my *rhu-tasiya*."

The second ear twitched as Ossy approached me again and cupped her hands. This time, I landed much lighter, and my thighs gripped tight. I could not keep the tension out of my body, expecting the mare to react immediately. She did rear, but only slightly, her front legs lifting from the ground in a slight hop, and her entire body going stiff. I drew a deep breath, and as I let it out, I closed my eyes and relaxed every muscle, picturing myself melting into the mare's back until we were one being. Rain pelted against my closed eyelids, and I heard the soft steps of Ossy moving away. Slowly, the more I breathed, the tension eased from Inara's body. I sat still and calm. I stayed that way for a few moments, much longer than was wise, until my breathing was slow and steady, and the mare bobbed her head with impatience.

I opened my eyes and looked down at Ossy, her brown hair plastered to her face in the pouring rain, and she handed my bow back to me. Beyond her, the other women watched us with shadowed faces. I ducked my head through the bowstring and settled it on my back, and then adjusted the quiver at my belt. I nodded to them.

"Let's go."

) (

Four women pushed the empty wagon to the edge of the grove, and Ossy and Tekmessa worked to fit the harness to the white mare. Once we had a few women holding reins and leads, the rest left to go into the village where they would help take what we needed. I was apprehensive Inara would not follow my direction, or leave the herd when I asked her to, but I need not have worried. She followed my legs and my hands with only slight resistance, leading me to believe she was already used to being handled, though had not been fully trained. Tekmessa drove the wagon, and Ossy trotted with a lead beside the white mare, just in case she bolted or became stubborn as we headed back to where my mother's body lay. I slid from Inara's back as soon as we reached the beech tree and looped her reins over a branch.

Quickly, the three of us loaded everything we could around the edge of the wagon, with the furs in the center, and finally, struggling because there were too few of us to lift her so high, we placed my mother's body into the middle. The rain began to ease, and when I looked up, I saw the clouds shift apart in the east, so that the sliver of moon peeked through like a silver bow in the sky. I had just pulled the edge of the lion skin back over my mother's lifeless face when cries of alarm echoed from the village.

This time, I did not wait for anyone's help in mounting. I unlooped the reins and leapt onto Inara's wet back. She reared again, higher this time, but I sat it out and squeezed her with my bare legs, reining her back toward the village. She galloped, and I clung to her back, letting her find her way in the dark. The rattle of wagon wheels echoed behind me, loud and brazen, faster and faster until I knew they had convinced the white mare to run as well.

Ha-mazaans swirled out of the night as Inara ran into their midst, some already mounted. Eri, her face set with determination, reined a dark horse in a tight circle, trying to keep it under control, and dragging another horse by a lead. Others were still on the ground, struggling to keep reins in their hands or hooves on the ground as the horses began to panic. I pulled Inara to a stop, and she reared again, more in protest than trying to unseat me. She wanted to run.

The frightened bawling of one cow, then two, then many pierced the dark, and the sound of hooves thundered on the ground. Shouts grew louder, and the ring of metal on metal carried through the faltering rain, echoing off the cliffs behind the village. Ha-mazaans shouted in the distance. Someone screamed. Acrid smoke filled my nostrils seconds before I saw the flicker of orange flame against the night sky. I reined Inara toward the fighting.

Shapes and shadows soon filled the path in front of us, forcing us to halt. Ha-mazaans had released cows and sheep from their pens, which were stampeding through the village, adding to the confusion, which was what we had wanted. Ahead, a hut's thatched roof was on fire, and one building built low on the terrace was already fully engulfed despite the wet rain throughout the day. Fire was not what we had planned.

As I steered Inara around a bellowing cow, I saw Leya, spear swinging above her head barely in time to intercept a long, curved scythe from splitting her skull in two. The man she fought was taller than her by a head and stronger. Dropping the reins onto Inara's neck, I unslung my bow from my shoulders and nocked an arrow in one smooth motion. Drawing the tight string and holding the bow far in front of me, I sighted, and the moment Leya jumped to the side to avoid another swing of the deadly scythe, I loosed the swan-fletched arrow. It buried itself up to the feathers in the man's throat, but I was already nocking another, kneeing Inara forward.

Leya turned, her eyes wide with surprise and the frenzy of battle.

"Go! The horses are ready!" I called, and she scooped up her plunder and ran toward me through the roiling herd of cows and bleating sheep. Inara danced again, but I squeezed my knees harder, and she moved forward readily enough, the reins still draped over her neck.

Ha-mazaans ran toward me out of the night, weapons in one hand and whatever they had grabbed from their raiding in another. Bundles of wool, copper pots, anything we could use and also carry. Alkippe clutched a screaming piglet under one armpit, the whiteness of it and her gnashing teeth bobbing through the air all I could see of her in the night. She leaped with a whooping cry over the back of a sheep that stood in her path, and I was about to turn Inara to follow her when I saw Prothoe's pale skin and silvery-white hair ahead of me. Aello was close behind her. She did not cry out when the arrow took her through the heart, but I screamed her name. Prothoe was still running, axe in hand. She, too, cried out and stumbled. She fell, axe skidding from her hand and an arrow sticking from her shoulder.

Frantically, I looked toward where the arrows had flown from and thought I saw the shadows move. I loosed my arrow, but I did not know if it had found its mark. It didn't matter. I ducked my head and arm through the bowstring and kicked Inara's sides with my heels, hard, taking up the reins again. She leaped forward, ears flat against her head, clearly not appreciating the rough treatment. Prothoe clambered awkwardly to her feet, clutching her shoulder and looking around wildly for her axe. She saw Aello, motionless, and lurched toward her.

"Prothoe! To me!" I shouted, and she whirled to see me and the mare heading straight for her. I reached my hand down, and she ran for me, reaching up and clasping my forearm. Prothoe was heavier than me, and even though it was a move we practiced often in vaulting, the weight of her almost pulled me from Inara's back. Prothoe used the momentum of the horse to pull her body up, though it was her injured shoulder she used to hoist herself behind me, and she cried out with the pain but clung to my ribs with her good arm. An arrow whistled through the air close by. I ducked, but it thudded into the clay wall of a thatched hut beside us.

Inara ran forward faster, and I tried to turn her, but her ears were pinned and her neck was tight and stubborn. I reefed cruelly on the reins, swearing, but still, she ran deeper into the village center. More cows poured into the path ahead, and they brought her up short; otherwise, I was sure she would have tried to climb the sheer face of the mountain. I had just pulled her head in a tight circle to veer away from the center of the village when I felt a thudding, searing pain in my left arm. The force of the blow knocked me sideways, but Prothoe managed to keep me on the mare with her good arm. This time, when I kicked Inara, she bolted back toward the other horses. Prothoe gasped and clutched at me as the motion nearly unseated her, but we were both clinging to the horse with the profound strength that comes from desperation and fear. I gave the mare her head, and we raced toward the screams of others. I glimpsed Eri's red hair and the horse dancing under her.

"*Go!*" I screamed at her, at all of them. More arrows whistled past us, and I heard another ha-mazaan cry out.

Eri spurred her horse, and it lunged forward. The one she led stretched its neck and didn't want to follow until I sped by with Inara, slapping my reins at its flanks. More horses ran beside us, and soon it was just the thundering of hooves on wet ground, the smell of mud churning under us, and the searing, white-hot pain in my arm as we raced up the road in the gathering light of dawn.

) (

We rode for two days, stopping once we were far from danger only to rest and water the horses, and eventually to tend the wounded. For me, that included having an arrowhead shoved the rest of the way through my upper arm, and the shaft snapped off so it could be pulled out cleanly. This was not done without a copious amount of mead first, and when I rode again, I was dizzy with pain and drink. However, it was the fleshiest part of my arm, and if it did not infect, the wound would likely not cause lasting damage. Prothoe had it worse, needing the arrow in her shoulder blade pulled back against the flesh, and the leather of her vest dug from the hole it left behind. I gave her most of the mead we had left, but when we seared the wound with flame, her scream set every raven and heron in the area to flight. Afterward, we pressed on, but it was with heavier hearts, for we left Aello behind. We thought of her, and thanked her, and sent prayers for her soul's journey to the Womb in the Otherworld. She was the first ha-mazaan to die in battle while under my orders, and I felt the weight of her life, of all of their lives, in my hands. It was not a responsibility I felt ready to handle, but it was mine.

The second night, we found a small knoll to the northwest of the river, far enough from the road that we could prepare for any unwanted intruders but still close enough that we could scout north and south, as well as water the horses and wash ourselves in the clear, easy-flowing water. Sagitta and I made our way through the young oaks and juniper to the top of the small rise and surveyed the area. There were enough trees to tie the horses and still allow them to graze, and we would be safe enough at the top, with a better advantage than lying about on the riverbank. We turned to beckon the others up the hill when I saw the tree.

My hand caught Sagitta's arm. She followed my finger to where I pointed, and then relaxed her axe to her side, frowning in confusion. The trunk of a young oak, barely fifty summers and still narrow and lean. From the roots twined the carved roots of another tree, and the trunk of that carving blossomed into square branches curling in on themselves. On the tree stood a horse, its feet bunched together underneath the body, and its head bowed toward the ground. On the back of the horse stood a deer, its antlers reaching high, and on the deer, a wolf. Finally, a great eagle, beak hooked and turned to the side to show its profile, its wings spread to cover all that stood below. And crowning the eagle's head, the rays of the sun, and the crescent of a moon.

"The Tree of Life," I said, my voice just a whisper.

"It is probably a boundary marker," Sagitta said but did not seem overly affected. Then I realized she had not been there to hear my mother's vision. I told her, my words halting and heavy, and she gave me a long, sorrowful look.

"It is here, in this place, that we must rest her body," I finished, and Sagitta nodded. There was a rustle of leaves as Ossy emerged from the brush at the edge of the hill, coming to investigate what held us up. When she saw where we looked, her face became a mask of grief.

All of us had put our grieving aside, as there had been no time, and something as sacred as death must be attended to with proper attention. With devotion. Now, as the hooves and the thundering of flight came to an end, so too did the blissful numbness that had shielded us from the pain of loss. Ossy disappeared again where she had come from, without speaking.

And so, though we had stopped, we did not rest. We dug a grave, and we gathered wood and stones with the help of horses and ropes and much sweat. We laid my mother's body, still wrapped in the skin of a mighty lioness, deep in the center of the knoll, on top of the logs we had cut and fashioned to hold her temple. The Fingers of the Great Mother, to hold her safe in her journey from this place. In her hands crossed upon her chest we placed her great axe, etched with gold, and a silver-tipped iron spear.

Sagitta took the copper wires twisted around her hair and placed them tenderly on my mother's black braids. Alkippe, her usually stoic face twisted with heartache, knelt beside her general and placed a hand on each shoulder. She said something in the language of her own mother's people, melodic and foreign to me, and then placed white rocks from the river upon my mother's eyelids. Tekmessa placed flowers and herbs from the forest all around Melanippe's body, singing sweet incantations as she did so, and then, taking the mixture of red ochre mixed with the blood each of us had squeezed from a cut palm, she drew a line across Melanippe's forehead, and down her bare arms to the tips of her fingers. She smeared it on the soles of my mother's feet, and last, across the blue-black tattoo of the *rhu-tasiya* above her heart. I shivered when she called the spirit of Zanas, far across the sea, to meet Melanippe in the Otherworld. Ossy removed the amulet she wore on a length of leather between her breasts, the stone blue and shining in the light of the fire we had built. She kissed it and murmured something before slipping it over Melanippe's head. Then she kissed my mother's pale cheek, the tears she cried falling freely onto the grey-blue of her friend's skin.

I led a black mare forward. Holding the lead loosely, I knelt at my mother's side, the ha-mazaans a ring of anguished faces around us. I leaned forward, the black hair that was like mine tickling my cheek just as it had when I was a babe. I whispered into her ear so that only she could hear. My promise to her spirit was the best gift I could give.

Finally, I kissed her cold forehead, my lips tasting the ochre and blood. I stood and drew my knife made from fallen stars. In the east, a small sliver of moon was shining above the sluggish river. I looked toward it, then into the eyes of the horse, black and mysterious.

The mare flinched only slightly. The blood gushed warmly over my arms. I held her steady, pulling her head down as the lifeblood leaked from her throat, the tears on my face mingling with blood until I thought perhaps I cried red. The mare knelt, the strength going from her, and I gently, tenderly pushed her body to the side so that her head lay next to my mother's, facing east, and her legs curled under her. As the light snuffed from her eyes, I closed them and thanked her.

The *zizenti* spoke the ritual prayers. When it was finished, I climbed out of the grave and stood with the rest of the women, facing my mother in a circle. One by one, we each threw a stone into the hollow, being careful not to strike the bodies of woman or horse. As each stone landed, a ha-mazaan said their farewell to the queen who might have been.

I was the last to cast my stone, heavy in my palm and black from the shadowed depths of the river below.

"Farewell, Melanippe, Mighty Black Mare of the Ha-mazaans, queen in her own right. Safe journey to the Womb of the Mother, Mother of my Heart."

Leya lifted the flute she had fashioned from the bones of the swans and played a mourning song. When the ha-mazaan's voices rose in song with her, my own would not sing. I wept and used my own hands to cover my mother's body with the earth, sending her back into the bosom of the Great Mother with my tears and my promises, which were all I had left to me.

PART III

DANGEROUS ALLIES

CHAPTER 18

OIRPATA

The morning crispness of autumn had given way to the heat of a midday sun. Col slanted an arm over his brow to block the blinding light and squinted toward the western horizon, where the golden eagle swirled higher into the sky. The sun blazed from the golden grass so that his eyes saw waves of people and beasts rising up from the dust, when in reality, there were none. As soon as his eyes moved away, the shapes disappeared, nothing more than mirages of heat in the afternoon glare. He whistled shrilly, one long tone of summons, and reined Faelan back toward the crossroads, satisfied there was nothing ahead to block the way of the wagons or to threaten the deer being herded between them.

He was still some distance from where he had left the others behind when he heard screaming. Even Faelan started at the ululating sound, his chestnut head flinging high into the air and his ears pricking in the direction of the crossroads. It sounded like a griffin. But it could not be. Not after all these years. The last in these lands had been killed long ago by his grandfather's own hand.

Col pressed his knees to Faelan's side, and the stallion leaped into a gallop. The screams soon changed, lowering to a harsh roar, and he distinctly heard his own men shouting along with them. The deer bawled and bleated with fear. Col's knees pressed harder as he drew his sword, and Faelan flattened his neck and reached with long legs to devour the ground in front of them. The wind of their speed caught at Col's sword, trying to tug it from his hand with the same fingers that furled his red hair with a grasping insistence. Faelan's white hooves fairly flew over the road, but still, it seemed an eternity before the crossroads came into view.

When he rounded the corner, the entire caravan was in chaos. Mounted attackers were slashing at his men with oddly-colored swords and strange-looking axes and stabbing at them with spears. Col thought for a moment they were the Black Cloaks from the north, the man-eaters who had been driven away from the territory many years before. But these men wore white or red or grey tunics and strange coverings on their legs with an unfamiliar zig-zag pattern that belonged to no local tribe he could recall. A few wore spotted snow cat hides or fur coats over leather. There were a dozen of them at least, all on horses, but he could not tell exactly how many between the sea of antlers and the buckle and sway of swords and men. The deer careened into each other, bawling and choking as they tried to escape the fray. And in the middle of it all, shoulders covered in a golden hide and torso covered with the scales of some strange beast, like dragon skin, one attacker stood on the back of a grey horse, aiming a curiously double-curved bow and a long, white-fletched arrow at one of the wagons.

Col screamed in fury, but the deer hampered his way forward, many of them stampeding toward the stallion and in every other direction in a frenzied panic. Faelan plunged through them as best he could, but already the man standing on the horse had leaped to the ground. Col heard the wheels of the wagons creak in protest as they turned too quickly on the rough road. Those wagons held all of their goods from an entire summer's worth of trade. And his father's chair that Col had carved especially for the king.

He shouted Faelan after the wagons jolting on wheels too old and brittle to be driven at such a speed. The stallion dodged more deer and leaped over two prone bodies on the road. Col could not tell who was down, but he saw at least one attacker lying in the dust, their strangely covered legs and braided hair identifying them as strangers to the Scoloti.

Faelan gained on the wagons quickly, though they were being driven at a breakneck pace. Even if the wagon's axles and wheels could sustain such speed, he was sure the horses would not last long before they broke a leg in the deep ruts. The thought made him angry enough to urge Faelan even faster, trusting the stallion would find the best footing on the road while he readied his sword to cut down the thieves.

The wind and hooves and thundering of the wagons roared so loudly in his ears that he did not register the hooves behind him until almost too late. He turned his head and ducked just as the arrow whizzed over his back. Cursing, he reined Faelan around and charged at the man, though they were already nocking another arrow. He fixed his eyes on their fingers, waiting for the release so that he could duck and swing his sword at their heart, hoping they would not aim for the horse under him. But the fingers did not move. Wide eyes the color of a full moon glared into his, set in a thin face that looked almost frail, as though the man had been starving for a considerable time. Then he was upon the attacker.

He swung his sword, though it was an awkward crossbody lashing with the weapon and their horse stepped to the side just as Col's blade slashed the air. He was about to round Faelan and try again when he felt a searing pain in his left arm. He looked down and saw red against the green of his tunic. When he looked up again, at least five more riders barrelled down on him. He could not defend himself against all of them.

Cursing the loss of the wagons, especially when they had made it so close to home, Col steered Faelan to the side. The stallion cleared the deep ditch with a long, gliding leap and was galloping again on the other side of it, away from the attackers, but they were not yet out of arrow's range. He flashed a look back and saw that the wagons continued south, and the attackers after them. They did not slow or pursue him, and no arrows were aimed at his back.

He did not have time to ponder who they were. The deer, untended and panicked, bleated their panic as they spread in every direction. The golden eagle circled above the crossroads, swirling high in the heat and watching the ground with sharp eyes. Col breathed a sigh of relief when he saw Esten, though bleeding from an arrow high on his shoulder, doing his best to round the deer into a tight circle again. He was losing the battle, but the attackers appeared to have taken what they came for and, thankfully, left his friend alive.

"What in Tabiti's blackened knees was that?" Esten shouted furiously as Col drew Faelan to a halt. Col sheathed his sword and swung from the stallion's back, sweeping his friend into a great hug. He was careful of the broken arrow still sticking from the shorter man's shoulder, but Esten flinched anyway.

"I don't know, but I am glad you are not among the dead, my friend."

"I am not so sure I won't be," Esten said dolefully, stepping away and looking down at his shoulder.

"I think you will live," Col grinned, clapping his friend on the opposite arm. "Unless they poisoned it."

Esten snapped his head up in horrified alarm, but Col was still grinning, his green eyes twinkling. Muttering, Esten shook his head and tried, one-handed, to wrangle the sweeping horns of a lost deer back to the center of the road. Col looked over the milling deer, and his heart grew heavier.

"Who did we lose?"

Esten frowned. "I saw Grigor down. And Anak. I am not sure who else. Most were wounded, but not killed, I think. I took one of theirs, though," the blonde man said grimly, and Col nodded.

"You did better than I," he admitted ruefully. "I didn't even draw blood."

Esten looked at Col's arm, slowly seeping red with blood.

"Not as bad as yours," Col said dismissively at the look and began to move around the edges of the deer swirling back into the road. They were looking for the safety of their wagons to huddle between, but that was gone. The stallion followed close behind him, dogging his every step, though Col did not lead him. He found several of his men along the side of the road, tending to wounds that were bad, but not fatal. He examined each man, asking what they had seen when he was sure they would live. Tanon had taken an arrow through the hand and another in the thigh, and Bren through the arm, both with white feather fletching that appeared to be from swans, the same as the arrow in Esten's shoulder. Shot from the one who had been on a grey horse, they reported. Col winced to see the sacred feathers used in such a way. Swans were the souls of the departed making their way to the Otherworld. It was sacrilege to kill them.

Arnan, passed out on the ground, had lost a hand to what Roldo described as a golden-etched axe, strangely double-bladed, while the other axes had been even stranger, with long pikes. Roldo made his reports as he wound a tight bandage around the stump of Arnan's arm and met Col's eyes with grim concern. Six had been killed from arrows or axe or blade. Others were unconscious, bleeding, or bruised, but not killed.

Col shook his head, stupefied. Though he had been scouting ahead for danger the entire trip down from the summer country, he had been looking for signs of wolves that might threaten the deer, or bears ready to move into hibernation needing an easy, fattening meal. An ambush on these roads was the last thing he had expected. Roads that had not known violence to travelers for three decades. Not since they crowned his father king, and the other tribes of the Ashkuzi had pledged their allegiance to the Scoloti. All tribes within their territory, whether they traveled with the herds of animals to summer pastures or not, knew well not to endanger the treaty of free passage on the roads. Especially since that free travel was offered in exchange for protection and allegiance from the king, and each of the king's three sons, who had territories of their own. It made little sense that anyone would jeopardize that allegiance now.

Col shook his head again and turned toward the stranger's body on the ground. Carefully, he turned them over, the white and grey spotted fur that had once belonged to a snow leopard matted with blood from where the arrow had pierced through their lungs. Were they from his mother's mountains, then, to the south? She had worn similar furs. But this man wore woolen coverings on their legs, fashioned in a way he had never seen before, and certainly not with the same markings as his mother's people. But when he turned their head, moving the thick brown braid of hair to the side, he froze in astonishment. Esten, who had finished corralling the deer as best he could, halted beside him and stared down at the face as well.

"A...woman?" Esten breathed.

Col muttered a prayer of contrition to Tabiti and unlaced the leather vest that covered the dead person's body. His breath, and Esten's, sucked in sharply when it parted to reveal a pair of perfect, round breasts.

"A woman," Col confirmed, covering her breasts and respectfully tying the laces again before standing. His eyes met Esten's. Together, they approached the second body, smaller than the first, lying face down at the edge of the road, blood pooling on the ground from an arrow in the neck. Yaro intercepted them on the way, and the three of them knelt and turned the body to lie on its back, black eyes staring into the sky. Their skin was brown, darker even than the tanned herders pushing the deer to their winter pastures, and still warm to the touch. The black eyes stared into his with disturbing intensity for all that they were deadened to life. Col gently closed the eyelids and reached for the laces of the simple leather tunic the person wore. Yaro made a sound of protest, for to disrespect the dead, even the enemy's dead, was a grave offense. Esten shook his head and put a restraining hand on Yaro's arm even as Col pulled aside the lacing to reveal a second pair of small, but undeniably female, breasts. Yaro gasped.

) (

It was a longer road home than it should have been. Without the wagons, and with only a few of their own horses left, Col was forced to move the six dead bodies of his own men to the forest just east of the crossroads, where he or one of his men would come back for them later. He mounted Arnan, who had regained consciousness but was in extreme pain and clutching the severed stump of his arm, onto Faelan's back, and walked home alongside the men who were not badly wounded. The horses left to them carried those who could not walk and the two dead women. His father would need to see them to believe it, even with these men as witnesses. Col helped keep the deer in line as best he could, but he was too distracted with thoughts of strangers and strange garb, and a pair of furious, shocked grey eyes, to be of much practical use during the long walk.

It was well after moonrise when the wooden gates of Gelonia came into view. The men dragged their feet with weariness, and Arnan had once more passed out, hanging limply over a perturbed Faelan's neck. Esten looked wan and paler than usual, and Col grasped his friend's shoulder as they made their slow and winding way down the hill toward the city walls.

"I am grateful, friend, that you journeyed with me this year," Col said. "But I am sorry it ended like this."

"It could have been worse, Colaxais," Esten said, his long yellow beard brushing his chest as he shook his head. "Could have been all of us dead." His eyes slid over to Arnan's limp body and away again. *Could have been our limbs*, Col was sure he was thinking, but his gentle friend would never be so unkind as to say it aloud.

"Aye," Col agreed quietly. "It could have been much worse."

But even as they ushered the deer through the narrow gates of the city, swinging long sticks to keep the animals moving, and the horse with the dead women moving behind them, Col frowned to feel a

prickling on his skin. He knew the matter was far from over, and Tabiti
sear him if he knew what to do about it.

)(

Col paced the length of the hall, the soft heels of his leather boots
making a swishing sound against the smooth, polished wood planks on
the floor. The sword strapped to his hips tapped against his dusty legs
like a fretful child trying to get his attention. He ignored it and made a
sharp turn, pacing back in the direction he had come from. A loud *clink*
of metal on wood made him glance up in surprise, as though startled to
find another in the room with him.

"Care to tell me why you are digging a trench with your feet in my
Hall?" his father drawled, raising a thick red eyebrow. The clink had
been the wine goblet, the contents quickly emptied down the king's
throat, being returned to the table. Col raised an almost identical
eyebrow back, and then raised the other.

"Oh," he answered breezily, halting his steps and waving a hand to the
door at the end of the hall. The door led to the kitchens, and beyond
that, the underground cellars. "Just wondering what we are going to
do with the bodies of those two women, other than keep them in our
cellars next to the turnips. Just wondering why we have the bodies of
two *women*. Just wondering," Col continued, his voice drawling out long
and slow with exaggerated indifference, "why we were set upon by an
entire band of griffin-shrieking, axe-wielding, terrifying *women*!"

He enunciated this last by flinging both hands into the air toward the
hearth fire, as though supplicating Tabiti to send him an answer in the
flames. But nothing came, other than the low chuckle from his father.
Col scowled and began pacing again.

"I'd imagine the 'why' is something we already know. They were after
the wagons," Targitaos said easily. "Since that's what they took. As well
as a few of my men's lives."

"Our men," Col said grimly. "And it was six of them they killed, before
we even knew what hit us. They could have taken us all if they had
tried." His green eyes grew distant. "I'm telling you, Father, they were
as fierce and as skilled as any warrior I have met in all our lands."
His thoughts shifted from his memories of the grey-eyed archer, who

had appeared like a centaur out of his grandmother's tales, to the man before him once more. His father was nodding in agreement.

"To be honest, I am sorry I did not see them myself. Women fighting as men! Such a curious thing. It would have been most entertaining. Alas," he gestured to his legs, withered and unnaturally thin against the wood of the chair.

Col stopped, his eyes going to his father's useless legs, and some tension leaked out of his tall frame. "I'm sorry, Father." He moved to lay a hand on his father's shoulder. "I know what the chair would have meant for you. If I cannot reclaim it, I will make another."

His father looked up at him, shaking his head. Sadness touched the edges of his face, turning his normally stern mouth soft with grief. "Do not worry yourself, Col," he said, reaching up to clasp his son's wrist at his shoulder. "Another chair will do, one day when you have time. We have lost more valuable things than that." The two of them, of a similar height if one were not confined to a chair, remained silent for a long, heavy moment. Col knew each thought their own thoughts of the most devastating loss of all—the golden-haired, laughing woman they had loved. Still loved, though it had a bittersweet ache to it, now.

Col squeezed his father's shoulder and then moved away, but the restlessness fading from his legs was not so easily banished from his mind. He stared into the flames, idly feeling the edges of the bandage tied tight around his left arm. He could not stop thinking about the women, with their painted wooden shields and swords and axes and strangely curved bows. Women who had killed six of his men with disturbing ease, one of which had come close to killing him. Twice. He could not think of much else since the caravan had returned to the stronghold the day before.

Everything about the attackers had set a flame in his mind brighter than his hair. The way they had shrieked and fallen upon his men without warning. And that archer. Something about that one, the way she had looked at him, had made his blade swing awkwardly when trying to kill her, but he couldn't put a finger on what it had been. Perhaps something in his subconscious, alerting that this warrior was not what they seemed? To harm the sacred bringers of life was a grievance against Tabiti herself; never in his life had he raised a weapon or a hand against a woman. Perhaps this had stymied his sword. But his mind had not known she had been a woman until well after, when he had witnessed the truth in the bodies of the dead.

Word of *Oirpata*, man-killing women, had spread like wildfire throughout the settlement already. It was only a matter of time before half the kingdom knew that a band of women had set upon and killed six men of the Scoloti, who were supposed to be protecting the rest of the tribes throughout the territory. Then he would surely have trouble on his hands.

Col's thoughts were interrupted as the heavy door of the hall swung open, and his brothers strode into the room. Arpoxais, always rushing everywhere he went, and hair the color of unripe strawberries sticking up in every direction to attest to his speed, reached their father first and quickly bent to kiss the king's wrist. Liopoxais, their eldest brother, strolled more slowly and did not even bother shutting the door all the way, much to Col's annoyance. Targitaos' eldest also took up the king's arm and kissed the edge of the golden cuff, but his eyes met Col's immediately as he stood straight again.

"Well, little brother, have you and our glorious king decided yet how we are going to subdue this wild bunch of *Oirpata* ravaging our roads?" Liopoxais raised a thin black eyebrow at Col, his dark eyes holding a mocking humor that set Col's teeth on edge.

"Subdue them?" he repeated.

"You don't plan on letting them wreak havoc on every caravan that passes from our lands to Arpo's, do you?" Targitaus interjected sternly, any of the grief that had been there moments before replaced by a disapproving scowl that fit more snugly on his harsh features. Col looked down at his father, a slight frown tugging his own normally congenial features downward, but he did not answer immediately.

"If they make it through to my territory," Arpoxais said, "you know our treaty with the rest of the Ashkuzi will be null and void."

"Aye," Liopoxais nodded. "It is already tenuous. I have heard rumblings against the Scoloti since last winter, when the snow took much of the crops early, and they did not want to give any grain for taxes."

"If their caravans are set upon by murderous bandits we did nothing to control, we would be forced to take the Heirophilus road in the spring," their father said. "And that would shave a full moon or more from the deer's grazing time at summer's beginning *and* end." His father shook his head again. "We can't afford it. The kingdom cannot afford it. Lio is right."

Col stared down at his father. What the older man said was right, as far as endangering treaties and peace agreements with the Ashkuzi tribes was concerned. It was a dangerous gamble to think of disrupting the tenuous peace they had established. Their father's rule was held firmly in place by each son occupying a territory and overseeing the distribution of taxes and grazing property for each tribe that paid them fealty. Still, the thought of subduing a spirit so fierce, especially as the one who had eyed him with moonlit eyes down the length of that arrow, seemed ludicrous. Col was still gazing down at his father's face, his expression enigmatic. It was Arpoxais who broke the silence, his voice a peculiar mixture of curiosity and slyness.

"Am I the only one who has wondered if these *Oirpata* are not, after all, the one?"

Three heads turned to him, and Col grasped for his older brother's meaning. "The one?" he repeated.

Arpoxais looked skeptical and glanced to their oldest brother for support. "Even you, Lio? Surely you have thought about it." When Liopoxais answered with only a raised eyebrow, Arpoxais spread his hands in a gesture of supplication. "I mean, their axes...don't you see?"

Col stared at his brother in astonishment. "You cannot be serious. They are women."

"Aye," Arpoxais agreed easily. "They are *Oirpata*. Man-killers. And one, at least as far as the story your men have told me, carries a golden axe."

"Be careful what you are suggesting, boy," Targitaos said. "Your mother already made this decision. The heir will be Colaxais."

Arpoxais looked between them for a long moment, but when his eyes fell on Col, they lingered, full of shadows.

"I know what our mother said," he said finally. "But that was when there was only the yoke."

The silence was tense, filled with unspoken words.

"And how do you propose to determine whether they have the Axe?" Targitaos said. "Are you going to take it and wield it against your own brother? Or wield *them* against your brother?" He made a scoffing sound and waved a hand in dismissal.

Arpoxais stared at Col, while Liopoxais grinned wide, like a wolf.

"I suppose that depends on who can tame them first," Arpoxais said and smiled a wolfish smile of his own.

CHAPTER 19

THE UNDERSIDE OF AN OAK LEAF

My mother had been traveling in the Otherworld for the span of one waning quarter moon to the next, and still, we had no firm grasp on how to take back our old life. Eleven full moons until *Alsanti*, although that matter was not at the forefront of my mind. It was there, but in the shadows, where I kept the memories of my time in Themiscyra, the images of the wound that had taken my mother's life, and my ever-increasingly haunted dreams, occasionally interrupted by the faint call of an eagle that came to me on the wind, and eyes the color of the underside of an oak leaf in spring. These things, along with thoughts of the *Alsanti*, stayed hidden in those shadows as much as possible.

We had not spent the month being idle. The raid for the horses and materials from the village had given us plenty to work with, and we had made the most of our time as we slowly moved north, following the road to…somewhere. Many of us worked with the horses, training them and making them familiar with our ways and conditioning them to the sounds of battle as we trained against one another every morning. Routine conditioned mind and body, and the same had always been done in Themiscyra. My wound was healing nicely and hardly caused a twinge when I drew my bowstring, but Prothoe still favored her left arm.

We made new clothing from the wool we had taken. Warm, tight-fitting trousers and new tunics with sleeves to keep the chill of the air from our bare arms. Leya had even secured thin bronze and bone needles from the weaver's hut, which we used to stitch the wool and make felted wool pads for a few of the horses. I sewed a short coat from the lion skin to fit over my vest on frosty mornings. We used the needles to tattoo each other's arms and legs and chests, using the fire to light our work while Ossy and Tekmessa and even Sagitta told stories. Soot from the flames and the blood from our hands, mixed with pigmented ink, pressed into the marks we made. I added a solid, thick ring of black on my left forearm, visible above my leather armguard every time I drew my bow, to remind me of my mother. A band of grief to match the one squeezing my heart. I tattooed that one myself, relishing the pain of the needle and the rough burning as I smeared bloody soot into the wounds. Ossy tattooed the *rhu-tasiya* on my right shoulder, and we spoke the words of binding, linking my spirit to Inara's. The mare's mane was a fantastic swirl of wind, and her hind feet twisted upward in the way we made all the marks of this kind, to show that her spirit walked partly in this world and partly in the Otherworld, protecting me in both places at once. As we tattooed and trained and sewed clothes or fashioned new sandals from the deer hides we cured, we discussed Themiscyra and our options to stay or go.

The ha-mazaans were split on what should be done. Whether we should move east or west. Whether now or in the spring. Because of geography and weather, going west in the spring seemed the more likely option, but the little we knew of that direction was that it was peopled with savage tribes of men, many of them either friendly with the Achaeans, or similar to them, and we were not keen on carving a path of blood until our ha-mazaan tribe was whittled down to a handful of war-weary women by the time we reached the banks of the Terme.

Or at least, *I* wasn't keen on the idea. A few women, missing their children, their sisters, their mothers, their men in Galatae, were adamant they were willing to pay the price and that anything less than this was cowardice and shameful.

For my own desires, I remained torn. Much of my dilemma stemmed from the Oracle's prophecies, both to my mother and to me. So much of it had come to pass that it now felt inescapable, and for this reason, I felt frozen in the inevitability of it. I was an arrow already loosed from the bow, and there was nothing that could change the direction of my flight. Something much more resolute and powerful than I was in charge of the winds of Fate that could alter my course. So instead of making solid decisions that might direct the steps of the ha-mazaans one direction or another, I waited for the Great Mother to impose Her will upon me and my people. Any choice I made would not matter, anyway. If the Great

Mother wanted me shipwrecked on a foreign shore, She would have Achaean ships steal me. If She wanted to take my mother back into Her bosom, She would take her, and nothing I, nor a *zizenti*, nor anyone else who loved her, could do anything about it. And if She wanted to make me some trivial joke of a queen over a rag-tag group of stolen horses and lost ha-mazaans, my palace the fields of grass and tall oaks of the forest, then She would do that. If She wanted me to rule in Themiscyra, then She would take us home.

What did it matter if I chose east or west? To go now or later? It did not. My choice played no part in the matter, no matter how much I had fought against that knowledge since my first moon-blood and my cursed prophecy. And so I waited, and while I waited, I began to despise everything, especially myself. There was an anger in me that crouched so deep it could not be expressed by talking. It could not be quelled by swinging a sword or loosing thirty arrows into a strawman, though I tried many times. It was just there. Deep in my womb and my heart and my mind it lurked, looking for a way out, or perhaps farther in. Inara bolstered my spirits, but even my *rhu-tasiya* could only do so much. Sagitta and Ossy and Alkippe tried to help, but I knew they could not understand. Eri had succumbed to her own grief, keeping to herself and training harder than I had ever seen and spending as much time alone away from camp as possible. I could hardly judge her for it. But when I tried to seek solace in the friendship that had carried me through so many childhood dramas, or worse, when I tried to offer comfort for my friend's expanding grief, I was met with sullen, unyielding silence.

Thus, when Alkippe returned from a scout to say there was a small caravan of people an hour's ride to the northeast, with horses hauling wagons and a few oddly antlered, elk-like creatures trailing behind, I would hear none of their refusals for me to stay at the camp.

"It will be a simple raid," Alkippe said, shaking her head at me. "We will take their wagons, that's it. If they have any wool or felt or even more skins, we will take them and be done with them," she said.

"And I will help," I said implacably, already removing Inara's hobbles from her feet.

"Cyra, it would be best if—" Ossy began.

"It would be best if all of you ceased treating me like a Xanharaspa and began remembering I am Ishassara," I said, more harshly than intended. Ossy's mouth closed with a snap, and I glared at the women gathered around the cold fire pit. "I've had enough with everyone thinking they need to keep me out of harm's way. I'm in the exact same position as you." I turned back to Inara and fastened the reins to her bridle in a quick knot, which I yanked harder than I should have, earning me a disapproving side-eye from the mare. "It's ridiculous to think I will not be participating in the same raids, fighting the same battles, and facing the same dangers as every other ha-mazaan here. I am to be the Defending Queen, not the Hearth Queen. I am coming with you."

There was a moment of silence until finally, Alkippe shrugged, her face grim. "I agree, Ishassara."

This earned her a fierce look from Ossy and an uncertain frown from Sagitta.

"Look, I know you are trying to protect me," I said finally, holding the reins and turning back to them. "I—"

"Yes," Ossy said grimly before I could continue. "The ha-mazaans have already lost two queens and one who was queen in every way but name. Losing an Ishassara for a few rags of wool and a pair of boots will not do anything to boost these women's spirits, Cyra."

"Good thing for them, I have no intention of being lost," I said. I finished adjusting Inara's bridle and turned to my goddess-mother. "Also, what about boosting *my* spirits? Do you want me to sit in camp all day every day, growing soft? You know I am the best archer here," I said, without bravado. This last was simple fact. However, no one, least of all me, had been sitting about in camp growing soft, with horses to train and food to gather and daily drills to attend, and I winced inwardly at the unfairness of my words. But my mind felt trapped in a cage, my throat increasingly tight as though in a noose, and I was not able to keep my words as controlled as I would have liked. "I will be glad to put my skills to some good use for the spirits of all."

With that, I looped my quiver and bow across my chest, adjusting it against the fur coat, and tapped Inara's shoulder. She responded quickly, bowing her head and tucking one knee beneath her until she bowed in the dirt. I swung a leg over her back, and she promptly straightened. There had been ample time in the last month to strengthen my bond with the mare, and she had grown familiar with my leg aides and the sounds I made with my tongue. Whistles and clicks and words, along with the subtle movements of my body, paired with her flicks of ears and head and the shimmy of her powerful body, were all beginning to be a familiar language between us. I still used the crude leather bridle I had fashioned, now without the makeshift bit, but it was more for my own piece of mind that I could tether her in place and she would not run off when I left her. I had decorated the reins with small strips of cloth, along with a piece of Melanippe's black braid, and they fluttered gently in the breeze under Inara's chin.

Ossy quickly realized the futility of dissuading me and mounted her own horse, a dark dun gelding that was almost the same color as Ossy's hair. Her shining axe was strapped across her back, but she had also brought a new bow and quiver. No one else challenged my decision, even if they disagreed. Sagitta, Ariadne, Eri, and ten others joined us, and when we finally set off in the direction Alkippe indicated, sixteen sets of hooves sounded conspicuously loud to my ears.

We traveled at a fast gallop, following Alkippe on her short red roan, until she held up a hand to slow and proceed with more caution. Eventually, she signaled a halt and dismounted, handing the reins of her horse to me. She motioned Sagitta forward, and together the two went on foot to scout ahead and find the caravan.

They were only gone for a handful of minutes when Sagitta came into view again, jogging lightly through the grass beside the road, the wicker of her half-moon shield painted a dark, blood red that mirrored the trousers she had sewn. The colder weather and the daily horse training meant we all needed our preferred tight-fitting trousers under tunics, and I wore dark grey ones, the same color as Inara. Sagitta was one of the few women wearing a hat today, though, a felted cap with a pointed top in honor of Matar Kubileya's breast, and with the flaps pulled low over her ears, I could not see more than the tips of her blonde braids. I thought she must be sweltering as the sun burned hotter, but she flashed a bright, eager grin as she came nearer and took her reins from Eri, swinging with deceptive ease onto the back of a leggy palomino mare.

"Twenty men, only five with horses, nearing a crossroad from the north," she said in a low voice tight with anticipation. "And a large number of strange deer, the likes I have never seen," she added. "There are two wagons, with rawhide covered holds. Those are what we want. First, we get rid of their drivers." She pointed at Ariadne and Phillipisa and said, "You two will drive the wagons as fast as you can as soon as they are clear. The rest of us will keep them occupied until you're away."

She took the reins of Alkippe's horse from my hands with a nod of thanks, but there was a patent question in her eyes when they met mine. I returned the nod, giving my go-ahead to advance. As we spurred the horses forward, I unslung my bow and drew an arrow. The reins hung loosely on Inara's neck, but she was running forward at a smooth, eager canter, her ears pricked forward in pleasure as the pounding of hooves echoed across the landscape.

Something of the mare's delight in the run seeped into me, easing the ennui that had worked its way into my spirit since my mother's death. I felt exhilaration and the thrill of danger. It made me feel alive. Racing to either side of me with weapons ready were Ossy with her arrow ready and Eri with her golden-etched, double-bladed axe. When we came upon Alkippe, Sagitta barely slowed, merely tossing the reins of the red roan to the new general and thundering on. Alkippe, despite having a wicker shield wrapped against her left arm, swung onto the mare's back at a gallop and was soon beside me, unslinging her axe from its belt and brandishing it into the air. We let out a loud cry as one, the shrieking, ululating sound of it piercing the bright morning and spurring the horses to greater speed.

We rounded the corner and came upon the wagons dead center in a four-way crossroad. The first thing I noticed was the many strange-looking deer or elk with enormous antlers sprouting from their foreheads like mythical, ugly unicorns. The men drew their weapons, but their horses reared in panic, and the suddenly terrified herd of animals scattered in every direction, which was exactly what we had planned on. My swan-fletched arrow took the driver of the first wagon as soon as he was in my sights. He screamed and clutched at his belly, toppling from the wagon seat. The second arrow struck the man walking next to the wagon, who was still in the process of unslinging his bow. The arrow buried itself into the muscles of his forearm, and he howled in pain, dropping his weapon. I preferred to disable rather than kill. I did not want to kill without just cause. It was not our Way. Still, we would do what needed to be done to take what we needed.

Ossy shot another arrow into a man's thigh as he rushed at us, sword held high. He stumbled but did not stop. She nocked another arrow, but my own was already flying, and the hand that held the sword aloft spasmed open as the arrow punctured the man's wrist. He screamed, clutching the wound, and dodged to the side to avoid being trampled under our horses' hooves. From the corner of my eye. I registered Eri swing her axe at another man reaching toward her with his blade. His sword flung into the nearby ditch with his hand still attached, and his scream blended with the rest of the bleating and cawing.

Animals scattered in every direction in an alarmed, raucous frenzy. Inara reared as one of them veered into her path, forcing me to pause in nocking another arrow. I took in the chaotic scene while the mare settled, watching Alkippe hew through a man with her axe and spur her mare toward another, knocking him off his horse. The men were tall and powerfully built, and mostly all had red or yellow hair like Sagitta and Eri. They were also armed with long swords or lances, and a few had bronze shields, which rang like bells when our ha-mazaan axes struck them. I noticed these details in a detached way, my fighting mind collected and calm as though this were just another training drill.

Abruptly, Ariadne yelled my name beside me, then tossed me her reins and leaped from the back of her horse onto the bench of the now-driverless wagon. Scooping the reins from the footboard, she smacked them with a loud smack against the backs of the two harnessed horses, screaming a mighty "HA!!" The horses bolted forward, more in panic than obedience, but they could not go very far because of the animals still bleating and blocking the path. Even as I tucked her reins under my thigh, freeing my hands to use my bow, an arrow pierced through Ariadne's ribs, and she gasped, hands dropping the reins and going to her bloodied side. She fell from the seat before I could move to help her.

I whipped my head around for the source of the arrow, but there were only horses, antlers, and rearing, bawling deer everywhere, so that all I could see was a writhing mass of animal flesh. Cursing, I flung the reins of Ariadne's horse over its head and smacked its rump, hoping it would seek its companions back at camp. Then, despite the fact that I had never tried the move with Inara, I placed my hands on her withers and pushed, lifting my body under me until my feet were firmly planted just behind her withers. I stood straight, adjusting to balance one foot in the center of Inara's back and the other on her hip while her ears twitched at me in consternation.

Everything became clear from this vantage point, and the swirling bodies of misshapen deer melded into a calm backdrop for my focus. I was directly in the center of the melee. A man with blonde hair and a long beard shining in the sunlight crouched behind the second wagon, nocking an arrow with the same fletching that had felled Ariadne. I raised my bow, but Inara tried to sidle out from under my feet, spooked by this new type of pressure on her back and also by the crazed swirling and shouting around us. I called out lightly, like singing, just as we practiced every day, while centering my weight against her movements. She settled again, though her feet still danced. I breathed deeply, centering down the shaft of the arrow, and let it fly. Just as it sunk into the man's shoulder, Eri cried out.

"Cyra!" I looked for her and instead saw a man racing toward me from behind my left shoulder. He swung his sword high, bellowing with fury. There was no time to nock another arrow. Inara reared and scraped at the sky with sharp hooves to warn him away. I ran down her tilting back with two quick steps and dove, catching the man off guard and requiring him to change course to meet me. He swung his sword, and it glinted toward my chest. It met nothing but air as I tucked my body and rolled from shoulder to hip under his very feet and under the swing of the blade. I swung my bow out and caught him mid-stride, the horn and hard wood of my weapon tangling easily in his running feet and sending him sprawling. I came out of the roll crouching on the balls of my feet, an arrow nocked and ready, and I sunk it into his back before he could regain his feet.

Inara whirled, head flinging into the air and eyes as wild as the deer careened about. She trampled the man's body into the dust, perhaps doubting my arrow's success. Behind me, I heard the clash of axe on shield and Sagitta shouting familiar frustrated curses. Snatching up the long sword of the man I had killed, I whistled shrilly to Inara as I ran. She followed me with fast steps as I found a path through the animals. The wagons were already lurching forward down the road with ha-mazaans at the reins, back in the direction we had come, and their wheels cracked against the ruts in the road as the horses picked up speed.

Men cried out in angry consternation, but they were too late to stop the wagons. The drivers were soon clear of the milling deer and away from the thick of the fight, the horses straining at their harnesses and thundering down the open road. But then a chestnut horse with white legs rushed through the mess of animals, the man on its back riding with his body tucked tight against the horse's neck. He spurred the horse after the wagons, sword held low to the side and teeth bared in a grimace of determination I did not like.

I glanced at Sagitta, who looked equally matched against a tall, heavily bearded man and his sword. I flung the sword I had taken into the bushes in the ditch and mounted Inara with a lithe swing of my leg over her back, not bothering to make her kneel. I still clutched my bow in my left hand, and as I reined Inara after the wagons and shouted her forward, I nocked another arrow and set my sights on the man who raced after them.

He rode like the wind; I would give him that. His horse was taller than Inara by a hand, and all legs, the four white socks a blur against the dust of the road. The two of them quickly gained on the shuddering wagons, but Inara was the fastest horse I had ever ridden. Even with the bow in my hands and my body firm and upright as I sighted along the arrow, I could feel the power of her body under me and the relentless resistance of the wind against my chest and face. We gained, and the man, hair as red as the horse he rode, glanced backward at the sound of thunder behind him. I loosed my arrow, aiming for the center of his back, but he somehow ducked flatter against his horse's neck and turned in a tight circle, faster than I expected he could at such a speed.

I leaned back, and Inara slid to a halt as the man galloped away from the wagons and straight toward me. I nocked another arrow as we slid to a stop and drew the string tight, the bow held far in front of me. I sighted more carefully this time through the dust from the horse's hooves, my eyes following down the straight arrow and past the flint tip to the center point between the man's eyes. The man's squinting, furiously glinting eyes, green as the underside of an oak leaf in spring.

The air caught in my lungs, and my fingers stiffened, paralyzed on the bowstring. I knew those eyes, just as I knew the copper of his hair and rusty stubble on his jaw and the irritatingly broad span of his shoulders. I knew them best surrounded by flames in an Oracle's cauldron, but I would know them anywhere. I froze for long enough that he was upon me, and if not for Inara's swift sidestepping dance, his blade would have sheared my arm from my body. The movement shook some sense back into my frozen muscles, and I shrieked at him, turning my body as he rode past and loosing my arrow with careless, desperate ferocity at the back of his heart. White feathers whizzed past his arm, although I saw him flinch and knew I had drawn blood at least. I ripped another arrow from my quiver, but then the rest of the ha-mazaans were thundering toward both of us, and the man must have known his chances grew slim. He spurred his horse off the road, leaping the ditch and galloping across the bracken, away from the hoard of women barrelling toward him. The chestnut left a high plume of dust in their wake, though I could still see the whirr of his white feet. I was still staring after him, stunned and hissing breath through my clenched teeth when Ossy reined in her dun gelding at my side.

"The rest of the men are attempting to gather their deer," she said, breathless, but eyes glimmering with the rush of battle. "If we are away now, they will not follow. At least not for some time. We still need to be ready in case they pursue."

I nodded and turned Inara to follow the others. We rode fast until we caught up with the wagons, and when we were a suitable distance from the fight, I re-slung the bow across my shoulders. Two horses with bare backs and reins held in the hands of another rider followed behind, and I wondered who we had lost in the skirmish besides Ariadne. Most of all, I wondered about the man who had escaped two of my poorly aimed arrows. I could not have forgotten his features if I wanted to, for they were seared into my mind's eye since my first moon-blood. The man with whom I would betray the ha-mazaan Way, if the Oracle never lied.

Red hair ahead of me made my stomach lurch with alarm, but it was only Eri. I kneed Inara toward her horse. "Eri!"

She turned to look at me, trepidation clear on her pale face.

"Thank you," I said as her blue eyes met mine. "For warning me. It saved my life."

She gave a terse nod, but she did not return my smile. We trotted side by side for a while, in a silence so fraught with tension I couldn't stand it anymore. "Eri, I hope you will forgive me for ignoring you when we were on the ship." Again, her eyes swung to my face, their expression indiscernible as I babbled on. "It was awful of me when your mother…" I trailed off as her face settled into stony lines, and she stared at me with a hardness I was becoming uncomfortably accustomed to seeing ever since my Ishassara ceremony.

Abruptly, she barked a laugh. "You think I wanted to be pet on the head and have a good cry on your shoulder, Cyra?"

The disdain in her voice took me aback, and Inara tensed her stride as she sensed my entire body stiffen. I stared back into Eri's glinting blue eyes and frowned.

"Well, you also didn't seem to be thrilled that I am Ishassara so soon," I conceded, unsure if I was ready to have this conversation now that I had started it. "I can understand how that's hard for you, to think of me being your queen, but we are friends and—"

"That is where you are wrong," Eri cut me off. Her words sliced into me like a sharp knife. "And, so we are clear, you will never be my queen." She pointed a finger to another ha-mazaan, Santo, on a small bay ahead of us. "And I can guarantee you she won't consider you her queen, either. No one who knows the truth of your mother should."

Her lips twisted at my shocked face. "My mother was in the Moon Hall when the crown was taken from your mother, as it should have been, though I didn't know until Ossy revealed the truth. Mother never told me why because she had given her sworn oath to never speak of it, but she did say you should never be Ishassara. I didn't understand before. I do now. Melanippe betrayed the Way of the ha-mazaans. And now you've admitted with your own lips that you would betray it, too."

I stared at her, a cold knot twisting in my belly and hot waves of something like shame blossoming everywhere else. She was not wrong. I had revealed it all the night my mother died, and so I could not deny it, though I wanted to. I wanted to say she was mistaken, that I would never betray the Way of our people. The Way which protected the rights—no, the very lives—of our women. Their rights to freedom, to choice. The Way which continued the line of the Great Mother and her wisdom from one generation to the next. I could say I did not want to betray anything, but I was very aware my own desires were flimsy against the will of the Fates. If the Oracle had spoken truly, Eri was not wrong, and there was nothing I could say in my own defense.

"If the story Ossy told is true," I said slowly, trying to order my thoughts in this onslaught of unexpected truths, "then the ha-mazaans themselves requested my mother's child be Ishassara. It had nothing to do with me." Then I looked at her sharply, some of the shame melting away. "What do you mean, your mother told you I should not be Ishassara?"

Eri's smile was tight and grim. "She knew as well as any of them, like Glaukia and Santo and Melo," she gestured to several ha-mazaans riding together farther ahead. Melo was back in camp. "My mother suggested long ago that we should choose another in your place. That the role of Defending Queen should go to the one who is best suited for the role. She suggested before our Trials that I challenge you. She gave me her axe and said if I defeated you, prevented you from graduating to Savaran, I could easily petition the queens and put my name forth for the role of Ishassara, though it had never been done before.

"I thought she was so foolish. I laughed at her, even, and told her you were my friend. But I thought about it, when we faced each other in the ring, because why shouldn't I? And now I wish I had tried harder, believed my mother, because now I know she was not so foolish."

I stared at my friend, or the person I had always thought was my friend, my mouth agape. She laughed, the sound brittle in the incongruously warm air. "You can pretend to be Ishassara, here in this strange land, Cyra, but there are many in Themiscyra and even with us now who will never follow you as queen. Not after everything. Especially not me. Do not expect *my* swearing stone in your hand at Alsanti."

Eri spurred her horse forward and cantered ahead of everyone, pulling in front of the wagons. I watched her go, horrified that the friendship we had nourished our entire lives was as the dust beneath her horse's feet. I thought back to Eri's face in the ring at our Trials. The animosity that had come as such a surprise. It was difficult to fathom that the one I had trusted so closely since I was a babe had meant to turn on me. Had already done so, though now she waited until Alsanti to make it official.

I thought of the man with green eyes, then. I thought of the Oracle's promise, or curse. I thought of my mother's last words to me.

It is only by following your heart that your true destiny will ever find you, daughter.

I wondered if I truly knew what my heart wanted. My destiny was finding me regardless of my wishes, and every step closer I came to fulfilling the Oracle's words, the people I loved fell away, as irrevocably as the dead fell from a spear to the heart.

CHAPTER 20

THE SOUND OF DAWN BREAKING

E ven with direction from the scouts, the women were not easy to find. There were no signs of smoke from their camp's fires, and even the horse tracks, or at least a great number of them, had been wiped from the dust of the road, except for the few sets of hoof-prints leading in both directions, clearly meant to throw off trackers. They had swept the dirt with fir boughs, making it difficult to find where their path left the road, and the grasses were further trampled on either side of the road to obscure their actual passage. If not for the cries of the eagle and the specific directions from the scouts, Col might have missed it.

It had been ten days since the ambush on the wagons, and the scouts had been sweeping the area on horse and foot for six days, mostly at Arpoxais' insistence. During the ceremonial burning of the dead—including the women's bodies—two nights before, the scouts returned with news. A small encampment, impossible to keep secret because of nearly fifty horses gathered among them, but hidden and well guarded nonetheless. It was more than half day's journey by horse to the west, they reported, with a long gully bordering the southeast side of the encampment. They observed a leggy red-haired one coming and going from the camp with a few others, sometimes on the back of a black horse, sometimes not, for several days in a row, while another equally tall black-haired one always left alone, and always to the same ravine. Most ventured in pairs or small groups to the northern meadow, where they made their horses do strange dances without bridle or lead. Every woman, in camp or beyond, was witnessed practicing with swords, lances, bows, and axes.

The scout's recollections had been tinged with fearful incredulity when they recounted their findings, while the whispers in Gelonia rose to a dull roar with the new information. The *Oirpata* are coming to find us and kill us all, some whispered. The Golden Axe has returned to us as promised, said others. All looked with renewed interest to the king, or more specifically, to his sons. Before, the Scoloti had accepted that only one of Targitaos' sons was destined by divine prophecy and the mother's Right of Choosing to inherit rulership of the clans. Now, they were less certain. Now, they were waiting to see if the Golden Axe was real. If it would choose for them, and perhaps choose differently than what had already been decided by the king's late wife.

"Surely you see that this would be the answer to your dilemma," Arpoxais had said in his usual forthright manner during the last meal the brothers had shared together. Col had raised his eyebrow, eyeing his older brother with wary skepticism.

"My dilemma?"

"We all know you never wanted it," Arpo said, leveling a challenging stare at Col, but there was no malice in his tone. There was no malice in his brother at all, but he was stubborn and consistent with his criticism of their mother's choice for king.

"It is not about what I want," Col retorted, setting his goblet of sana down with more force than necessary. His brothers never failed to ruffle his normally calm feathers, and this matter was especially irritating. "What's done is done, Arpo. Leave it alone."

"Is it done, though?" Lio put in from the other side of the fire. His eyes smirked at Col over the rim of his own goblet. "If the Golden Axe has finally come, the tribes in and outside of Gelonia will not think the matter so settled. And we all know Arpo is more skilled at matters of state than you, little brother. And at wielding a weapon. Despite how crafty you are with your hands." His smile at the end made Col grit his teeth, but he was used to their jabs by now.

"Like I said, if the Golden Axe has come, then you might once again have a choice, Col," Arpo said. "Isn't that what you would want? For the tribes to have the best king? The one who is truly destined for it, and not our mother's favorite?"

The words of his brothers had gone deeper than either of them would ever know. Col had agreed to be part of this ridiculous nonsense for the primary reason that, if he failed in convincing the people this was not the Golden Axe of their legends, he would never have the full support he would need from the majority, something he would desperately need to continue the peaceful relations amongst the tribes. But the secondary, more personal reason was to prove to himself that he was indeed his mother's best choice and that he would be a good ruler of the tribes, but that was a problem he did not think would be solved by finding a fancy weapon in the hands of an *Oirpata*.

He would admit he was curious as to who the women were and what they wanted, however. This curiosity, alongside the glimmer of silver eyes in his dreams, had driven his suggestion to Esten that they approach peacefully, giving no reason for anything to escalate beyond hopeful communication. If he could find out who they were and why they were here, perhaps it would be simple enough to rule out Arpoxais' wild theory. And if Arpo was right... Col was not sure what the consequences would be, but he would rather have the women's army on his side than have to convince, or even fight, his own brothers for a position his mother already covenanted to him.

Arpo and Lio had already skirted around the encampment, each with their own small contingent of men, and set up camp. Each brother, including Col, had brought enough soldiers that, if it became necessary, they could engage in a small skirmish with the *Oirpata* without too many lives lost, but not so large as to make it seem war was being declared outright. Col chose a spot to the east of the ravine to make his own encampment, and it was there he instructed the men to remain while he and Esten rode on unattended. Or, as Esten put it, "completely fucking vulnerable."

Col looked up into the sky where the golden eagle spun above them, then glanced over his shoulder at his friend, whose horse was keeping a respectable distance from Faelan's unpredictable hooves. The morning was bright, though not clear. There was a haze hanging high in the air from many hearth fires that had burned in the night to keep the chill of the autumn air at bay, and the smoke had nowhere to go. He gestured to Esten, signaling they should dismount and tie the horses. Col dropped Faelan's reins without tying them, but Esten wrapped the leathers of his stout bay around the branches of a pine sapling, fixing them in a knot. Col unbuckled his sword belt, laying it over Faelan's saddle, and motioned for Esten to do the same, ignoring the look of unrestrained incredulity on the man's face. Once Esten disarmed, thoroughly begrudging the process, they moved forward cautiously, mindful not to disturb fallen branches or rustle the drying grass underfoot. Above them, the eagle gave a soft, petulant sounding cry.

A hidden twig snapped under his foot, and Col froze, as did Esten beside him. Their eyes scanned the gully, then the opposite ridge, looking for signs of movement, but Col saw none. Again the eagle shrieked overhead, almost insistently. Slowly, he and Esten crept forward once more, both of them scanning the creek bed below and the ridge to the west and north for any signs of movement. The forest here was thicker, with dense trees of fir and beech, oak, and willow farther down the embankment where the water ran clear. The eagle screeched, low and soft. Col's eyes grew more intent and more cautious.

They were just nearing the inner edge of the trees when Esten stumbled slightly, his foot twisting as a rock moved under him. He sidestepped to catch his balance, and another twig snapped, shockingly loud in the stillness. Both froze. It was only because Col turned his head to throw his friend a scowl of irritation that he caught sight of a flash of blue.

He gripped Esten's arm in warning. Slowly, he pulled his friend backward a step, then down into a crouch. Staying low to the ground, he put his finger to his lips and pointed toward the north end of the ravine where he had seen the flash of color. Esten nodded, fretful hands reaching instinctively for a weapon that wasn't there. Warily, they made their awkward way, crouch-walking toward the north. The eagle's shadow swirled on the ground in front of them as they placed their steps with careful precision, moving as softly as the bird overhead. Col's eyes scanned every tree, looking up into the branches, and searched every bush, looking for shadows out of place. He was looking directly into such a shadow when an arrow buried itself into the slim trunk of the tree close beside him. Extremely close. Esten cursed and flattened himself to the ground. Col ducked down instinctively, but his eyes caught sight of the white feathers, still vibrating from the impact. He stood straight once more and scanned the forest, slowly raising his hands into the air. He saw nothing.

"We have no weapons!" he called, and at his feet, Esten hissed, not quietly,

"Are you *insane?*"

Col held his arms higher, far above his head.

"I come to speak with you!" he called, only his eyes moving in an effort to see her across the gully.

A second arrow split the first directly down the middle. It was a clear message that the initial strike had not been a mistake in missing him. A shiver moved down his spine. He swallowed.

"Tabiti help me," he muttered, but he kept his hands in the air, fingers splayed. "Stand up, Esten. They need to see we are unarmed."

"You *are* insane," Esten answered his own question in the same hissing whisper. "I am not standing to make myself a perfect target. Get *down!*"

"If they had wanted those arrows through either of us, they would be there," Col said with, he was proud to think, an admirably convincing show of conviction. "Stand up."

Slowly, extreme reluctance adding sluggishness to every movement and regret for being friends with an insane man etching deep lines into his face, Esten stood. He raised his hands into the air in an imitation of Col's stance, his eyes squinted almost shut, clearly expecting to be skewered by an arrow at any moment. They stood like that for ten breaths or more, with no movement of any kind from the forest ahead. A drop of nervous sweat trickled its way down his spine. He wondered if she had already crept behind and an arrow was about to plant itself between his shoulder blades so that he would have swan feathers for wings even as he drew his last breaths.

A dark blue shape emerged from the trees.

She held her strange curled bow far in front of her, just as he had seen her hold it on the horse. The string was drawn taut, ready to fire, and the sacred-swan fletching gleamed like snow between her fingers. She took another step, but sideways, her strangely covered legs moving like a cat's, with bare toes feeling the ground first before her heel placed with stealthy, steady precision. Her hair glistened wet in the dappled shadows under the trees. It was not wrapped in the braid he had seen her wear last time but spilled down over her shoulders and behind her in a black wave, like shadows falling at twilight. Even from a distance, he could see the distinctive markings on her arms and also the flint of her eyes as they stared into his. She looked deadly as a winter's storm come at the witching hour.

She looked magnificent.

"We come in peace," he called when his breath returned. He tried not to speak too loudly, lest she startle like a wild animal. That is what she seemed to him—a wild animal of the Old Country, from the mountain places where his grandmother had traveled from, bringing her stories of fae folk, and djinn, and animals which could speak in the tongues of man. Animals which could take the shapes of men. Or women.

She stared at him, her arrow pointed squarely at his heart.

"Taksulya?" the wild creature spoke abruptly, sounding puzzled but not hostile. Not exactly.

Col studied her. He did not understand the word she had said, though it had been a questioning tone. It had almost sounded like his own word for peace. He repeated it.

"Peace. Yes. We are unarmed. No weapons. I just want to speak with you."

She stared stonily, unblinking, and took another sideways step, one long leg crossing behind the other and the top of her body swaying slightly to the side like a willow branch moving in the wind. Graceful, lithe, supple. Wild.

"Taksuliya," she said, her mouth turning down in a frown, a detectable skepticism tinging her voice. She continued to stare, and he met her eyes calmly, resolutely. Without looking away from her face, he said to Esten,

"I am going to remove my vest and tunic and show her I have no weapons. That I am not a threat."

"You've got to be fucking with me," Esten said flatly, but Col's hands were already moving to the laces at his vest. He loosened them and shrugged the hardened leather from his shoulders. It dropped to the ground with a thud. She did not lower her bow. His fingers went to the laces at his throat, untying them enough so he could get the tunic over his head. A flicker of surprise crossed her face, but he definitely noticed the string of her bow pull tighter, so he took a deep breath and continued, pulling the tunic over his head and tossing it aside, while praying that the ancestors in those swan feathers would have mercy on him, and redirect her arrows. He wore only the short leather loincloth and boots now, but he didn't think she would appreciate it if he stripped fully nude. The wind was a welcome chill on the nervous sweat gathering on his back. Behind him, Esten's breath squeaked from his lungs in a strangled, wordless expression of either disapproval or shock. Probably both. But the woman simply stared. She did not loose her arrow.

"Strip," Col ordered his friend, increasing conviction adding authority to his command. Every moment she did not let that arrow fly was another in his favor. He had not felt this determined since spotting young Faelan, frolicking wild and untamed on the plains, and knowing the horse would one day carry him across the plains. He would approach this woman the same way, without guile or violence. It was the only way to approach something wild. Let it know it could remain that way. Unharmed. Free.

Esten stripped his tunic and tossed it aside, muttering something about "cursed company" and "well-deserved" and "fucking loyalty" and "sana," which was the strong drink he preferred over wine. Col ignored him and kept his eyes fixed on the woman.

Her bow moved, and his heart tried to jump into his throat as though to hide itself from an incoming arrowhead. But the tip of her arrow only jabbed pointedly at the boots he wore, then moved back to his chest. Col nodded his understanding, feeling far more pleased than the situation warranted.

"Boots too," he said eagerly.

"Colax—" Esten began, but Col was already balancing on one foot, pulling the soft leather loose from his leg and tossing the boot behind him. He took the short dagger from the second boot and tossed it away behind him, far from his reach, before taking that boot off too. He thought he saw her shoulders relax slightly, but he could not be sure.

"I cannot believe I let you talk me into this, Colaxais son of Targitaos, bane of my existence." Esten sounded genuinely disturbed. "If I had known you wanted to strip in the forest for an *Oirpata* she-panther, I would have stayed behind with the cavalry. Or joined one of your brothers on the hunt for them!" he exclaimed. "I would expect Lio to strut naked in front of them since the man will fuck anything that moves. And I can guarantee Arpo is not foolish enough to approach them unarmed. *He* at least has the sense Tabiti gave him. Clearly, I chose the wrong brother. Blackened tits of Tabiti, you are—"

"Just take your boots off, Esten. She isn't going to shoot you if she hasn't already." Col smiled, placing a hand to his chest, and called to the woman again, while Esten huffed and tugged off his boots, muttering.

"My name is Col," he said, tapping his chest. "Col."

This time, he read her confusion clearly. He thumped his bare chest. "Col." Then he held out the same hand to point at her, raising his eyebrows. "Your name?"

"Col?" she repeated doubtfully, and the name sounded round and lovely on her lips.

"Yes!" he nodded, patting his chest again. "Col. And you?"

White teeth flashed as she chewed her bottom lip. At that moment, she appeared much younger than her previously fierce expression had led him to believe. He thought of the bodies they had burned alongside their men, one of whom had seemed extremely young to be using the spear she had died holding, even if she hadn't been a woman. The other had been older, although it was hard to tell by how much. Her skin had been dark and unlined, but age was there in her features just the same. This one appeared younger than both, though—

"Cyra," she spoke hesitantly, but it was not a question.

Col smiled triumphantly. He turned to Esten and slapped the shorter man's chest with enthusiasm, ignoring his startled grunt. "Esten," he called to her. "Col. Esten. Cyra." He pointed to each person as he said their names. She shifted from one foot to another.

Slowly, her voice clear and firm, she repeated both of their names and looked them in the eye.

Col felt a wave of triumph wash over him, and he smiled wider. He watched her scan the rest of the forest, looking again for more men, and breathed a sigh of relief that he had only brought Esten today. His confidence as high as the sun, Col stepped forward. He had not quite planted his foot back on solid ground when the arrow planted itself between his feet.

"Fuck," Esten said.

Col did not see her draw another arrow, but a fresh one was already nocked and pointed squarely at his heart when he looked up from the one between his legs. Slowly, he held his hands out to his sides and took another agonizingly slow step forward, meeting her eyes. Her bow remained taught, but the arrow did not fly.

Col began moving down the steep slope toward one of the large boulders wedged into the bank of the ravine. He glanced up from his feet every few steps and spoke to her while he walked, knowing she could not understand him, but hoping it would soothe her, as it would a spooked horse. He spoke of the sunlight, and the fine day, and his intentions for peace, though the words did not matter. Her light eyes watched him, wary and sharp, and the bow followed his every step, until finally, he sat on the end of a rock outcropping. It was not as comfortable as he might have liked to look up at her rather than across, but it seemed less arduous than shouting at her from so far away.

Though he wished she might come closer, or put down her bow, she did not move. With a glance back at Esten, who was standing awkwardly in just his loincloth at the top of the bank, arms akimbo, Col tried to think of more words they could share other than names. He was just about to point to the thin stream of water running in the gully when she laughed, clear and bright and strong, the sound of it echoing in the narrow gully.

The breath caught in his throat, and he looked up at her in wonder. If ever he had believed in fae creatures of the forest, it was now. There was a sound in her laugh that he had never heard in the voice of a woman before. It sounded like the cry of the eagle above him, but not shrill. Free and fierce. It sounded like lightning might, if it had a sound. It sounded like the dawn breaking. He looked at her, and something in him knew a truth in a way he had never known anything before.

The words he said then came from the deepest part of his soul, as though pulled from within by an outside force rather than of his own choosing. He meant every one of them. She stopped laughing, though a smile played at her lips and her glinting, silver eyes, bright and mysterious as the moon, studied him as a cat might look at its prey. He said the words again, as though to make them true, and help her know them, and believe them.

She whistled abruptly, loud and clear and sharp, piercing as the eagle's cry. She watched him even as she sounded it through her teeth, and he stood quickly, eyeing the top of the ridge uneasily. It was entirely likely he was about to have fifty bows drawn on him rather than one. She smirked down at him, and he cursed softly, turning to clamber back up the bank to where Esten was frantically gathering up his tunic and boots, putting them on in a frenzied rush. Col was just yanking his second boot on when he heard the unmistakable sound of swiftly pounding hooves. He was ready to follow in Esten's footsteps and duck behind a too-thin tree for cover when a grey horse emerged from the trees at the far end of the western bank.

The woman, Cyra, whistled again, and the horse trotted with long strides toward her. Col stepped forward again, shrugging the heavy leather vest over his shoulders as he watched.

"Let's get out of here, Col. Now," Esten begged.

"Yes," Col murmured, taking another step forward to have a better view. He tied the laces of his vest distractedly as the horse reached the woman. She finally lowered the bow, loosening the string slightly, but she did not un-nock the arrow. Instead, she tapped the horse's shoulder with the back of her hand, and it promptly bowed in front of her, tucking its nose between one extended foreleg and kneeling on the other knee. She stepped delicately over the horse's withers, and it rose, turning its head to stare curiously directly at him. Cyra held her bow low to the side and nodded to Col slightly as though saying goodbye. The horse was without reins of any kind, and yet it backed into the trees as carefully as though she was guiding it with her hands.

"Wait!" Col shouted. The horse paused in its steps, but again he saw no movement that would have caused it to halt so quickly. "Come back tomorrow!" He pointed up at the sun in the sky, then down to where he stood. Then he whistled a shrill sound of his own.

The eagle appeared within seconds of his call, diving from the smoke-hazed sky. He held his arm up, great talons wrapping around the leather padding sewn to his sleeve. *Both of us can have our tricks*, he thought, satisfied with her startled reaction. He pointed at the sun again, and back to his feet, but before he could make her understand his intent, the shrill sound of a horn echoed from the direction of the women's camp. A warning, without a doubt. The women knew they were surrounded.

Woman and horse wheeled away as though one being and disappeared into the forest in a thunder of hooves and a stream of unbound hair as glistening black as a stryx's belly.

CHAPTER 21

WARMED MEAD ON A COLD DAY

We broke camp the morning after the ambush against the men at the crossroads and retraced our steps north with the pillaged wagons. The wagons were a greater boon than we had hoped for; though they had no wool, they were full of various brightly dyed and delicate silks, much like the ones the traders brought to Themiscyra from the Indus Valley. From these, we made new tunics, though they were rather richly-colored and stood out against the landscape like the peacock bird of many colors Camilla's mother, herself from the Indus region, often told us about. With our leather armor and woolen trousers, however, it was only a small worry for camouflage, which we gladly traded for the sake of luxurious comfort against the skin.

The wagons were also full of fresh grain, from which we made hardtack and flatbread. There were jars of rich olive oil, the same design as the ones left over from the Achaean ship's galley, marking them as a product of the western isles. These raised our suspicions and our hackles as, once we found them, we feared stumbling across Achaeans trading their distinctive wares around every bend in the road, but finally, the ha-mazaans agreed the goods had more than likely been traded somewhere along the same coast we had been shipwrecked upon. This led to a contentious debate, which was never settled to anyone's satisfaction, as to whether using the treasure buried back on the beach to buy passage upon a ship, along with enough men to sail it back to Themiscyra, might be possible. Most agreed this would be too risky, and place us in the same danger we actively tried to avoid—being in close and inescapable quarters with a contingent of men.

In the wagons, we also found an odd wooden chair with four rolling wheels, beautifully carved with deer and bees along the back of it, and several wooden boxes of beeswax, both raw chunks and finely crafted candles. Perhaps to our greatest delight, the wagons were also full of wine, and we were in no way hesitant to drink our fill.

Despite the heaviness of my heart from Eri's earlier confession, the evening after the wagon raid, I drank wine and laughed and danced to the drums with the rest of the ha-mazaans, whooping and stomping with wild abandon around our great fire. We danced for Kubileya, and pounded our spears, and told stories, drinking well into the night. We mourned the loss of two more brave warriors in this way, and, though it had been but an echo of what might happen in our Moon Hall at home, the ritual was a balm to our soul after so many nights of simply surviving in this unknown wilderness.

Now, as our growing caravan of horses, ha-mazaans, and three wagons moved closer to the crossroads we had assailed the previous day, I felt the cumbrous weight of being Ishassara upon me once again. Flickers of the man's green eyes danced in my mind, setting me further on edge. I felt raw and exposed, perhaps because of the night's revelry and the aftereffects of sweet wine, but perhaps also because of the discomfort in my spirit, as though it were a wild horse lassoed by some unknown force, and that noose was tightening every day, dragging me forward toward a fate I wanted no part in.

I no longer thought the Oracle a liar. She had spoken truly, and now it felt futile to fight against the inevitable. The noose would simply tighten, and whichever Fate held the end of the rope would haul me forward whether I went willingly, or whether She must drag me.

When we left camp, the tug of that rope was exactly what I felt when I rode Inara into the crossroads. The physical crossroads mirrored itself inside of me, with the responsibility of choosing one direction or another simultaneously weighing me down and radiating a forceful pressure from the inside out until I felt I might be crushed from every direction. And yet, I felt a tug of that fateful rope, just there beneath my breastbone. Following the rope seemed to be the only way to ease that pressure.

"That way." I pointed to the northeast.

Alkippe eyed the ground from the back of her red roan. "It looks like the herd of deer went that way. Where the deer went, so did the men."

"It also looks like there's forest that way," I said, looking north to a thin line of treetops barely visible in the distance. "Or at least, a bigger stand than we've run across so far. We will take our chances for better shelter." *And I will surely meet my destiny, and be done with it, and with this cruel game,* I thought.

"Utter foolishness," Eri said harshly, moving her horse to the front of the line. Apparently, her confession from the previous day had lent courage to her opposition of my every suggestion. It did not help that she was absolutely right.

"If we go that way, we almost certainly end up in the midst of those men. We might as well hand them the wagons and a few extra horses when we get there!" Her scoffing did nothing to ease the pressure suffocating my lungs. I chose for more than my own life, I knew, and every ha-mazaan would suffer if I chose poorly.

"Aye, Eri speaks wisely." This time, it was Glaukia. The tall ha-mazaan, a few years older than my mother had been, spurred her horse forward. Her blue-grey eyes met mine with quiet defiance. "If we go east, we enter the griffin's nest, one way or another. But if we follow the western road, we head toward our home. Our families."

Glaukia and I stared at each other for several breaths, the tension transferring from our bodies to our horses so that they fretted and jostled on the road with barely restrained agitation. Glaukia looked away first, a slight redness staining her throat and then her cheeks under my resolute gaze. The lasso tightened, choking me until I grew angry and reckless.

"For now, we go east," I grit out. "Any ha-mazaans who wish to go west today, and therefore actively chooses not to follow me as Ishassara, may have the horse they ride, the weapon they carry, and a skin of wine for the road, but no more," I said, unrelenting. "All who follow me east will remain loyal to me, until the day of Alsanti, under the pain of death. At that time, each of you may choose whether I am your queen or not, as is the Way set for us by Themis and Matar Kubileya. Am I understood?"

I did not give them the chance to voice their dissent or agreement before I nudged Inara into a trot, then a swift canter, heading down the eastward road. Hoofbeats followed immediately, and then the squeak of poorly constructed wheels, but I did not turn my head to see who followed or who did not.

When we made camp just after midday, near a ravine and a small stream that ran through it, every ha-mazaan was there, even Eri. True, she had not faced much of a choice. Fierce as they were, three or four ha-mazaans who disliked my decision would be no match for the elements, or the savages, or the thousands of leagues between where we were and home. It was a bitter, heavy-handed victory, and I knew it had come at a cost I would pay for later. I hoped it would be at a time when the price did not cost me everything I had left.

"It is a foolish, headstrong thing to have done, Cyra," Ossy said later, and, though she kept her voice low so that no others overheard, her censure stung all the more for its accuracy. We sat together under the awning of hides and fir branches, each twisting scraps of deer hide into braids we would use for bridles or bindings. "Would you like to tell me why we are in this forest, a day closer to whatever trouble we found yesterday, and at least three ha-mazaans less of a loyal contingent?"

I looked to where Glaukia, Eri, and Melo sat by a fire with a few other women. Ossy looked as well and nodded.

"Aye, they are here with their bodies," she continued, "but I can tell you for certain their hearts are no longer with you." When she turned her gaze back to mine, it was with a searching intensity. I returned her stare with a stern look of my own, my agitated hands twisting pieces of the hide over and under, over and under.

"I think you knew very well what they thought about my mother," I said. "And so I think you also know that I didn't have a choice. Their hearts haven't been with me for some time." I tried to keep the bitterness of betrayal from my voice, but was unsuccessful. "It was either call them out or wait for them to declare a mutiny at a worse time. Something like that could cost a ha-mazaan their life."

I did not look away, and Ossy shook her head slowly before a slight smile touched her lips. Her eyes grew wistful. "You are more like your mother every day," she said quietly, her hands stilling for a moment in her lap. "Especially when your eyes go dark and angry. Sometimes I wonder if Melanippe's furious stare killed that griffin rather than her arrows."

I was startled out of my grim countenance enough to bark a laugh at the scene Ossy painted. Ossy shook her head again. "Either way, you have your mother's strength, and her wisdom, for all that you are rash. But, I do wonder what made you decide to go east," she finished, taking up her length of leather braid and continuing to twist.

"We needed better shelter," I hedged, eyes on the work in front of me. It was not a lie.

"Mmmm, yes," Ossy agreed, too easily.

Our fingers twisted and turned as we fell silent, and finally, I tied the end of my four strands in a knot, pulling it tight so that it would not loosen. I swallowed heavily before saying, "The man on the chestnut horse with white socks. The man with red hair."

Ossy looked at me expectantly, as though she had been waiting for me to say exactly that. "Yes?" she urged.

I frowned at her, suspicious. She stared back with guileless golden eyes.

"I need to meet him," I said finally, unwilling to say more yet. I could trust Ossy with my life, I knew. But until I understood what was going on, until I felt I had some semblance of control over my life and the lives of the women I was supposed to be leading, there were some things I needed to keep to myself. Such as the fact that I had seen his face before, in a fire.

Ossy nodded again and said nothing. For the first time in my life, I wondered what prophecy my goddess-mother had been given and what things she kept from me. We all had our secrets, it seemed.

☽ ☾

I lay on a wide, warm rock, letting the sun dry my bare skin and wet hair after a swim in the frigid stream. My woolen trousers, itchy and uncomfortable at the best of times, were stretched out underneath me with the sleeveless blue silk tunic on top, a semi-soft blanket between my skin and the hard surface of stone. I watched an eagle, magnificent against the hazy sky, circle above. Every so often, it gave a lazy, petulant screech, as though annoyed it could not find a mouse or a hare big enough to bother diving from such a great height.

Inara and I had worked hard this morning, as we did every morning, and it felt good to lie back and let the increasingly sporadic warmth of the sun heat my tired body. I wondered how much longer the sun would provide such comfort and how much longer the nights would be bearable with just a fire and our wool and furs to keep us warm. There had been many discussions in the past few days about building a more permanent shelter and how to go about it. Whether we should rely on what we had already constructed, which were simple conical huts of wooden poles covered with the thick deer hides, with a chimney hole at the top for fires in the center. These would be fine if the winters grew no colder than in Themiscyra, where it simply rained day and night for three months. But we were farther north now, and none of us knew exactly *how* far north. Alkippe had suggested we prepare for worsening cold by digging into the earth, and burrow into the Great Mother's bosom like foxes for the winter. Neither of these options, building or burrowing, suited me. But we did not have many options, and every day the sun set and rose again, granting less daylight and even less warmth, the fewer options we would have.

A crackling in the distance made me raise my head from its hard pillow. I had left Inara in the camp, preferring to stretch my legs in a short walk after all the riding I had been doing. I lay at the far northern end of the ravine, where the creek trickled downward and into the rocks and crags below, and my rock bed was low to the ground and surrounded by tall grass, so I could not see much of anything when I raised my head. I heard nothing more, though, other than the eagle screeching insistently overhead. I sat up, peering around at the sun-dappled landscape. No deer, or horse, or other ha-mazaans wandering in search of a bath. I looked for several minutes but saw nothing, although the southernmost part of the gully was obscured by trees. Most likely, it had been a deer wandering in the brush. But the hairs on the back of my neck stood on end when the eagle screeched again, soft and quiet.

Without standing, I pulled my newly stitched blue tunic over my head, then the scaled vest over that. I tightened the buckles and laces and slung my belt over my shoulder and hips. I tugged the trousers over my legs, the wool scratchy against my still-damp skin. Perhaps we should abduct another wagon full of silks, I mused, so that we could make a second pair of trousers to wear underneath the woolen ones. I smiled, pleased with the idea, and bent down to pick up my bow.

A twig snapped. I froze.

I listened for a long, still moment, moving only my eyes to scan the land, the sky, the forest. I stayed crouched low and nocked an arrow, keeping the white feathers of the fletching loose and supple between my fingers. I saw nothing. There was no movement other than the bird above me. That was the problem, I realized. Every day when I came here, the birds from the far end of the ravine were usually kicking up a racket. Today, they were quiet and still, as though they mimicked me holding my breath. I moved backward, still crouching low to the ground. When the gully bottom was no longer in my sights, I moved more quickly to my left, keeping the far southern ridge of the gully in my sights. I was almost as far as I could go before the trees would thin too much to keep proper cover when I saw him.

He was attempting to hide, but his hair shone such a brilliant red against the shaded green of the trees that he might as well have been waving a firebrand beside his head. Beside him cowered a shorter man with yellow hair and a ridiculously long beard. I was fairly sure I had put an arrow through that one already. They shuffled upright again, creeping in my direction. My eyes slid back to the red-haired one. My chest squeezed slightly with the familiar knot of anxiety that had become the constant, unwelcome companion to my thoughts and memories of this man's all-too-familiar face. It was only the second time seeing that face in the flesh, but it was unmistakably him.

I should have turned back the way I had come. Disappeared without a trace into the forest, returned to the camp, and rounded up every hamazaan to join me in riding the men down and trampling them beneath our horse's hooves. I should have whistled and brought Inara to me and ridden them down myself. I did neither of these things. Instead, I heard the rustle of the leaves overhead and thought of my mother. My lips compressed into a hard, tight line. I pulled the arrow back, sighting along it just as I had in the crossroads, now ten days ago.

The arrow lodged in the trunk of the thin tree between the two men, but the blonde one fell to the ground as though hit. The red one flinched but stayed standing, his body going still and his eyes scanning the very ridge I stood on to see where my arrow had flown from. His eyes passed over me twice, and the second time I had to pause in the act of drawing another arrow from my quiver, lest he catch the movement. Then, slowly, he raised empty hands high into the air and called out across the gully.

"Weje ne ghuisos," he said, speaking gibberish. "Eg oano garsiyo!"

I loosed the second arrow and bared my teeth with wolfish pleasure when it split the first one down the middle. The flame-haired man's eyes were all that moved to look at it. His hands moved higher into the air. His lips moved, and something hissed from the man on the ground. The red one spoke again, not looking away from the ridge I hid on, but he was too quiet for me to hear any words. The blonde man slowly, painfully slowly, climbed to his feet and raised his own empty hands in the air. *What are they playing at?* I frowned and readied another arrow, my movements slow and measured so as not to catch the eye.

They stood still as the trees. I watched them for several wary moments, considering. I saw no swords or spears, axes or bows, and had not seen them lay one down within many steps of where they stood. They appeared unarmed, other than whatever knives might be hidden in belts or boots. When they made no move toward me, or to lower their hands, I took a deep breath and swore.

"Kubileya curse me for a fool."

I stepped out from the edge of the forest.

My bow drawn and ready, I aimed at the man's heart, but his hands did not move downward when he saw me. He stared, and I stared back. The familiar features of his face were open to my gaze, and the lines of his body, less familiar, showed me that he was strong and healthy and accustomed to being outside in the sun. His skin was not pale like Eri's, though they shared the same color hair, but rather dun, though not as dark as my own. His shoulders were broad and his chest strong, but he was not bullish like the Achaean sailors. His legs were too long for that, his hips lean and square in such an unfamiliar way compared to a woman's body. He was dressed in wool and leather, the former a deep green that matched the shadows in the forest. *He should shave his head,* I thought nonsensically. *That way, he might not stick out like a blazing bonfire when he's trying to hide.*

"Weje cemyen taksudya!" he called out, catching me off guard and snapping my attention away from his body and back to the situation. His voice was rich and smooth, like warmed mead on a cold day. I did not know the language, but one word sounded...familiar.

"Peace?" I said the last word back to him, almost as a reflex, uncertain if I had heard him correctly.

He nodded and said the word again, along with the rest of the gibberish. I frowned more deeply, unsure of what he was up to.

"Peace," I repeated dubiously.

We stared at each other a few more breaths, and the yellow-haired man said something, his eyes darting at me and then away, as though the sight of me burned his eyes. The red man called out more nonsensical words. His hand went to the laces on his tunic. My breath stilled, and I pulled the string of my bow completely taut with a low creak of sinew and wood. His fingers threaded through the laces on his chest, pulling at them to loosen as though he would draw a knife from within the folds.

Should I loose an arrow and run, or run and save my arrow?

It was absurd to think he could throw a knife at me from this distance. It had been foolish to engage with him at all, or give away my position, and if I did not leave now, there would be consequences I, and the rest of the ha-mazaans, would not like. And yet, my feet rooted to the ground like any tree, and the arrow languished between my fingers.

The man lifted his tunic over his head in one smooth motion and tossed it to the ground. He stepped forward one step, bare-chested, arms splayed wide to the side now rather than above his head. There was a slim bandage tied around his arm, where my arrow had drawn blood over a week ago. It was in the same place my own arm healed from the arrow I took while stealing Inara.

Even from this distance, I heard the yellow-haired man groan, long and anguished. Then he, too, began removing his tunic. Astonished, I watched as both of them stepped away from their clothes, only a thick loincloth of soft leather wrapped around their hips and their tall boots covering their legs. I considered the red-haired man, whose gaze did not falter, although his expression was difficult to read from this far away. A flush crept over my chest and up my neck until it tinged my face with hot, prickling points of... of I didn't know what. I tried to push the distracting feeling aside and ground myself. I shifted my arrow down in a quick, commanding gesture to his boots before re-centering it on his heart.

He nodded, and without looking away, reached both hands down to hold the foot of his boot and slowly slide the length of it off. The second boot he slid a dagger I had suspected was there from its sheath, but he tossed it far behind him before removing the boot.

The yellow-haired man shook his head, muttering. The tall one answered without looking away from me, his arms down at his sides now, his shoulders squared confidently, and his hands relaxed, as though it was as normal as the sun setting in the west to stand naked in the woods with an arrow pointed at your heart. The leaves above my head stirred and rustled, the breeze lifting a piece of my still-damp hair and floating it across my face. I thought I could hear my mother laughing. The red man raised a hand to his chest.

"Maj lamman Col," he tapped his chest. "Col." He thumped his chest again. Then he held out a hand and said, "Vaz lamman?"

I frowned.

"Col?" I repeated stupidly. This entire situation had turned into something much different than I expected when I had sent that first arrow.

The man nodded, excitement brightening his face so that his green eyes sparkled ridiculously bright, even from a distance. He tapped his chest once more, said "Col" again, and once more extended his hands, repeating the other words. He was asking for my name. I bit my lip, thoroughly confused and uncertain. Not about what he was asking. Just why.

"Cyra," I said tentatively, and immediately felt foolish. I scowled to quell the feeling.

He smiled, teeth flashing, but not at all like a wolf. It was a genuine, sunny smile. It reminded me of Ossy's obnoxiously cheery morning face, which I was constantly irritated by. Then he turned and smacked the yellow-haired man's chest, the sound reverberating into the gully, and called,

"Esten!" He tapped his own chest, then his companion's again. "Col. Esten. Cyra." He nodded excitedly as he pointed back to me. It was strange to hear my name on his lips.

I shifted my feet, realizing I was still poised to flee, automatically repeating the names back to him. He smiled again, somehow even wider so that a dimple flashed. I scanned the forest instead of his distracting face, wary that he seemed so at ease while unarmed, with an arrow pointed at his heart. I didn't know when his other men would arrive, but surely he would not be so naive as to approach with such confidence if other armed men were not hiding nearby.

He stepped forward. I planted my arrow between his feet before his foot touched down. He froze. I had already nocked another before he splayed his hands out to the sides and met my gaze with calm resolve. He stepped forward again, more slowly, and began descending the steep side of the ravine. For some reason, I let him, though my breath felt tight in my chest, and my arrow followed his heart the entire way down. He simply chattered unintelligibly until he had made his way to a crumbly-looking outcrop of rock, which he sat on. Once he was still, my breathing eased, but the flush in my skin had deepened, and my heart pounded in my ears. The second man, Esten, stayed where he was, nervously hopping from foot to foot in his loincloth.

A wave of something close to hysteria rolled through me. This was without a doubt one of the most absurd situations I had ever found myself in. Two men, both of whom only ten days ago had been close to dying by my own hands, were almost completely naked, dancing around in a gully and chattering at me in some foreign tongue. And one of them was as familiar to me as the rhythm of my moon-blood, for I had thought of his face every time I bled. Thought of how it smiled at me from the flames of the Oracle's cauldron. Thought of our marking on his chest, which he clearly did not have. I never could have imagined that this was the full picture of that flaming prophecy.

It was too ridiculous. I laughed at the absurdity of it, and even as the unexpected sound sprang from my lips, the tension eased from my body. Some inner coiling behind my breastbone smoothed itself, untangling the prickling vines of anxiety that had been curling and rooting there for weeks. Perhaps years.

The red man said something when I quieted, gazing at me with an earnestness in his green eyes that caught me off guard. He repeated the words when I didn't respond. Something about the way he was saying it made the flush travel through my body again, tingling in my womb and back. I could almost understand him and knew he was desperate for me to listen, but the way he said the words made the heated flush prickle at my skin.

I didn't like it.

I set my teeth together and whistled for Inara, loud and shrill in the quiet air. I hoped I wasn't about to make a fool of myself by making the call only to have nothing answer it; I had not practiced with the mare from this distance, but I did not relish walking out of this situation by trying to pick my way backward through the brush. I did not trust that I would not trip on my own feet and humiliate myself in front of both of them.

The whistle had barely ended when Col, his face comically chagrined, scurried up the side of the gully and began putting his clothes back on, alongside Esten, who was much faster and more determined about the process. I watched the red man's muscles ripple, strong and lean across his back as he pulled on his boots. He was not uncomfortable on the eyes, that much was certain. The prickling sensation intensified, but I could not look away. When Inara came through the trees, pulling my attention away, I was almost disappointed. I whistled again, and she moved toward me with quick, smooth steps along the ridge opposite the men.

They had finished dressing and were about to disappear into the trees, but the red man stopped as Inara's nose touched my arm. He stepped out of the shadows again. I will admit to showing off slightly when I made Inara kneel so I could mount, but it was also the most practical solution, as I did not want to un-nock my arrow. As soon as she stood, I looked to the man, our eyes meeting for a long moment. I would have preferred the feeling of the noose tightening on my spirit, but all I felt was a further unraveling, a loosening deep inside. It was terrifying, and exhilarating, and strange. I knew with that quiet knowing deep in my womb that this would not be the last time we met.

I motioned with my seat for Inara to back up, but the man shouted again across the gully, pointing first at the sun, then at his feet. I paused, wondering at his meaning, but then he whistled, very much like I had done moments earlier.

A shadow moved across the gully. I reacted immediately with my bow, and then, genuinely surprised at what I saw, lowered it again. The eagle that had been circling folded its wings and dove straight toward him. It pulled up in a grand display of wings, longer than Inara's entire body from head to tail, and alighted on the leathered arm the man held out. I gaped. The man grinned. Then he pointed toward the sun again and back at his feet, repeating the same words.

The brazen, urgent call of Alkippe's horn shook me from my dazed gaping. I whirled Inara away, breaking eye contact but not the feeling deep inside of me, like a knot had just been tied in the tapestry of my Fate.

CHAPTER 22

SHADOWED WATER

Both of his brothers set up camp to hem the women in, Arpo to the west and Lio to the north, expecting Col to move his men closer from the south, but instead, he kept them at a distance and returned to the ravine the next day on his own. He went when the sun was in exactly the same position in the sky, hoping she had interpreted his message. It was naively, desperately hopeful to think she would want to meet again, especially after being well aware their camp was surrounded, and so he was disappointed but not surprised when she did not make an appearance. Still, he returned alone a second day, and a third. Each time, the small valley was empty, and though he searched with caution each time, he did not feel the prickle on the back of his neck that told him he was watched. Even the eagle above was quiet. He considered simply crossing the ravine and walking into their encampment, but reason decided against venturing straight into a viper's nest. The only thing that gave him some small hope was the fact that the gifts he had brought each day were gone by the next.

He climbed down to the rock just as he had the two days before and laid his offering there. He was not sure Cyra was the one finding them, but he could only assume that either the gifts or the message of them would find its way back to her eventually. Disappointed nevertheless, he left the day's offering and made his way back through the forest to where Esten waited with the horses.

"Back again so soon?" Esten said, sounding both irritated and aggrieved as he mounted his horse. "I was hoping this day to finally be rid of you, preferably by the she-cat's hand. Alas, Tabiti is not with me."

"I thank the flames she is not," Col grinned, scooping the reins from the ground and swinging easily onto Faelan's tall back. The horse pranced with energy, hoping they might race the wind this morning, but Col turned him back toward their camp and set a leisurely pace. Faelan's ears pressed flat against his neck, his tense body radiating displeasure with every plodding step. Esten followed dutifully behind for a few moments before finally asking, his voice thick with unconcealed frustration,

"*Well?* Are you going to share what has taken over that fire-singed mind of yours? What are we doing, Col?" Esten's exasperation had been simmering for days, and it finally spilled over. "We should either capture them or leave them to your brothers. You said yourself you don't believe the Golden Axe nonsense."

Col frowned, reining Faelen in as the stallion attempted to break into a run. "I don't like the idea of either of my brothers getting their hands on an entire tribe of *Oirpata*," he said finally.

"You heard for yourself from the scout last night that Arpo has gotten more than just his hands on one of them. If he's to be believed, that is. And why the *Oirpata* did not kill him is a bigger question. Makes me doubt his story tenfold. But then, she did not kill you..." Esten frowned in frustrated confusion.

"Arpoxais is simply trying to win at a game no one else is playing," Col said easily, ignoring the last part.

"No, *you* are not playing a game that *everyone* else is very committed to," Esten said bluntly. "Lio and Arpo are definitely playing, perhaps against each other, but most definitely against you. So if you don't think these *Oirpata* are actually the Golden Axe, and your claim to the throne is safe, then I ask you again, what in Tabiti's blackened knees are we doing here?"

There was a long pause, and Col shifted in his saddle, gathering the reins more tightly as Faelan reared slightly and tossed his head in anger. "I feel a pull toward her," he finally confessed, more honestly than he had intended. But this was Esten, his friend since childhood. One of the few friends who had not betrayed him and left to make new tribes with his brothers once the line of kingship had been declared. After several days of twisting it around in his own heart and trying to make sense of it, maybe talking about it out loud could help. "It feels...it feels as though some unseen thread connects us, and I am simply obeying its draw."

He considered the truth of this even as Esten snorted with annoyance and muttered curses to himself. Col felt a deep admiration for the extraordinary woman, Cyra, that went beyond the twilight of her hair or the mounds of her olive-tinged cheekbones. She was beautiful, yes, in a striking, utterly foreign, mysterious way. A dangerous beauty, like that of a panther or wild horse. That wildness was exactly what he admired. The way her spirit shone from her eyes. The way her chin tilted up with defiance, her shoulders stiff with pride. The way her arrow had quivered with deliberate power when it struck the tree. She was deadly, without a doubt, but she had spared his life for a reason. He thought she might feel it, too. That thread that connected them. Only, she had not returned to the ravine, and now he was beginning to doubt she had felt anything similar at all.

"She's a she-cat and will rip your throat with her claws the moment your eyes are turned," Esten was saying. "We should be returning to Gelonia. We should be bringing enough troops to round them up like your father wants to do. We *should* be acting like sane men, but we aren't, and why I am still here with you three days into this madness is far beyond me." Esten moved his wounded shoulder back and forth in an uneasy fidget that made it clear he had already suffered at the *Oirpata's* hands and wasn't keen on repeating the experience.

Col smiled easily, though Esten was becoming increasingly agitated.

"You remain with me because you are the best of friends, and I am glad of it," he said. Esten snorted again, muttering something unintelligible.

They rode in silence once more, but Faelan still pulled at the bit, eager to stretch his legs. They were far enough away now, and the forest thick enough in these parts, that the sound of hooves would not echo back to the encampment, so Col gave him his head and clicked his tongue. He shouted back at Esten to follow as the tall chestnut leaped into a gallop, and the wind caught in red hair on both horse and man. They had not gone no more than ten strides when Esten shouted in alarm from behind. Col twisted to look and immediately drew Faelan to a rearing halt, spinning the horse in a tight turn and drawing his sword. Even as he charged, he knew it was futile.

Six horses quickly surrounded Esten, and glittering spear-points held him in place from every direction. Several more horses and riders intercepted him and his friend, and in the lead, a grey horse, dark and dappled like shadowed water in a stream, bearing a black-haired woman. Cyra. The arrow in her bow fixed on him with steady, practiced aim, even though the horse danced like rain under her, the reins completely free on its neck. He reined Faelen to a stop far closer to her than was wise, but she did not move back nor, more importantly, shoot him. Her arrow motioned to his sword even as she spoke words he did not understand. There was nothing to misunderstand in her tone, however. It was one of command and easy authority. He tossed the sword to the ground as more women on horses circled around him. Her head twitched backward, toward Esten, her eyes still fixed on his.

"Give them your weapons, Esten," he called out and watched as his friend grudgingly dropped first his drawn sword to the ground and then, at Col's continued prodding, his dagger. One rider slid from their horse and crouched to collect the weapons, handing them to another rider before mounting again with practiced ease that did not go unnoticed by either man.

Once Esten had surrendered his weapons, Cyra looked pointedly at Col's left boot, raising an eyebrow, and he grinned. He slid the knife from its sheath and flipped it in the air, casually, catching it by the blade. He spurred Faelan forward, ignoring the spears gathering closer to his chest and back. There was a spattering of unfamiliar, urgent talking, but Cyra held his eyes steadily as Faelan sidled closer to the grey until he was within arm's reach of her. He held the knife out, handle first, offering it as though it was the most beautiful of flowers. She lowered the bow slightly.

A lean woman with barely discernible tattoos across her dark-skinned cheekbones, making him wonder if Tabiti Herself had come to take him, appeared on Cyra's other side. She moved her horse in close and hissed something urgent to Cyra, her face emanating admonishment and concern. Cyra answered calmly, almost thoughtfully, without breaking eye contact with him. She reached one slender hand, marked with heavily tattooed zig-zagged triangles, crescents, and circles from wrist to elbow, to take the knife. Col relinquished it with a smile and said, genuinely,

"How wonderful to see you again."

The dusky skin on her high, sun-weathered cheekbones turned darker with a flush of red, and he wondered if she had understood him. She said something else in that commanding voice and pointed back the way they had come. Back toward the women's encampment. He made a gesture as though asking her to lead the way and was rewarded by the most imperious scowl he had ever seen. Even worse than his father's, which he had never considered possible. A sharp prodding in his back made him turn to see a mousy-looking older woman poking at him with the pike on her axe, frowning and pointing down the road. There was nothing mousy or old about the weapon, however, nor the way she held it. He nudged Faelan into a walk and met Esten's eyes with an apologetic shrug as they came abreast.

"I don't think they mean to harm us," he called reassuringly, as the women around them moved to a trot, then a steady canter, pressing both of them forward with the points of their weapons.

"I don't think they mean to offer us sana, either, you love-struck idiot!" Esten called back, but the thunder of hooves drowned the rest of his words.

They rode quickly, and some of Faelan's itch to gallop had been scratched by the time they arrived at the women's encampment, though Col now realized the stallion had sensed the women following them all along, and he had been too preoccupied to listen. The camp was large, crowded with women and horses milling about the semi-circular clearing. The spot was well chosen, hidden from the southern road by almost a full league of forest and surrounded by trees on two sides, as well as the gully to the southeast. Several tent-like structures, built from freshly cut saplings and draped with deerskin, were erected close to the trees around the edges. There were other makeshift shelters set up, with awnings to keep the rain off but with no walls to retain heat. A few women sat under these, their hands busy with various tasks, including, Col observed, sharpening their weapons. One woman stood out in stark contrast to the rest in their tight-fitting leather vests and leg coverings; her once brightly dyed red robe, dirty with stains and long wear, swept the ground when she walked, and her head was shaved completely, revealing tattooed markings on her forehead.

Col also saw his two wagons, plus a third crudely made one, off to the side near a rope paddock where horses grazed. He felt mixed emotions on seeing them—sorrow for the dead that had tried to protect them and irritation that these women had been brazen enough to steal what he would gladly have offered them under the gift of hospitality. The camp looked exactly as his own did not three leagues west, as though these women were on a military reconnaissance of their own. The thought chilled him. There were no men in sight, but these women had already proven to be as deadly as any man he had ever known, and why they had a small yet undeniably fierce army camped within Scoloti territory was still far beyond his understanding.

Every face in the camp turned to watch their entrance, and none of them were welcoming. Col felt a second, stronger twinge of apprehension. He could only imagine what his father would say right now if he knew of his son and heir's reckless gamble. But something deeper in Col felt still and calm, rather than aroused to danger as his mind told him he should be. He suspected Cyra did not intend to harm him. She had already had the chance several times. No, there was something else she was after; he was almost certain of it.

They stopped in front of one of the conical structures, forcing Faelan to a halt also, since they still surrounded him with spears and axes. The one with skin as black as Tabiti's prodded Esten to dismount. Cyra moved the grey mare toward Col, her torso swaying with a snake-like, side-to-side movement as the horse walked, her bow slung over her chest and white-fletched arrows peeking from over her shoulder. She held his eyes with grim determination, but before she could reach him, a voice called out from across the clearing. A shadow crossed her face as she reined the mare to a halt. Her features pinched into a frown, and anger clouded her expression as her eyes slid away from his to the woman approaching. She spoke, her tone harsh.

Col looked down at the other woman, who had hair the same color as his own. She could not have been over twenty summers; her face was youthful, and her long, lean legs were bare under a blue tunic, though she wore leather sandals that laced from the ankle to the knee, covering much of her legs. In one hand, she held an axe, decorated with gold etching along the face of the blade.

The Golden Axe his men had spoken of. Col's gaze grew sharper.

The red-haired woman replied equally harshly back to Cyra, gesturing angrily with her axe in his and Esten's direction. Another woman, older, her scarred face making her glower more pronounced, came to stand next to the red-haired woman, her arms crossed in a universal gesture of defiance that required no translation.

Every woman Col could see carried at minimum a small knife at their belt. Almost all carried a deadly weapon of some fashion. Some had half-moon-shaped axes with long pikes strapped on their backs, or on their hips if the handles were short. A few had swords, some of them drawn and ready, or spears gripped comfortably in hands obviously familiar with holding a weapon. They were all strong and muscled, some lean and some stocky, and their skin ranged from pale cream to the darkest of red-browns or black. Their eyes were stern but bright with everything from curiosity to distrust, and all were unabashed in meeting his eyes or the desperately uncomfortable Esten's.

Cyra, her silver eyes flashing incongruously bright against skin like a toasted nut, answered the women challenging her with a tone of finality, and a tense hush fell over the gathering. Faelan sidled under him, and Col met Esten's eyes with increasing apprehension. He was fairly certain Cyra did not mean him harm, but he could not vouch for the rest of them. Their eyes might as well have been spears themselves, for all of the sharpness they leveled at the men. But then the red-haired woman turned abruptly away, and as she did so, Col's eyes met hers. She stopped, axe held low, and stared up at him with what looked like shock or recognition. Then she was gone, pushing her way through his spear-holding guards and away from their circle.

Cyra spoke, suddenly close beside him, jolting his attention back to her. She pointed at him, then at the ground. He dismounted in a smooth drop, letting Faelan's reins fall to the grass, and was immediately prodded toward one of the tents. When a young fair-haired one reached for Faelan's reins, however, he moved to stop her with a sharp "No!"

His eyes met the woman's icy blue ones even as she leveled her axe and stuck it firmly into his leather vest, directly over his heart. She held it there with deliberate pressure, and then looked at Cyra, who had dismounted and was now eyeing him with intense disapproval.

"The horse must be free," he motioned to Faelan.

"Ekwos?" Cyra repeated curiously, pointing at Faelan. He nodded and pointed to the reins on the ground. "Ekwos... He cannot be tied. He must remain free."

"Free," she repeated slowly. The word rolled in her mouth with an unfamiliar tightness, accenting it with a foreign crispness he had never heard before meeting her in the gully. Her eyes slid from his face to the horse and back again. Finally, she gestured to the woman, who stepped away with an expression that reminded him strongly of Esten's, though his friend had long disappeared to who knew what fate inside a tent. Something about the interaction between the two women made him glance back at Cyra in renewed surprise as he was prodded forward at axe-point to the tent. She appeared to be in command of these *Oirpata*. With that bit of curious knowledge, he ducked his head into the flap opened for him and entered the darkness of the tent, wondering exactly what he and his foolishness had gotten them into.

Chapter 23

ISHASSARI

followed Col into the tent and watched as he stood in the center, scanning the walls of hide curiously, turning in a full circle until he was facing me again. Our eyes met as he completed the turn. He smiled, almost expectantly. He did not appear afraid or worried that we had brought him into our midst, unarmed and with only his yellow-haired friend as unlikely backup. He seemed almost pleased, if I didn't know any better.

This annoyed me even more than Eri's continued attempts to undermine my authority. I slowly, pointedly drew the small dagger from my leather armband and motioned sharply to a small stool on the far side of the fire pit. He promptly went to it and sat, stretching long legs to each side of the cold stones like a spider, hands resting easily on his thighs.

"This has not won you any favors from Eri or Glaukia, Cyra," Ossy's voice, muffled as she ducked through the flap, was tight with irritation—at myself or the indignant ha-mazaans, I wasn't sure. Likely both.

"No," I agreed shortly, not looking away from Col. "But I could have removed these men's hands and heads and mounted them on spikes for the carrion eaters, and still Eri would have found error in my decision."

Ossy frowned at me and then put her hands on her hips, surveying Col with a judicious stare. He smiled nonchalantly. My frown turned to a scowl.

"Col," I pointed at him with the knife, then at Ossy. "Ossy."

"Ozzy," he repeated congenially, nodding at her.

"Ossy," she corrected curtly. She moved sideways around the tent, keeping as much space between his body and hers as possible and holding her short blade lightly in her hand just as I did; there was no room inside the tent for swords or axes, if it came to a fight. This was exactly why Ossy had argued the men be kept tied to the tree outside. A plan I had refused, despite the repetitive requests that I be reasonable. I needed to speak with the red one, and not in public. And I needed to speak to him before any, or all, of the three encampments surrounding ours advanced any closer.

"Kuwabi Esten?" Col said, pointing toward the flap.

"He is in a tent nearby. Unharmed," I said. He stared at me, uncomprehending. How was it that he used so many words similar to ours, or to the Achaean tongue, and yet he understood nothing of what I said? Perhaps he was simple in the head. I pointed, again with my blade, to the south wall of the tent and said, insultingly slow with my words and tone, "Esten. There. Safe." A slow light dawned in his eyes. Either the words or the tone conveyed the meaning to him, as he finally nodded.

I stood in front of him with only the cold fire pit between us, but rather than intimidating him with my height as he sat on the low stool, I only felt awkwardly conspicuous being this close to him. He showed no concern for his situation but rather a curious interest in everything he could lay eyes on. His eyes moved from me to Ossy, and again to the poles of the tent, all the way up to the open flap above him that let in fresh air, and acted as a draw for the smoke of our nightly fires. He looked at my bare feet for several heartbeats, and I resisted squirming my toes. He looked at the furs Ossy and I used for our bedding and the wooden chests that were behind me, stolen from his own wagons. He looked at the deer hide walls and the woven reeds laid over the deadened grass to keep the dust down.

As his eyes passed over the wooden chests again, I reached behind me and pulled an object out of one of them, holding it in front of me. His eyes brightened with recognition and met mine once more.

"Why did you leave this on the rock?" I asked. He stared at me hopefully.

"Assu hekwos?" he said.

Ossy peered at him.

"Assu," she repeated, and he turned to her, nodding. Then he looked back at the object in my hands.

"Assu?" he asked again and looked up at me, still with that hopeful expression like a dog waiting for its rib bone after a feast.

"His words are almost familiar to me," Ossy mused. "Like I have heard them before, or knew them as a child. I think he is asking if you… covet the horse? Desire it?"

I examined the small wooden horse. It was crudely carved, but not poorly done, as though it had been made quickly, yet still by skilled hands. The mane and tail had been carved to show a horse in motion, and the legs, though square and not well defined, allowed the figure to stand upright while set at an extended trot. The small body had been rubbed with soot, and patches rubbed away to resemble tiny dapples. It was Inara, without a doubt. He had even captured something of her fierce pride in the way the head tilted up and the typical undecided flip of her mane over both sides of her poll.

Sagitta had found the carving the day after I had met the men in the gully. I had gone back with her, Ossy, and Alkippe, to canvas the area after scouts returned with word that we were surrounded. No men had been in sight, just this carving, which Sagitta handed over to me with a raised eyebrow and blue eyes full of mischievous questions that remained unanswered. The next afternoon's scout had found another carving. I pulled this second, more elaborate shape from the chest and held one horse in each hand, the hard wood clanking against the blade of my knife.

The second showed Inara bowing, with one foreleg extended in front of her and her head tucked between her legs. I did not doubt there was a third waiting in the gully today, but we had been busy preparing our ambush to take the two foolhardy men and had not yet had time to fetch it.

Again, his face showed hopeful eagerness as he clearly recognized the second piece. His eyes met mine again, and he flashed a wide smile at me in a dazzling display of strong teeth.

"Assu?" This time, he said the word very softly and with the same intensity as he had said the unknown words from the bottom of the ravine that first day. A flush, similar to what I had felt then, once again crept up my neck, and I turned away to set the carved horses back in the chest, taking the moment to hide my discomfiture. Taking longer than was warranted to tuck the pieces away and cover them with stolen silk, I finally turned back to face him, breathing deeply to settle myself.

"Yes, they are very nice," I said, not wanting to reveal to Ossy—or him—how they made my heart squeeze a bit to see them. "But why?" I demanded. "What is your game? Why do you approach every day with only your friend? Why are there small armies camped around us, and no one has attacked us yet? What are you doing here?"

Col sat uncomprehending under this barrage. I wondered if Sagitta and Alkippe were having any better luck with the yellow-haired man and the language. I doubted it. Most of us spoke Palaic, Hattic, and the Achaean tongue of my grandmother's people, and some, like Alkippe, had their own mother-tongue besides. But though the men's language shared similar words as those I knew, Col did not seem to recognize anything I said.

"Why are you leaving me gifts? We killed your men. I can still kill you, yet you keep coming here without your men. It doesn't make sense." I glared at him in frustrated confusion.

"I don't think peppering him with questions is going to do much when he clearly has no understanding," Ossy said. "However, I can probably answer the question of why he is leaving you gifts." Her voice was sly and suggestive, and I glared at her next.

"Who are you?" I asked him again, slower but more aggressively. He stared up at me dumbly. "I know your name is Col. I want to know why you are coming *here*." I punctuated the last by pointing at him and the ground in front of me. "Why?" I demanded, drawing the word out slow and succinct, my eyes boring into his.

"Khuvi?" he repeated uncertainly. It was not quite what I had said, but it gave me some hope.

"Why?" I nodded, enunciating the word. He repeated it back, and I saw a glimmer of recognition. He raised his eyebrows and looked at Ossy and then at me and said something as though explaining. Ossy sighed, and my shoulders slumped.

"I didn't understand a word of that," Ossy shook her head, echoing my thoughts. "I don't know what you were hoping would come of this, Ishassara, but they speak nonsense and don't understand a thing we say. Best to kill them and have done with it."

"We are not—" I began.

"Ishassara?" Col interjected the perfectly pronounced word as a clear question. The term was comfortable on his tongue, though slow to form, as though molded from melted honey.

We both looked at him in surprise. Ossy nodded and pointed at me with her dagger. "Yes, Cyra is Ishassara."

"Cyra Ishassara." His eyes glittered as though he had just heard the most interesting secret. He raised a hand to his chest.

"Colaxais, Ishassari."

"You are the son of a queen?" I said the words hoarsely, stiffly, my mouth abruptly dry.

"Or a king," Ossy offered thoughtfully, almost to herself.

Col nodded and pointed to Ossy, seeming to understand her. "Pahattur Hassuri."

Ossy's eyes met mine. Her expression was grave, and a chill swept through me. Then she shook her head and covered her face with a hand, letting out a low, long groan. Then she crossed her arms in front of her, the blade sticking out from behind her elbow in one tightly clenched fist, and gave me a disbelieving stare.

"Matar Kubileya, Cyra! Now what? If this man is the son of a king, there is about to be an entire army coming for him, you can be sure. And they are going to be a lot more aggressive than they have shown the last few days." She let her head fall back as she spoke the rest to the sky. "Melanippe, forgive me for not realizing your daughter would be as much trouble as you," she finished, speaking her frustration to the empty air and brandishing her dagger as though trying to jab her old friend with it.

I bit my lip as Col sat back from the jabbing blade, eyeing Ossy warily. She was right, but it still did not make sense to me why a king's son and his army would be camping near the people who had attacked his caravan and then leaving trinkets in the wilderness rather than engaging in battle. Not to mention choosing to strip basically naked in front of a stranger to prove he was unarmed. Ossy was lost in her own thoughts about the matter, still muttering to herself. No doubt trying to figure out ways to be rid of a king's son, now that she realized he would not be so easy to kill. Well, easy, perhaps. But there would be no wisdom in it, with at least a hundred men surrounding us within a league in every direction.

I stooped to grasp the lip of the wooden chest, dragging it closer to the fire pit. I reached in and pulled out my sharpening stone before closing the lid, and then I sat on it. I was directly across from him now, close enough that our feet could touch if we each stretched out a leg over the cold ashes between us. I smiled an easy, superior smile. Then, I began sharpening the star-forged blade of my dagger.

Col grew visibly uncomfortable, sitting straighter on the stool, though he had in no way been slouching before. The strong, square fingers splayed across his thighs flexed, as though he wished for his own dagger, now tucked into my belt, to be between them. His eyes met mine steadily enough, though. He was not a coward. I rang the blade over the stone with a swift singing motion and then held the dagger up. I pointed to the blade.

"Blade."

He looked at it, confusion warring with wariness. I set the stone on my thigh and pulled his dagger, which he had handed over in such a display of cockiness, from my belt. The blade was longer than mine but entirely made of bronze and neither as sharp nor as well-made. The handle, however, was finely carved from some kind of horn, the knob a delicately worked eagle's head, banded with strips of gold, and the eyes of the eagle two glittering garnets. Now that I knew he was the son of a king, I wondered if they might actually be rubies. The eagle was much like the one he had called down from the sky several days before. Like the one which had circled the ha-mazaan camp for many days now, making me irrationally suspicious, as though he watched us through its eyes.

"Blade," I repeated the word, pointing at the blade of his dagger and then mine.

"Blade," he repeated my word slowly. I nodded and pointed to the eagle on the other end.

"Eagle," I said. Then I pointed my finger up toward the sky and made a swirling motion, as though following a bird drifting on a hot wind. "Eagle."

"Eagle," he nodded, rolling the word I was using carefully on his tongue as though tasting it. But then he said, "Hewis." He pointed again at the handle and swirled his finger in the air like I had. His words had a slowness to them. A languid, lazy, summertime sleeping in a ray of sunshine quality.

I frowned. "Howis?" I said, plucking at a fold in the grey trousers I wore because the word he had used was so similar to ours for "clothed." He looked at my fingers, confused again.

"Hewis," he repeated, pointing at the knife's handle and once more in the sky. He screeched suddenly, loud and piercing, exactly like an eagle, and flapped his arms at his side. Ossy stepped forward with her dagger ready, but he stilled himself and, smiling at my startled face, said again, "Hewis."

"Hmmm," I said, resisting the urge to let my lips twitch into a smile. Ossy barked out a laugh of her own and then shook her head at me.

"If learning his speech is what you had in mind, goddess-daughter, I think it will be a longer and more arduous task than you thought."

"I don't doubt that," I said, considering him. He had seemed so...boyish, making sounds like an eagle, and yet even sitting unarmed and captive, there was something about him that exuded confidence and strength. I realized it was the same thing I had recognized in Inara that day when I first laid hands on her. Power. There was a power in him, and it came from a place deep inside. It was a power that had no need of weapons or great displays of might. It simply was.

I picked up the sharpening stone again and slid the blade of my dagger over it, my hands steady and firm. His eyes watched with wary curiosity, but not fear. After a few ringing swipes of the blade, while I considered what to do, I heard a commotion outside, and the flap of our tent flung open with a whoosh of air.

"Ishassara, forgive me!" Prothoe's pale blonde head ducked through the door, and as soon as she straightened, clutching something in her fist, I could see that her cheeks were flushed from exertion or emotion. Her eyes flickered briefly over Col, who watched her with unconcealed curiosity. "It is Eri," she said then, and paused, looking once more to the red-haired man.

"He understands nothing," I waved my hand at him dismissively as I stood to face the doorway, frowning at Prothoe. "What about Eri?" I asked, but something hard twisted in my stomach.

"She leaves the camp on horseback, with others," Prothoe said, clearly agitated. "Glaukia, and Melo, and Santo. And more. Maybe ten in all." She looked at Ossy then. "She said something about going to be with the side that will win this fight. I do not know what she is talking about. But," she stepped forward and held her closed fist out to me, her fingers slowly, reluctantly opening to reveal what she held. "She left this."

The rock, a grey granite worn smooth by water, such as the waves of an ocean on a beach, was crusted with dried blood. My dried blood. Eri's Swearing Stone from my Ishassara ceremony.

The hard thing in my belly became cold, spreading through my body until I was as chilled and stiff as the stone I took from her.

"Bring them back," I said when my lips could move again. "Take as many ha-mazaans as you need, though leave enough that we are not undefended. Alkippe will lead you. Go. Now," I said, and Prothoe ducked through the flap again, hurrying to obey. I turned to Ossy, aware that Col watched every move being made with green, perceptive eagle eyes of his own.

"Ossy, go with them. Make sure Erioboea knows what the consequences will be if she does not return to camp before nightfall." My tone was grim. I did not want to think what would happen if Eri didn't—or did—return. Either situation would be ugly for the both of us. I clutched the stone in my hand until it cut into my barely healed scar with a sharp, head-clearing pain.

Ossy hesitated but said, "I will go as you wish, Cyra, but the men should be—"

"I will stay with this one. Sagitta will stay with Esten." I cut her off and held up my hand to stop her protests as she shook her head. "This one will not harm me. You must trust me in this, goddess-mother."

She held my gaze for a long moment until the shouts from outside and bustle of horses being rounded up and weapons being readied intruded into our silence. She looked at Col finally, then stepped close to him so that he was forced to tilt his neck in order to meet her eyes.

"Ishassara Cyra," she said, pointing at me with the tip of her knife. "You, Col," she said, and the tip of her knife appeared under his chin. Then, it lowered to the place between his thighs, not so lightly pressing into him. "First, much pain, and then a slow death, if she is harmed."

He may not have understood her words, but he understood their meaning, I was sure. His eyes moved to me, and I shrugged. Then she stepped away, and with one last look of warning as she strode past me, Ossy left.

I turned to Col and smiled grimly.

"Shall we continue?" I said and sat once more, tucking Eri's Swearing Stone into my belt with forceful finality. I took up the sharpening stone, ringing my blade over the roughness of it. "This is a stone," I said slowly, holding it up at eye level. "Stone. What is your word?"

CHAPTER 24

BETRAYED

---

waited as Alkippe and Ossy dismounted, the knot in my stomach a persistent ache. I saw no red-haired ha-mazaan on a dark horse amongst those returning. I glanced over my shoulder to make sure Col was still behind me; he stood obediently next to the tent, watching the proceedings with interest, his hands tied tight in my own knots in front of him. I had needed to let him out to relieve himself, well after I knew he had grown tired and weary of my language lecture, but we had not made it back into the tent before the search party returned. I turned back to the ha-mazaans as a horse approached from the middle of the line, prodded forward by Prothoe. Glaukia. My eyes went to Ossy and Alkippe, questioning.

"The others are gone," Ossy shook her head.

"Aye, but not toward home," Alkippe's words were heavily accented, as they tended to be when she was angry. "Gone to be with these kind." Her disparagement was unequivocal as her hand waved in Col's direction. Her eyes flicked down to his tied wrists, and then back to my face, disapproving.

I shook my head in confusion, ignoring her concern. "They were captured by his men?"

"No," Glaukia said, stepping forward, and before Alkippe or Ossy could hold her back, the tall woman knelt in front of me. My mouth set into a flat line as I looked down at her.

"Explain," I demanded. Glaukia worked her mouth as though chewing over what words would not enrage me. She remembered my mother well. She knew the same rage slept within me and was awakening.

"Erioboea…has been meeting one that looks and speaks like these for several days, Ishassara," Glaukia said, pointing at Col. "She has gone to be with him."

"Meeting him?" I repeated slowly. "Be with him?"

Glaukia peered up at me with worried blue-gray eyes. "They found each other in the northwest forest, Ishassara. They...Erioboea told me she had been bathing in the stream, and the man came upon her." Glaukia's eyes slid away from mine as she said this. I felt a knife twist in me.

"He raped her?" My voice was thick with rage, and there were angry mutters from the ha-mazaans looking on.

"N-no, Ishassara," Glaukia said, growing even more uncomfortable. "She chose to lie with him. She told me that night. Me and Melo and Santo. She told us she offered him her body, as she desired him. And she told us they had agreed to meet in the same spot in the woods the very next day. She told us he would bring others if more women would come. Somehow, she understood this, though...though their language is not ours."

I could not believe what I was hearing. Eri had lain with one of the same men she had so adamantly wanted us to avoid? Had learned his tongue already? And then abandoned our camp—and her Swearing Stone—to be with him? "But why?" was all I could think to say.

Glaukia paused, swallowing, and looked at the ground for a long time before answering, so quietly I almost missed the words, "It was her prophecy, Ishassara." She looked up finally, meeting my eyes. "She told me her prophecy when we rested on the beach, after the ship and the storm. She told me of the golden-haired man who would find her and take her as his bride, but only after she had crossed an ocean of water to be with him. That he would make her a queen in his own lands. That only then could she...find her home again.

"The Oracle told her that where there were once two sister queens, in this new land, there would only be one. That those who did not follow her would be...would be forever wandering. She told me that Hipponika knew from her own moon-blood prophecy that her own daughter would be queen. That it should not be you." Glaukia swallowed again. "It was only later...last night she told me what she had done in Themiscyra. I swear it, Ishassara." Glaukia's voice became urgent, her words spilling over one another in her haste to speak them. "She told me how she helped them. The Achaeans. I did not know before, I swear it. She kept that from me because she said she was ashamed and had not known where everything went so wrong. But she said she knew now, and if we listened to her, we would find home again."

Her throat moved as she swallowed again, holding back her tears. The coldness I had felt earlier was a faint chill compared to the icy rage coiling its way around my heart. My teeth clenched, the sound of their gritting loud in my ears and the breath could only fit in my lungs in small, shallow puffs.

"What do you mean, she helped the Achaeans?" I ground out. I don't think I had ever spoken words so coldly. Glaukia shifted her knees on the ground, the gravel digging painfully into her flesh, but she did not rise. Alkippe and Ossy stood behind either shoulder, and Sagitta stood close to my side. All held their axes ready and their mouths in grim, unforgiving lines of disgust.

"She confessed much to me last night, Ishassara," Glaukia hedged. When I did not look away, she swallowed again and finally elaborated. "She confessed to taking the one they called Theseus as a lover because she thought he was the golden-haired man of her prophecy. She said he promised to take her across the ocean to be his bride. He asked for her help in subduing the rest of the ha-mazaans because...because Heracles wanted to take Hippolyta's belt. Theseus told her that if she helped him and his friend, he would make her his wife. But she said everything went wrong and that Theseus betrayed her. That they wanted to steal the queens, not just the belt. But it was too late. She had already poisoned the *kimiz*, and the water from the spring, on the night of...of your ceremony." Glaukia looked increasingly miserable with every scandalous, traitorous word, but I could not muster any pity for her. There were varying expressions of shock and disgust on the ha-mazaan faces gathered around. Glaukia avoided everyone's eyes.

"And this new man that she has gone to be with?" I said finally, as though I had not just heard that my best friend had been moaning between the sheets with an Achaean, with Theseus, and plotting the destruction of our city. When she had not even made First Blood yet! And yet she sought to challenge my right to the throne because my mother had been too young to have me? Had whelped me outside of conscription for *matar*, when she should have been Defending Queen all along?

"Erioboea feels she has been given a second chance to fulfill her prophecy, Ishassara," Glaukia said. She shifted her knees again. I wondered distractedly if tying her in such a position would be a fair reward for her treachery.

"She said as soon as she saw him, she knew he had been the one in her vision, not Theseus. So she...lay with him to keep him close. And she asked the others and...and me...if we would come with her the next day, to lie with them as well, and prove our loyalty to...to her. To her vision."

"And did you?" I asked. She was silent for a moment and then nodded once. "All of you?" She nodded again, the movement stiff with shame. My lip curled, but there was an uncomfortable feeling of guilt within me. Had I acted any differently? Had I not thought about the same, dreamt about the same? The man who had been in my thoughts and dreams since my first moon-blood stood within a spear's length of me even as we listened to this treacherous tale. And did my prophecy not demand the same betrayal of our ways in order to further the cause of our people? Confusion swirled in me, mixing with the white-hot anger I felt toward Eri.

She had betrayed me. Worse, she had betrayed all of our people and helped the cursed Achaeans to bring all of us to this place. To our dooms. She had been the reason for her own mother's death. As the realization dawned on me, I thought back to the way Eri had been on the ship, and the days after it, sunken in a misery that I had assumed was grief. And it had been, but now I knew it had gone far beyond mere grief. Guilt had magnified that grief a thousand-fold. Guilt for betraying every ha-mazaan. Guilt for Hippolyta's death. Guilt for Antiope being stolen away, for her rape and imprisonment, and perhaps her death. Guilt for the death of her mother before her very eyes. Guilt for Ifito, Pisto, Aello, and every other woman we had lost. Guilt for Melanippe, my beautiful, powerful, Nightmare mother, who had died slowly in front of her, reminding her of her treachery until she very likely went mad from the weight of it. My lips curled back from my teeth.

"And today?" I said finally, as the silence stretched out into a fragile, painful thing. "Why did you go with her today?"

"I...after she told me the truth last night, I realized I could not follow her as Ishassara, though I had promised to," Glaukia said slowly. Her eyes could not meet mine, so she stared at the braid hanging over my shoulder, and the tattoos on my arms, then the tops of my dusty bare feet. Anywhere but my eyes. "But I thought if I went with them, I could find out what she meant to do, Ishassara. And, once I knew what she planned, I could come back and tell you. To prove my loyalty is to...to you." Her voice became hoarse at the end, and I thought she might actually cry. She did not, though her lips trembled pitifully. I stared down at her, unblinking.

"Glaukia was riding to us when we came upon her, Ishassara," Alkippe said reluctantly, though her voice was still flat with anger. "She surrendered her weapons and led us to where the rest had merged with...these ones." Alkippe used the pick on top of her axe to point at Col. I glanced back at him, almost having forgotten he was there, and when our eyes met, his expression grew worried. I had not bothered hiding the fury boiling inside of me. I turned back to the ha-mazaans.

"It appears they have a large number, but they did not go east, where this one and the yellow one camp. They went west," Ossy said.

"And what did you learn when you lay with their man, Glaukia?" I asked. She flushed, and the color looked odd on her swarthy, weathered skin.

Eventually, she said, "I did not understand much of what was said, Ishassara." Her voice was thin, weakened by shame.

"You would have had leave to lie with any one of them. You know that, right?" Something in my voice made her look up at me. "It is your right to lie with whomever you choose, even if the choice is foolish. What would I care?" I shrugged. "However, you did so at a traitor's request. You listened to her lies and her treachery, and you would have brought destruction down upon what remains of our people in this land. For what reason? Because you did not think my mother should have borne me under that sycamore so young?" The fury in my voice whipped the air like a lash. I thought of my mother again. Her cold body as I kissed her lips. The blood of a horse that was not her *rhutasiya* gushing over both of us. All for the selfish desires of one whom I had always thought of as my friend. And yet, Eri was young and naïve like I was. Glaukia did not have the excuse of youth. "Do you imagine I will grant you leniency because you returned to give this news? Do you really believe that is enough? You betrayed two Ishassaras if you truly thought Eri was the one destined to be queen."

Glaukia paled. She had not thought of it that way, clearly, and had indeed thought returning would save her. She also thought I was young and inexperienced at being Ishassara. She would learn how much such a thing could not matter here when our women were surrounded by wolves creeping closer and more trying to tear us apart from the inside.

I spun abruptly and went to Col. He stepped backward in trepidation as I reached out to him but then held his ground as I wrenched his arms forward, untying the knot that bound his hands. Avoiding his wary, questioning eyes, I yanked the braided leather free of his wrists and turned back to the others.

"Tie her."

I gestured to Glaukia, dropping the rope into Alkippe's hands. The general did not hesitate, winding the length around the older woman's hands with quick precision while I instructed the others. "She will remain tied to the uncovered wagon until I decide what fate is suitable for a traitor twice over. Make sure she does not sit comfortably." I turned back to Col and motioned for him to go inside the tent ahead of me. Holding the flap open, I turned to summon Ossy, who was looking both sorrowful and angry.

"I will need you, Ossy. The rest of you," I looked out across the serious, stony faces of the ha-mazaans, my heart hurting for them as much as for myself. "Be prepared. We may be fighting against our own sisters soon. Make plans accordingly."

CHAPTER 25

CHOOSING

M y anger at Eri's betrayal had me feeling anything but hungry, but I asked for venison and what wine was left from Col's own wagon to be brought to the tent. I also called for Esten to be brought over, and though we did not bother binding them again, we sat the men on either side of the fire pit, well apart from each other but still able to talk. Esten seemed tired but no worse for wear after his doubtless harrowing afternoon being drilled for information by Sagitta.

He'd proved as incapable as Col at offering anything of the sort. It did not seem like the best course of action to whittle them down with constant questions they could not understand, so I let them eat their dinner in relative peace. What peace is available while in captivity, that is. I kept an eye on them as they spoke in low tones, likely hashing plans to escape. They ate with calm unconcern, or at least Col did. Esten acted as though he had not eaten in a week, and the food disappeared quickly from his wooden plate before he licked his fingers in satisfaction.

Ossy ate along with the two men, but I watched in silence, my plate ignored, fidgeting instead with my dagger. My mind was a maelstrom of emotion. The knowledge that Eri had been part of the Achaean plot to take ha-mazaans from Themiscyra was still so ludicrous and abhorrent that it would not sit as fact within my mind and instead slid about like a fish through fingers in turbulent water. I wondered if Glaukia lied. Then I wondered if Glaukia could ever manage to conjure such a horrible lie. The latter seemed less likely to me. But every time I thought of the details, my mind hazed over with a dull cloud, as though trying to block the truth from forming in any discernible, understandable way. Distasteful as it was, however, I could not think of a reason Eri would have had to lie about her part in the ordeal, nor for Glaukia to fabricate such a tale after Eri's disappearance. It certainly did nothing to make the older woman appear in a better light. To admit the one she had chosen to follow as Ishassara, rather than myself, had turned out to be a vicious traitor to us all only made Glaukia more culpable for her misplaced loyalty.

I had been angry enough at the damage done to ha-mazaans, the havoc wreaked on all of our lives, at the hands of Heracles and Theseus. Adding one of our own to the forefront of responsibility lent a tinge of bitterness that coated everything I looked at, including food. I watched as Col chewed the venison appreciatively, and then as he ate a few of the plump, overly ripe blackberries Tekmessa had found the day before. His eyes sparkled with appreciation when he tasted the sweet berries, and I stared at the way his cheek dimpled with pleasure. He seemed content enough to be here, captive among us, eating as though it was the finest meal offered to a favored guest. This should have irked me, but instead, I found it a testament to his courage.

Melanippe would have approved of his backbone. But thinking of my mother, and how she had been robbed of her chance to meet this man who was, apparently, an irrefutable part of my destiny, only deepened the bitterness. Col sent me a questioning look as my roiling emotions boiled over into an inarticulate sound of vexation.

"Duhor?" He held out a fresh piece of smoked venison to me. Ossy watched him like a hawk, as she had since stepping back into the tent with us. I shook my head. He chewed his own piece while watching me with thoughtful eyes, and I began to feel the annoying flush creep up my face as the intensity of his gaze became uncomfortably intimate. I looked everywhere but at him, finally choosing to focus closely on my blade, pretending to buff out a fingerprint on the well-polished metal. Esten looked between the two of us and rolled his eyes. Ossy cleared her throat.

"What are your plans, Ishassara?"

"To keep this Ishassari and learn his language," I said, waving my knife toward Col, whose eyes sharpened at the word for heir. Esten also sat straighter. "And then, hopefully, we will use him as ransom."

Ossy's eyebrows climbed toward her hairline, but she took another careful bite of food and chewed rather than commenting.

The hauntingly lonely cry of a golden eagle sounded close by. Closer than it should for a bird of prey, but it had been creeping closer throughout the day. I looked to Col, suspicious. His eyes twinkled into mine even as he whistled a lilting tune toward the opening in the tent, but there was no rush of wings as I feared. Only silence. My hands stilled on my knife.

"I don't know what to do, Ossy," I said finally. My voice sounded childish to my own ears, and my shoulders slumped as some part of the rage uncoiled itself from my spine and left me feeling limp and tired. "I don't know what is best for every ha-mazaan, and yet I am tasked with making the decision for all. How can I fault Eri for following her prophecy when I am simply doing the same?"

Frustration squeezed between the spaces of my words, warbling under the pressure of speaking them out loud after crowding my heart and mind for so long.

"Either Kubileya blesses our path, or she does not. I did not go searching this man out," I waved the knife toward Col again. Esten's eyes followed the blade warily. "The first time, at least. Nor the second. Yet here he sits, straight from the flames of my vision and a thousand leagues from where I first saw his face." I shook my head, running my fingers along the blade, just near the edge of it. When I finally met Ossy's gaze, the loving compassion in her eyes was nearly my undoing, but I finished my confession. "Destiny rushes toward me by no choice of my own, yet my destiny affects us all. Just as Eri's will affect us all. I don't understand enough of it to make the best decision. And I think, perhaps... perhaps it does not matter what I choose anyway."

I had hoped it might feel better to finally admit what had been weighing on me so heavily for so long, but saying it out loud merely made it feel more concrete, more real. No longer a dilemma of internal struggle, it was now a substantial, seemingly insurmountable stumbling block.

"Kubileya plays cat and mouse with us all," I shook my head wearily. "Why would she give this vision to Eri and a different one to me? How can they both be true?"

Ossy regarded me solemnly, nodding slowly. "Yes, it is certainly a mystery how Kubileya is working through this one," she said eventually and looked over at Col.

When I had revealed who I suspected he was, after bringing the second carving back to the camp, she had not seemed overly surprised. She still did not trust him, of course, as I did not, but her own trust in my vision from the Womb of the Mountain was much stronger than my own. Perhaps it was because she had more faith. Perhaps it was because she had seen how Melanippe's own prophecy had come true, from beginning to terrible end. That thought did nothing to bolster my own faith.

"Cyra, perhaps you do not understand well enough the point of Kubileya's gifts from the Oracle, rather than not understanding the prophecies themselves," she continued, turning soft amber eyes back to me.

"What do you mean, 'the point'? The point is to reveal our path so that we may follow it and bring honor to the Way of the Ha-mazaans."

"No," Ossy shook her head. "The point is to reveal what may happen if you remain true to your heart, to the desires that sleep there, and to prepare you to choose accordingly. That is why Eri has thrown her lot in with both an Achaean and a stranger in a strange land, without regard for the effect on herself or her people."

"But... she was just—she was following her vision," I argued haltingly, not sure why I was offering any kind of defense for Eri.

No. I knew why. It was because I feared we were too similar in our motivations and in the inevitably devastating outcome each of us would have for the other ha-mazaans.

"Or at least she thought she was," I continued, increasingly defensive for the both of us. "Perhaps her prophecy revealed to her that she should lie and scheme with Theseus."

"I cannot presume to know the Oracle's exact words to Erioboea, goddess-daughter, but I cannot think they included 'And you shall betray your people, and be the cause of many deaths of those you love, including your own mother,'" Ossy said firmly. She did not add, *And your queens. And Melanippe,* but we both thought it. A shadow crossed her face, but she continued.

"Eri acted according to her own heart, and in this way, the prophecy found her a willing party to anything that might increase her chances at power. She chose at every moment according to what her deepest desires were, and her desires were selfish and harmful to herself and others. This, then, is the point of the Oracle's message. Do you see?"

When I shook my head, even more confused, she sighed and put the piece of meat she had been about to eat back onto the platter. Col had finished eating and was holding the cup of wine loosely in his hand, regarding us with quiet, too-perceptive eyes. Esten looked ready to fall unconscious but remained too vigilant of my knife to close his eyes. I wondered absently where they were going to sleep tonight. I supposed they would need to be locked in the wagons. I wondered how difficult that would be. If they would put up a fight.

My mind circled back to Ossy's question, and I shook my head again.

"No, I don't see," I said slowly. "What the Oracle says is what will be. So there really isn't much choice involved, good or bad. Eri made a mistake thinking Theseus was the one in her vision, obviously. But is that really her fault?"

I glanced at Col, wondering if I had mistaken his face. The way his eyes glinted assured me I had not, even if he did not carry our *rhu-tasiya* mark on his chest as the vision had shown. "Eri is fulfilling what has already been chosen for her. The Fates wove her destiny before she was even born." We both knew I was no longer speaking about my friend.

"They weave our destiny as our hearts beat, according to the longing of our souls," Ossy corrected gently. "Our paths do not stray far from what we truly desire, and they are not decided beforehand, even by the Weaving Fates. They Weave as we walk. Only when our lives are finished may the threads be followed backward and the pattern known by all. However," she said, "they intertwine our lives with the destiny of all others, as you have already said. It is out of this intertwining that we make our choices, and our destiny unfolds." She paused, then said, carefully, purposefully, "Eri *could* have revealed the Achaean's plan to the queens. To her mother. Or to you, her closest friend. But it was not in her heart to do so because there was something she wanted more. She chose from her own desires and followed her own vision, which she *decided* was her prophecy.

"There is no absolute truth in any vision from the Oracles, or the *zizenti* cauldrons, or even our own dreams. There are ideas, possibilities of what could be if we stay true to our hearts. And not everyone makes sure their heart is clear of malice, and hate, and greed. Not everyone makes sure they align their heart with the Great Mother. The Oracle may see truly, but she may only see what is in the hearts of those who appear before her."

"So was Eri not destined to make those choices, and have those desires, simply from knowing her prophecy?" I said, even more overwhelmed by confusion.

"She was not. Even the prophecy you have told me does not include how you will get there, does it?" Ossy asked, and I knew the question was not rhetorical. She expected an answer.

I thought for a long moment, remembering as a familiar dream the vastness of the Oracle's cavern, the amber of her eyes and those of the lionesses, the prickle on my skin as the flames, silent and unburnt, revealed a man's face within their flickering light. I looked over at Col again, and he met my eyes calmly. His own sparkled with the same flame I had seen back then and dreamed of ever since.

"Well," I said slowly, swallowing, "she said I would bind myself to a man and be queen only with him by my side. That he would be a king in his own right. I don't see how that is not telling me how things will end. I didn't make the choice to come here, to this land. I didn't make the choice for my queens to be murdered and stolen or my mother to be killed." I frowned with frustration. "And I certainly didn't make the choice to meet him. But it was not by chance, either."

Ossy neither nodded nor shook her head; it was something in between the two. "You did not choose those things, no. They were in some ways a part of many destinies colliding," she admitted. "But." She looked me in the eye, her expression grave. "You *did* choose, in every moment, how to react to those circumstances. You chose to fight and kill the Achaeans on the ship when you could have betrayed Tekmessa to the boy and doomed us all. You chose to pursue capturing the horses and following your dreams of your *rhu-tasiya*. You chose to help your mother despite the fact that she was dying, rather than toss her to the waves or slit her throat and be done with the trouble." She smiled slightly at my indignant gasp and raised a hand.

"Of course you would not have, because it was not in your heart," she said pointedly. "You chose to go north after we captured the horses when you could have chosen any other direction. You chose to go east when we came to the crossroads, though again, you could have chosen any other direction. You chose not to shoot this red-haired one with your arrow when he was a free target," she waved a hand casually at Col. "We both know you could have chosen to kill both of them and be done with it. Yet, you did not."

We both looked toward the men, and Col met my eyes once more, perhaps waiting to be addressed. If it annoyed him that we were clearly talking about him, our words and intentions a mystery, he did not show it. I chewed my lip, then stopped when his eyes were drawn to the motion. I looked back at Ossy.

"Nothing in your prophecy told you to do those things," she finished insistently. "It is up to you, and your heart, and the choices you make, for your destiny to find you."

"But," I insisted, still not finding this new line of thinking a comfortable fit, "that could also mean that someone could choose differently than their prophecy, to make choices to oppose it and negate it, and I tried that." At her questioning look, I squirmed in my seat, the lid of the carved chest increasingly uncomfortable. "After the Oracle gave me my prophecy, I thought it was shameful. A curse. I vowed to never betray the ha-mazaan Way. And yet..." I did not want to say it out loud, but I waved my hand toward Col.

"And how have you betrayed the ha-mazaan Way with this man? Or in any fashion?" Ossy asked, raising an eyebrow.

"I haven't," I conceded. "Yet."

She snorted. "Pah! I hear nothing in your prophecy that says you will betray who we are. I hear that you will sit as queen, and a king of his own right shall sit at your side. If this is the man, he is already Ishassari. If you choose to lie with him, it is your choice and your right. Tell me, what in this says you betray us?"

Her tone demanded a response, but the questions made my thoughts spin.

"She said I would...I would bind myself to him..." I began weakly, and Ossy made another scoffing sound, adding a dismissive wave of her hand to emphasize it.

"Ha-mazaans are not forbidden from marrying, or binding, or living with men. Many other cities have done so for hundreds of years before your great-grandmother Marpesa and her sister thought it best they live separately from men. Even still, some have husbands who live apart. You know this, but it is neither here nor there. To bind yourself would not be a betrayal of our ways. It would be a divergence from a custom for our queen, nothing more."

"Our queens have never married men," I insisted. "Even my mother refused to marry my father when he asked it of her. And she loved him. And he loved her," I said.

"He did," Ossy nodded. Her eyes became far away for a moment. "He certainly did. But, because of the customs, which are not Laws," she emphasized, "your mother would have been required to challenge her family, and bring one lone man to remain amongst only women, or leave Themiscyra and be with him in Wilusa, which she was free to do, despite the cost. She could have even traveled back and forth, even. The choice that Melanippe made was to allow for Themiscyra to remain a refuge for all women, and for herself to remain in Themiscyra, where she had a purpose. A purpose greater than her feelings for your father. She could not find a way to have both because your father would have demanded much of her time and did not understand our ways. She followed her heart, just as she did by choosing to bear you and sacrifice her right to the crown. Do you understand?"

I did not, really, but I nodded anyway. There was a long spell of quiet, in which I considered Col with a level, thoughtful stare.

"So, I could kill him," I finally said. Ossy choked on her mead and set the cup down before fixing me with an incredulous stare.

"You could," she agreed, her thin eyebrows climbing high. "I am not sure how you came to that conclusion from what I just said. Is this what you desire to do? What your heart says is right?" Her tone was genuinely curious, and though she obviously tried to keep it neutral, it was clouded with doubt.

I *could* kill him. That would remove the possibility that I would betray the Way of the Ha-mazaans, even indirectly. Except, killing indiscriminately and without reason was also not our Way. But would the act be without reason? I had killed his men in order to gain simple goods like clothing and food; surely, if I killed him now, it was simply a delayed outcome of something that could have happened the same day? And yet, killing prisoners of war was also not our Way, and he was essentially that, as I had kidnapped him well after the raid.

The only real reason I could think of to kill him now was that I feared what his presence might mean for me and the future of my people. Because I feared the inevitability of being tied to him and prone to the downfalls that came when men found themselves jealous of a woman's connection to the Great Mother's Old Magic. I feared what could happen between us, what I felt when he looked at me, and whether it was wrong. I feared my own culpability. I feared myself.

"No, it is not what I want," I murmured, and Ossy nodded.

"I did not suspect so. Even so, whatever you choose regarding this man, for yourself, the direction we travel, and the future of the ha-mazaans—that you can possibly know about—" she stressed the last with a pointed look, "is still, ultimately, a choice you will make from within your own heart.

"This is what it means to be Ishassara, Cyra," she said solemnly. "It means choosing that which is best for all, from the most noble and knowing place within you. But it still means choosing. This is all we have with our time outside of the Great Mother's Womb. We choose in every moment who we will be, and we pray that when we return to Her Womb, we will find our choices worthy of seeing ourselves born through Her again."

We sat once more in deep silence until it was interrupted by a soft snore. I glanced in surprise to the far side of the tent where Esten leaned precariously against one of the slanted saplings supporting the tent walls, his mouth slack and his eyes closed. Col shrugged, and my mouth quirked. Neither of them seemed too upset at their continued captivity, nor did they seem intent on planning or executing an escape after all. I sighed and looked at Ossy again.

"Then, my answer is the same," I said. She looked a bit lost. "About my plan," I reminded her. "I think we should keep this one and learn his language. Then we go east, and we hope he is important enough to use as barter for our freedom and safety on this land. And the supplies we need to see us through winter. If he truly is an Ishassari, he will be worth at least that to his people. I hope."

"It is as fine a plan as any, Ishassara," Ossy said, and a glow ignited at her praise. Her steady support meant a great deal to me while everything was so tumultuous. Once more, I was doubly thankful for her wisdom and kindness. I told her so, but she simply smiled at my solemn thanks.

"The promise to support you is a promise I made to your mother when you were just a child," she said. She fixed me with steady, solemn eyes. "However, you are no longer a child. You are a young woman, and the leader of our people. And it so happens that, though I see much in you that is a reflection of your mother, I see also a light that is entirely your own and a strength that is from your spirit alone. It is also for this reason that I am proud to walk with you and pledge you my support, Ishassara Cyra."

I blinked away the sudden tears in my eyes, and she smiled at me fondly, cuffing my arm lightly.

"Now, have you decided what must be done with your red one and his shy friend for the evening?" she asked, businesslike once more.

"We will lock them in the wagons, with a guard posted to each."

"I suppose that is wisest," Ossy nodded sagely, then tipped her head to the side, her eyes sliding to Col. "Or," she continued lightly, "I could move my furs to Sagitta and Alkippe's tent, and only the shy one goes to the wagons."

I shot her a shocked glance, aghast. I could not suppress the flush darkening my face. Ossy chuckled.

"Come now! You fancy each other. You have earned First Blood, and more besides. You can defend yourself if needed, which I doubt it will be, so it is well within your right," she said.

I snapped my mouth shut when I realized it was still hanging open.

"Ossy!" I hissed, unable to form any kind of coherent protest. Mostly because I could not deny having thought about it already. Ossy smirked knowingly. She stood and picked up the wooden tray of food, holding it out to Col with a raised eyebrow, but he waved it away with a polite nod of thanks.

"Perhaps the two of you could take a turn about the forest, and figure out the words for lips, and bed," she suggested archly, making her way to the tent flap and completely ignoring my strangled sounds. She looked back at me before leaving. "I will send another to stay near you in case the yellow one wakes up. But if you decide only one wagon needs guarding, just know, Cyra, it is your choice. There is nothing about a prophecy that makes it so. If you do not wish it, then do not choose him."

With those words, she stepped out of the tent, leaving me to face a pair of curious green eyes, my face uncomfortably hot with chagrin.

CHAPTER 26

SEEN

Despite Ossy's unsubtle prompts to take the red-haired Ishassari to my bed, I did no such thing. Instead, I led them outside and handed Esten off to Leya, instructing her to guard him while he answered the call of nature, wandered the camp, tended to his horse, and slept in the wagon. Once he understood what was happening, he seemed reluctant to leave his friend, but the ha-mazaan nudged him silently with the butt of her spear, and he quieted. I left them to sort out communication regarding the evening's particulars.

As soon as we were outside the tent, Col's tall stallion, apparently not interested in the mares throughout the camp, immediately appeared at his shoulder. I watched them greet each other, noticing with increased curiosity how attentive the horse was to Col's every gesture. When I motioned to Col that I would like to walk into the forest, just the two of us, he hesitated for a moment before gesturing to the horse and speaking a low, drawled murmur of words. The stallion dropped its ears in a distinct display of displeasure, but he remained standing at the edge of the trees as we made our way into the darkening forest.

I motioned for Col to walk ahead of me, and followed at a slight distance as he followed, without hesitation or stumbling, the same path that I had taken for the past week. He either had a tracker's eyes, or he had watched me walk it. Neither possibility brought comfort. But when we finally came to the edge of the ravine, his shoulders straightened in the dim light of the moon, the tension going out of his spine as his muscles relaxed, as though he had expected something sinister to be waiting for him. Yet, he had followed anyway. He stopped at the top, looking back at me questioningly, and as I came to stand beside him, my eyes moved to the rock at the bottom of the gully and the small figure on top of it.

He smiled, then, and said the same thing he had earlier in the day when I had held the other figures.

"Assu?"

Before I could respond, he began making his way down the steep side of the ravine. I thought about ordering him to stop, but as I had not brought my bow and there was not much I could do other than bury my knife in his back if he ran, I stayed quiet. It was highly unlikely he would leave without his friend or his horse, and for some reason, I got the feeling he wanted to stay. He had certainly not shown resistance, even when we first took them on the open road, and had cooperated easily enough for the remainder of the afternoon. I was not sure why it would be so, but he seemed as curious about us, about me, as I was about him.

As Col hopped the stream at the bottom with a nimble leap, I wondered idly if the prophecies of Matar Kubileya were ever given to those who did not follow our ways. If those who knew Her by another name saw similar visions and had Spirit dreams. It was possible he had seen me before in a vision, and this is why he had been so brazen that first day in the forest. Even with my arrow quivering in the tree next to him, he had stood bravely, confidently, though not mockingly. No, he had seemed very aware that I could have sent the arrow through his heart as easily as my dagger spearing venison on a plate. Yet, somehow, he had also believed, rather foolishly, I mused, even if he did know my face from a vision, that I would choose not to do so. But then, I was relying on the same foolishness, simply because I had known his face for years. It did not mean I knew *him*.

He retrieved the third carving and promptly made his way back to me. Twilight gathered quickly here in the shadowed forest. I could barely make out his features until he was close to the top as the darkness collected more densely inside the ravine. It had not seemed so late when we left the glade, and I wondered at the wisdom of coming alone with him to this place, but I wanted to see what he had left for me. His eyes twinkled curiously as he held the tiny figure out to me, cradled in both palms. He smiled.

"Assu?" he asked again, very quietly, and this time, along with the hopefulness, there was something else in his voice. He sounded... anxious.

I looked at it but did not take it immediately. How he had carved the first two with less than a day spent on each was a mystery to me, but this one even more so. Where he had found time to sleep, I couldn't imagine. Perhaps he had not slept. Perhaps he was some kind of strange being that did not need sleep. Or, perhaps he was some kind of strange being that had used magic to make the carvings. As I looked at it, and finally took it into my hands, I felt a strong suspicion this last theory was very much the case.

It was a horse again, but this time a figure sat on its back. The horse was more crudely done than the first two, with the legs carved only as a rough outline in the solid wood underneath. The head and neck and tail were clearly defined, though, with all the wood cut away and even the fine details of the hair perfectly defined. He had spent more time on the person, etching as many details as possible in the short time between one morning's delivery and the next. The scales of my vest were perfect, and the cuffs of trousers over my bare feet, with slender toes cut just so, so intricate that I could not picture a blade shaping them. The hands were not fully formed as they rested on the mane, but they were still tapered, and slender grooves revealed my fingers, with tiny bumps as my knuckles. The hair was long, tiny notches cut all the way down to resemble the braid that often swung over my left shoulder, just as it was depicted. Best of all were the fine markings of soot he had once again worked into the figure like paint. They showed Inara's dapples again, and the darkness of my hair. They also showed my tattoos. Though they were slightly misplaced, he had drawn the crescents of the Great Mother's moon cycle as they traveled up my arm. He had not captured the open triangle at my wrist, but the lines that showed my unbroken heritage, and the thick line that expressed my grief and loss of my beloved mother, were clear. He had even captured a crude outline of the *rhu-tasiya* markings on my right shoulder, with her hind feet twisted upward to show she walked with part of her spirit in the Otherworld.

I was stunned. Speechless. I stared at it for a long, bemused moment, and when I finally looked up into his face, there was a tenderness there that I could not fathom. He smiled, nodding, as though pleased with what he saw in my face. Still, I said nothing, though I clutched the piece tightly, protectively, to my scaled vest, careful not to smudge the soot.

It was not as though it was the most magnificent carving I had ever seen. It was not even the best likeness of Inara or of me that could be imagined. But the details he had managed to place, to *remember*, even, were of such significance, even though he had only seen me briefly during our skirmish, and from a distance in the forest, that I could not help but feel exposed. Vulnerable. *Seen.*

"Thank you," I whispered hoarsely, and meant it. He nodded again, though we had not covered those words in our language lesson. I began to turn away. His hand caught mine by the wrist. Surprised, I looked down at where his long fingers easily circled my arm, following the line of the thin tattoo. His hand immediately released me, but he took a step closer so that I had to look up at him. He raised a hand then and slowly, as though to not startle me, tucked a loose strand of hair that had unwound itself from my braid behind my ear. His fingers traced lightly down my cheekbone and along my jaw before they slowly dropped away. He said something quietly, looking into my eyes as though waiting for me to answer his unknown words. Before I could think of anything in my suddenly sluggish brain, he raised his head and turned toward the woods and spoke loudly, in a completely different tone. I spun, looking into the darkness of the trees, my hand going instinctively to my sheathed blade that I realized too late should have made an appearance the moment his hand touched mine.

There was only a whisper of sound, but I saw pale blonde hair and skin in the thin twilight as Prothoe stepped out from behind the narrow trees. She held a bow, the arrow notched and ready between her fingers, though she did not usually carry anything but her axe. She had been guarding me the whole time, of course. A flush rose on my face, burning hot. She would have seen everything Col had just done.

"Ishassara," Prothoe said easily as she came closer. "I thought it best that you have an escort."

"It is good, Prothoe. I thank you," I replied, more formal than the situation warranted, hoping the darkness hid some of my awkwardness as I recalled his fingers stroking my face. How I had leaned into the touch, almost automatically. She seemed to give no notice to my discomfort, and her bow was relaxed now. She stared at Col with a considering gaze, then said to us, "We should be back at camp. Ossy has already moved her furs from your tent."

I made a strangled noise, and she paused, turning back to look from my reddening face to Col's passive, unwitting one.

"Is that not what you desire, Ishassara?"

"He will sleep in the wagon," I said loudly. Too loudly, and with too much barely concealed panic in my voice. I was aware that Col was eyeing me curiously, wondering at our conversation, but Prothoe merely shrugged and gestured for me to lead the way.

) (

Col did not remember the walk back to the wagons. An unexpected turmoil of emotions, not to mention the heat of desire that still coursed through his body, jumbled his mind from the moment his fingertips had brushed Cyra's skin. He had wanted to kiss her so badly, as unwise as that might have been, and had only resisted because he knew they had been followed to the ravine by one of her guards. He could not forget the wonder of her face shining up at him in the moonlight. Nor did he want to.

When they arrived back in camp, fires burned inside closed tents, and a few women talked quietly at one of the outside fires. Several turned their gazes to stare at Col in open curiosity as he followed Cyra toward the wagons. Another woman stood between the two covered holds, presumably guarding Esten already, hopefully, safely inside one of them. Cyra turned as Col stepped up behind her, and she gestured to one of his own wagons.

She said something unintelligible, though it sounded shy and awkward, and then moved away on stiff legs, back toward her own tent. Col watched her go, and when she pulled the flap aside and glanced back at him, he smiled, though his face was in shadow. The pale-haired woman prodded him with the end of her bow.

Col climbed awkwardly into the wagon, forced to duck his head and crouch because the wagon had been built as a storage and transport unit for Scoloti supplies, rather than the more spacious living quarters of the housing wagons. The light from the outside fires seeped through the rawhide covering, lending a warm glow to the inside. Once inside, he was happy to find the chair he had carved for his father intact, though it did mean the available floor space was considerably cramped for sleeping. There were furs piled inside, though, and he stretched out with a grateful sigh, the weariness of the day's tension slowly easing from his muscles.

"Esten?" he called softly through the rawhide covering. He listened for a moment until the sound like a hibernating bear might make drifted from the wagon beside him.

Satisfied his friend was well enough, Col's mind immediately went back to Cyra. He thought of how she had sharpened that gleaming blade with practiced precision for most of the afternoon until he thought the blade might be whittled away to a needle. The sound it had made, and even the color of it, had been spinning ideas in his mind of what it could be made of. Not bronze, of that he was fairly certain. He pictured the fierce intensity of her face as she demanded words from him, pulling the language out of him as though he were a deep well and she the bucket, filling herself with every drop of water she could find. He thought of her eyes. The way they had gleamed in the darkness when he had fetched the carving from the ravine. He thought about the soft skin of her cheek under his fingertips, and the silk of her hair, and wondered how he could ever have mistaken her for a man. She was very obviously woman, but she was also so strange. Fierce, but in other ways tender, even vulnerable. Mostly fierce, he thought to himself, smiling into the wagon's darkness.

He wondered how she would have reacted if he had done it. Pressed his mouth to her often compressed, irritated lips. Likely slid the knife straight through his ribcage, he thought. Perversely, the scenario made him feel honored. Honored that, so far, he had not given her cause to use her blade. He had no intention of becoming her enemy, but it would be a difficult task to convince a wildcat to be friends.

He thought then about the scene he had witnessed earlier in the day and the moment he had lost all doubt she was the leader of this odd group of women and their horses. He had not understood much of what happened, or anything that had been said, but he did not need to know their words to recognize commands and obedience to those commands. From the way Cyra had spoken to the woman kneeling in front of her, he knew she was angry. Furious. Col wondered if it had to do with his brothers. He could not see Arpo making such a rash decision. He wondered if Lio had advanced somehow and engaged in a battle with the women, and there had been losses. It was very unlikely that so few women, well outfitted and practiced as they were, could overpower his brother's men. And yet, two weeks ago, he would never have believed it if he was told an army of women would descend on his lands, fully experienced with sword and spear, and successfully ambush his own caravan.

Because of this, the idea that Arpoxais was possibly on to something with his outlandish theory had been swirling at the edges of his thoughts all day. Could these women have the Golden Axe? Had he seen it in the hands of the red-haired one? Or, as his time with them today had made him wonder with increasing unease, could they actually be the Golden Axe? The dual interpretation had long frustrated his father and his brothers, but Col had never before given it much thought, neither before nor after his mother had named him heir. But Arpoxais seemed certain one of them carried the actual axe, and his certainty was driving a wedge of doubt into Col's mind. What if the opposite interpretation of the prophecy were true? What if the Axe was, as the legend so obscurely indicated, an army in itself? What if these women were that army, and Cyra their leader?

It seemed so implausible. And yet...and yet, they were so fierce. Strong, not just in body, but in mind, in discipline and strength of will, he could see it. It was clear in the way each of them went about their errands with firm precision and none of the mewling complaints some of his own men gave when tasked with cutting wood or cleaning the stables. They were so strange and mysterious, like every fantastical tale his mother or mother's mother had ever told him from their homeland.

Like every story of the Golden Axe that was prophesied.

Col turned again on the hard floor, the wagon's axle creaking in protest. He stuffed his leather vest beneath his head and tried to steer his thoughts away from the Golden Axe, real or metaphorical, and from his brothers, and from the fact that he and his closest friend were captive to the most fearsome group of women, and possibly people in general, that he had ever known. Cyra's eyes came to his mind unbidden, bright, and translucent like a polished silver mirror. This, he did not push away.

He had not been wrong about feeling a connection and of her feeling it as well. He knew she wanted something from him, as well, and sometimes when she had looked at him today, he had thought she was studying him for some sign, some message that he did not know how to give. That they could not understand one another's language seemed only a minor inconvenience. Words would come in time. For now, he would show her that he meant her no harm. Perhaps he would carve her a new horse since she had looked so pleased by the last one.

Col smiled, picturing it. Then, he slept.

☽ ☾

I let the flap fall after Col disappeared inside the wagon, and made my way to the now smoldering fire pit. I set the small figurine down on top of the wooden chest, making sure it was steady, and stared at it as I untied the laces of my vest. I added wood to the fire and thought about what the carvings could mean. When I lay down on the mattress of dried grass and pulled the soft furs over me, I thought of his fingers, the way they had gently, oh so gently, tucked my hair behind my ear. I thought of his eyes and the way they shone when he looked at me. I thought of the way I wanted to feel his mouth on mine and his arm around my shoulders.

I thought of Eri.

I could hardly judge her for choosing as she had, at least here in this land, if she, too, felt these things with such disarming pressure. If she followed her prophecy and her heart, wrapped into one. And it was this thought, deeply disturbing in more ways than one, that kept me awake long into the night, after all of the fires in the camp had gone out.

CHAPTER 27

FREE TO GO

I awoke bleary-eyed and tangled in furs well after most of the ha-mazaans had already eaten a hot meal and finished leading the horses to their morning grazing. Shamed at my own lack of discipline, I made quick work of dressing and smoothing out my braid. When I finally flung aside the tent flap, Col and Esten were already seated in front of the group fire pit, their feet tucked easily against the rough stump seats, their hands filled with small bowls of food. Ossy and Alkippe sat nearby with several other ha-mazaans, and all seemed to be relaxed and unconcerned at the mixed company.

Col looked up as I approached the uneven circle, immediately coming to his feet and offering me the stump he had been using. I shook my head slightly, but smiled my thanks, motioning for him to sit again. He did, and Esten nodded a reluctant greeting back to me as I acknowledged him.

"Where is Glaukia?" I asked Alkippe.

She scowled, her dark eyes hard onyx and the tattooed dots on her cheeks dancing under tense muscles. Her long, pink-tipped finger pointed toward the first wagon we had stolen. I saw a pair of hands tied to the heavy spokes of the wheel and Glaukia's tall frame folded on the ground beside it. "There," she said. "I released her for a few moments at dawn. She tended to her business and ate. What would you like done, Ishassara?"

Her clipped tone made it obvious she was impatient for justice to be meted out, but I shook my head. "I have not yet made my decision. I will speak with her first." Alkippe made as though to follow me, but I held out my hand to stop her. "No. I will hear what she has to say alone, and

I will make my decision alone. She is my responsibility. My burden." I looked at the others as I finished. Ossy nodded.

Glaukia's head hung to her chest as I approached, but she raised it as the sound of my bare feet crunched the dried grass. Her eyes were bleary and pained, and I was sure a night spent in such a position could not have been comfortable. The way her hands were tied to the top of the wheel, she could not quite reach the ground to fully sit. I squelched the pity threatening to soften my resolve and stood over her, motioning for her to stand. She struggled to get up, her legs most likely numbed from kneeling for so long, but I made no move to help her or steady her as she swayed on her feet, merely watching her impassively until she had braced herself enough to look me in the face again.

There was pain, there, and fear, and a small shadow of something else. Sadness, perhaps. Regret.

"Why?' I asked simply. She opened dry lips, her brows knitting in some confusion at the broad question. "Why did you choose her over me, as your Ishassara?"

Glaukia closed her mouth, her eyes sliding away to my shoulder, and licked her dry lips nervously. She thought carefully for a long moment before her blue-grey eyes met mine again.

"I missed my husband," she said simply. The confusion was plain on my face, and she shrugged, her tied hands making the gesture awkward. "I knew you would follow in the same path as your mother, and your aunts, and your grandmother, Otrera, and her mother before her," she explained. "Your great-grandmother Marpesa killed her husband, and her sister Lampedo the same, and forbade men to live permanently in Themiscyra. Yet, the other cities allow men. They allow ha-mazaans to marry, and to keep their boys into adulthood rather than foster them to other families, or banish them to their fathers in Galatae." There was true resentment in her voice. I frowned.

"Marpesa killed her husband because he was a scourge among men," I said. "A vile man who beat her and came within one knife's width of stilling her heart. She killed him in self-defense and barely lived to tell of it. You know this. It is why she and her sisters founded Themiscyra and Sinope. To provide refuge for those who would flee such troubles and live freely. As women should." I was so familiar with the story that the words had taken on a vaguely rote sound, as though I were reading them from an instructional tablet rather than feeling the truth of them. Glaukia was nodding.

"Aye, Marpesa had good reason to rise up as she did. To learn the bow and the sword and take back her life. Her daughter Otrera also liberated many women in this way. But her insistence that this was the *only* way cost many of us. It cost us our fathers and our brothers," Glaukia said. "It ultimately cost me my last years with my husband."

The pain in her poured out, the floodgates of truth now opened.

"Then your mother forfeited her crown by becoming a *matar* rather than adhering to the Ways of the Sister-Queens. Many of us were angry that her daughter should have unattested rights to be Ishassara, after everything." When she continued, her eyes could not meet mine. "We were angry that one law could be broken, but...but not others. That because of whose daughter she was, she had rights we did not have. We were angry that her daughter would be queen, yes. That our loved ones were being sent away, and the law forbidding men in Themiscyra could not be broken, while she had broken such an important law and was rewarded rather than punished."

She glanced at my stony face and swallowed, licking dry lips. "Hipponike spoke often, and bitterly, about how she felt oppressed by Otrera before your grandmother died. And then even more so by Hippolyta and Antiope, who took Otrera's place with no contest and with no willingness to change or listen to the people. It was Hipponike that put it into our minds that maybe Themiscyra could be different," Glaukia said. Her voice grew quieter and less confident.

"When...when her daughter shared her own prophecy of being Chosen Queen, of leading a new tribe of people by casting her lot with a man of golden hair, I thought...I thought it was a sign from the Great Mother that a new way was possible." She shook her head, squinting as though she might be able to see something just out of reach. "But then you shared your own prophecy, and I felt so confused, Cyra. They seemed the same. They both seemed to promise the freedoms I wanted, but...but I had already pledged to help Eri. I swear I did not know about her treachery with Theseus," she said in a rush, her head shaking from side to side with desperation. "If I had..." Her eyes met mine again in desperate entreaty, but I kept my face blank. Glaukia ducked her head to her chest and stared at her bound hands.

"When she told me about the men here wanting to...meet more

women…and that she had already lain with one of them, something came over me, Ishassara. A desire. Not just for the flesh. I am lonely. It has been so long since I have been with my husband. He died many winters ago, and I never traveled from Themiscyra after his death. It was a longing that I thought could be satisfied, and no harm done. It was not against our laws. You said it yourself!" Her speech was fast, then slow again, changing tempo with every new thought.

"And yes, I thought it might help her cause if she had been chosen as a queen who would lead us in a new way. Lead us home. But then, after Eri confessed to poisoning the *kimiz*, I knew I had chosen the wrong Ishassara. You must believe me, Cyra. I would never have betrayed you or your mother if I had known. I will never betray you again!"

Her eyes pleaded even as tears fell onto her weathered, almost leathery face, the scar and small tattooed dots on her cheeks glistening under the wetness. I pictured her practicing with axe and bow next to my mother's tall, leanly muscled frame, a sight I had seen many times before. I pictured her in the Moon Hall, happily performing the ritual dance we made to celebrate Kubileya's light in the full moon. I pictured her drinking with the queens and laughing with the Xanharaspas. All the while wishing for a different life.

"And what of your own prophecy?"

It was taboo to ask such an intimate thing. Prophecies were gifts from Kubileya to ha-mazaan, and no other had the right to ask the details. And yet, I felt Glaukia had waived that right. She had made choices based on the prophecy of another, after all. "What did the Oracle show you that made you choose this way?"

Glaukia blanched. Her mouth made a round "O" with the shock of the question, but she firmed her chin and stood straighter, as though the memory of her own time in the Oracle's cave renewed her confidence.

"The Oracle foretold I would choose a way different from my sisters. That I would light a path for other ha-mazaans by revealing another's treachery and save lives with the truth that I spoke. It is why I returned rather than stay with young Eri. I fulfilled my prophecy, just as it was shown to me. I have done right by you, as it was foretold."

She nodded passionately to convince me of her sincerity. I tipped my head, and something in my eyes caused her eager smile to fade. The hopeful conviction on her face flickered and died at my words.

"You could have fulfilled that prophecy the moment Hipponike spoke of betraying the queens in Themiscyra. Or on the beach when Eri revealed her intentions for betrayal, is that not so?" I asked, my voice mild. "You could have revealed treachery long ago and saved many more lives, including Hipponike's, and now Eri's. And yet, you did so when it was too late."

I pulled my knife from its sheath, and her eyes widened. The blade flashed as it cut through the ropes on her wrists, and her shoulders sagged, her entire body trembling with relief.

"Come and face your chosen path, then."

Without another word, I turned and walked away, her voice crying out hoarsely to my stiff back.

"Ishassara! Cyra!" she called, pleading. "Please! I did not know..."

I heard her stumbling footsteps behind me, her legs no doubt still numb. I did not turn to her weeping. As we approached the circle again, it had grown with more ha-mazaans, perhaps all of them, and all were quiet. There were fewer now that nine others had deserted with Eri. Still, there were a lot of faces to look upon and remain firmly resolved to what needed to be done.

Glaukia's muffled sobbing continued behind me. Col stood once more and stared at me, his expression grave, as though he could sense the seriousness of the mood that hung over the camp. Perhaps he knew, as Ishassari, what difficult decisions felt like in the gut, twisting with the weight of twenty stones. Perhaps he knew what it meant to have the weight of someone else's life clutched in the palms of your hands. How it felt to have no good way to set them down again. I looked over the composed and serious faces of the ha-mazaans and straightened my spine.

"We cannot stay here much longer," I said. "Our source of food from the northern forest and from the eastern and western plains has been cut off. Eri, who seeks to betray our every move, has joined the army to the west. Winter descends, and we do not have adequate shelter or provisions for a long cold. For these reasons, we will move east as soon as I have learned enough of this man's language," I announced, looking around at the ha-mazaans. They were confused, as I expected.

"This one," I pointed to Col, his red hair bright against the blue of the mid-morning sky, "is the son of a king. An Ishassari."

Shocked murmurs, astonished expressions, and furtive glances between Col and myself at this announcement.

"We will use him and his friend to barter a deal for our safe passage, or hopefully for adequate supplies for the winter, for ourselves and our horses. When we have assessed who his people are and how strong, perhaps what is not offered freely can be taken, if there are enough of us left."

Concern and doubt blossomed on a few faces. I nodded to them, specifically. "Any ha-mazaan who feels this is a foolish choice may speak freely, now, without fear of repercussion. This is my sworn promise. However, I will also tell you that this man," I gestured to Col again, "is the same one that was shown to me in my vision from the Great Mother, at my first moon-blood. If I understand the vision, which I do not claim to, he is the one I am prophesied to bind myself to."

Surprise turned to shock. Ossy had been sworn to secrecy, so even Alkippe and Sagitta wore expressions of consternation as they looked at him with renewed interest. Col looked uncomfortable for the first time among us, as everyone stared at him with a new, curious intensity. He shifted his feet as though preparing to run and looked back at the women cautiously. His eyes met Esten's before he looked back at me, questioning, but my concern was for the women.

"I feel I must be honest with you so that you, in turn, are free to make your best choices. For these reasons of shelter and food, and from the time I have spent speaking—or trying to speak—to this Ishassari, I have decided I must follow what I feel is the right thing to do, for our safety. This is not something I say lightly or expect you to understand. I do not expect you to trust him." My eyes met each of theirs for a long moment before I shifted my gaze to the next ha-mazaan.

"However, if you do not trust me as your Ishassara, then we are doomed to fail. This is what I must know, now, before we move any further. Whether you will trust me, or whether you wish to go your own way, like Glaukia and the others. Like Eri."

A hushed silence descended as my words ended. Then, a tentative, quiet voice from the far side of the circle.

"What about Glaukia? What will become of her?"

I hesitated. Glaukia's quiet sniffles had quieted behind me.

"Glaukia has confessed that she did not hold with the ways of my grandmothers long before we came to these shores, and that she no longer wanted to live the Ways of the ha-mazaans in Themiscyra."

There were startled voices from the crowd and a low murmuring of questions. Perhaps, for some, a fear of discovery. I raised my chin.

"Her choice to believe or desire differently is not the issue. Her choice to hide this belief and pretend to give her support, when she was only waiting for her best chance to flaunt our Laws, to undermine the authority of the queens and betray the new Ishassara—this is what I will not forgive. But I cannot find honor in killing someone who has only followed their prophecy, even if it has led them down a dark path."

I turned back to Glaukia. Her blue-grey eyes were rimmed with red, and the scar on her face was glaringly white on skin grown pale with terror.

"You wanted so badly to go your own way, Glaukia. To not have a granddaughter of Otrera and daughter of a lawbreaker as Ishassara. But you also did not want to stay loyal to the Ishassara you freely chose. It is your right to choose, and you have chosen according to your own heart. So you will have your right to choose freely now. Forever.

"You are no longer ha-mazaan. I release you from our Ways and our sisterhood. You are free to go. North or south, east or west—I do not care. But you will go without your weapons, without axe or sword, and you will go without a horse. And though I give these women the freedom to choose whether they will trust me or not, to follow me from here, none will leave with you. You will go alone, as you have chosen. Or, you will choose to die, and I will wield the axe myself."

There were many indrawn breaths. No ha-mazaan had ever been outcast before. Death was more honorable. I wondered which she would choose, and which she would find any honor in, now that the damage had been done. Glaukia paled so that her whole face was a scar. I turned my back to the agony in her face. This was who I had to be, now.

"I am asking you now, ha-mazaans, if you do not trust me, and if you have doubts about me as your Ishassara, then this is the time to make your decision and not pay the price for it. I do not need to wait for the Alsanti to free you. You will not be outcast like Glaukia. She has brought this on herself by treachery that was two-fold and can never be trusted again. But I will not move forward with anyone who hides from me, or, more importantly, the world, what they truly are. What they believe of the ha-mazaan Ways. The dissent of a few will mean destruction for all."

I scanned their stricken faces. Many looked uncertain, even grim, but for the first time in a long while, I felt sure of what needed to be done.

"Mistrust between us will be a sickness that gathers in the roots and spreads to weaken the entire tree. We must work toward the same vision if we are to survive. The time for division is behind us. This is the time for unity, and unity will require honesty. Tell me your hearts so that we can work together as one toward the same goal."

This time, the silence stretched out uncomfortably long, while inside, my heart beat loudly, pounding its tempo in my ears. I gambled everything with my speech. If even a handful of women chose to break away now, we would not have enough numbers to defend ourselves in an attack or organize raids for new supplies. Or if any of the surrounding camps descended on us, to reclaim this son of a king. But a decision had to be made, and that was what I was doing.

Thraso stepped forward then, and I steeled myself for her words.

"I do not know entirely what Glaukia believes, Ishassara," the tall woman said slowly. "It is true, the Laws have sometimes been restrictive." Thraso looked around, her mouth a serious, thin line in her broad face. "However," she continued, meeting the eyes of several uncertain-looking ha-mazaans, and then my own, "those of us who lived in Themsicyra, rather than Chadesia or Lykipe or Thrace, where the men live freely, chose to do so. Many of us because of these very restrictions. It was easier to know our freedoms to live and fight, to bleed and dance, to worship and speak, would not be hindered by a man's control, or jealousy, or even his affection." She shrugged. "I never felt like I was oppressed or restrained from seeking out a man's company if I chose it. I do not think you will deny us the same. The Laws were there to protect the freedom of the ha-mazaans. The freedom to dance, and bleed, and fight as we wish. I would only ask that these rights remain, even if new ways and new laws are inevitable."

"Aye," another voice said, and Asteria stepped forward, her hand resting lightly on the sword at her hip. "I ask the same, and would ask it of any who leads us. To freely live and choose within the rights gifted to us by Marpesa and Lampedo, by Otrera, by Themis, and by the women who have fought for our freedom since man began to remake a god in his image."

Leya moved forward, her dark eyes unreadable. "My own moon-blood prophecy has long seemed impossible. To have a child, a son, and to raise him at my side to become a warrior as honorable and strong as his mother and grandmothers and sister ha-mazaans. Perhaps there will be new laws, now that Themiscyra is so far from us—possibly lost forever. We all know it is true," she said, though her voice shook as she met other ha-mazaans frowns. She raised her chin and forged on, meeting my eyes with a steady determination. "New laws that allow for where we are today. I would have been *matar* already if it had been allowed. But I was too young. Now..." she shrugged, and there was sorrow in her eyes. Her eyes flickered to the two men standing silently amongst us. "Now it may be too late, I don't know."

I nodded my understanding. Leya was my own age. I had not known she wanted children. And though her moon-blood prophecy shocked me, it was no more aberrant than my own, and I could hardly fault her for it.

Phillipisa spoke next. "We only ask for the rights Kubileya granted us and calls us to fight for. No more, and no less."

But then Thraso spoke again, and her eyes were troubled. She did not look at me, though. She looked at Col.

"Will you make this man your husband, then? And seek to have him rule us? As king?"

When she finally looked at me, I met her eyes with all the honesty and strength of will I could muster. "It is not my intention to make him your king. It is not my desire to see any ha-mazaan subject to any man in such a way she would lose her right to choose, or fight, or love, or bleed freely. This is a vow I swear to you on my life. But I cannot answer the rest of your question, Thraso. I have known him one day, and yet his spirit I have known almost ten years. I hope you understand what I say."

She pondered my meaning a moment before nodding, accepting the truth of my answer as I was able to give it. "Our freedoms, and the right to choose. This is what I will lay down my life for," she said.

There were other murmurs of agreement. No one stepped forward to proclaim their dissent. I nodded, easing the breath out of my lungs, and met their eyes with solemn earnestness.

"I swear to you that your choices, and the ability to live as you have, will never be taken from you. To choose freely, with honor, is the value that makes us worthy to be ha-mazaan. Makes us willing to be warriors who protect the Way with axe and bow when we are called upon to do so. Otherwise, we kill without purpose, and that is not our Way. Our

Way is what keeps us, and those we have sworn to protect, free. I will only be Ishassara to serve that freedom. This I promise you."

)(

We took Glaukia to the farthest southern point that we could, away from the armies on the other three sides of our camp. I let her ride her own horse as we went so that she would remember what she was losing. Her face was ashen when I took her reins and ordered her to dismount. Alkippe handed her the skins of water, the furs, and supplies that would keep her alive for long enough that she could find her own path. And she handed her the green bow and quiver of arrows that Ossy had convinced me was fair to provide since the weapon would not mark her as ha-mazaan. Only a survivor. I had agreed reluctantly, but when we left Glaukia, her face watching us go as an abandoned dog says a final farewell to its master, I was glad they had convinced me to give that small mercy, at least.

That night I dreamed of her, walking alone in the wilderness. She was lost, and a tawny-red lioness hunted her. Her bow was broken, her feet ravaged. She was bleeding blackened blood from her heart, and the wound looked old, infected by time and exposure.

She cried out the name of the man she had been married to many years ago. When he did not answer, she cried for her father. Other voices joined in her crying, women and men, until they filled the landscape with weeping, and I heard every name of every broken heart cried from their invisible lips. I heard my mother's voice. She was young and unseasoned, and she wept for something that could never be.

I awoke with their voices shuttered in my heart and the sound of the eagle crying mournfully from the treetops above Col's wagon.

CHAPTER 28

SWEETGRASS AND LEATHER

I was peppering Col with further questions, Esten snoozing rather uncomfortably against the stump on the ground when Tekmessa approached. Col ceased his attempts to explain the various words for "mine," which I was struggling to comprehend in any meaningful way. He had been in our camp three weeks, and I was still unsure of most of what was said. And yet, there had been some progress, at least on my end. Two paces forward and one back. Today had been one long debacle of hand gestures, frustrated pointing, and, occasionally, excited congratulations when a word was finally understood. Too occasional. Therefore, when he turned to Tekmessa with a respectful nod, I was quite grateful for the interruption. I looked up from my seat and smiled as she entered the circle.

"Ishassara," Tekmessa smiled back, her left hand holding her long red robes high of the dust and ashes beneath our feet, while her right hand carried what looked like an ornately decorated jar we had taken from the Achaean galley.

"Hello, Tekmessa. Are you well? I feel I have not spoken with you in too many days," I said, genuinely apologetic. I missed the *zizenti's* gentle demeanor. My days had been filled with horse training, weapons practice, defense strategies, and now, hostage minding and language lessons. There had been little time for idle talk with friends.

"It is no worry, Ishassara," Tekmessa smiled. "I have been busy foraging and preparing. Here," she offered me the jar. I took it, looking at it, and then her, questioningly. "It is for preventing a child," she said calmly.

I stared up at her, and definitely not at Col.

"I did not think you would want to be with child now, here," she spread a graceful hand to indicate the grove, but she meant much more than that. It was her way of saying that the choice would be mine, despite my age and the expectations that my role as Defending Queen should prohibit me from becoming *matar*. It had become clear that the strict rules of my grandmother and great-grandmothers had become archaic to the true hearts of the ha-mazaans. A new Way was emerging in this new land, and the realization both terrified and gladdened me.

I opened my mouth, about to protest much of what was being suggested, but then I closed it again. Finally, I said, earnestly, "Thank you, Tekmessa."

Esten awoke with a start at the *zizenti's* feet and, seeing her red robes so close to his face, jerked his head backward and lurched to his feet, still sleep-fogged. Tekmessa smiled at him kindly as his bleary eyes took in her shaved head, fuzzed with long stubble, then the tattooed marks on her forehead and collarbone, and the tiny ones on her hands. When he looked into her face, which was calmly watching him watch her, he reddened to a deep magenta and stammered out a garbled mix of our words that was possibly meant to be a greeting.

Tekmessa's smile widened, and she held out her hand to the stocky man. Esten took it as though transfixed, his hands almost bearlike over her slender fingers, and he bent to kiss one of the tattoos on her thumb. I looked up at Tekmessa curiously as she stepped back and then glanced at Col. He was watching the two with an amused twinkle.

"Once a day, Ishassara," Tekmessa said suddenly, as though no interruption had occurred. Esten stood conspicuously still, staring at her, but the *zizenti* was unfazed. She gestured at the clay jar I held. "Best start now, unless you are going to make the poor man sleep in the wagon another night."

With what I feared was a very obvious wink, the priestess turned and made her graceful way back to the covered awning she spent so much time under, drying and crushing various herbs and preparing tinctures for our camp's needs. Esten watched her go, and I eyed the jar in my hand. After a few moments of consideration, in which I steadfastly avoided Col's eyes, I pulled the cork stopper and took a swig of it. My face involuntarily screwed tight with disgust at the bitter, acrid taste, but I choked it down with determined gulps. When I did look at Col, he was watching me with an increasingly familiar glint in his eye.

Defiantly, I took another drink, sealed the bottle with a decisive shove of the cork, and stood.

)(

Col stood to follow Cyra as she spoke in hesitant Scoloti, asking him—no, definitely ordering him, even if she didn't have the right words—to prepare his horse. When she motioned for Esten to stay behind, shooing him toward the awning where the red-robed priestess worked every day, Col's lips twitched as he watched his friend turn from pink to dark red in embarrassment. He clapped Esten on the shoulder as he left him there in the circle, the poor man's feet rooted to the ground in fear.

He bridled Faelan as instructed, leaving the saddle with the rest of the tack, also as instructed. Cyra emerged from her tent with her bow slung over her chest and a full quiver of arrows. He adjusted the knife in his own belt and raised his eyebrows, wondering what she was up to. She had returned his knife to him a week before, but this was the first time he had been allowed to ride out with her rather than stay with one of the many women set to guard him while the others went about their morning training routines. Cyra gave him no clues of what she was about, though, and only looped a thin rein of leather around her horse's neck before swinging easily onto the mare's back. She looked down at him with a particularly challenging glint in her eye.

Col grinned up at her and swung himself onto the chestnut's tall, bare back with equal ease, meeting her gaze and her challenge with raised eyebrows. She rewarded him with her own grin, a fierce and determined flash of teeth, and then they were both cantering into the forest. She called back to the women about to rush after her, waving her hand for them to stay behind as the horses disappeared into the trees, and Col felt for the first time in many weeks a welcome freedom from the oppressive, sometimes hostile glares of his guards.

They rode at a steady gait until the northern meadow opened before them. Col knew Lio was still in the northern forest with his army, though Cyra had communicated in broken words that the western army had moved farther away. He wondered what Arpo was up to. He had seemed so adamant about the Golden Axe. And neither brother had even attempted to rescue him, which he did not regret, as he didn't want the women hurt. Still, he had thought they might make some effort—

Col's ruminations on his brother's strategies were cut short as soon as the meadow opened up to them, and Cyra shouted a loud "Ha!"

Her dappled mare, Inara, lunged into a gallop, and Cyra's laugh echoed back to his startled face before he shouted his own encouragement to a more than willing Faelan. Col was delighted to feel free again after so many hours sitting and constantly talking misshapen words. The stallion stretched long legs into the wind, and his head was low and soon level with Inara's; both horses laid their ears flat and ran faster, and Col heard Cyra laugh again. Col could see the mare's refusal to allow another horse to take a lead, no matter how long its legs were. *Like mother like daughter*, Col thought, and spurred Faelan faster.

When the northern treeline came into view, Cyra nudged the horse to the right in a wide arc, and Col followed. They raced in a circle all the way back to the opening in the forest, and Col thought she might head back to camp already. His heart fell a bit in disappointment as they slowed. Faelan let himself be reined into a long-legged, impatient trot. But as both horses settled into a fast walk, snorting air through wide nostrils more from the thrill of the race than the effort of it all, Cyra kept going past the entrance to the camp, following the same track they had just raced over. Above them, the golden eagle screamed petulantly.

Cyra glanced up at it at the same time as Col. The raptor was flying high against the sun, her wings a gliding spot of darkness against the blue of the sky. She, too, had not felt free to roam while she watched over him in the camp. But she was well enough, he knew, and technically free to roam where she wished. It was her own choice to stay near him. He realized Cyra was looking at him and met her gaze with a steady, curious one of his own.

He saw the flush start in her throat, and her expression shifted from searching to haughty in a heartbeat. She fixed her gaze ahead, and they rode further in silence. Both of them brought their horses up short when a sound crackled from the path ahead of them. Cyra had drawn her bow over her head and notched an arrow before Col could even turn his head for a full scan of the field. But all he saw was grass waving in the sun and the trees to the far north of the meadow. If Liopoxais had scouts in the middle of the field, they would be well hidden in the thick grass and impossible to see from this angle.

A movement from the corner of his vision made him jerk his eyes back to Cyra. She knelt on the mare's back, holding her bow in one hand and balancing herself with the other as she brought one foot under her, then two. He raised his eyebrows as she stood fully, just as he had seen her do the day she ambushed his caravan. Back when he had so foolishly assumed she was a man rather than a creature of the fae. Her arrow aimed where the sound had come from, and when she clicked the mare forward with her tongue, she swayed gracefully on the mare's back, her feet planted firmly and confidently.

The grass rustled again, and Cyra loosed her arrow an instant before an enormous shadow of golden wings unfurled over the mare's head, diving into the grass. The mare reared, shying away from the surprise of the eagle's dive. Col watched helplessly as Cyra flew toward the ground. She tried to roll, but the bow hampered her, and she landed instead on her face and stomach in a rush of air and dust. Col flung himself from Faelan and rushed to her, reaching for her arm.

"Are you alright?" He feared something would surely be broken, but she flipped her head back to glare up at him before he could touch her, trying to suck air into lungs that had been knocked empty.

Her mouth was gaping like a landed fish, but she did not seem badly hurt. Col grinned down at her. The breath wheezed into her lungs, and he laughed aloud, recalling the sight of her shocked face as she had flown toward the dirt. She scowled, sucking another pained gulp of air into her chest and crawling to her knees. She ignored the hand he held out. Undeterred, Col put it under her elbow and helped her rise, shaking his head from side to side as he continued to shake with laughter.

Cyra wrenched away from him, and Col stopped laughing, putting both of his hands in the air. "I'm sorry," he said. "I only want to help." She understood help. They had gone over that one. Her silver eyes were dark with wounded dignity and suspicion, and Col made sure to keep his lips straight.

Her mare stepped forward then, snuffling at Cyra's back with a contrite expression. Then she took Cyra's black braid in her mouth and began to chew it. Col laughed again and threw caution to the wind, stepping forward to extricate the length of black silk from the horse's muzzle. He stepped away once it was free, though now wet with slobber, and watched her brush her clothing free of dust and debris, satisfied she only had bruises to her knees, and her dignity. When she had finished, she looked to where her arrow had landed. The eagle was happily tearing apart the rabbit, using the swan-fletched arrow as a brace for its great talons to hold the poor dead animal down.

Cyra slanted a look at Col, and he shrugged. He watched her lips curl into a rueful smile, and when she laughed, her shoulders slumping in defeat, Col wondered if it might be possible to hear that sound every day for the rest of his life.

$$) ($$

My mouth curved into a rueful smile, and I shook my head, laughing in defeat. I took hold of the loop around Inara's neck and clicked her forward, and Col took his horse's reins in hand. We walked side by side for a bit as I stretched the shock of a hard landing from my muscles, breathing deeply to relieve my chest of the crushed feeling. My dignity would take longer to recover. Once in a while, Col would chuckle softly and shake his head, clearly thinking of my humiliation. This irritated me and also set me at ease at the same time. Somehow, many opposite feelings were co-existing in me, making it difficult to reconcile how I really felt about the man.

He was an unknown piece of my destiny, a tiny thread in the fabric of the Great Mother's tapestry, and yet I felt drawn to him of my own accord. I wondered how it would have been if we had met in the Moon Hall. If he would have noticed me. I surely would have noticed him. He was attractive, of course, but it went beyond the ridiculously adorable dimple in his cheek, or the distracting span of his shoulders, or even the sparkle of intelligent humor in his eyes. It was something about his presence. Like his soul extended out from his body, and the part of me that could sense such things knew that part of him.

He was a stranger who felt familiar. He was a potential threat, yet I felt at ease. He was a man, but he followed my direction, difficult as it often was to communicate, without question, and had only ever been respectful toward me and the other ha-mazaans. He was strong, powerful, yet he moved and spoke with genuine gentleness. He was considerate in ways that made me feel boorish and unkind, though he did not mean to make me feel that way, I was certain.

I flushed again as he caught me staring openly at the broad span of his shoulders and the red hair that brushed against the collar of his tunic. He stopped walking, and I did as well, our eyes meeting in a long, meaningful conversation that needed no words. He let the reins of the stallion fall to the ground and then reached a hand toward me, palm up. I took it without thinking and let Inara's rein fall to her neck. She immediately began grazing, but I barely noticed. I could only notice the heat of his hand gently engulfing my fingers and the way his eyes gleamed at me. He smiled, the dimple peeking out, though he was no longer thinking about my ungraceful fall, I knew.

Before it could drag out any longer, I raised myself to my toes and kissed him, full on the lips. I felt his body go rigid with surprise, and my own was stiff with apprehension, both for the unknown motions of the action and also fear of his reaction. Or of mine, I was not sure.

His lips were not rigid, though. Firm, but not hard. The stubble of his rusted beard scratched my chin, and the smell of his skin, warm and dusty, with a dark musk that was purely, wholly male, filled my senses. He tasted of sweetgrass and leather. I began to step back, to open my eyes and meet his squarely, when his arm wrapped itself around my waist, his skin scraping against the scales of my vest. He drew me into him with a smooth, unrelenting pull, pressing our bodies close from collarbone to knee. His other hand settled on the back of my head, his fingers digging into my braid, cradling my neck with splayed, gentle, perfectly strong fingers. I gasped at the feeling of it, and then his mouth was on mine once more, and I did not try to step away again. When we did separate, only slightly, my arms were wrapped around his neck, my body a tingling mass of fire. This time, the smile I gave him was purely wicked, and I saw it mirrored in his eyes. They were as dark as the moss under an oak.

When I pushed him to the ground, his hands gently guiding me to lie on top of him, I did not think of the sentries posted throughout the forest in front of us, for the grass here was tall and thick. When I unbuckled my belt and flung it away into that thick grass, and the scaled vest after it, I did not think of the horses, for they both ate contentedly, muzzles pressed to the fertile ground and noses touching. When he sat up to bring his lips to mine again, to cup the back of my head as a man holds water to his lips, I did not think of the open sky above us, with lazy clouds that watched everything, for they could not tell their tales to the world.

I thought only of the look in his eyes and the tender, hungry way his hands traced over my lips and down my throat between kisses. The way his face reflected awe and something strangely akin to pain when I pulled the tunic over my head, the autumn air cold on my breasts, and pulled the warm palms of his hands up to cover them. I thought of how he no longer looked just kind but rather starving. How I felt the same. I thought of how we needed no words for this. It was a language I had never spoken, but it did not matter.

And when his hands touched me, traveled over my ribs, my throat, my back, as I sat astride his hips, feeling every inch of me as though he was a worshiper and I the one worshipped, I eventually thought of nothing at all.

CHAPTER 29

EAST

Col turned slowly on the thin mattress of dried grass and linen, careful not to rustle it too loudly. The dying flames sent fingers of light to dance and glide on Cyra's bare skin, over her ribs and flank, and down the long muscled length of her leg. His fingers itched to follow them, to mimic their playful dance, but he did not want to wake her. Instead, he reached over her waist and pulled the doubled fur of the lion skin over her waist, then eased himself close to her back to share his warmth. She murmured indistinctly in her sleep, stirring, but she did not wake.

Two and a half fortnights since she had brought him into her camp. One fortnight since she had invited him to share her tent. Just half a moon since their race in the north meadow, when he finally stopped wondering how it might feel to kiss her, hold her. Be a part of her. Not all the wonder had been lost, though. If anything, it had heightened. Now, he wondered if this was real, or if he was fever dreaming, and all of his days and nights were simply a boyish fantasy conjured from an injured mind. Whether it was or was not a dream, Col wondered how he could possibly keep it from ending.

Desire to reassure himself everything was indeed real overrode his caution, and he stretched out a gentle finger, the calloused tip of it tracing lightly over the delicate swirl of the twisted horse on her arm. She used many of his words now, but she did not possess enough to explain the markings to him. Still, he could feel their magic. Old Magic, as his mother would have called it. The primal kind that lived in trees of the great forests and in the animals that roamed them. The kind of Old Magic Cyra was entirely sculpted from.

She knew enough of his words to explain what she wanted from him.

The thought made him smile, more a grim creasing of his lips than a happy curve. The irony of it all was too much. He had not needed to convince her, or any of them, that they should come with him. They were not offering to be allies, but if he took more than forty warriors back with him as willing guests and gave them shelter for the winter or for however long they needed to stay, it would be an undeniable sign to both of his brothers—to all the Scoloti tribes—that these women were under his hospitality, and that there existed a semblance, at least, of allegiance between them. That they belonged to him in a way that neither of his brothers could claim.

Guilt swirled in his stomach like eels in a bucket full of swampy water. He would provide them shelter for the winter whether they were the Golden Axe or not, of course. And he would happily make Cyra his wife, his queen, even if she were not a princess of her own people. If she would have him. But knowing why he had come to her and why his brother had taken some of them away made his guilt stir and fester some days, especially now that they would move east with him to Gelonia.

He did not know her well, but what he knew from careful observation and simple proximity, what he sensed from the grounded, strong spirit that exuded from Cyra and needed no words, was that she was proud and had much reason to be. She would not take kindly to the thought that three different armies had come to claim her and her people to their own ends. Not that this had been Col's intent. He didn't think. But his people would think it had been. And his brothers, perhaps even his father, would most definitely believe it was.

Col pulled the furs higher over Cyra's shoulder and lay back. He knew better by now than to wrap his arms around her while she was sleeping. She did not like to feel caged, even in her dreams. Cyra sighed softly, nuzzling back into him. He smiled, and the soft shadows of the fire danced their flames high on the sloped walls of the tent as her skin pressed into his side. Some of his guilt eased, then. In his heart, he had no desire to claim her or her troupe of ha-mazaans, as they called themselves, for a throne or power or prophecy. Even if he wanted to, it could never be done. She was a wild creature, born to be free, and would be claimed by no man, he was sure.

) (

I gave orders for the camp to be disassembled as soon as we had finished our morning meal. Before I had even finished speaking, the first snow began to fall from the flinty sky. This, as much as the knowledge that we had somewhere specific to go, made everyone turn to their tasks with quick hands.

Together, Ossy and I folded the furs inside the tents, then the skins of the walls. We piled them in heaps that we wound tight with cords of braided leather, and these we tied to the pack horses or piled into the wagons. We loaded the chests as well, and as Col took the handle of one, helping me walk it to where the wagon sat, I smiled at him. We had worked together over errands often in the last few weeks, as I learned his words and he learned our routines. It had proven a pleasant venture. Almost as pleasant as our evenings in the tent and our rides to the northern meadow.

With everyone working, it did not take long to break camp, and we moved eastward well before the sun had centered in the sky. Col rode next to me in the lead, with Sagitta and Ossy and Alkippe, never far from me, directly behind. Esten stepped onto the wagon next to Tekmessa and took up the reins. For all that the yellow-haired man had seemed unnerved and uncomfortable during his first week as our captive, he had come to life under Tekmessa's gentle care. So much so that he had even come back to our camp rather than leave when Col had sent him as a messenger to the surrounding armies, giving them notice to disperse, and that we would travel east within the next few days.

Even though he assured me his people knew we would be moving east, Col made it clear to me we must go carefully and that he should be clearly visible in front. I gathered from this that if his people did not see him amongst our party, they would not hesitate to engage us in combat as intruders on their land. I had returned his sword to him some days ago, which he wore on the beautifully tooled belt at his waist, and his dagger was sheathed inside of his boot, and as the two of us rode ahead of the long line of ha-mazaans, I felt a strange pride well up in me. It seemed so... right, to be together like this. For his knowing smile to be only a glance away and for my own to answer so easily. For the ha-mazaans to be united in a destination, and that our path was weaving together much more beautifully than any could have expected when we found ourselves stranded so far from home.

We rode until the sun lowered toward the broad horizon behind us, and though I made several concerned comments that we should halt and set up camp for the evening, before the light disappeared, Col shook his head. "We are close," he assured me. "We will be home before the light is gone."

So we rode on, and the snow that had fallen in the morning, threatening what was to come in the days ahead, had all but ceased, leaving our way clear and tinged golden by the light of the setting sun under the clouds. But the farther we went, and the closer we came to Col's home, the more uncertain I became. The problem remained that I did not know what we were headed into. My conviction from the previous month that this was our best option of finding more permanent shelter from winter was now creased with heavy folds of doubt, like an old shawl I had worried at over and over with my fingers until it was a shroud of wrinkled misgivings. Col described his home as a small city, or at least that is what I understood, but I did not know in what context he thought of a city. Would it be a small encampment, or an entire village, or a city like Themiscyra, with hot-spring baths and cobblestone streets and tiled mosaics of hunting scenes in a great Moon Hall? I gambled everything on the tenuous notion that he and I had established some sort of truce, if not an understanding, both with our words and our bodies. I was relying on the idea that this thin thread of connection would guarantee not only my safety but that of my people. If I gambled poorly, there was much more at stake than some nights of pleasure or intriguing conversation.

I looked over at Col, and his face was calm, without either excitement or evasiveness as he met my gaze. Despite my words to the ha-mazaans about trust, and despite the fact that he had shared my tent for more than a fortnight, I did not yet trust him. Not as I trusted Ossy. How could I? Ossy had dangled me on her knee as a babe, brushed the sand from my own knees when I had taken my first tumble from the back of a horse, and listened to my ranting tirades about how unfair my mother was when I had not yet grown accustomed to the vast emotional landscape of womanhood. I was making a choice to trust him based on very unreliable circumstances. I was having doubts about how much I trusted myself, now, for making such a decision. But it felt too late to turn back. I sent a prayer to the Great Mother that any poor consequences of this choice would befall me only, and not the other women. She owed me that much, I figured, after everything She asked of me.

We crested the hill as the sun set, spreading its orange-red flame across the sky so that it seemed on fire as the city came into view underneath the conflagration of clouds. The sight of the burning expanse did nothing to ease the knot in my stomach. The city was large, though not as large as Themiscyra. I could see the reflective glimmer of a wide river to the northeast, and around the entire city stood a tall wall of timber effectively keeping intruders out. *And captives in.* I pushed the thought aside, trying to take in the details while the knot of anxiety tightened in my stomach. Squat buildings perched on the land at haphazard intervals, with smaller houses in between. Dotted amongst them were the deer we had seen traveling with their wagons, recognizable even from this distance because of their great forward-protruding horns. The ha-mazaans paused to take in the sight, and I wondered if the other women felt the same fear that I did. No one spoke, either to confirm or deny their hesitancy, and so I nudged Inara after Col's stallion and followed him over the crest of the hill.

We moved quickly down the winding ribbon of road, our strange contingent of ha-mazaans with their spears surrounding a broad-shouldered, straight-backed Ishassari and his yellow bearded, shy, infatuated friend. Sooner than I would have liked, we were dwarfed by the unexpectedly tall timber walls, with brass-bound gates that stretched high into the glowing sky the closer we came, the entrance flanked by twin wooden towers that sat square and ominous against the flaming clouds. The enormous gates swung closed as we came within shouting distance of the walls. I glanced at Col uncertainly. He did not look at me but kept his gaze on the battlements and on the men who gradually gathered along the top with their bows drawn.

When we drew within arrow-shot of the gates, I unslung my own bow and nocked an arrow, ready to draw at the first hint of betrayal. Alkippe and Prothoe surrounded Col, and Sagitta and Asteria rode near Esten, making sure he could not flee. What Col and I had been able to communicate about this situation was one thing. What I would leave in his hands alone was another.

He ambled forward a few more steps, and my thoughts raced as I wondered if he would simply keep going, leaving us to choose whether to risk enemy arrows to fetch him back or let our chances of bargaining disappear through the gates with him. I wondered whether I should, or could, put my own arrow through him to stop his escape. But he reined his horse to a halt and called something to one of the men who sat ready with his own bow in one of the tall towers. I did not understand the words, but Col motioned that he needed to move closer.

Warily, I nodded to Alkippe and Prothoe, who prodded Col forward, their wicker and leather shields prepared for a flight of arrows. I did not carry a shield, but I signaled for the others to remain behind and nudged Inara forward as well, ignoring Ossy's hiss to stay back. The horses moved slowly closer to the gate, Col's expression mild and his hands crossed idly on his horse's withers.

He exchanged more words with the man in the tower. I was sure I understood Col say king, and their word for warrior, though he ended with our word of ha-mazaan. The man atop the gate disappeared briefly, and the uneasy shuffling and sniffing of the horses scenting out our new surroundings were the only sounds to interrupt the ominous silence. My skin crawled with the waiting, and my thoughts raced into the dark rabbit warren of every scenario. Did Col truly understand what we wanted? Was he betraying us even now, discussing how easily we could be overcome by numbers and his freedom gained, all while speaking so calmly?

A different man appeared at the top of the wall, leaning from the battlement for a better view. His hair was black, his eyebrows sharp lines against equally sharp features.

"Colaxais!" the man called down, grinning, as he rested one elbow on the railing in a casual gesture. His eyes flickered to me, then over the ha-mazaans behind me. He gave a low whistle, his grin widening.

"Liopoxais," Col answered easily, a wry grin tugging at his own lips, though I could only see the corner of his mouth from this angle. Col's brother. Oldest brother, if I had understood my vocabulary lessons correctly. Liopoxais looked down at us with curious intensity. His eyes came to rest on me, and he asked a question, one-winged eyebrow raised.

I looked at Col, understanding far less of their speech than I had expected or hoped. Whatever Col said in return made his brother bark out a sharp laugh. I looked back to him, tensing. Inara shifted under me, sensing my anxiety. The gates made a loud creaking sound, opening. Liopoxais disappeared from view.

I raised my bow, and ha-mazaans who had held back urged their horses forward with their own weapons raised, as they expected to be met with a hundred mounted warriors ready to defend their town and take revenge for killing their men and kidnapping their Ishassari. But then a hand was on my arm. Col's fingers gently pressed against the tattooed band that marked my grief. His face smiled gently when I looked up, and he motioned for me to lower the bow even as the opening gates revealed a simple, empty dirt road ahead of us.

"Peace," he murmured. "You will not be harmed in my home."

He took it upon himself to turn and wave the rest of the caravan forward, and then he waved his hand in front of us, offering for me to lead the way. I hesitated, still unsure, doubt twisting in me as I had second and third and fourth thoughts about the wisdom of this decision I was making. Had I let my feelings for this man lead my people directly into a den of griffins?

Liopoxais appeared in the road, and though he had a sword, it was sheathed. He made a grand gesture, bowing from the waist to usher us through the gate. Something about his smile and the way he flicked his hair back when he stood straight made me think he was mocking us. When I looked over my shoulder to Ossy, who had ridden forward as the gates opened, she shrugged, offering me no direction.

I prodded Inara forward, though I did not shoulder my bow. An eerie feeling tickled my shoulders as I passed through the gates. It felt similar to having an arrow aimed at my back, or to being watched when the moon is high and the night is dark, and you are not sure what kind of creature sees you with its night-sharp eyes. Inara felt it as well. Her knees rose high as she pranced in place, moving sideways in a skittering dance. I wished I could take credit for the movements, since they normally took several years of battle practice to achieve with a horse, but I could not. She was only expressing her own jittery nerves, or manifesting mine. The other ha-mazaans followed warily, some of their horses snorting air as they passed through the unfamiliar boundary. No ha-mazaan shouldered their weapon, although Col smiled at some of them in reassurance as the tall gates of split trees and bronze dragged closed behind us, effectively shutting off our escape.

I studied the city with wary, curious eyes as we followed Col down the central street. There were a variety of small log buildings, and as we passed, people came out of the doors to stare at us curiously. None hid their astonishment when they looked at us, taking in our clothes of leather and silk, wool and animal pelts. They gawked openly at our weapons, especially my bow and the unfamiliar shape of the ha-mazaan axes. Many of the children giggled and screeched when my eyes met theirs, and the familiar, innocent sounds tugged a smile from my stiff lips.

The place was filled with myriad wagons of the same sort we had taken in the raid. All were covered with rawhide or wood, and some were almost twice the size of the ones we had taken, likely requiring at least three or four horses or perhaps even a team of oxen to pull them. From these wagon's rear doors, more people emerged to whisper behind their hands and eye our party with ill-concealed astonishment. Some regarded us with blatant fear. This assuaged my anxiety, restoring some of my confidence in our small band of warriors. It was good if they feared us a little, though too much fear could cause them to act rashly. I shouldered my bow again, not wanting to incite anything, and signaled for the other ha-mazaans to do the same. Some holstered their weapons. Some did not, and I did not make them.

Milling amongst the wagons and the houses were a few horses and many of the odd-looking deer. Their huge antlers extended out over their backs when they raised their heads to view us. They were not wild deer by any means, and acted as the horses did when they saw us pass, though their eyes watched us with more wariness.

Eventually, the hardened dirt of the road ended in a large circular courtyard, where an enormous oak rose from the center, its limbs spreading wide to shelter the entire path looping around it. It was the only tree in the entire city, as far as I had seen. Underneath its thick branches sat a great red wagon, its paint fresh and untarnished by weather or time, its massive yoke resting on a delicately fashioned brace.

Behind the wagon hunched a long, low building, built of stacked logs and covered with a thickly thatched roof. Smoke curled from a chimney, and in the fading light, it appeared as an old folk tale my grandmother had told me when I was just a small child, about the hill-folk who had lived in the northern country of her childhood home in Mycenae.

Col dismounted, letting the stallion's reins fall to the ground. Liopoxais, who had strolled comfortably beside Col and chatted agreeably the entire way, clapped his brother on the back and gave him a wolfish grin. It was only once they stood side by side that I noticed how closely they resembled each other, though Col's hair was like burnished copper and his brother's shone like obsidian. They shared the same long, almond-shaped eyes and high cheekbones, though Col's had never looked as sharp as his brother's. Even their beards grew in the same shape, trimmed close to their faces to show the strong line of jaw and chin.

Col approached Inara. I lifted my leg over her withers and slid to the ground before he reached me. He instructed me with carefully pronounced words and gestures to leave my bow with Alkippe. I hesitated a moment, and then unslung it. Alkippe scowled when I handed it to her. I gave her reassurance that she and the other hamazaans could storm the building if I did not emerge before dusk. Though she did not seem mollified, I left her there with the others and motioned for Ossy to follow.

The three of us entered the low building through a thick wooden door. It was carved with a great twisting tree surrounded by foreign symbols that could have been writing, but in no script I had ever seen. There were bees sculpted into the honey-colored wood, flying and resting in the branches of the tree, and I thought of the wheeled chair Col had insisted on bringing back with us. As soon as I stepped through the threshold behind him, the smell of burning beeswax and fresh-cut wood filled my nostrils, along with wood smoke, and a charred, thick tang like wild onions and roasted meat. The floor under my bare feet was polished planks of wood, worn smooth by years of use, and swept clean of mud and dust. It was strange to feel the hardness of a floor under my feet, as I had felt only dirt and grass and woven rushes since stepping off of the ship that had brought us here.

Col shut the door once Ossy stepped through with hesitant, wary steps, her eyes moving to every shadow just as mine had done. The two of us stared at the great fire burning in the center of the room. It looked familiar. I thought of the fire in the Moon Hall, but no, that was not it. My mind filled with an image of a cave, and a soundless fire, reaching out to singe my eyebrows. Perhaps it was because there was a cauldron hanging from a tripod above the flames, and steam rose steadily from the great bowl of it. Once again, I smelled the meaty, salty aroma of food. My stomach growled.

A man sat at one of the long wooden tables near the fire. Col led us forward, but the man did not rise to greet us. His lap was covered in wolf pelts, though it was not cold in the room with such a great fire, and his right hand toyed with a golden skull-shaped goblet on the wooden table next to him.

"Atta," Col said. Father. He left my side to step forward and took hold of the man's outstretched hand, turning it and kissing the inside of his wrist. His father, the king, replied easily in words I did not recognize.

I studied his face. It was weathered, and older, but not so old that he appeared decrepit. His eyes were dark, and where his hair had once been a deep red, the copper in it had turned mostly to pewter, like rusted star-iron returning to its original form. On his arms were cuffs of gold, thick and encrusted with the biggest precious stones and jewels I had ever seen. Around his neck, he wore a circlet of gold that ended in two opposing deer heads, their noses not quite touching, but resting comfortably on the dark, hollowed skin of his collarbone. Their sapphire eyes glinted blue in the light from the fire.

The king looked his son over briefly as though searching for signs of harm after his long stay in our camp. Finding nothing amiss, his eyes traveled briefly over Ossy. She met his stare evenly before his hooded eyes shifted to me.

The weight of his gaze settled into me as though he saw more than my wrapped braids or the scales on my vest. He studied both thoughtfully, then the marks on my bare arms and shoulder. When his eyes met mine, they were thoughtful and profoundly intense, like his son's. But they were not Col's eyes. There was not the same… kindness. I held his gaze with my chin firmly set, fighting my urge to scowl at being studied so. Finally, he nodded, as though whatever he had seen confirmed something he had already suspected.

He uttered a command in unfamiliar words but an unmistakable tone. Col immediately reached out and took hold of my hand.

"Ishassara Cyra, my father, King Targitaos," he said, pulling my hand forward. He shifted his hold on my fingers as he held my hand toward his father's face. I did not resist but felt rather awkward when the man bent and brushed his lips lightly over the inside of my hand, just below the first of my moon-marks.

"Ishassara Cyra," he said.

Then, the king held his hand out to me. I glanced at Col, who flicked his hand in an unhelpful, encouraging gesture. I reached out and gingerly held the king's wrist, repeating his gesture by kissing the base of his palm. I was unsure what it all meant, other than a sign of respect, but I didn't want to start off on the wrong foot, for the sake of my people. When I stepped back, Col took my hand once more. My face flushed at the intimacy in his gaze; this was his father, after all. The king. But I held my chin high and met the king's gaze until Targitaos spoke again. I looked at Col, hoping for a translation I wasn't confident he could provide. Col smiled and squeezed my hand, not letting go.

Slowly, in words partly his own, and partly my language, he said, "Ha-mazaans. My father welcomes you all. He welcomes Ishassara Cyra home."

PART IV

THE GOLDEN AXE

CHAPTER 30

GELONIA

"Good eve, Ishassari Colaxais!" a woman called out.

"Good eve, Mura," Col replied, reining the stallion to a stop as she lumbered down the back steps of her wagon and came toward us.

"Lady Cyra," Mura nodded to me with considerably less warmth, but I smiled at her as kindly as I could.

"Hello, Mura."

"How is your son?" Col asked. "Has his arm healed?"

"It is better than before, Ishassari," Mura nodded, but her brow creased. "He's already busy with his father tending the deer. Too soon, I told them both. He should rest it longer, I say. And with the babe so close..." her hand pressed against the side of her enormously round belly as her gaze slid over me, avoiding my "witch-eyes," as some of the women called them, before looking toward the great paddocks that held the deer.

The men, because it had always been a man's role in Gelonia, were busy feeding the herd bales of dried vetch and buckets of grain that kept them during the winter months. The long, interminable winter months, which had dragged their cold, icily dripping fingers over the landscape for far too long now. I did not see her son amongst the antlers and shaggy hides, but when I looked back to her, she was still staring out at the paddocks with a worried frown. Her hand massaged her belly with absent-minded strokes as though the babe bothered her with its jostling.

"Tekmessa would be more than happy to tend your birthing, Mura, if you want help with the babe," I said, though I knew my attempts at connection were futile.

The women here had their own midwives, of a sort, but though they were wise with their herbs, they were less knowledgeable about the workings of the body. Some of their practices were simply archaic, often even brutal for mother and child, much to Tekmessa's dismay. But I also knew they did not trust the *zizenti*, because of her tattoos. And because she was ha-mazaan. *Oirpata*. A man-killer, and unnatural, and likely a witch besides. Just like me.

"So kind," Mura said noncommittally.

I tried not to let my frustration show, deliberately relaxing my tensed mouth, but Col smiled down at the woman, and she beamed back at him, happily ignoring me once more as they talked grains and the sure signs of spring everyone here kept insisting they could see.

Mura, or indeed anyone in this city, would talk to Col for hours if they could. And he would be happy to oblige. Everyone here adored their Ishassari. In turn, he looked after them well, making sure every family had enough food or fuel for their fires and that their wagons were maintained to the best of his abilities. Abilities which I now suspected were well-nigh magical when it came to anything needing the touch of his hands. Even me, perhaps.

Winter had provided plenty of opportunity to observe how much his people respected him and how careful he was to serve them when they were in need. I had walked beside him every day for five months, not helping him exactly, for I knew nothing of carpentry or wagon-building or wood carving, and even less about food stores and planning provisions, or making conversation around the hearthfire. But I offered my support where I could when he visited with his people, just as he offered his when I tended the horses or worked with Camilla in the smithy to create new weapons, or trained and hunted with the other ha-mazaans, and sometimes even the few people of Gelonia who wished to learn to fight as we did.

Sometimes it was an awkward threading, trying to weave one way of living with another. The seams of that particular tapestry did not lie flat. There were few ways our two peoples saw eye to eye or practiced the same customs. Eating in the central hall together was one similarity. Some ways in which the hearthfire was revered was another. Both our peoples acknowledged an animal's sacred gift when it gave its life for our survival, though the ha-mazaans always asked for a life before taking it. Profession of loyalty and service to a promised heir, though always a male Ishassari here, was similar, though there was no trial year required to prove one's abilities before an *Alsanti*. These small things kept our respective followers from being at each other's throats too often, but more times than not, there was a tension in the air that followed both his people and mine. Sometimes it was after a fight about a ha-mazaan insisting on scouting alongside the men, who were not accustomed to their own wives leaving the wagons. On a few occasions, tensions became high after men became careless with their words, or their hands, either before or after our women had taken pleasure with them. It was something ha-mazaans were not used to experiencing. Or, perhaps those who remembered those issues all too well had thought they escaped those problems long ago.

The winter had been long, and colder than any of the ha-mazaans had ever experienced, but despite these tensions, we remained safe and relatively warm. Warmer and safer than in our makeshift shelters with our furs and tiny fires. Perhaps we would have survived on our own, but even so, though we did not thrive here in Gelonia, we did not suffer, and for that reason, I remained grateful for the hospitality offered.

"Whatever you need when your time comes, Mura, you will have it," Col promised and kneed Faelan forward again. "Tell Scoti that I will need him soon to help with Faelan's tack, so he had better take care of that arm!"

We rode away to her wave of thanks and made our way toward the horse paddocks nestled close to the great hall. There was nothing for me to do with Inara, as I had not been using any tack, but I helped Col store away his saddle, and then we fed all the horses, making sure each had enough food for the long night. I eyed the quickly dwindling supply of dried fodder in the store shed, frowning.

"It will be enough," Col said, finishing his tasks and coming to stand beside me.

"We added over forty horses to your burden. And the ground is still frozen..."

"It will be enough," he repeated firmly. "The deer are less, now that some have given their lives over the winter. Soon, the others will travel north with those who pasture them over the summer months, and their horses will go as well."

"But is there enough to last until then?" I asked doubtfully, turning my steps to follow his as I clutched my coat tighter around my shoulders. I had lengthened the short coat of lion skin I had made in the fall, all the while thinking of the beautiful grey cloak embroidered with silver that Ossy had gifted to me. But such a fine piece would not have suited this place, anyway, with its hard snow and forever rolling hills of mud when it thawed. I wondered if I would ever see grass again, despite that being all I had seen when we first came to this land.

"They will probably leave for pasture later this year than last," Col admitted. "But there will be enough fodder to keep the horses. This is not your worry, Cyra. Let me carry at least some burden for my own city."

He smiled at me fondly as he said it, and I returned the smile the best I could but could not erase the worry. Especially when another wet flake of snow touched my lips. I looked up into the sky, lightened against the blue of the twilight with fresh snow falling once more. I sighed. Winter had never been so long, nor so snowy, but even with its struggles, I did not know if I wanted it to end. I didn't know what would happen when it did. My excuse for being here would melt with the snow, and then...

$$) ($$

"How much longer is this snow going to last?" Cyra asked, eyeing the white flakes falling to the ground. Col shrugged, raising his face to the darkening sky and letting the cold snow fall on his cheeks and beard. When he opened his eyes again and looked down at her, she smiled crookedly, but she looked cold and miserable. He knew she and her southern ha-mazaans hated the cold of winter, but he couldn't help wishing it would never end. Once it did...

"Hard to say, really," Col answered finally, pushing open the heavy wooden door of the hall. "It's the longest winter I can remember since I was very young. Even then, we didn't have as much snow as this." *And Tabiti has been answering my prayers that this winter never ends, so...*

"Snow would never stay so long in Themiscyra," she said, moving ahead of him into the long hall and immediately hurrying to stand close by the lingering fire. It had gone too long untended and was dying a slow death of starvation. She poked it futilely with the nearby stick before holding her hands to the smoking ashes. Col wondered, not for the first time, how she and the others would have fared without their new boots of wolf fur and the thickly lined capes they had stitched from the furs that had once been their only protection from the cold during the long nights.

"At home, it's mostly rain all winter. Cool rain, bone-chilling rain, icy rain, light rain, heavy rain, sideways rain. Never-ending rain." She smiled at him ruefully, rubbing her hands together over the now twinkling coals. "We rarely see snow, and it never stays. Not like this."

Col's lips mirrored her smile, though his was more wistful. "I would like to see it one day," he said, hefting a bear rug from the bench. "The palace at Themiscyra, and the Moon Hall. The great stables." He motioned for her to sit underneath the bear skin, though she was already wearing the long lion skin cloak. She sat, and he sat next to her, tucking the thick fur over her legs before hugging her close to share his warmth. "And I would also like to see how your blacksmith works with the starstones. Perhaps when spring comes, we will find some in our own lands, with your help. I'm sure if I could watch her work, I could decipher the secret for such sharp metal," he mused.

"Aye, well...as soon as you craft me a ship, I will take you to Themiscyra, where we have plenty," she said wryly, and he chuckled.

"Give me a few more years," he said lightly, "and I will craft you a ship bigger than the one that brought you to me. As long as you promise to let me watch you dance naked in the Moon Hall."

"No promises," Cyra said archly. "I already told you men should not be present for such holy things."

"I would not want to anger Matar Kubileya," he said earnestly.

She peered at him from the corner of her eye, wrapping the cloak tighter around her shoulders as the flames from the hearth fell quiet, their warmth barely reaching them. The hall was not usually so cold, or at least had not seemed cold for the entire winter, but dry wood had become scarce weeks ago. The city was relegated to mainly horse dung as fuel, and it meant the fires were smokier, not as warm, and definitely not as pleasant smelling as wood. Col leaned forward to scoop more bricks of dried dung into the pit, which succeeded in increasing the smoke tenfold. Grimacing, he sat back onto the cushioned bench and slung an arm across her shoulders once more, hugging her close.

He was always warmer than her. Even though Tabiti's flames ran hot within her, they mostly burned in her eyes and in her words when she was angry and did nothing to warm her body as they did his. Col smiled, thinking of it, and watched as the flames sputtered and then caught on the dung, the slow tongues of orange licking around and up until they had taken hold, and some of the smoke eased away.

"To think someone can have such skill lighting shit on fire," Cyra said dryly. But then she gave him another sideways look, and her black brows drew together ever so slightly. "Do you ever wonder," she said slowly, being careful with the words that were still quite foreign on her tongue, "if perhaps your Tabiti and our Kubileya are not one and the same?"

Col raised his eyebrows at her. "Of course they are," he said.

"Why do you think that?" She sounded slightly taken aback, though she had been the one to ask it.

"Because there is only One," he said simply. "One Creator, One Mother. There is only One Light in the sky."

"Two," she corrected. "The sun, which you say is the face of Tabiti. And the moon, which we say is the face of Kubileya. And who some call Cybele." Her brow creased in the way it often did when she became confused or agitated by something that would not obey. It was an expression he was now well accustomed to. "Anyway, there are at least two lights in the sky," she said firmly, but Col shook his head.

"No, Tabiti shows Her face in the day as the sun. And at night, She watches us go about our ways with a more forgiving eye in the ever-changing moon. And at all times, She is in the glow of the flames. All Light is of the same source."

"Perhaps," she eventually conceded, though it did not sound like any concession that could win a man a victory. "Although in other lands, they worship many goddesses and even male gods. Which is preposterous, of course." Col nodded in agreement, but Cyra continued before he could ask more about these male gods. "It is still strange to me that She might show Herself in such different ways and require such different forms of worship from all people."

Col thought about this for a moment, his eyes on the slowly writhing flames. "I do not think She requires any such thing," he said carefully. Cyra turned to look at him, and her eyes moved across his features until her own became soft with affection. Even after all these months, the beauty of her caught at his breath and made something inside of him ache a little. It was a good ache, but it was the only way he could describe it.

"I truly do not think She requires anything of us, other than to remember Her. It is why we keep the ever-burning hearthfire," he continued, his words slow and precise as always so that she could understand them. As soon as all parties realized it would be the ha-mazaans who must learn their words rather than a mutual sharing of languages, communication had developed more quickly. It had taken only a few months for her to become familiar with the speech of the Scoloti. Col's people, though nomads in this vast land, simply did not have experience with multiple languages that she and most of her ha-mazaans did. Still, the strangeness of some words often left her grasping for the correct meaning, and it was very easy for the most innocent of conversations to quickly go awry. Then Tabiti's fire would cover her countenance like lightning in a spring sky. He had learned this far more quickly than he had learned any of her words.

"But why do your people not have *zizenti*? To lead in sacred rituals and honor that remembrance?" she asked. He tipped his head thoughtfully.

"I would say we have our wise women, though they do not call themselves priestesses. But they know their herbs and healing, and they help with the women when they are with child. Much the same as Tekmessa."

She made a noise that was not quite a laugh. More of a *pshhh*. "Tekmessa, and all *zizenti*, do not deal with *only* childbirth and healing. They birth souls in *and* out of this world. They prepare ha-mazaans for death as often as they prepare for new life. You have not shown me how your own people handle this," she said frankly. "Even your wise women seem afraid of death or of touching the bodies of those who journey through the Gate. Plus…you burn their temples." She shuddered under his arm, and Col felt a twinge of guilt as he remembered her and her women's horror when he had told them the fate of their dead he had brought back from the crossroads. But he had not known what it meant to them when he had done it.

"I cannot see how any of your people find their way," she finished. Her voice was filled with chagrin as though it had been weighing on her. "They do not even know their *rhu-tasiyas*."

"I think," Col said slowly, "if more in the world than your ha-mazaans have such a thing as this carrier of the soul, this *rhu-tasiya*," he said, the word awkward on his tongue, "then the deer, which we have always sacrificed in the Holy Fires, guide the souls of my people. The deer are sacred to Tabiti, as the horse and lion are to Kubileya." He considered for a moment, watching the small flames in the hearth. "Faelan surely protects and guides my own soul here. As does the eagle, though I have never heard her name. Perhaps they will do so in the afterlife, as well. I do not know."

She hugged the lion skin closer. Col watched the flames and felt Cyra's skin slowly warming next to him. But when he glanced at her, she did not appear to be feeling any less miserable than when they had been outside.

"You will have no lip left for me to kiss if you worry at it with your teeth any harder," Col teased, and she stopped chewing her lip, a light flush traveling up her throat. He leaned down and placed a quick, affectionate kiss on her lips. He might have pressed for a more passionate one if not for the cold gust of winter air as the heavy wooden door behind them banged open.

"Little brother! Little panther!" boomed Lio's strident voice.

Cyra stiffened under Col's arm as Lio strode into the hall, his bold steps quickly outpacing even those of the tall ha-mazaan who walked with him. Sagitta's hair had clearly been tousled by more than the wind, and her blue eyes sparkled with a particular mischief. She grinned at them as she shoved the door closed behind her with her foot, teeth flashing against the redness of her cheeks. Whether they were tinged by cold or recent athletic pursuits, he did not know.

Col smiled back easily. Lio blew air loudly through his mouth and clapped his hands briskly before holding them out to the fire. Cyra stayed still and watchful under the furs, eyeing his brother with the wary expression she reserved especially for Lio.

"Our father wishes for the ceremony to be held on the new moon," Lio announced abruptly, stretching his hands to the flames and then grimacing when they offered scant warmth. He tossed several more bricks of dung into the smoldering coals, scattering them and effectively smothering what little flames had been there. He swirled his heavy cloak off his shoulders, scattering damp snow to the floor, and hung it haphazardly over the tripod sitting to the side. He looked about pointedly for a place to sit close to the fire. Col regarded his brother steadily, making no move to adjust his position on the bench until

Sagitta came closer, and then he shifted closer to the edge, allowing her to squeeze in next to Cyra.

"Does he?" Col said, frowning. "There will still be snow and frozen ground. I hardly think it is the best time."

"Targitaos wants what Targitaos wants," Lio said, grimacing at Sagitta as she sat in the spot he had been eyeing. Sagitta ignored him as Cyra shared the edge of the bear rug with her.

"He says it will be best to have it done with, and to have your ha-mazaans there as a sign of support, if Arpoxais means to challenge you," Lio continued. Cyra looked at Lio with sharp, ice-grey eyes. She looked back to Col.

"Challenge you?"

Col looked into the smoky pit and leaned forward to heft the long stick, which he used to prod at the bricks and create some breathing room. He waited until there was a slight flicker of renewed flame before he spoke, trying to keep the irritation with Liopoxais out of his voice.

"Aye," he said. "Word came three days ago that our brother wishes to contest the Kingship decision." He paused for a long moment before continuing. "Apparently, he sees his new…acquisition…as a sign that he is the rightful heir."

He felt Cyra's eyes boring into him and continued to prod at the fire, giving it room to breathe, though it suddenly felt very warm in the room. Col wondered why he had thought it so cold before.

"What acquisition?" Sagitta asked.

"A pretty axe. And a few lively and hot-blooded ha-mazaans with it," Lio said cheerily, smiling at the two women and ignoring Col's forbidding glare.

"You do not mean Erioboea?" Cyra said, her tone doubtful. She was looking at Lio with inscrutable eyes, but then she looked at him.

Col hesitated slightly, then nodded.

"Why would he think that?" Sagitta asked. "I thought you said your mother had been given the right to choose the heir. Isn't the matter done? What does Erioboea have to do with anything?"

Lio grinned down at his younger brother, but Col ignored the look and kept his gaze focused on the fire pit. Lio sighed up at the ceiling as though greatly aggrieved.

"It seems," he said, "that both of my little brothers have found new she-cats with fun toys, when it was only supposed to be one of them,"

Lio spread his hands wide in a supplicating gesture. "Who can tell what games Tabiti plays with us? Who knows which of you has the Golden Axe that was promised? Who knows which of my brothers is the Chosen One?" His dark eyes glinted down at them as he spoke, completely ignoring Col's severe frown of warning. "Arpoxais believes he knows. Whether my littlest brother can decide what *he* knows before it is too late...that is another matter." His smile grew wider as his eyes slid to Col.

Col grappled to control a rare flare of anger that made him want to plant a fist in his brother's smirk, and he did not bother hiding it as he stared up at his oldest brother. "Enough, Liopoxais," he said stiffly.

"What does he mean?" Cyra asked, though she also did not take her eyes from Lio's face. When Col did not reply immediately, she finally turned her head, but he did not meet her eyes.

"Col, what—" she began, but he stood, wafting cool air under the bear rug and making Sagitta exclaim a frustrated curse as she clamped it over her thighs.

"Not now, Cyra," he said. There was an uncommon hardness to his voice, and he saw her jaw stiffen from the corner of his eye.

"Don't you *dare* speak to me that way. I deserve to know what he is talking about. Especially if it has to do with me. *Or* with Eri."

"It does not," Col said, too harshly, turning to her. He tried to look as conciliatory as possible, but his anger at Lio and his own guilt made his expression more cross than he intended. She stood, the bear skin falling from her lap unheeded so that Sagitta had to make a desperate grab at it with more irritated cursing.

"I think it does," Cyra said, meeting his cool gaze with a flinty one of her own. "Tell me what he is talking about. What Golden Axe? What does he mean by 'there was only supposed to be one'?"

"Ah, I see that there is much for you to discuss, little brother," Lio interrupted smoothly, moving between them so that they both had to take a step back. He scooped his cloak from the tripod hook and swirled it over his shoulders, spattering more drops of water into the fire, where they hissed steam. "Sagi, care to join me while I check the deer? I daresay their company is going to be less...how shall I say it? Ahh...volatile." He smiled and waited expectantly as Col and Cyra stood awkwardly on either side of him, glaring at each other.

Sagitta frowned at him and crossed her legs. "I am interested to know the answer to what my Ishassara asks."

Lio's smile faded into an irritated frown.

"Come now, woman," he insisted. "You can't wish to listen to this eagle and she-cat squabble. We will tend the deer, and you can show me again how you keep warm in this mythical homeland of yours."

Sagitta regarded him coolly, not moving. All traces of her former mischievous glow had faded. "Pass," she said flatly and turned her eyes back to Col, raising an eyebrow. "Well?" she said to him.

His brother scoffed and turned away from the three of them, making his way back to the door. "Good luck, little brother," he called, and though his tone was light, there was an edge to it that cut colder than the evening air as he wrenched the heavy door open. "I have to say, I don't envy you or Arpoxais these days. One of you will be king, but both of you will be castrated fools, even more so than our father soon will be."

Before he could go through the door, however, Alkippe appeared on the threshold, her dark head shrouded in a ring of black wolf fur that edged her even blacker cloak. Only the white of her eyes showed against the indigo twilight. She looked like night itself had come knocking. Lio scowled darkly at her, and Alkippe scowled back, pushing the hood away from her face. He did not stand aside for her, so she pushed her shoulder into his as she strode into the room. With one last grimace at her and the room in general, he disappeared into the snow, pulling the door closed with a *whuff* of icy air.

Alkippe approached the fire with her usual unhurried swagger. She removed the bulky rabbit fur covering her hands, dropping the gloves to the bench before holding her hands out to the warmth of the flames. Col took the opportunity of her arrival to move the tripod over the fire and heft the kettle onto its hook. He stirred the heavy ladle and frowned down into the day-old stew as though the very sight of the deer and onions disgusted him. The eels twisting in his stomach did feel like disgust, though. Disgust with his brother, and with himself.

Cyra waited, her chin set at a determined angle. Alkippe gave Col and Cyra a measured look, feeling the tension she had walked into. When Col finally looked up at Cyra, the anger had gone from his chest, only to be replaced by a great weariness.

"Well?" she echoed Sagitta. "What was Liopoxais talking about?"

"I have already said it does not concern you, Cyra," he said, more gently than before. "There is nothing to tell you. If our father wishes to hold the Kingship ceremony on the New Moon, then our people will do so. That is all that matters."

Our people. He heard how it sounded and winced as her eyes flashed.

"Is it?" she said flatly. "From the sounds of it, there is much you have kept hidden about this ceremony, or the reason for it. I ask you again, what is this promise your brother spoke of? *What is the Golden Axe?*"

CHAPTER 31

THE GOLDEN AXE

Col did not answer immediately. His eyes shifted from Cyra to Alkippe, who watched with a level, guarded expression in her black eyes that gave no indication of her thoughts, as usual, then they moved to Sagitta, who wore her frown of disapproval much more openly.

"What...or who," he said with resignation, stirring the ladle in the cauldron one more time and then slowly lowering himself back onto the bench. Cyra looked down at him, frustration making a quick resurgence on her face. Col cut off her next question. "My brother thinks the Golden Axe is a 'what.' But some say it is not a thing at all. Not an actual golden axe. Sit, Cyra, and I will explain." He put a steady hand on the space between himself and Sagitta. Cyra crossed her arms with stubborn slowness.

"I will stand," she said stiffly. "Tell me."

Col sighed, knowing it would be fruitless to push her too far with any kind of order to desist or comply.

"My mother," he began. His mother's beautiful face and green eyes rose immediately in his mind. "She..." he paused again, frowning, unsure of what words he could use. He didn't want to use any of them; that was the problem. He'd thought he would have more time before this became an issue. He'd hoped it would never become known at all so that it never needed to be an issue. The eels of guilt twisted in his stomach. He looked down at his hands so that he would not have to meet anyone's eyes.

"There is an old prophecy that began with my mother's many-times mother," he began again. The attention of all three women in the room sharpened as he said the word prophecy. He did not know why, but

Cyra had drawn the definition from him early on, along with the words for destiny and fate. "Part of this prophecy is the reason she named me heir, even though I am the youngest. Because she claimed I had fulfilled a piece of the destiny that my brothers did not. Or could not." He halted again and looked up at Cyra, once more running out of words.

"What was this prophecy?" she asked.

"Where mother's many-times mother...from?" Alkippe asked, her words stilted and uncertain. Though she understood their speech well enough, the native tongue she had spoken for much of her childhood made pronouncing many of their words awkward, so she generally avoided speaking to anyone but Col and a select few who were patient enough to make conversation.

"In the mountains to the southeast," Col said, looking at her with slight surprise. "Why?"

"Mother of mother of mother have much...wisdom in their...roots. They see," she said, but she put her hand low on her stomach. Col followed the movement and raised a questioning eyebrow.

"Womb wisdom," Cyra explained, with an impatient gesture of her hand. "All women have it, but it is easier to sense many generations ahead. The vision becomes more clear. This is well known."

"Ah," Col said, though it was not well known to him.

"What was the prophecy?" she prodded again.

"Mother's many-times grandmother, Brin, made a cauldron. The cauldron that sits in our chambers," he explained. Once he began, the words rolled more easily, and he did not worry if they understood them. He just needed to tell it, so that he could assure Cyra it all meant nothing to him. To *them*.

"The cauldron was of the Old Magic. Brin gathered earth from the banks of the sacred river and molded the clay of it together with her own blood. She melted down the gifts of gold her own mother had given to her on the day of her marriage. She decorated the cauldron with all the gold she had left in the world. Once the cauldron was ready, she went into the forest, where the griffins hunted and the snow-cats prowled after great tusked beasts as big as this Hall, and she brought back the three plants that she would make a potion from. A potion to finally beget a child, for Brin had spent many years barren, and her husband demanded an heir.

"In the cauldron, she had fashioned of Old Magic, she boiled the plants, and when she drank them, she fell into a deep sleep. The sleep was meant to heal her, for her body had grown weary in her travels with her husband, and his hands had not been kind to her. This is why her belly would not swell with a child, she knew. However, she also knew that if she did not give him an heir, her husband would cast her aside, or kill her, as he had already sworn to do this."

Col paused. The three women stared at him with increasingly severe frowns. He shrugged in a feeble attempt at agreement with their anger before continuing.

"While she slept, the husband came upon her, for she had not returned to his wagon to help with the plowing, and he had been searching for her in a rage for days. He found her there in the forest, asleep under the stars, and it was the one night where Tabiti did not watch over the earth with her moonlit eye. The husband shook her to wake her, but she slept too deeply. He...had his way with her...while she slept."

Col was forced to pause again as Sagitta shifted on the bench so she could peer into his face more closely, her expression incredulous and her fierce blue eyes trying to read the sincerity of his words. Alkippe wore a sneer of disgust, so he was certain she had understood enough of what was said. Cyra's eyes might as well have been ice, and her mouth was a thin dagger ready to cut someone. Col looked to the three of them and raised his hands in a paltry effort to fend off an oncoming attack.

"It was wrong of him, of course," he said quickly. "If you want to know the prophecy, I must tell you the entire story. Peace," he pleaded and darted an uneasy look at Sagitta. She did not have her spear or axe, but all of them carried some sort of dagger, even though most Scoloti frowned at them for it still. Sagitta kept her blade safely sheathed, though, so he went on.

"When Brin finally awoke, she knew what her husband had done. He laughed at her angry accusations and, taking his hands from the plow he was using, struck her to the ground when she raged at his denial." Again, Col made a calming motion with his hands and hurried forward with the story, slightly louder to cover the angry hissing.

"For this, and because she knew her belly quickened with his seed even though he had come upon her with the deepest disrespect, Brin spoke the Old Words. The Words that held the power of her own mother's mother, who had told her people's stories of when the ice covered the land and the tusked beasts were their prey," Col said solemnly, looking at Alkippe. "These were Words that had the power to shape the future. They were Old Magic."

The women nodded as though they knew exactly what he spoke of.

"She told her husband that because of his dishonor, the traditions of his forefathers would fall into ruin. She proclaimed to all that she, Brin, and all of her daughters afterward would choose who would lead their people, as it had been in the days of her mother's mother's mother. If this was not honored, the sons of his sons would fall to ruin and despair. But that was not all.

"She took hold of her cauldron and smote it against the earth so that it split with a deafening crack from bottom to top. Then she took hold of her husband's axe, and she severed the yoke which harnessed the horses to their traveling wagon. She cut through it as though it was the most slender of twigs. Finally, she turned the blade to the plow, and she smashed it apart with two mighty blows. The axe, too, was split asunder in her fury, and she cast the pieces of it into the fire, where they were consumed in the heat of Tabiti's flame and anger.

"Her husband cowered to see the wreckage his wife wrought upon all that which was dear to him. But Brin was speaking the Old Words, the Old Magic blossoming into a powerful, inescapable force in her, and there was nothing he could do to stop her.

"'By the breaking of this yoke, I break our marriage,' she declared.

"'By the splitting of this plow, I split the destiny of your sons from the ways of their father's father. No seed of yours shall inherit without a woman's blessing.

"'By the melting of this axe, I promise that no weapon you or your offspring wield as king shall prevail over your enemies, lest another weapon forged of the Old Ways, with the same magic that flows in my veins, be found, and can be wielded with more honor than you have shown to me this day.

"'And by the breaking of this cauldron, I vow that no son born from your dishonor will ever be crowned king, without first repairing at least one damage that has been done this day.'

"And with this, Brin ordered that her once-husband be held down, and the others in their camp were so frightened by her power that they obeyed. As his punishment, she tied a string around his testicles, and she tied it tightly so that his screams could be heard at the farthest wagons on the high plain."

Col paused, his throat thirsty for water, dry from rising anxiety.

"I like many times mother," Alkippe interjected approvingly. "She strong woman."

Col's lips twisted wryly, though he did not disagree with her. Cyra turned her back to him and went to the table with stiff strides. She poured water from the earthenware jug into a leather mug and carried it back to Col. He took it with a soft smile of thanks, but she regarded him levelly, unsmiling. As soon as he had taken a long swallow, she jutted her chin at him.

"Continue," she commanded.

He shifted on the bench, but all three women pinioned him with their eyes, and he could neither escape nor leave the tale unfinished. He sighed and stared down at the cup of water for a moment.

"My father was the first in many generations to fix something that was broken that day," he said. "The day he met my mother in the fields, he found a plow, half-buried in the dirt, too broken to till the fields or aid the planting for many generations. He fixed it, and though his people were wanderers, he planted fields of grain and tended them with his own hands, so the people did not have to wander so far to feed themselves or the deer they held sacred. For this is what the woman—my mother—wanted, to be able to live in one place and not spend her life wandering from one pasture to the next.

"When he had grown the finest crop their people had ever known, he bid her to marry him, and she did. And when the people saw he had fixed the plow, which they believed to be the one from Brin's story, they rejoiced, declaring he was chosen to lead them. And so they crowned him king, though our people had not had a king in many generations."

The women watched him, transfixed, but the words would not come as easily now. Now that he was closer to the truth.

"So what happened with the other things Brin destroyed?" Sagitta asked.

"Well," Col said, and he gave Cyra a cautious look. "It appears perhaps I have some Old Magic as well."

Cyra frowned down at him. "A man with Old Magic?"

"I think perhaps the Old Magic is more common where you are from," Col said wryly. "Here, anyone with it is considered odd."

"That's because the Old Magic is a woman's domain," Cyra said matter-of-factly. "And we are a city of women."

"Even so," Col said, "I took the yoke from the ground where it lay buried, and I...fixed it. I did not really consider what I was doing. The history of the thing," Col shrugged. "Repairing it seemed easier than waiting for the crafters to fashion an entirely new one when I needed it soon, for our yearly migration to the feeding grounds. And when my mother found me using it on our wagon to lead the deer..."

"No one try...fix it...or fix other things...before?" Alkippe asked dubiously.

"Some did. Most were too superstitious to even try. But those who were not afraid to touch them were never successful. I was too naïve to be afraid, and I thought the stories were just that. But the yoke just sort of...came together for me. Allowed itself to be reshaped. As all wood does." Col shrugged, not understanding it himself.

"So your father fixed the plow and was chosen as the first king," Sagitta said slowly. "And now you fixed the yoke, and that is a sign you are the one your mother should choose as the next king, even though you were not firstborn?"

"In a nutshell," Col said.

"Why no queens leading your people?" Alkippe said, thrusting her chin toward him accusingly.

Col shrugged. "I don't think anyone ever really thought about it. Perhaps no women wanted that."

Alkippe grunted. "Doubtful. Men did not listen. They tell own tale of grandmother's wishes."

"Perhaps," he agreed, shrugging.

"What about the cauldron?" Sagitta asked.

"Still broken. Perhaps it waits for another king. Or queen."

"And the axe," Cyra said. It was less of a question than a reminder to get to the point.

Col paused for a long, tense moment, not looking at any of them. He swirled the water in his cup, focusing on it intently.

"You said some think the axe is a 'who' rather than a 'what.' But clearly, it was a weapon, and it was completely destroyed. Does it mean you must forge a new one? Is that why you are always asking about my star-forged dagger?"

Col looked up at her, keeping his expression neutral. "It was made clear through the stories of many mothers that the axe must be found, not forged," he said carefully. "And in the retelling of those stories, it became...legend, shall we say, that perhaps the weapon that could defeat our enemies would not be made of gold, or bronze, or any metal, but that it would be an army unto itself. An army that could not be led by a man without honor."

Understanding dawned on Cyra's face. He braced himself, holding her stare with a steady, forced calm, but her eyes might as well have been stone.

"You think we are that army," she said. He winced at the cold accusation in her voice.

"Some think so," he finally admitted, but his eyes slid away from hers, and the eels twisted.

"What about you? What do you think?" Cyra's voice was normally firm, but now it was hard as rock and sharp as the blade she wore on her arm.

"I think prophecies are a way for people to make sense of the world," Col said carefully. "And not very good ways to make decisions or choose kings."

She stared at him. She might have swallowed the moon; her eyes were so round with fury.

"But your people believe these prophecies. Your brother and those who follow him believe it. Believe he has an actual Golden Axe. And you have fulfilled a part of it yourself, with the yoke," she said. "So if you had both the yoke and the Golden Axe, you would have more claim to the throne than he would. Am I wrong." Again, it was a command and not a question.

"If the prophecy had any meaning, what you say is true, but—"

"You brought us—*me*—here to lay claim to the ha-mazaans. To *use* us." She said it so softly that it cut through his heart more painfully than if she had screamed at him or lashed out with her blade.

"No!" he said sharply and stood. "No," he repeated, more gently, but still urgently. "I brought you here because you would not have survived on your own through winter. Because it was what you wanted! That was before...before I knew how you came to be on this land at all. I brought you here to help you. And because I..." he trailed off as the door swung open again, and several people bustled noisily into the room, bringing a deluge of colder air with them. Still, it was not as cold as Cyra's eyes, and Col could not stop the eels from twisting.

CHAPTER 32

PAWNS

---

tried to scowl at the opening door, but my face was frozen. Shocked into immobility. Pain twisted deep in my chest, clawing at my heart. A pain I had never felt before, not even when I had learned about Eri's betrayal. I had not had any part in that. This, though.

This was my own fault. I had chosen to bring the ha-mazaans here. Chosen to lead them straight into a game of men and prophecies. Or had I? Had I chosen, or was I fated to be here? Once again, the noose tightened around my neck with yet another prophecy that choked me, pulled my steps in one direction or another regardless of my will. Another tether on my soul, pushed and pulled by the Fates, leaving no room for me to find my own way forward.

Ossy and a Scoloti woman carried two enormous legs of smoked meat into the hall. Tekmessa and Camilla followed with several more Scoloti women behind, Essri and Aife and Petar, their hands full of platters of freshly baked bread cooked fresh in the stone ovens. Somewhere behind the pain, irritation flashed. It was always women preparing the meals in Gelonia. It had always been women in Themiscyra, of course, but that's because there were no men. Here, it was simply the women's role, and that was that.

I looked back at Col, who made a forlorn gesture with his hands that did nothing to quell the cold knot of anger building itself into a tempest in my chest. Alkippe and Sagitta remained silent as the room filled with people, and both of them met my eyes with troubled wariness.

Ossy heaved the flank of meat onto the table, then turned to me. "Why so grim, Ishassara?" she said, clapping me solidly on the shoulder. "We will eat real garlic tonight with the venison. I even found you some old withered apples in the northern forest, close to the river."

I replied with a distracted thank you, and she gave me a searching look. She looked to Col, taking in his pained expression. "Hmmm," she said and turned away as the heavy wooden door opened once more.

Liopoxais entered, carrying Targitaos. As one, every person in the room turned their back and averted their eyes. I stared with the rest of them at the far wall as the room grew silent, waiting for Liopoxais to finish seating his father and for Col to finish arranging his furs and fetching the gruesome gilded human skull the king used as a goblet.

I had thought it a strange royal custom at first, this averting our eyes, and though I had wished to show respect for their ways, it also was tiresome and disruptive to always be ceasing sword practice or horse care or an evening meal, simply to turn one's back on the king as he was carried here and there. Once I finally understood enough of the language, Col explained that his father saw his paralysis as a weakness that threatened his rule. Targitaos believed that if the people constantly looked upon his withered legs, and his inability to move away from Col's carved chair without being carried, they would consider the power of his rule equally withered and either challenge him or, worse, scorn him. Plus, a king who could not ride to battle was hardly a king to be respected. In this, I could not argue.

"Proceed." Targitaos' voice was in no way withered, however. When I turned back to face the table, he was seated comfortably in the rolling chair Col had fashioned, his lap discreetly covered by warm furs.

"Thank you, Father," Col said, moving to the man's side and taking his hand. He kissed the inside of his father's wrist, just below the gold cuff.

"My Lord," I said stiffly when it was my turn, bending over the same wrist. His eyes, dark and rheumy with a winter illness, pinned me with their sharpness. He expected that I address him as "my King," but this was something I staunchly avoided, as did the rest of the ha-mazaans. It seemed enough that we were following their ways as best we could, keeping our heads low and helping with any work over the long winter. Subservience was too much, though. Targitaos did not like our refusal. His annoyance radiated from him now, and since the mood was already set, I decided to go all in.

"King Targitaos, I trust you will clarify for me something that your son has been reticent to share," I said, ignoring Col's warning frown and the impish grin that slid onto Liopoxais' face. More people entered the hall and took their places around the table. Essri cast more dung onto the hearth fire, causing more smoke to fill the room before the drafting vent in the ceiling could coax it outside.

"What is that?" Targitaos asked, his words blunted like a dull sword. He was not a man of many words and rarely spoke in the hall unless it was to give commands about deer husbandry, or spring migration plans with the wagons, or to settle disputes amongst rival families that Col had not already handled.

"I was hoping you would tell me, and my ha-mazaans, the purpose of this New Moon ceremony you are arranging. Since it has been made known to me that our presence is requested."

Targitaos considered me, his fingers twitching on the fur on his lap, and finally, he reached out an unsteady hand for the goblet brimming with wine. He lifted the gilded skull to his lips and drank heavily. A few streams of red ran from the corners of his mouth, dripping onto the darkly dyed wool of his tunic. I often wondered how much pain he suffered, though according to Col, the accident had been several years ago. The accident that had killed his wife, and Col's mother. A runaway team of horses, Col had said, dragging the wagon off the edge of a steep embankment, killing themselves and the queen and crushing the king's back so that his legs no longer moved. Killing his dreams of conquering more lands and requiring he live vicariously through his sons. This had become obvious to me during our first days inside Gelonia's walls, but Col did not seem to see it. I knew this desire to use his sons as pawns, as copies of himself, was why Targitaos sent Liopoxais to the south and Arpoxais to the west with many of the king's own men, to conquer new lands in his name, even though he already possessed everything he could possibly need for a successful kingdom.

Targitaos set the golden skull down with a resounding thud that echoed in the sudden hush of the Hall. I looked around and saw all the Scoloti were occupied with a strange intensity that involved looking everywhere but at the king or me. The ha-mazaans, however, watched Targitaos with frank curiosity. A few, like Ossy, were frowning slightly, their eyes on me. I made it a rule to keep my head down and my mouth shut during these dinners. I already felt unwelcome enough by some, especially Arnan, who had lost a hand in our raid, and by the others I had shot with my arrows. Talking usually made the feeling worse.

"It is a Kingship ceremony," Targitaos said finally, his voice an odd mixture of impatience and reluctance.

"And what does that entail?" I prodded.

Targitaos frowned, but I didn't know if it was because I, a woman, continued to address him so openly in mixed company or because he simply did not want to answer the question. Being part of his court was the first time in my life I had ever experienced what it might feel like to not be thought of as equal to a man. Many of these people could not see us as anything but freakish aberrations who dressed as men and played at things men should be doing. Col did not seem to notice this, either, though he was one of the few who also never treated us that way. I was not sure how or why he was different. There were others like him, but they were not as many in number as the ones who resented our free and forward ways.

"It entails the beginning of the end for an old king and the initiation of a new," Liopoxais answered, his face twisted in his customary smile. His hands were busy tearing chunks of meat from the flank on the table, and he pushed the platter toward the king unceremoniously. Targitaos frowned at the plate, or at his son's interruption, I wasn't sure.

"It is an old custom," Targitaos grumbled, staring at his food. He stuffed a morsel of meat into his mouth. As soon as he had taken his first bite, the rest of the table began tearing their own chunks of meat and bread and slicing thick pieces of the odorous hard cheese made from deer's milk.

"As old as a grandmother's grandmother," Col said, shooting me a pointed look before sliding a platter of food across the table and motioning to an open space on the bench. "Please," he said. When I stubbornly hesitated, he sighed. "I will tell you what it entails, though it is not considered words most of our women would hear over a meal."

Our women. He meant the Scoloti women would be offended, or scandalized, or sickened. Perhaps all of that. He also meant the hamazaans had proven to be very different from their women and by now had earned a classification all our own. This made me smile grimly, and I took the seat at the bench. Many of the Scoloti women would not meet my eye. The men did easily enough, though, and while some looked at me with uncomfortable intensity, others had a curious glint in their eye that I could not grasp the meaning of.

The women, though. They were why I usually kept my head down at public gatherings. They rarely spoke with me, and if they did, it was to relay a message or answer a direct question, which they did in as few words as possible before scurrying on their way. I think they hated me. Hated us. They would have had enough reason if we had simply been strangers who had abruptly entered their lands at the onset of winter, putting strain on their resources. More reason, then, that we were women. They found offense in our easy ways with their men, our lack of prudishness toward sex, which the ha-mazaans enjoyed without binding themselves or bearing children like the Scoloti women were required to do. They suspected immediately, just in the way he had introduced me, that Col had been claimed by an outsider. This effectively stymied their hopes, for themselves or their daughters, of being the wife of the future king. The women would have hated me for this alone, I knew. But there was also the matter of the six men we had killed. Husbands and sons, nephews and fathers. Many had lost a man to our arrows and axes or knew someone who had. Others had been wounded by our hands. This, they would never let us forget, I was sure.

The fact that all the ha-mazaans quickly realized the women were merely glorified scullions, that their days consisted of embroidery and cooking, childbearing and then childcare, of stitching boots for their husbands from the skins of deer and wolves they were not even allowed to hunt, made us curl our lips with disdain.

The few, perhaps fifty in the entire city of almost a thousand, who had come to us and tentatively asked to learn to fight as we did, to shoot a bow or hold a sword and make their steps swift with courage, were required to do so in secret. Col knew, of course, but we kept it between us and my ha-mazaans. Scoloti women here were not supposed to fight because they were considered *too precious*. We had flaunted this rule without compunction, as it was never ours to begin with.

But I could not help feeling that the women hated *me*, specifically. Perhaps it was my eyes, which they called witch-eyes, whatever that meant, because only men were witches, or my tattoos, although most of the ha-mazaans had similar markings. The women claimed I had bewitched their Ishassari, put a spell on him with my eyes, and bound him to me with the markings on my body. This, and the fact that I still rode out with the ha-mazaans any day the weather would allow, practicing our skills with our horses and bows, spears, and axes. Leading them and Col outside the walls to hunt, providing as we could for the resources we had taken from them. This was not their way. But I refused any ha-mazaan to be relegated to the wagons to stitch fancy embroidery during the long, dark winter days, as was Scoloti custom. They saw me as dangerous, first because I was a woman, and second, because I was a warrior. Because I was *Oirpata*, ha-mazaan, and I protected our ways with fierce, unapologetic pride. I did nothing to make them love me, I will admit.

Col did not seem to notice any of this, either.

"No," Targitaus said bluntly. He did not look up from his plate.

I stared at him in confusion, wondering what he was saying no to after my thoughts had spiraled away from the conversation for so long. He continued, still looking at his meat.

"We will not discuss the ceremony before it happens. It is not necessary." He tore another bite from the hunk of meat in his hand and chewed with steady resolve.

"I—" I began, but Col placed a heavy hand on mine and squeezed. I turned to him, frowning, but his eyes held a solemn warning as he shook his head.

"I will tell you later. It is a delicate matter," he said quietly so that his father could not hear.

Liopoxais grinned tightly across the table. Sagitta and Alkippe ate without speaking, but they both glanced at me thoughtfully in between bites. I turned my focus to my meal, but I barely tasted it. Ossy nudged me again and leaned in to whisper into my ear.

"Rumor has it, the middle brother moves this way from the west with an army," she said in our own tongue. Her words belied the lightness of her tone, and she kept her voice low and her face pleasant. "Rumor *also* has it that a red-haired *Oirpata* rides beside him, and her axe gleams golden. Has this rumor reached you?"

I pasted a wan smile on my face as I pretended to be amused by her words. "Something of the sort," I replied, keeping my eyes on my platter. "Col was just telling me a rather revealing story. I'm afraid he and I have some important things to discuss."

"Yes, you could try hiding how you really feel once in a while, you know," Ossy said dryly, still smiling sweetly. "When I first came in, I thought you were going to stuff the young Ishassari in the cauldron and make a tasty stew for us."

"Mmmm," I said, pursing my lips. "Perhaps I still should."

"Perhaps. But he is not all bad. Considering," Ossy said, and I glared at her from the corner of my narrowed eyes. "Considering some of the others, is what I mean," she clarified.

"I must agree with you there, goddess-mother," I said finally. We ate in silence then, each of us wandering in our own thoughts.

Before too long, the people in the hall had eaten their fill, and the room slowly emptied as women and men excused themselves from the king and made their way to their evening chores. I averted my eyes with some relief when Targitaos finally signaled to his sons that he wished to leave the hall. As Col carried his father away, I snatched a piece of dark bread from the table and stuffed it in my cloak for later, when I hoped that my appetite would return.

I would rather eat away from this place, anyway. Evening meals were the most dreaded part of my day, for they were the only time I was required to sit politely and play the Scoloti housewife for longer than a few moments. The rest of the day, I could go about my business, and at night, it was only me and Col, which I looked forward to with more anticipation than most anything else during the tedious winter days. Where I found the women awkward and stilted in their conversation, Col had proven to be a vast and varied font of interesting knowledge, especially once my language had improved. Our evenings were as filled with hours of sharing and debate as they were with passion and tenderness. It was an easy intimacy that I had taken for granted. Now, I wondered if that, too, had all been a part of his plan to bring the legendary Golden Axe under his sway.

Ossy waited beside me until Targitaos had been carried out before she gave me a pointed look. "Shall we inspect the horses?"

I nodded, lifting the fur-lined hood of my cloak over my head. Sagitta and Alkippe joined us, their expressions serious. We made our way in the snowbright night to the edge of the paddocks where our horses grazed.

"Timuë will birth her foal soon," Sagitta said as we neared the fence that ran the perimeter of their nighttime enclosure.

"Aye, and the sorrel," Ossy said, though it was dark enough that they were all just black shapes milling against the white ground. Soon after we entered through the swinging gate, a nose pressed into my arms, looking for treats.

"Sorry, girl. I only have bread."

Inara snorted indignantly but took the small piece of the loaf I tore for her. I smoothed my hand down her nose, and she dropped her forehead into my collarbone, resting it there. Heavy as it was, I did not push her away. I needed the comforting touch as much as she did.

"What will you do about this Golden Axe business?" Alkippe said, her teeth flashing the same bluish-white as the lightly falling snow settling to the ground. She did not bother to keep her voice low. No one else knew our words.

"I don't know," I shook my head, and Inara pressed into me.

"What's this?" Ossy said.

"Seems the family legend predicted our arrival," Sagitta said from farther away, where she was smoothing her hands over a heavily pregnant mare. "In the metaphor of a Golden Axe, that is. I can think of worse things to be called." She sounded amused by it. Alkippe did not, as her grunt confirmed.

"A Golden Axe that can make a king. And the brothers are not as decided as their mother was on who deserves to be that king, either," Alkippe said.

At Ossy's look of lost confusion, I filled her in on the more important bits of the story Col had told us.

"So this is why Eri marches with the brother from the west?" Ossy mused. "They intend to challenge Colaxais for the throne?"

"Perhaps," Sagitta joined us so that we stood in a small square, our breaths mingling in the dark hollow between us. "According to Col, Arpoxais and his army believe he now has the Golden Axe in the form of Hipponike's—now Eri's—blade. And also according to Col, the rest of them believe we ha-mazaans are the promised Golden Axe in the form of an army."

Inara shoved me so hard I barely kept my feet underneath me on the slippery ground. I turned to her, stroking the warmth of her neck.

"Who sits on their throne is of no concern to us, anyway," Ossy said. Then, slower, she said, "Is it?"

I knew what she was asking. I hesitated too long before answering. "No," I said, but there was more confusion than conviction in my voice. Another long silence, where the soft crunching of snow under hooves was all that sounded in my ears.

"I...I don't know," I said finally. My shoulders were heavy and sore, like I had carried too many pails of water or spent too long stacking rocks. I lifted them up to my ears and rolled one and then the other, trying to ease the tension in my body. The others waited, expecting more from me, but I did not know what to say to them.

"He would make you his queen if he takes the throne," Ossy said.

"I do not need any man to make me queen," I said sternly. I whirled to face her, fists clenched. "I would be queen in my own right, at the *Alsanti*, if I have earned it. *Me alone*. Not as someone's wife." I snarled the word at them. "That is not why I am here. You know this."

"Why are we here?" Alkippe asked, her voice not revealing any emotion.

"Because we needed a safe shelter for winter," I answered. "Because we needed time to figure out our path. To figure out our way home." I paused, feeling the weight of their eyes on me like a palpable thing, pushing the weight heavier upon my shoulders. "To find out whether we can ever go home at all."

Alkippe shifted her weight, the leather of her vest creaking in the night air. No one spoke for a long moment.

"You love him," Sagitta broke the silence. It was not an accusation, but I felt like it had been, like a punch in my gut.

Tears stung my eyes, and there was a growing lump in my throat that had been threatening to expand itself through my entire chest since Col admitted his truth.

"The fact that I love him does not change that I am your Ishassara," I said as firmly as I could. "I will do what is best for all of us. Whether it is deciding to go east and south, through the hostile mountains, or west and south, through the hostile peoples, will be decided once we know what is best. And if it means staying, rather than losing all my people to cold or battle or every danger on a thousand league journey... then that is what I will decide. And you will decide if I am right at the *Alsanti*."

"And if his brother challenges him," Sagitta said, "and we are in the midst of a civil war that is not of our people, what then? Will we hide in the wagons like their women and wait to see which brother wins? Or will you have us fight in a war that is not of our making and likely die anyway?"

I flinched. "There need not be a war. And if there is, I will order no ha-mazaan to risk their lives where their loyalty does not lie."

"But your loyalty, Ishassara Cyra," Ossy said gently, "is not so easily reconciled. And where our Ishassara fights, we will fight also."

"I..." I did not know what to say. Would I fight at Col's side if it came to a war with his brother? I could not imagine sending him into battle and not being at his side. It felt wrong. Like a betrayal. But if I and my soldiers had merely been pawns in his game of prophecies from the beginning, what possible loyalty did I owe him? I tasted blood and realized I had bitten my lip.

"I ask no one to fight for Col, or for me," I said again. "I do not know more than that. I must speak with Col. I need to know..." my voice trailed off again. What did I need to know? What did I truly want to know?

"Yes," Ossy agreed, although I did not know what she was agreeing to because I didn't know what I was saying myself. She stepped forward, the cool fog of our mingling breaths parting as she stepped through it. "Ishassara, your heart is wise. You have learned your path well, even though it has been a difficult one. Remember the words of your mother. If these things guide you, then you can guide us. I trust you."

)(

Col had hoped Cyra would be busy with her ha-mazaans and horses for much longer, but she came into the hall shortly after he reentered with his brother. He had also been hoping his brother would not follow him back to the Great Hall, but Lio seemed intent on making his life a twisting pit of vipers.

"You cannot expect me to choose between my brothers in a battle," Lio said in a tone bordering on affronted astonishment, but Col heard the thin thread of mockery in it.

"That is exactly what I would expect, if it comes to it," Col said grimly, even as Cyra approached where they stood at the hearth, her steps less wary than her eyes. They both turned to greet her, Col with a curt nod and Lio with an exaggerated smile, which she did not return. Col glimpsed blood on her lip, and his frown deepened.

"My lady Cyra," Lio said with his best attempt at charm. "Perhaps you can convince your prince that it would be most unseemly for me to interfere in the squabbles of my younger siblings? Especially not when he has such talented warriors at his disposal." His smile was saccharin. Cyra looked as though she had swallowed a hornet.

"My people are not at anyone's disposal," she answered scathingly, glaring at both of them. "But perhaps one of you would be so generous as to fill me in on what is happening with the army that approaches?"

Col shifted, trying to ease the tension in his shoulders. But it would be better if she heard it from him than from his brother.

"Arpoxais marches on Gelonia with his men, now that the snows have eased enough for travel," he said. "He brings your friend with her golden axe, and the other women as well. The spies tell us—"

"My spies, little brother," Liopoxais interjected smoothly. "You cannot say I have not helped you, after all."

"Liopoxais' spies, if they can be trusted," Col continued coolly, meeting his brother's eyes with a level stare, "tell us that between them, your friend and my brother have agreed it is fitting for them to rule over the Scoloti, and even over your ha-mazaans, because of a prophecy." Col's eyes slid tentatively back to Cyra. He was not wrong to anticipate her anger as the grey of her eyes darkened like smoke from a forge. Her tongue tasted the blood on her lip as he continued. "Apparently, the red woman claims she is a Chosen One of her people, from a destiny promised when she was young. But it does not matter what my brother wants or what this wayward ha-mazaan thinks she should have. My mother already made her choice."

Col was entirely unsure if his words were true, that Arpoxais' wishes did not matter anymore. He wished he felt less doubt about everything. About his mother's choices, about Arpo's insistence that things would be better if he was king, about Col's choice to bring Cyra and her ha-mazaans into such a tangled mess. Doubts or not, he was determined to play down any harm that she or her ha-mazaans might think was imminent.

"Yet your brother does not agree," Cyra echoed his thoughts. "But does he expect to stand outside the gates with a village of men and a few ha-mazaans and be able to shout you into handing over your throne?"

"There is more than a village of men," Col said evasively.

"How many?"

"Five hundred strong at least," Lipoxais answered with relish.

Cyra's eyes flashed. "But...how is it that so many would challenge the laws of kingship in your lands? Only because of this...this axe?" she asked, her black brows knitting together like a raven's wing folding for a downward dive. When her teeth bit into her lip again, Col was sure the blood had come from a previous worried gnawing.

"Because they make their own laws," Liopoxais said. "Our father has done well to keep unity among the tribes for so long. Alas...I fear my little brothers will not be able to keep it so, with both edges of the prophecy so sharply dividing the people. And with many preferring a man of Arpo's...strength, shall we say, to lead them." Lio smiled apologetically at Col, though Col knew his brother meant every word.

"And how long before they are at the gates?" Cyra asked, ignoring Lio's jabs.

"Before the New Moon," Col said gravely, meeting her eyes. Five days.

Her eyes moved back to his brother. "And you do not defend your Ishassari?" she asked coldly.

Lio spread his hands in a wide shrug. Col almost smiled to see her lip curl in a sneer.

"How can I choose?" his brother replied glibly. "It would not be right."

"You do not know right," she said flatly. "And you do not know honor, if you would sit back and let this happen. You are a coward, not a brother." She ignored the expression of pale fury that stilled his face. Col interrupted before one of them met with harm at the other's hand.

"It does not matter," he said. "When Arpoxais comes, he will not win the throne so easily, to make a mockery of all the hard-won peace my father has brought for the sake of a twisted piece of prophecy. He will meet my sword, and the swords of the men who support me, with or without Lio's help."

The words that went unsaid seemed louder than any he had spoken, though. *With or without the Golden Axe in the form of a ha-mazaan army.*

She stared long at both of them, her shining eyes almost level with theirs and her back as straight as any sword. She said nothing as she turned away from him. Col felt, beneath the sloshing of the eels in his gut, that much of his strength went with her when she walked out the door.

CHAPTER 33

SALTED WILDFLOWERS

When Col came into our chambers, I was huddled on the floor near the fire, the paltry warmth of it not managing to penetrate the cloak still wrapped around me. I wished for the hot sun of Themiscyra to melt the ice inside my chest, but home had never seemed farther away than now. He shut the door softly and lowered the latch. I did not turn to him as he came across the room on silent feet, but I felt his warmth more than I did the fire's when he finally stood close to me.

Tabiti's flames, I thought miserably. I wanted to rage at him and have him wrap his arms around me at the same time. When he sat on the bear rug next to me, I looked at him, almost scared of what I might see. His eyes were equally wary and pained, as though he expected me to scream at him like a Scoloti housewife.

"I am sorry I did not tell you before," Col said. His eyes were their darkest green and shadowed with weariness.

"Which part?" I asked dully. "The part where your brother is marching an army against you? Against us? Or the part where myself and my ha-mazaans are just a tool in a game your family has been playing for some time?"

"That is not what this is. But yes. For all of that. I'm sorry."

"Is it why you came to me in the forest that day? To capture me?" I asked bluntly. He paled, but I would not waste time on niceties when my heart was hurting as it was.

"No," he said slowly. "And...yes." The pained expression amplified. I stiffened, feeling my chest compress tighter, the protective wall of ice grow a sliver thicker.

"So...it was all for a purpose, then? A plan?" My voice sounded far away. "The carvings were a clever hook for a gullible fish?" I looked at where they sat lined upon the mantle of the hearth. Clever icons of my *rhu-tasiya*. Clever hooks. I shook my head. "Letting us take you hostage without even putting up a fight." I laughed a high-pitched, single syllable that sounded harsh and bitter in my ears but still far away. "I practically threw myself right into your plans."

Col was shaking his head. "No," he said firmly. "No, that is not how it was, Cyra."

"Then tell me how it was!" I said fiercely, viciously, my lips thinning to show my teeth. I leaned forward, my palms on the floor as I spit the words at him. "Tell me you and your brothers did not discuss this 'Golden Axe' after we raided your caravan. Tell me that is not why you sent your armies, to see who could win it—win *us*—first." My anger congealed into an icy rage when I saw the truth of it on his face. My tone became scathing, although it was mostly self-hatred I was feeling. "Tell me you did not thank your precious Tabiti when I threw myself at you. Opened my legs for you. Brought you to my bed, and you didn't have to even *try*."

"*No*," he said fiercely, almost a shout. His eyes flashed angrily, and he lurched forward to grasp my arms with hard fingers. "I came to your bed because I already—"

"Unhand me, or you will lose your fingers to my blade," I said lowly. His fingers eased from my arms. He looked down at his hands as though he had not known where they were.

"Do you know," I asked, still dangerously quiet, "why we have the rite of First Blood among my people?" He shook his head stiffly, his shadowed eyes on mine.

"So that we do not hesitate when it matters. So that any man we choose to lie with will know we will have no hesitation in taking the hand, or the life, of the one who harms us. Do you understand this?" My words were slow and bitten off at the end. I thought my fury would eat me alive.

He looked into my eyes for a long moment. "I understand, Ishassara Cyra." Another long look. "And I would never harm you. Do *you* understand this?" His voice was quiet, and a little sad, but he did not back away.

"I understand only that I am a fool," I said, slowly sitting back and slipping my blade all the way back into its sheath. I had not drawn it, but I would have, if needed. The very thought of it made me feel tired and heavy with grief. I tensed as his hand returned to where it had been on my arm.

"I am sorry. I did not mean…I should not have grabbed you like that. I…" His throat moved as he swallowed. "I need you to believe me. I did not come to your bed for anything but…but love."

I stared at him. His eyes were still pained, but they were sincere.

"You did not even know me," I said, unsure of what else to say. Part of my heart wanted to sing at his words, and the rest of me wanted to scream he was a liar.

"I knew enough. I knew the first time, in that ravine when you laughed like the dawn, that I wanted to make you part of my life. You may ask Esten what I said to you that day," he said, and his tone was earnest. His hand still lay on my arm, but gently. "I knew enough, then. I knew more by the time we lay together in that meadow. And I know more now." His face was as grave as I had ever seen it.

"I know how you like to feel the earth sing under your bare feet. That you listen to the Great Mother in this way, and that these boots we wear chafe at you. Make your feet deaf and slow on the ground, at least in your own mind. I know you are the best archer in your band of mighty ha-mazaans, and the most stubborn. I know you are the most gifted with the horses, and that you speak their language in ways others cannot. I know you guide your people wisely and protect them with courage and greater honor than I have ever seen in any man. I know that you could have killed me that day in the ravine. Or any since, except for your honor, which would never allow it without reason. May I never give you one.

"I know you have a mind as sharp as the star-forged blade you sharpen every day. I know, if you truly wanted, you could flay my skin from my body and feed it to the ravens while I beg for mercy. I know, Cyra, that if I ever raised a hand to hurt you, it would be the least I deserved. I know there is a fierceness in you, a wildness that can never be tamed. I know this now like I could not have known it then. But I knew enough of it. I knew I loved you, or that I would love you, if given the chance. There is no other reason I lay with you than this."

To my absolute horror, I began to cry.

It was not a sobbing, blubbering cry, but I could not keep the hot tears from welling over. It was infuriating. I wanted to scream, not cry.

Col looked as horrified as I felt and began making inarticulate sounds of distress, trying to put his hands where they would do any good, but mostly just waving them helplessly. I thought he might even cry with me. I could tell he was holding himself back from holding me. I wished he would not hold back. I wished I did not wish that. I cried harder.

"What am I supposed to do now?" I asked through my tears as soon as I was sure my voice could move through my tight throat. Col added a perplexed look to his helplessly distressed face. "I will not ask my ha-mazaans to fight for you, Col. I cannot do that."

Col shook his head. "I never said I would ask them to fight for me," he said carefully.

"Well, you could not ask them, because they don't belong to you! But do you expect me to just let you go into battle alone?" Col went back to looking helplessly confused. "Liopoxais already said he will not bring his men to support you. What does that leave you? Four hundred men? Your women are useless!" I said savagely, my mouth turning down in disgust. "So what do you expect me to do?"

"I—" Col started, and then stopped, clearly at a loss for words. He tried again, even as the tears fell hot on my face and the pressure inside of me expanded unbearably.

"I would never expect you or your women to fight my battles for me," he said. "It is not why you are here, Cyra. I thought you *wanted* to come here with me," he said this a bit desperately, spreading his palms out in supplication.

"I did," I snarled. "That is what makes me so *angry*!"

Col blinked and sat back, running a hand through his hair and then rubbing both hands over his face.

"How do you not understand!" I cried unfairly, since I didn't understand any of it myself. "I have spent my entire life trying to escape a destiny that would lead me to betray my ha-mazaans and the Way of my people. Ossy kept giving me all these talks about choice and how it is up to me. But it sure doesn't seem that way! And if it is, either my Kubileya or your Tabiti—maybe they are one and the same, I don't know!—but either one or both are playing a cruel joke on me!" I realized I was sounding exactly like a Scoloti housewife but did not care. I rambled on.

"Because I did choose some things. Maybe the wrong things? I chose to not kill you. I chose to lie with you. I chose to come here with you.

And now, I do not see that I have any other choice than to fight for you, even if none of my ha-mazaans will fight with me." I did sob then, but it came out as a frustrated growl, like a trapped wildcat might make.

"Cyra, you do not—"

"I DO!" I yelled, and he flinched back with a stricken look. "Because I love you, you great fool! So I *don't* have any other choice! But you can take your ideas of a Golden Axe and shove them where Tabiti does not shine! I will not ask my ha-mazaans to fight for me because I was stupid enough to fall in love with the very person I spent most of my life trying to avoid!"

) (

Col stared at Cyra, joy and distress warring for supremacy in his chest. She seemed stricken by her own words and was more upset than he had ever seen her. He knew he was risking his safety after the unwise way he had grabbed her earlier, but he could not watch her suffering any longer. She fixed him with wide, wild eyes as he came toward her, like a wildcat caught in a trap. She put her arms between them when he drew her close, but her push against his chest was feeble, as though she expected herself to do it rather than wanted to. Gently, carefully, he pulled her to him, his hand on the back of her neck and his arm pulling her body into his lap, though she was not light by any standards. She remained stiff with resistance, still fighting the tears that he could feel dripping hot against the skin of his throat. But she did not pull away. Or put a knife in his ribs, which had been equally possible. Even that thought could not quell the smile that spread slowly across his lips as they pressed into her hair, or the warm glow, like molten gold, flowing through his chest.

"Cyra," he whispered into her hair. It smelled of horses and smoke. "Your love is the only gift I want, and I will treasure it for as long as you offer it. Your freedom is why I love you, do you not understand this?" She pressed her face into his neck. "Love is not fealty," he said. "Love is love. I want nothing more from you."

"But that is the problem," she said quietly, her body relaxing into his muscle by muscle, though he knew she was fighting it. "I would give you everything I have." She swallowed. "But I cannot ask those who would swear fealty to me to fight for my love of you. This is not their battle. Your games of kingship and squabbles amongst men are not for us to settle. When we fight, we fight to protect our Ways and to honor the sacred path of the Great Mother."

"I know. I know, Cyra. I am not asking anything of you or any of your ha-mazaans. You must believe me."

She was silent for a moment, then said, so quietly into his chest that he had to strain to hear her, "But would you fight for me if I needed it? If my ha-mazaans needed you?"

"Yes," he said without hesitation. "But that is—" he stopped.

"It is *exactly* the same," she said firmly, hearing the words he did not speak.

They fell silent. Col battled the opposing feelings of helplessness and joy within him. Joy was winning.

"Will you say it again?" he asked.

"Say what."

"That you love me."

She tensed again, and this time pushed both fists hard into his chest to lean back and scowl at him. Her eyes were red and puffy, which he had never seen on her before. Even her nose was red, and where the tears had streaked her face, the skin seemed almost burned, as though she was allergic to tears. Allergic to crying. He grinned. Her scowl grew fierce, and much of the flint returned to her silver eyes. She was the most beautiful creature he had ever seen.

"Is that the only thing you heard?" she said, sounding slightly strangled.

"Yes," he lied. "Please?" He smoothed a hand across her cheeks, wiping the tears off one, then the other. Her face moved against his hand, but he was not sure if she was rubbing it against his hand like a cat would or trying to bite him, also like a cat would.

"I love you," she growled. His smile widened.

"And I love you, Cyra Ishassara. That is all that matters." He squeezed the arm around her waist. "The rest is something we can figure out together."

She stared at him for a long time, until the storm in her finally subsided. He waited until the fire in her eyes had simmered to the usual spark, and then leaned in to kiss her. Her lips were warm and tasted of salted wildflowers, and spices kings paid a fortune to taste only once.

When he had sufficiently drowned himself in the taste of her lips, at least for a few moments, he untied her cloak, and her belt, and her vest. She made quick work of his own belt and tunic. And when he lay her naked on their bed, her body sinking deep into the mattress, he stretched her hands high over her head, holding them there. He smoothed a hand from the inside of her palm to her hip to the tip of her toes, raising gooseflesh all the way down. He knew well enough they were not from the cold.

She watched him with those glittering eyes the whole time, even as her breathing changed. He brought his hand back up her body, his eyes following his fingers as they traced the incredibly strong length of her thigh, lean and muscled from daily riding and training. He traced the small lines and dots tattooed on her hips and belly, new from this winter, noticing her stomach suck inwards as his fingertips tickled her flesh. He traced upward, through the center of her perfect breasts, where indented lines from her belt keeping them firmly pressed against her chest were still fresh on her skin. He traced these, marveling that a warrior so fierce could feel so soft, and still she watched him. Her eyes were full of everything he could not fathom but that he wished to spend a lifetime discovering. He traced up her throat, over her chin, and lingered for a moment on her full lips, so often frowning with concentration or being bitten by her own doubt, but full and parted now with desire. He brushed a light finger over the cut on her lip, put there by her own worry. Worry he had caused. He brought his palm against her cheek, his fingers splayed out in the hair around her face, and looked into her eyes, matching her enigmatic stare.

"There is nothing I would not do for you, keeper of my heart. And there is nothing I want from you, other than your love for as long as you will give it. But I promise that in all my ways of loving you, protecting your freedom and keeping you wild will always be how I serve you. My love will never be a chain that binds you. This is my solemn vow."

) (

"What did you mean about your destiny?" Col asked, his fingers busy in the loosened waves of her hair. He had discovered early on that she enjoyed it being brushed and would practically purr like a kitten if he did it well. Therefore, he did this as often as possible. It seemed to set her at ease tonight.

He'd often wondered how much she truly enjoyed her hair confined in braids and her breasts bound by belt and vest. Both were necessary to do what she did as ha-mazaan, but she seemed restricted in so many ways when what she really wanted was to be free. But he was wise enough to keep such thoughts to himself. She tipped her head back and sighed as his fingers grazed her skull. He thought she might not answer, and did not press her, but eventually, she answered in a voice heavy with spent passion,

"I knew you. Your face. I knew I would meet you."

Col stiffened with surprise, then eased the tension from his body with deliberate intention, lest it discourage her from speaking further. He stroked his hand down over her black waves again, waiting.

"I saw your face in the flames of our Oracle when I was twelve summers," she said. "Do you know, I think I even saw your horse? I did not realize it until now."

He bit his tongue to keep from interrupting with questions. Already there were so many, but he did not want to risk it.

"Yes, Faelan *was* there. His long white socks. How strange. I did not see Inara." She paused for a long moment, humming softly while his hands combed. "I was told I would never be queen of my people unless I met you. Bound myself to you."

Col's hand stilled, tangled halfway through her long strands.

"You must understand," she said imploringly, still into his chest, "to bind ourselves to men is not our way. It is against our customs. I thought it Law, even. But..." her voice trailed off. He finished the downward stroke more slowly, keeping his lips firmly shut. She shifted her body against him, hooking a long leg over his knee under the furs.

"But I saw your face, in the flames. Saw that it was my destiny to break from the ways of my people, and that this would be my price to be queen. I did not understand. I still do not understand," she said. "Ossy said it was my own choices that brought me to you, after the Achaeans took us. But... it does not feel that way."

"Is it only your Ishassaras who are bound by such prophecies?" Col asked curiously, feeling this was the safest question of the hundreds pounding at the back of his teeth like they were trying to storm through a gate.

"No," Cyra said, strangely grave. "No. But it seems that my own prophecy and yours have intertwined, to become a destiny neither of us could have chosen. I do not see how it is otherwise."

He thought for a moment. "That day of the caravan raid. You could have shot me with that arrow. Is this why you did not?"

"Yes."

"And in the ravine?"

"Yes."

"And if you had?"

"I don't know."

"But you still could," he said slowly. "If I were not in your life…had never come, or were…dead…your people would most likely still choose you at this ritual you call the Alsanti. You could still be rid of me and be queen."

"If I am found worthy, yes," she said earnestly and propped her head up to look at him. He felt slightly chilled at her casual acceptance of this scenario. It did not seem to be the first time she had thought about it.

"Then I would have nothing to do with you being queen. So why did you not do it when you first saw me? Why do you not…do it now?"

"Kill you, you mean? Because I was curious, then. And I love you, now." She said this very matter-of-factly. "And I don't see what killing you will accomplish anymore."

"How very reassuring."

She laughed lightly, and the pique eased from him at the sound of it.

"I think…it has always been my struggle of not being able to choose that confounds me. Frustrates me," she said, laying her head back on his chest. He ran his hand through her hair again and felt her lashes flutter against his chest like delicate wings. "I want to choose my own path, make my own destiny. But, without my destiny, I would not have met you. And now it seems another prophecy not of my control binds me to you further."

She said this last with simple finality, and Col stilled his hand on the back of her head.

"Perhaps," he said finally. "I fear it is all beyond me. Destiny. Fate. The workings of Tabiti, whom you call Kubileya. I do not understand any of it. I would give back to you what you lost, Cyra," he said, apologetic sorrow coloring his words. "If I could. Your home. Your city." He paused. "Your mother. I know what that kind of pain is." He thought of his own mother and the grief that still clung to him like a dark shadow that never felt the sun.

"I wish you had not suffered. But I cannot find it in me to regret this destiny of yours, whether it was chosen or not. I am only a man, and selfish besides." He braided his fingers into her hair and squeezed it tightly. "My love for you has nothing to do with any prophecy. I know that if I had not met you, my soul would have wandered empty and barren my entire life, and I never would have known the reason."

They were quiet, then, and her hand traced invisible patterns on his chest. When her fingers stilled, he knew from her breathing that she slept, but his eyes could not close to join her. He did not know about destiny, or prophecies, or what Tabiti asked of him. He had never been a particularly devout man, but he prayed with more than his lips as he held her. He prayed to his own Tabiti, and to her Kubileya of the Moon, though they were one and the same. He gave thanks for what She had brought to him. He gave promises and made bargains in exchange, if he could only keep the gift She had brought him.

Then he prayed he was wrong about what he knew inside. In the end, he simply prayed to have more time.

CHAPTER 34

TAKEN

"Ishassara Cyra! *Ishassara*! Wake up!"

Alkippe's voice. Not my dream. Col lunged out of the bed at the same instant a heavy fist pounded on the door. He did not bother to cover himself before opening it, and I sat up in bleary-eyed confusion to see Alkippe's unconcealed revulsion as she stared at the naked man in front of her.

"Is good I desire women," she said bluntly in broken Scoloti, staring at Col. Her eyes went past him to me, even as he scrambled for his tunic.

"Ishassara. It is Erioboea," she said in our tongue. There was an unfamiliar urgency in her voice.

"What about her?" I asked, sleep falling away from me along with the fur blankets as I sat up.

"She has taken your mare. Inara."

I was dressed in tunic and trousers and boots and moving out the door before Col could finish lacing his boots. When I found the rest of the ha-mazaans under the great oak in the main courtyard, I knew by their faces it was not some cruel joke.

The traces of snow and ice had melted overnight in a sudden thaw, turning the ground soft with mud, and as I moved closer to the huddled group, a raindrop splattered against my face. I ignored it.

"How?" I looked from Ossy's grave face to Sagitta, and Thraso, and Leya. Even Tekmessa was there, though she hung back, her red robes grimy along the edges like she had walked a great distance in the mud. "Tell me."

Col's distinctive step sounded behind me, and the women's eyes moved as one to watch him approach. Though he often watched our practices and sometimes set his skill against ours, unless invited, he usually left us in privacy to meet or discuss our plans as we wished. The ha-mazaans regarded him warily now as he came to stand silently at my side.

"Tell me," I said again, more insistently. "Col will not know our words, anyway."

"We rounded up the herd as usual, Ishassara, for their morning water at the river," Sagitta said grimly. "But Inara was not with them." The tall woman shifted uncomfortably in her long boots, wet with mud and melted snow. "We searched the entire city for her. Then, the sentries came. The morning sentries," she explained, and this time her eyes moved to Col. "They killed the night sentries, Ishassari Colaxais," she said in Scoloti.

Col stiffened beside me.

"Arpoxais is not yet so close with his army," he said. "Our scouts would have warned us."

Sagitta shrugged. "I cannot say. But they were killed in the night, and no one knew until it was too late." Her blue eyes swerved back to mine. She continued again in our own tongue. "The morning sentries found the dead and saw Inara outside the gates. Eri holds her, and a few ha-ma…a few women. They have sent you a message, Ishassara."

"Eri has taken Inara?" I repeated dumbly, barely registering everything she said. All the ha-mazaans stared at me. "Taken my *rhu-tasiya*." I tried to make it a question but could not summon the proper inflection.

"She holds her outside the western gate right now," Alkippe said reluctantly. "Within arrow's reach, even. She knows what she does. The sentries tell us she gave a message for you. She has challenged you to battle, Ishassara. Alone. Two mornings hence. Otherwise, she will kill the mare."

I stood mute and stunned, my mind not knowing which words to grab onto and make sense of and which to let slip through the fog, never becoming real enough to fully comprehend. Rain began to fall in earnest, pattering against the ground around us. The bare oak offered little shelter.

Vaguely, I heard someone explain to Col in Scoloti what they knew, but their words and his response were far away, through the dense fog as I stared at the splashes of rain on the muddy ground. I could not fathom that one who knew our ways, who knew the significance of our *rhu-tasiya*, would even contemplate such sacrilege. It was not done. It was not even dreamed. I would not have conceived of such a thing for my worst enemy, I was sure.

I raised my face, the rain stinging in my eyes.

"Then I will meet her."

"We will—" Alkippe began.

"No," I cut her off. My eyes moved from her to Ossy, to Sagitta, and to the rest, whose faces expressed horror, disbelief, anger. Fuel for my inner flame, to burn away the fog. "I will do this alone. This is my fight."

"That is what she wants, Cyra," Ossy said.

"Yes."

"Don't be foolish! Our strength will always be in our togetherness. You will play right into her hands because she knows you will behave recklessly," Ossy chided, her own anger making her words uncharacteristically harsh. I simply nodded.

"Yes," I said. "But it is between Eri and me now. This cannot be your fight."

They fell silent, though their frustration was palpable.

I turned to Col. "I tell you what I tell them, Colaxais," I said and told him in his own tongue.

His eyebrows drew together, and he glanced up at the ha-mazaans' grim faces. "Cyra—" he began, but I would not waste more time.

"I will see Inara now."

I turned in a daze and walked westwards. Col caught my arm and whistled sharply. He looked down at me, his face grim with concern. Faelan's hooves, always free to roam where he wished, yet never far from Col's side, sounded from the distance. Col shouted an order to young Scoti, who watched the proceedings from a shadowed doorway, and his slight frame disappeared in a flash.

Faelan slid to a stop in the mud, coming dangerously close to both of us. The young boy ran out with a bridle, handing it to Col with his unbroken arm, the other still bound in a sling. Col tucked the bridle over the stallion's head. Then, he swung onto his back and leaned a hand down to me. We grasped each other's forearms, and I swung onto the tall chestnut's back, wrapping my arm around Col's waist as he shouted the stallion into a gallop.

When we reached the western gate, the same one we had entered on our arrival, I slid from Faelan's back before Col had drawn the horse to a halt. I took the steps of the watchtower two at a time. The sentry at the top was busy aiming his bow at something—or someone—beyond the gate, and his eyes bulged when I breached the stairs, shoving him aside.

She was there. Inara. Cinched around her neck were three cruelly tight lassoes, the tension of them pinching her flesh into wrinkles as she strained and screamed with fury, trying to pull loose. But it did not matter which way she tried to escape. In every direction that her neck pulled, there was a traitorous ha-mazaan pulling her back to center, strangling her in their trap. They could not get any closer to her lest they lose a hand to her teeth or feel the sharp, deadly knives of her hooves. Inara reared in fury, and when her striking hooves were finally hauled back to the ground by their tugging, rope-burned hands, great splashes of rain and melted snow splattered the air.

And there was Eri.

She sat astride her own dark horse high on the ridge above the mare, the flaming copper of her hair the only way I knew it was her from this distance. She sat unmoving, the golden axe that had once been her mother's slung comfortably against her shoulder blades, unthreatening. I wanted to unsling my bow and put an arrow between her breasts. But she was not within reach, even of my arrows. Only Inara was. Eri was taunting me with my own *rhu-tasiya*. The fog on my mind lifted away completely as rage burned through it.

Only when I heard more horses and turned to see several ha-mazaans approaching the gate and Faelan waiting below did I become aware that my face was wet with tears and that Col's arm was around my shoulders as he looked out at the scene of my traitorous friend and my *rhu-tasiya*. I turned away from Ossy's worried face looking up at me and looked back to Eri.

I could not see her face, but I was sure she saw me there in the watchtower. I watched with helpless fury as the women tugged harder at Inara's neck, slowly, inexorably drawing her back, up the hill, and into the trees. Eri's horse stood on the ridge a while longer, long enough for the rage in my chest to spread into my arms and up into my cheeks, making my face burn. Then, she turned her horse, moving into the trees where Inara had disappeared. Her body rocked easily from side to side as her horse's slow, mocking steps took her into the forest until she had disappeared, and my *rhu-tasiya* with her.

) (

I spent the rest of the day in silence. My inner landscape was now both frozen and roiling at the same time, like a spring river jamming ice into a great dam that could break at any moment. My thoughts of Eri were the water battering at the ice, pounding relentlessly with rushing, tumultuous thoughts of betrayal, and prophecies, and treachery. The ice was where my thoughts ended, cold and hard, frozen emotions encasing the truth that my beloved Inara, the carrier of my soul, was in the hands of a traitor.

I knew Eri would kill her if it came to it. She would follow through because she was nothing if not committed to achieving what she wanted, whether it was first prize for a footrace or, apparently, the rulership of the ha-mazaans. I wanted to think differently, to believe the best. To believe Eri was not capable of this. Or, to believe that it would be an easy victory, me over my old friend, whom I had fought a hundred times before. Therein lay the problem. Eri was skilled with an axe, while I was not as good with an axe or sword as I was with a bow. And if she meant to face me in hand-to-hand combat, she would have the advantage. Of course, I could always simply kill her with an arrow from a distance. But I knew enough to know Eri would not leave the mare unattended. If I did not meet her as agreed, Inara would die, whether by Eri's hand or someone else's. Yet if I did meet her, and somehow prevailed, what reason was there to think the other women would let Inara go, after everything?

These swirling thoughts made it impossible for me to engage with anyone. I assured Col I would be alright while he undertook preparations for battle, and locked myself in our chambers, alone. But while I was silent, my hands were busy, and the work became a meditation of sorts, calming the flooding river or, at the very least, acting as an embankment to keep the waters from spilling over. I inspected all of my armor, old and newly made over the winter, and made sure each of my weapons was ready for fighting. Even the bow, though I could not use it against Eri. There were still Arpoxais' men advancing, though, once I finished with her.

I replaced the hand-grip on the bow, using leather from Col's plentiful stash of tooled scraps and leavings. I inspected the arrows, checking that the swan-fletching was tight and smooth and thinking of Col's admonishment for killing and using the feathers of a bird so sacred to his people. *Fair exchange for burning our dead*, I thought, but without rancor. I double-checked the newly cast bronze heads from Col's armory were sharp and firmly fixed in place with their rawhide bindings. Last, I took my sword from the bracket where it hung next to Col's larger one. The leather scabbard he had made for me was smooth and heavy in my hands, the tooling a beautiful pattern under my fingertips. I spent a long while sharpening the blade, the singing of the stone against the metal satisfying something in my soul that helped keep the worst thoughts of water and jamming ice at bay.

As long as I did not think of Inara and those ropes.

Instead, I thought about my ha-mazaans. I thought about the Scoloti. I thought about dinners to come in the Great Hall, though I would not attend this evening's. I thought about Tekmessa, and Esten, and the others who had taken lovers here. I thought, and wondered, and these thoughts, too, kept the ice wedged firmly in place as the river thundered against it, trying to break loose.

)(

When Col returned to our chambers, after Tabiti's hearthfire had been stoked for the evening and the rest of the city had gone to make their last supplications of love or prayer, I turned to him with a quiet grief that had no voice. He held me, thinking it was only about Inara, and I let him think it, hoping the river inside of me, bigger now with a grief that had not yet even happened, would not break through the ice after all.

When I calmed, more from exhaustion than anything, he told me what he had learned throughout the day.

"You are certain of this?" I asked.

"The numbers do not lie. At least another four-hundred men, on top of the first contingent."

Almost a thousand men marching. We were silent for a bit, and when I finally offered my suggestion, he fought it, as I knew he would. But I knew it was the best way. The right way. It calmed me to have a clear purpose. Finally, when I had led him to see reason, we spoke at length about our plans and what they would mean for the people. For both our people, all together.

Afterward, he covered my body with his hands and his mouth, and I did the same to him, drinking him in like he was the last drop of water in a wide desert. I did not allow the savage, icy thoughts to break free while I was with him. Instead, I thought of how bright his eyes were and how Tabiti's flame never burned low inside of them. How they glowed warmer than the hall's hearthfire when he looked at me. I thought about how his smile curved when I touched him. I thought about how his body went hard with just a glance at my most wicked smile, and I teased him with one until he groaned with impatience. I thought of how well we fit together. I thought of how complete I felt when he held me and I him. And then, I thought of nothing at all.

When he finally slept, I slipped from the bed and took the furs he was not using. I crept from our chamber and into the courtyard, and I laid my fur down between the roots of the old oak. I lay there in the cold, thinking of my mother, the bare, finger-like branches of the tree cracking their knuckles in the wind above me.

When I slept, I dreamed of Inara.

She walked toward me, three tight ropes circling her neck while the long, frayed lengths of them trailed on the ground behind her. Instinctively, I put a hand to my own neck as though the ropes were there, digging into my own throat, and they were. I tugged, feeling the air being choked from me, but they pulled tighter as I struggled.

Inara came steadily forward. There was blood on her neck, where the flesh had rubbed raw in her furious fighting. When I brought my hands away from my neck, the same redness was there on my fingertips, and it was not only from where my nails had broken from clawing at the rough ropes. I pulled at the tightness again, desperate to be free.

Cyra.

I stopped clawing at my throat, dropping my hands to my sides helplessly.

You choose well, my child. Her languid black eyes were steady and free from pain.

I felt a tightness that did not come from the ropes but rather began inside of me. I cried, and the tears stung on my bloody neck.

"But I love him," I said, and it was more of a cry. A plea.

I know, Inara said, lifting her head and sniffing the wind. The breeze lifted her mane so that the hair stood straight along her neck, waving high in the air.

I know, she said again.

"Is this the only way?" I asked.

Inara dropped her head and blew air through her flared nostrils. I thought she shook her head.

There are many ways. Any way you choose is a way.

This was not an answer, but I did not know how to rephrase my question. She stared at me, implacable.

Do you trust me?

I stared back at her. I did not know if it was the mare asking or the One who had given me Her name.

"I don't know," I said finally, truthfully.

It is alright, Inara said, still gazing at me with those wide eyes. Her eyelashes were impossibly long, and the stars swirled in her eyes.

I will take care of you anyway.

Then she was gone, and I awoke to tears on my face, but when I put a panicked hand to my throat, there were no ropes. There was no blood. Just the knot of grief, of pain, and perhaps all the tears I would cry for the rest of my life, blocking my ability to breathe.

When I finally slept next to Col again, I did not dream.

CHAPTER 35

WAR COUNCIL

n the morning, I dressed to seek out my ha-mazaans, but they came to me first. Col had already left to speak with his scouts and gather his men for the war council convening in the great hall. When the knock came at the door, I knew it was not Col's hand. I opened it to find Ossy, her forehead etched with concern.

"Cyra," she greeted me with uncommon gravity. I stood back to let her in, but she shook her head. "The others would meet with you. In the Hall."

I followed her wearily, wondering if they meant to try and convince me not to meet Eri's challenge. They were solemn when I entered, many of them avoiding my eyes as I made my way to the great fire in the center of the room. I could feel their anger and their grief for me. I did not want their pity, though. And as Ishassara, it was my duty to lead, to be strong, and to guide them even when a piece of my soul was being torn away. I turned to face them, squaring my shoulders.

"Well?" I said.

"Ishassara," Alkippe began, and I steeled myself for her recriminations. "We know that you must do this thing with young Erioboea," she continued, surprising me.

It did not escape my notice how she called Eri young. I wondered how often they—rightfully—viewed me the same way and simply caught themselves before saying it out loud.

"But we also know another battle comes after," Alkippe said.

I frowned. "I already assured you I would not—"

"We know," Alkippe interrupted, her black eyes unwavering. "We know. But we also know you will not let your man go to battle without you. And we want you to know we will not let you fight alone."

I stared at her, and then at the others. Every woman had a look of quiet determination that did more to deflate my oncoming argument than if they had been yelling their objections.

"I cannot ask that of you."

"You do not need to ask it of us, Ishassara," Ossy said. "It is our battle, now."

"Aye," Thraso said, her voice grim.

"Aye," Sagitta said, hopping down from where she perched on the long table. "We do not need to fight for *them*, Ishassara, though some of us might." She glanced to Tekmessa when she said this, and the *zizenti* nodded calmly. "Some of us have found friends here. More than friends, even. But at the end of the day, we will fight for *you*. *With* you. As is our right."

"Aye," said forty more voices, and my tears spilled over.

I nodded, both reluctant and relieved at their unwavering loyalty. Eventually, because they expected me to say something, I said, "Then it will be so, if it comes to it."

They visibly relaxed. I looked over their faces again, studying them. I had not expected to say anything just yet, but it did not seem there would be much more time for conversation.

"Ha-mazaans, answer me truthfully when I ask you something."

I looked at Camilla's youthful face, her childish plumpness faded now after training with us for so many long months, though her hands had been accustomed to molding silver and gold rather than swinging swords. Still, she had not hesitated to offer her blade or bow on my behalf today, and she was only fifteen summers. I looked at Thraso, broad-shouldered and stoic. I was not even sure how much of the Scoloti language she spoke because, like Alkippe, she mainly kept to herself. Tekmessa, who had shared almost as many nights with Esten as I had with Col, and yet never spoken about it to me. She was private that way, and I respected that, but I did not think she would keep the man around if she did not care for him. Sagitta, who had spent time with several of the Scoloti women, and men, never choosing one for longer than a few nights. Not even Liopoxais, which had not lasted long. Leya, whose friendly, easy nature had won her many friends here. Ossy seemed to have made friends of a sort with Essri and Eife, but beyond those women, I could not say. I looked at Alkippe. Even in our life before, safe and naïve in Themiscyra, I had wondered about her happiness when I noticed the way she looked at Sagitta, and never saw her act on her feelings. In Gelonia, she had retreated even further into herself, hidden behind an impenetrable wall of solitude and silence.

Each ha-mazaan returned my regard with respectful, curious expectation, while the silence drew out like a thick thread caught in a thorn, pulling taut.

"Yes, Ishassara?" Ossy prodded, tilting her head to the side slightly.

"I would know," I said slowly, my eyes moving over each of their faces, looking for the truth of their responses, "if any of you are truly happy here."

"Happy?" Alkippe said, her pink mouth pursed in confusion.

"Yes. Happy. With your daily routines of horses and practice, of sharpening swords and eating in this Hall," I swept my arm to the long table. "More specifically, happy making conversation with men's wives who talk almost entirely of embroidery and whom we will never be liked by. Happy with these walls of wood that surround us. Happy to know day in and day out that this is what your life is. That these men humor us and think they allow us to play games with our horses and weapons while they wait for our bellies to grow round like their own wives', as they think is proper. Happy with the friends you have made and the new ways in which our days are shaped by the pattern that life in this city weaves. Happy with your nights of passion, or with the ones you might even love. Are you *happy*?"

They stared at me in consternation, unsure of what to say. I had not meant to say most of it, but it was all what I had thought about while I sharpened my sword and made myself ready.

Their silence was enough of an answer.

"You must know that I see this. I see the way your shoulders stiffen and your eyes look beyond the walls, for the spaces you can be free. I see your teeth clench when we are forced to speak their words and then talk only of sewing or cooking or deer when in mixed company. I see how you hide who you are to be with them, to be with your lovers or friends. And I think you would continue to live this way if I asked you to. Because I love Col. But I will not ask it of you." I raised my chin.

"And I will also not allow you to settle for this, even though I know some of you have found love as well. I will not see you die slowly, withering away while you play nice. I will not see you lose freedom for safety. This would be the greatest tragedy I can think for any of you, beyond dying at the point of their swords. There is honor in that, at least," I said. "So if it needs to be, we will fight because one of our own has savaged our sacred Ways. But I do not expect you to fight for their king, ha-mazaans. I expect you to fight for what is right. And when we have done what we must, we will take our freedom back. We will move east. Maybe toward home, and maybe not, because it may not be possible. But we will not stay here. Not while I am your Ishassara, and you are my responsibility to protect and defend—from *all* harms."

There was a stunned silence, but I also thought there might have been a flicker of relief in a few eyes.

"But what about Colaxais?" Tekmessa asked softly. I wondered if she would rather have said the name Esten.

"Colaxais will be king of his people, as is right. But if one of his people wishes to join you, then let it be put to a vote by the rest of the ha-mazaans, if they are allowed to leave. I will not stop them from coming. And if one or more of you truly wish to stay..." I swallowed. "My wish is for you to be free and for our ways to not be lost. But I need you to see that they will be lost if all of us stay. This I know."

"But Col loves you," Ossy said. "Needs you, even."

"No," I shook my head. "He does not need me. He will be king whether I am here or not. And though I love him, I will not be a queen by his making. Especially not of people who cannot love me and whom I cannot respect because they prefer to live so small. It is not right for me to stay." I looked at her, my face set.

"You told me I could choose, Ossy. That my destiny was only made by my choice. Well, I am choosing. A prophecy will not hold me hostage any longer. There will need to be a new way. That is my choice."

Ossy's face was etched with misgivings. I did not think she wanted to stay here any more than I did, so it surprised me that she was the only one openly challenging the idea.

"You are my people," I said, looking at each one of them. "My sisters. My responsibility. I will not watch you die a slow death of captivity because I love a man. And it is my duty to ensure the same does not happen to you."

There were a few nods, though many of them still looked unsure. They would need time to process.

"I also request one more thing."

"Anything, Ishassara," Alkippe said without pause, and others nodded. The lump came back to my throat.

"You will tell no one, especially not Targitaos or any of his sons, that we leave when the battle is over."

"But you will tell Colaxais?" Ossy said, her face pulling tight with an unfamiliar frown.

"Eventually. When the time is right."

They shifted uncomfortably.

"He cannot know before the battle," I said. "Not until we are ready. None of them. Is this understood?"

I waited for their agreement, which they gave with nods and reluctant murmurs, and then I waved my hand at the door. "Go then. Prepare what you must. For battle and...for leaving."

They went, and for the first time, I felt an emptiness threaten to overwhelm me, but I fought it down. There was neither the time nor the luxury for that. I needed to get Inara back. I needed to plan for our safe journey away from Gelonia. And I needed to steal my heart for its inevitable breaking, and for the look in Col's eyes when he watched me leave, for that was surely going to be the worst of it all.

) (

"Arpoxais approaches east of the crossroads, my King," the scout said, somewhat breathless from his long ride. "Where—" the haggard man's bloodshot eyes flickered over me and my few ha-mazaans only briefly before looking back to the king. "Where the women camped, before winter. The one who killed the sentries and her small group of *Oirp*—of women still remain close to Gelonia, beyond the western ridge."

"And my son's host?" Targitaos asked.

The scout shifted his feet. "Many hundreds, my King."

"Many hundreds of my own men turned against me," Targitaos shook his head, biting the words short with scorn. He raised the skull to his lips and took several long, deep swallows of wine.

"I would think it is my little brother they turn against, Father," Liopoxais said. His dark eyes glittered as he looked down the long table to where Col stood staring into the hearth, the light of the flames turning his hair into a fire all its own. Col turned to face him, raising one eyebrow.

"And what reason have I given them to turn against me?" he asked.

"What reason have I?" Targitaos growled back.

"They turn because Arpoxais has sold them a dream. A fantasy," Col insisted. "They turn against their own people for the sake of a children's night-story."

"How insightful," Liopoxais said with deceptive lightness, his hands busy with the straps of his vest, tugging them tighter across his chest. The hard leather creaked in protest as it stretched taught. He looked back up at Col. "Although you are here with your pet she-cat, believing in the same story. Selling our people on the same foolishness to convince them to fight."

I struggled against the heat that rose swift and fast in my chest, trying to burn its way out in the form of several curses directed at most every man in the room. Alkippe, Sagitta, and Ossy were also with me, but what they had intended as a strategic meeting of a war council was quickly devolving into the petty squabbles of men.

Col's face settled into an irritated frown, but he met my eyes, and those of my ha-mazaans, with calm assurance while he responded to Liopoxais. "I have sold the people nothing," he said. "My path was chosen for me many years ago by our mother. Our father has asked me to fight this battle, as he cannot. It is his throne I defend. I did not ask for it. Nor have I claimed that these warriors fight for me." He nodded his head in our direction.

"Yet, here they are at our father's war council," Liopoxais said, waving a graceful hand over our small group. "Ready and willing to die for you because you captured their hearts." He tipped his head and placed a graceful hand on his chest, eyes glittering. "It's really very romantic."

I tucked my chin close to my chest and breathed deeply, to keep from using my dagger to widen his mocking smile further.

"We fight for Ishassara," Alkippe announced firmly in her thick accent. She so rarely spoke, especially in their tongue, that most everyone looked at her in shock, as if one of their deer had opened its mouth and sung. Their consternation could also be because she was a woman daring to speak so forthrightly at a man's war council. She stared at Liopoxais with flat disdain, ignoring the others. "We fight for Ishassara's *rhu-tasiya*. We fight for right way. Not you. Not king," she looked pointedly at Targitaos. "And not throne." She looked at Col and did not soften her stare.

"You would have us believe you enter this battle to fight for a horse?" Liopoxais said with incredulity, and he barked a laugh into the tense room, slapping his palm onto the table. I steadied my cup as it teetered, fighting to control my anger.

"We would," Sagitta answered calmly, but her blue eyes glittered harder and brighter than the sapphires in the king's torc. They fixed on Liopoxais for a long moment. Then they turned to Targitaos, who grunted and waved his empty goblet in the air as a demand for it to be refilled. "And for our own Way, which is not that of men," she said, still calm. I envied her control.

"There are forty of you," Targitaos said dismissively. "Forty women, dressed up in men's clothes, as children playing at games. What you think you fight for is of no concern. You will be like flies at a rock wall, with your axes and green, barely dry bows. You will disappear into the carnage like wide-shot arrows into a forest, and be broken the same." He shook his head and laughed, but there was no humor in it. "This is not child's play. All of my sons are fools if they think women are going to make a difference in an actual fight." His eyes were hard on both Liopoxais and Col. He did not even bother to look at us.

My fiery anger was fast turning hard and cold. I kept my chin down, busying my hands with re-tying the leather laces of my armguard. Silence filled the room as the scout shuffled his feet, and many of the men at the table nodded their agreement with the king. Col stood stiff and uncomfortable by the increasingly smoky fire.

"And if there is no fight?" I said finally, straining to keep my voice measured and even.

Targitaos frowned again, and he was forced to look at me in order to say, "What babble is this?"

I looked up from my laces, pulling the last string tight. "What if the people have no doubt which 'fantasy' to believe in?" I shrugged. "Liopoxais thinks his brothers fight for a prophecy. I cannot be sure, but I would think at least some, if not most, who fight for Arpoxais do so because he has convinced them, with Eri's help, that the prophecy is on his side. That the Golden Axe is in his possession, and therefore the throne should be as well. And some," I glanced at Col, "will fight for loyalty, for the wishes of their former queen, or the established way of things. But also for the same prophecy. The other interpretation of it, since Col's claim to the throne came through its own fulfillment of that story.

"Either way," I said, looking between Liopoxais, who was tapping his fingers on the table, and Targitaos, who drank more wine, "the simplest way to end a battle where hundreds of your men will surely die, no matter which brother they fight for, is to not let them fight at all."

I felt Ossy's astonished glance, but I kept my eyes on the king.

Targitaos' sneer when he lowered his goblet and wiped the back of his hand across his mouth could not have been any more contemptuous. "This is why women have no right to carry a sword or call themselves warriors," he said coldly and shook his head. "To suggest that we surrender—"

"I suggest no such thing."

"Don't speak in circles, woman!"

I bit back a sharp retort and smiled tightly. "If the people fight because they believe the one who claims the Golden Axe is the rightful heir to the throne, then we will simply take the Axe and settle the matter."

Everyone stared at me.

"I thought we were also considered the Golden Axe?" Sagitta said, leaning back in her chair to have a better view of me.

"So some say," I nodded. "And Eri and her women are considered to be as well, partly because she has the actual golden axe of Hipponike," I said, finally meeting the eyes of my own council. I had not discussed this with them first because I knew they would not like it. "But Eri does not have our numbers. And if the people think we are this prophecy, then we will be the whole of it. So I will take them back, both Inara and this Golden Axe. One Axe, one loyalty. There will be no need for your army to fight against Arpoxais'. His claim will be eliminated."

Liopoxais scowled almost as darkly as his father. "I don't—" he began, but Targitaos waved a hand.

"And how do you propose we do this without a battle?" the king asked, unwaveringly stern. It was still a victory. He would not ask if I had not piqued his curiosity.

"Oh, there will be a battle," I assured him. "But it will not be between your army and Arpoxais' men." I regarded him levelly, my jaw firm and back straight. "It will be between me and the one who has betrayed our

Ways. She has long wanted to prove herself against me. Now can be her time."

"Arpoxais will never concede defeat because of the scratching of two she-cats," Liopoxais said. "Whether he believes he has the real Golden Axe, or simply uses it as a symbol to rally the men to his cause, he will not back down without attempting to take the throne with a fight."

"Then I will convince him to fight me. Alone," Col said, and we locked eyes. "If Arpoxais defeats me, he will have the throne as he wants. Unless, of course, you suddenly consider having a hand in the matter, brother?" he said, eyes flashing as they met his brother's. Liopoxais shrugged, hands splayed wide in a gesture of helplessness.

"Cyra is right," Col nodded. "There is no need for his men to die, nor mine. Not when all of them are part of this kingdom. I will convince Arpoxais it is best to settle this between ourselves rather than waste the lives of any more men. I know he cares about the people he leads and the ones he would fight, just as I do. Cyra will challenge the one who carries the Golden Axe. And if we win, the throne is mine. If we do not...men do not die needlessly, simply because we did nothing to prevent war."

"Arpoxais will not agree to this," Targitaos frowned, but he did not sound convinced of his own words.

"Then someone here should convince him it is the best way forward. For all of us," Col replied, eyes still on his brother. "Since you claim to be taking such a neutral stance in the matter, Liopoxais."

"Claim?" Liopoxais repeated stiffly. Though the change in him was slight, barely noticeable, the tendons in his throat stretched taut with strain, and his nostrils flared wide.

"You have as much reason as Arpoxais to challenge for the throne. Perhaps more, being the king's firstborn," Col said. "But you pretend to be disinterested, impartial, worried about picking between brothers as though one of us will take offense. One cannot help but think it might be easier for you to watch our armies slaughter each other while you sit back and drink wine, ready to swoop in with a helping hand and finish the job for both of us. Not so hard to take the throne once there is scarcely a stable boy left to defend it."

"Colaxais—" Targitaos began, but Liopoxais' indignant huff cut the king's warning short.

"I don't know what you are on about, but—"

"Did you think I would not have spies of my own, brother?" Col's stern voice cut through the blustering like the lash of a whip. "Did you honestly believe I would let the lives of hundreds of good men, and of these warriors we have offered our hospitality to, rest in the hands of a sly trickster? Do you really think I am such a fool?"

Liopoxais' face was white as frost. He bared his teeth, furious, but there was a hardness in his eyes and an unwillingness to meet his father's stare. Alkippe studied Col with a thoughtful frown as though seeing him for the first time.

"What is he talking about, Liopoxais?" Targitaos asked. But his oldest son merely fumed, lips compressed and white.

Col sighed, his temper subsiding. It was hard for him to hold onto anger for very long. I had seen it myself. It was like it burned him on the inside until something calmer, like a pool of cool, pure spring water bubbling from a mountain, would rise up to soothe the flames. It was so different to how rage overtook me, consumed me, that even now, it befuddled me to see his mastery over himself.

"Your plan is very clever, brother. I could fight one army with what I have, but not two." Col's face was set like granite as he looked around the table. "My men will not have the stamina to meet yours after fighting such a great battle already. Nor would Arpoxais'. But if I take Arpoxais' army by defeating their leader, and Cyra takes their Golden Axe, we will defeat your army. Together. And if I do not win, Arpo will have support from my men. Either way, we will defeat you."

Col's eyes met mine, and I nodded, smiling a slightly crooked smile.

Ossy gaped at me.

"You knew about this?" she asked.

Targitaos looked from me to Col, to Liopoxais, then back again, for once stunned into uncertain silence.

"It is your best hope," I said to the room as a whole. Most of the men did not look at me but frowned down at the table, uncertain what to make of Col's revelation or of the plans he and I had already made. "I will face my kinswoman and reclaim what is mine, and also what Col needs to settle this. If you sacrifice countless men so that a few of you may satisfy your egos," I shook my head, and my smile turned grim. "No son of Targitaos will have a kingdom worth defending, if that happens."

"Col speaks truly, Liopoxais?" Targitaos said, ignoring my words. Liopoxais could barely keep his teeth covered; his lips were drawn so tight. Finally, as though his eyes had become weighted and difficult to turn, he edged them from Col's shadowed face to their father.

"You should have done what was right to begin with," he said coldly.

"Your mother—"

"Had no right to make the choice she did," Liopoxais interrupted hotly.

"She had every right!" Targitaos said harshly, slamming his goblet onto the table. Wine sloshed onto his hand and dripped to the table, but he gave it no notice. "She spoke from the same authority that made me king. The same authority that forbade you and Arpoxais from making any claim to my throne. She followed her right as it was foretold in the prophecy."

Liopoxais sneered. "The same right that brings these women into your company and proclaims them your salvation?" His eyes moved over us with cold contempt. "They make a mockery of you, Father, because you are playing into their hands by believing any of this tripe."

"I do not care what these women—"

"Ah, but my little brothers do," Liopoxais said, his customary slyness returning. "And whether or not you will admit it, you want to believe they are the Axe, even if they are women. Don't you, Father?"

Liopoxais smiled, and for a moment, I saw only Theseus' wolfish grin that day in the Moon Hall. "Because believing it helps you believe in your silly fantasies that have kept you king, even as your legs wither and your decrepit body shames us. You lost your right to the throne a long time ago. You are simply too stubborn and weak to accept it."

"How dare you speak so to your king! To your father!" Targitaos' voice shook with fury, but also shame. Liopoxais had hit a nerve the king himself had been poking, peeling it raw and trying to hide the aftermath of doubt and insecurity for years.

"I dare because I am right," Liopoxais said bluntly, looking around the table. The men did not meet his eyes, but they did not look as upset as one might expect when their king was being insulted. "All of you know I am right. Even your precious Colaxais," he sneered, and finally he stood, moving the heavy wooden chair back with a screech of wood on wood. He placed both fists on the table, knuckles down, and leaned toward his father at the far end of the table. His voice was low and tight when he continued, and he met every face with a gimlet stare.

"*I* am right, and *I* am the firstborn. The throne *will* be mine, as it should be. If I have to fight both armies together to have what is rightfully mine, then that is what I will do."

He swung away from the table to leave the room, but Col's words stopped him.

"And how many of your men believe the prophecy, Liopoxais? Do you know?"

Liopoxais half turned back to the room, raising an eyebrow at his younger brother.

"How many will still fight for you, even if *I* have the Golden Axe? The whole of it?"

Eyes locked, the two men stared for so long that I felt the tension in my teeth. It vibrated in my bones, and I glanced at Col, unsure of how I felt about his meaning.

The whole of it.

It was one thing to offer him assistance. It was another to feel claimed.

"I will take my chances, little brother," Liopoxais said eventually, with a last glance at me. Then he was stalking out the door in a shadow of black cloak and anger.

Targitaos watched his eldest son go with a troubled expression, his features settling into weary lines of pain. "When did you know of this, Colaxais?" he asked finally.

Col moved to stand behind me, his feet quiet as ever on the smooth wooden planks. I would not have known he was there if every nerve in my body was not attuned to his, sparking along the entire length of me.

"Several moons past. His army is almost the same distance as Arpoxais'. Four hundred strong, plus those within our walls he has turned against me. Against you."

Targitaos pierced him with a furious glare, some of the strength coming back into his face. "And you did not tell me? Warn me?"

"What good would it have done?" Col shrugged. "I have been doing what needed to be done. I did not think it wise to cause needless worry."

"What needed to be done? Meaning convincing these ones to side with you," the king said, sparing us a brief look. "And a traitor roaming free in my city, while he—my own *son*—and his spies report every move I make?"

"And what would you have done?" Col asked coolly. "Killed your own son for wanting his birthright? Or would you ask me to do it for you, as you now expect? For me to kill my own brother, whom I love?"

Targitaos regarded his son in astonishment, sitting back slowly in the tall chair. His next words were far more measured, more uncertain than before. "You do not believe the throne should be yours?"

The leather of Col's vest creaked behind me. If I knew him well, it was a slow, casual shrug. "I believe I need to do what is best for as many people as possible. But as for the throne..." he moved again, and his hand settled on the back of my chair. "If it comes to it, I will fight Arpoxais, now that he has been convinced by this woman that the throne is his, and I will fight him alone, sparing the lives of good men in my army, and in his. And then I will lead all of them against your oldest son. You had better pray that I win, because I know Liopoxais. If he wins, he will still slaughter all who believe—either because of a legend or my mother's wishes—that I should have taken your place." He paused. "If it weren't for these things, I wonder if it would not be better to hand the throne to either of my brothers and let it be. But I cannot stand by and let innocent people die."

"Then I suppose you had also best pray," Targitaos said after a long silence, in which the breathing in the room became stifled and thick, "that you and your she-cat can do what you say. Else, I will be at least two sons lost and no kingdom to speak of."

CHAPTER 36

SPIRIT FOR A SPIRIT

"Tell me again about this," Col murmured, tracing a finger around the twisted horse on Cyra's shoulder. Their chambers were still dark, and he had not had the will to leave the warmth of her arms to light a fire. Even in the dark, though, he knew the lines of it. Knew every mark, whether ink or freckle, scar or dimple.

She shivered under his fingertips, maybe from his touch, or maybe, as he suspected, from memories of the mare standing captive in the rain, the ropes tightening around her neck. Col tried to imagine how he would feel if Faelan were in the same situation. He could not.

"It is my *rhu-tasiya*. Inara," she hedged.

"I know. But I also know it is Old Magic, even though you have not said so. I would know how it works."

She was quiet for several breaths.

"Please," he said. She pulled back a little to try and see his face in the darkness, but everything was shadowed and dark.

"All of our marks are Old Magic," she admitted. "But these..." she moved her hand over his, and her fingers pressed his hand into her flesh as a guide as they traced over the horse's neck and down the curled forelegs. "With these, the *zizenti* bind our spirit with our *rhu-tasiya's*. There is only one, who protects us through this life, and will meet us in the next," she said finally. "A spirit companion which guides us and defends us. We should go together through the Gate but...eventually, both will be there, in the Otherworld. The binding is eternal."

Sorrow deepened her voice, and she trailed off. As her hand stilled on his, he turned his palm and laced her fingers between his.

Col listened to her breathing for a long moment, feeling the warmth of it against his bare chest. "Tell me how you knew Inara was your *rhu-tasiya*." He felt her lips tug into a frown against his chest.

"She spoke to me. In my dreams. Called my name and told me her own. And she was half-wild, yet she let me capture her. Then, once I was with her, had touched her and poured my heart out to her, I just knew." She stopped, and her body tensed along his.

"What Eri has done is the most wicked thing I can imagine," she whispered hoarsely.

"Inara will return to you," Col said firmly. "We will take her back."

"She will kill her," Cyra said, and a chill skittered through him. He did not know if she meant the woman would kill the horse or the horse would kill the woman. He struggled to think of what he could say, but all of his reassurances seemed trite, and he did not want to lie to her. Finally, he said,

"I want you to have my mark."

"Your mark?"

"Yes. And I want you to mark me."

"Mark you?" She was obviously struggling to understand his meaning.

"Yes. Today. With the Old Magic."

She raised herself on an elbow, untangling their fingers. Dawn's light seeped around the edges of the oiled skin over the window, but it was only enough for him to see the moonlight of her eyes peering down at him. "Mark you with what? The stallion? Faelan?" she asked.

He shook his head. He reached a hand up and twisted her long black hair around his wrist. "With you," he said softly.

She let out a small huff. When he said nothing more, she pushed away further and perched on the edge of the bed, facing away from him.

"What do you mean, me?" she asked cautiously. He could not decipher what was in her voice. Fear? Doubt? Reticence?

"I mean that you are the carrier of my soul, Ishassara," he said simply. He had thought of it for many moons, and now he was sure of what he wanted. Needed.

"But I know you are also half-wild. That one day—" he stopped himself, sitting up behind her. He sensed her stiffen, and she kept her head turned away. "I know that when I see you, I see the Old Magic. And I know that when I face my enemies that it will always be your face and powerful spirit that give me courage. Whether...whether you are by my side or…far from me," he said. There was much he did not say. He had made his promises.

"And if there is some secret way this mark protects a person, then I want you to have mine as well. Most of all, Cyra, I would have the promise that if…if one of us were to die, or be…parted…my soul will find yours in the Otherworld. This is what I want."

"People are not *rhu-tasiyas*," she said without conviction.

"Their spirits are. Horse or woman, we are all born from Tabiti's fire."

She turned slightly, and he could imagine her scowling into the darkness. He pressed on.

"If these marks bind spirits together, if it means you have my protection, and I yours, here or in the Otherworld, then I would have this promise. This hope."

She turned around then, and in the dimly growing light, he could make out the grave lines etched between her raven brows.

"Then I would have the same, Colaxais. Spirit for a spirit," she said. "For this life, and the next."

They were both silent, then, and she leaned forward to press her mouth to his in a long, hard kiss that made something in his heart feel like it was breaking. Snapping in two with the cleanest of sounds. The kind of quiet sound that can kill a man if he hears it too many times.

When it was light enough, Cyra gave orders to the servants to fetch various supplies: copper spoons, a flat rock, sap from the pine trees in the eastern quarter of the city, ox bile from the slaughter yard, tallow and dried berries from the dwindling supplies in the kitchens, and honey. Col helped where he could, but she insisted the preparation of ink and the binding of the needles be done by her own hands.

For the ink, she used the last of their precious wood supply, burning the thin oak twigs down to rough charcoal and crushing it to a fine powder in a stone pestle. To this, she added precious tallow from the dwindling winter supply in the cellars and the few dried hawthorn berries the servants had somehow scrounged for her.

Once the more obscure supplies had been found and brought, Cyra explained to him their purpose as she added them to the mixture. Ox bile to set the dye more firmly in the skin, and honey and sap to act as binding agents while also keeping infection at bay. She ground all of this together with the back of the copper spoon, the metal making a satisfyingly rhythmic scraping on the stone as her slender, deceptively strong hands moved it back and forth, back and forth. She bound the needles together in bundles of three and five, their sharp points pressed close, and held these in the flame of the beeswax candle for several moments. Col watched everything, mesmerized and mute, a sense of reverence filling him as the ritual unfolded.

Last, she ordered copper pots of heated water brought to their chambers. Col helped the servants carry them from the tripod over the large hearthfire in the Great Hall and back to their room. When he set them down, steaming on the hearth of their own slowly warming fire, Cyra shut the door and dropped the latch. She turned to face him.

"Strip," she ordered. He obeyed, the chill in the room raising gooseflesh along his shoulders and bare legs. He stood in front of the fire, next to the small bench and table, covered now with various supplies. To his pleasant surprise, Cyra removed her clothes as well, the lean length of her beautifully-colored skin slipping from her tunic with a stretch as lithe as a cat in a sunbeam. She placed her star-forged knife on the table and moved the beeswax candle closer. Finally, she bent to dip a soft linen rag into one of the steaming buckets.

He gasped softly when the scalding water touched his skin, the droplets running down his chest turning quickly to icy fingers trailing down his stomach and legs. He looked down at Cyra, but her face was composed, contemplative. She moved the cloth unhurriedly from the base of his neck, across his chest and back again, moving from shoulder to shoulder with a smooth, ritual-like efficiency. She squeezed the water into an empty pot and then dipped the rag into the water once more, and this time she wiped it down first his right arm, then the left. She repeated the wringing and dipping many more times, moving around his body and touching every part of him with it, her hands at once firm and tender. She washed the small of his back and his thighs, the tips of his fingers, and the hard muscles running to his groin. She even washed his feet, and he stood awkwardly as she held the first one and then the other, tickling between his toes. When she finally stood, laying the rag aside, she looked into his face.

She placed both hands on his chest, on either side of his heart. Softly, she said words in her own tongue, and Col bit his tongue to stop himself from interrupting to ask their meaning. She pushed him down onto the stool. When he sat, he did not know if it was the harsh winter chill against his damp flesh or the feeling like Old Magic had completely filled their room that made him shiver uncontrollably.

When she picked up the dagger, he eyed the blade warily as it came to his chest. He did not flinch when she set the sharp edge of it to his skin, but his breath caught and puffed out again when she quickly dragged the edge over his heart, skimming the hair off at the base. She shaved a large circle with the blade, using the rag to wipe away hair until the skin was perfectly smooth. Once finished, she cleaned the knife with customary care, then brought the candle closer to the edge of the table. She pushed his legs apart, her fingers gentle but firm, and as she knelt between them with her knees on the thick fur of the bear rug, she smiled tenderly up into his face.

Col tried to smile back, but his face had frozen into a stiff mask. He realized the feeling that churned in his stomach was nervousness. He had not felt this anxious since he had been a boy of thirteen or fourteen summers, and his father had pressed a sword into his hand, telling him his first proper battle would be fought within hours.

"Shhhh," she whispered, smoothing hands both calloused and gentle down the sides of his face and neck, stopping over his heart. "Be still, my love. The pain is brief. Only the binding is eternal."

He did not have the heart to tell her it was not the pain that made his skin want to shimmy itself away from his body. That it was not fear of himself being hurt that made his stomach clench and quiver, and the taste of bile rise, bitter in his throat. He simply nodded and watched as she took up a small length of burnt willow, the tip of it sharpened to a point. She held it lightly between her fingers and pressed it to the smooth skin above his heart. She looked up at him, then, her teeth biting her lip in the first sign of uncertainty since beginning the preparations.

"You are sure this is the shape you want?" she asked, a furtive cloud of doubt and, perhaps, insecurity slipping through her moon-bright eyes.

"I am," Col said quietly, firmly, some of the anxiety easing away with the conviction of it. Her eyes held on his for a long moment, and then, nodding, she set to her task.

The charcoal felt strange scratching against his skin, giving him something to focus on other than uneasy thoughts of the future. He watched Cyra's white teeth pick at her lip as she concentrated on drawing the design. He even managed a slight smile when she pursed her lips and poked her tongue out, absently licking a finger, using her saliva to rub at a line she did not like and then re-draw it with a satisfied nod of her dark head. She had not bound her hair in its braids yet, and as it fell over her shoulder and across her naked breasts, he resisted the urge to twine his fingers in it. She was not his lover in this moment. She was a priestess of the Old Magic, and he the sacred offering.

When she had finished, observing her work with a critical tilt of her head, he braced himself in preparation for the sharp needles. But she did not take those up. Instead, she reached for the small stone bowl of thick ink and held it out to him. He took it, the hollowed rock rough and chilled against his palms. She took up her dagger again. He watched in some consternation as she held the blade against the palm of her left hand, where she already had a fresh pink scar, and quickly drew it down. She made no sound. She did not grimace. Her face was fierce, intent, focused. A long line of blood welled quickly, and she closed her hand into a tight fist, squeezing it. As blood welled over the tips of her fingers and down, dripping, Cyra held her hand over the stone bowl and spoke an incantation that made the hair on the back of his neck and arms stand on end. His body understood the words his mind could not. When she finished speaking, she moved the bowl to his right hand and took up his left. She looked up at him, bringing the cold metal of the dagger to the same place in his palm.

Col nodded once, and the knife sliced into his skin as her words repeated, haunted and lilting. Old. The pain soon blossomed, and the chill of the room intensified as his body beaded with sweat. He kept his face set, determined to follow her lead. Cyra closed her own bloody hand over his and squeezed his hand until the blood dripped into the bowl, mixing with hers in glistening pools of inky blackness. She took the bowl from him, stirring the thick substance with her finger.

This time, when she placed it back into his hands, the stone had warmed from their touch and from their blood that had begun to dry sticky and rough on the outside. She took up the bronze needles, running the ends of them through the candle flame once more before dipping them into the ink. She set them against his chest, her arm braced against him, and began to work.

Col gasped as the first piercing pain touched his chest, but then he bit down on his tongue, setting his jaw against the sting of it. Within a few moments, he leaned into the pain, relished it even. He let it burn bright and sharp in his mind and bared his teeth as though challenging it to be worse. When the sting of it fogged his mind, he dug hard fingers into the cut along his palm, keeping the pain alive.

When he did this, the pain underneath the tattoo could not unravel itself. The shadow lurking under his heart, behind the newly forming mark, the shadow that was the reason he asked for her mark at all, could only whisper softly, instead of scream. With the pain in full blossom, the shadow's tortured cry could not be heard as clearly. The hurt of his body was welcome, if it kept that dark knowing at bay, even for a time.

At one point, when the pain made him feel oddly light-headed, he inspected Cyra's face with a rapturous intensity. The way her mouth murmured words he could not understand. The way her raven hair brushed her cheekbone as she leaned forward, eyes squinting in concentrated effort. But when he did this for too long, studied her too closely, the shadow tried to sneak from its hiding place, and its whispers grew louder. He looked away, eyes stinging.

When she finally wiped his chest with a rag, the water in the copper pots had long cooled and the candles were stubs on the table. Col felt dazed, and his heart was thudding fast and loud in his ears. He gathered himself with some difficulty, trying to focus as the blood rushed in his head.

"Well?" she asked, tentative and weary. She turned to lay the bundle of needles on the table, stretching her cramped fingers.

Col looked down at his chest. Thick black whorls curled into the lithe body of a panther, wrapping itself entirely around his heart so that its mouth captured its own tail. She had drawn the lines across its legs and back exactly as he had asked, and its eye was the round orb of the moon. Crescents and lines, two thin and one thick, curled over its forelegs, straight and precise. When he looked back to Cyra, she was watching him closely, her face full of apprehension.

"It's perfect," he said softly. "Your spirit. My *rhu-tasiya*."

Her lips curved into a wry smile then, and her hand smoothed over the tattoo once more, smearing blood that seeped from the wound, her fingertips careful on the raised and swollen ridges of it.

"I want to say it is strange that this is how you see me," she said. "But you have always seen into the heart of me."

He noticed how different his language sounded on her lips after she had been speaking her own for so long. How her mouth was so careful with the words, as though they were sharp glass, and he regretted not making more of an effort to learn her tongue. He pushed the shadow back down as it tried to whisper something about time and being too late for such things.

"Always," he said finally, letting his hand reach out and settle on the darkly gleaming crown of her head. He tried to keep his touch light, despite the heaviness in his heart.

When it was time for them to trade places, Col called for more hot water to be brought, along with more candles, and he stoked the fire in the hearth. Both of them drank wine while they waited, but they did not speak many words. He offered her the same cannabis she had given him, to relieve some of the pain his clumsy, untrained hands would inflict, but did not push her when she declined. Instead, he washed her body with the hot water just as she had his, and with every gentle pass he made with his hands, he marveled at the magic of her and said prayers of his own, both in his heart and into the air. The lean muscles of her arms, the tapered softness of her waist, the gentle curve of her hip, and the supple arches of her feet heard his whispered pleas, if she did not. The shadow tried to climb out of his heart and cry through his lips, but he bit it back and set his mind to think of only the present. Her.

When he knelt between her supple thighs, it felt like an act of worship. It was. When he drew the mark on her chest, his fingers were sure, as they were familiar with such things. When he finally dipped the needles into the ink, hesitating for a moment above her delicate skin, she smiled at him encouragingly. And there, behind her silver eyes, he saw the same shadow that was behind his heart reflecting back at him, though she had not yet admitted what it was. She only nodded, and he bent his head to the task, steeling himself against the thought of causing her pain. Her hands guided his fist for the first few pokes to help him find the right depth. The first push that her hands did not guide, she hissed softly, and he knew he had gone too deep, but she set her face quickly, and he went on. Eventually, he focused on the pain in his knees and the meditative silence that did not let his shadow speak, or at least not loud enough to hear.

When he had finally finished, her face was pale, a crease of pain etched into her forehead. His own hand was cramped, and his back was sore, and the mark on his chest blazed with a fire he hoped he would feel for the rest of his life. He wiped her chest gently with the wet cloth, blood and ink smearing across her perfect skin. Her nipples were hard from the pain, her entire body covered in gooseflesh.

When she looked down at the mark he had made, he felt the same apprehension he had seen on her face when she waited for him to see his own chest. The same whorls and curled lines showed the neck and sweeping antlers of a deer, but where its nose would be was the beak of a golden eagle. The same beak was at the tip of each antler, and along its flank were the same knots, without beginning or end, that showed on his shield. She nodded, wordless, and pressed a hand against it. Her left hand, the blood from the cut crusted and dark. She moved that hand to his chest and took his left hand to place it on her own mark. She spoke something, clearly enunciating words he could not grasp but didn't need to. Old Magic. Col felt the panther on his chest writhe like a cat curling into a sunbeam.

When she looked up at him, her eyes were fathomless and dark as the craters in Tabiti's nighttime eye.

"Spirit for a spirit," she whispered.

"For all eternity."

When he kissed her, he was sure the panther on his chest sunk its claws into him as though trying to crawl inside of him.

CHAPTER 37

A FINAL RECKONING

I awoke in the morning to the sound of rain against the oilskin window and the tattoo on my chest burning with fresh fire. I hoped to feel it there for the rest of my life, untempered and raw. A tangible memory. I rose, weary before my battle had even begun, but ready to do what must be done. For Inara. For Col. For me. For my ha-mazaans to be free.

I ate what Col put in my hands, and answered his questions when he spoke them, but otherwise, my mind remained focused on what the day would bring. When it came time to put on my armor, my movements were stilted and fitful. I dragged the scaled vest over my tunic, tightening it against the fresh tattoo between my breasts. My fingers fumbled with the straps and buckles at the side when Col's fingers, steady and warm, pulled my hands away. He did not interrupt my thoughts with unnecessary words, and I was grateful.

With a calm efficiency that quieted some of the inner storm pelting inside of me, Col fastened each buckle, making sure it was neither too snug nor too loose. Then, he wrapped the wide leather belt over the vest and fastened that as well. He had made me a new buckle of silver and ivory engraved with the arched neck and rearing hooves of Inara. I could not look at it without thinking of the mare, and so I kept my eyes fixed on Col's red hair as he fixed it in place. Next, he slid my arm guard over my hand and onto my forearm, the dagger already secured inside of it, carefully tugging the laces until it fit snug against my skin. He gestured to the wall where my weapons hung.

"The sword," I said. Then, because it seemed wrong to ride out without it, I added, "And the bow."

He retrieved the sword and the new leather scabbard he had tooled with beautiful scrollwork and never-ending knots and buckled it to my belt. Then, he swirled the cloak of lion fur over my shoulders, and I fastened the chain across my chest. The weight of it was a warm embrace, solid and comforting. Col handed me my bow, and I slung it over my shoulder as he attached the quiver to the rings on my belt.

I left Col alone to fasten his own cloak and sword, lest he act on the look that had crept over his face; I could not tell whether he wanted to talk me out of this fight or make love to me, but either one would distract me in ways I was not prepared for.

The rain had begun in earnest. Ha-mazaans waited, armored and ready in the courtyard, the breath from their horses steaming in the damp cold. Even Faelan stood with them, his ears flopped in their usual sideways posture. The women had readied a mare for me, and I knew it had been a kindness, but I could not take her reins. Instead, Col pulled me up behind him on Faelan, my sword and bow and cloak making the jump awkward.

We rode out in full battle formation, the sound of our horses' hooves and snorting, the tinkle of bridles and thunk of spear or sword against ha-mazaan shield a meditative, familiar refrain that eased my soul. I pondered the ha-mazaans as we rode, drinking in their faces and relishing in a fierce pride of belonging. I did belong to these sisters, and the knowledge gave me strength. *They* gave me strength. Prothoe, with her white hair and broad shoulders and loyal heart. Ossy, my wise goddess-mother with her worried bronze eyes and ready axe. Sagitta, her blue eyes bright with anticipation and some other emotion I could not guess at, but who had become as a blood sister to me. Alkippe, her face hidden within the shadows of a helmet, but her steady, solid presence reminding me so much of my own mother that I swallowed a knot of grief and looked away.

I would not fight only for Inara today, nor only for the Golden Axe that would seal Col's claim to his throne. I would fight for these women, my sisters, and the Ways which had not only brought us together but which would also keep us together and keep us free. The Ways which Eri scorned when she poisoned our city and lent aid to Theseus, and when she threatened my *rhu-tasiya*.

When we reached the western gate, I slid from Faelan's flank before Col had brought him to a halt, already unfastening my cloak. Col dismounted, and the others made a semi-circle around us, watching silently as he took my cloak and tucked it behind Faelan's saddle. Reluctantly, I unslung my bow and unbuckled the quiver. They would only be in the way, though it felt foolhardy to leave them behind. I held them out to Col, and he took them, his mouth turning down at the edges and the worried crease between his brows deepening.

"Cyra," Sagitta said, and I turned, preparing to repeat orders to stay behind, but she held her wicker and leather shield out to me. I took it with a nod of thanks, threading my arm through its braces. I turned back to Col.

"Open the gate," I said.

He stared at me for a long moment, and I wondered if he would attempt to stop me now, at the last moment, but he finally nodded stiffly and called to the guards to open the gate.

I kissed him, then, quick and hard, and pressed my hand hard into the center of his chest where the tattoo was raw and burning, so that he gasped at both the pain and surprise of it. I darted away before his arms could close around me. I could not go through with any of this if I let those feelings overwhelm me.

This, then, is what our mothers and grandmothers meant when they said women could not fight well when they had men to think about. I pressed my left hand, still crusted with dried blood, to my own chest as I stepped away and gave him one final smile, as bright and hopeful and intimate as I could manage.

The heavy wood gate swung inward with a groan of wet hinges. The horses behind me stamped their hooves in the mud as though anticipating a run when they saw the open land in front of them.

I saw only Inara.

Held by ropes far away against the rise of the hill, well beyond even the farthest-flung arrow, she reared high with a flash of wet hooves, and Eri's horse danced back to avoid them. The women who held her, traitors of the worst kind, yelled and shouted to each other, though their voices were like magpies at such a distance. I walked toward them, breathing deeply into my constricting lungs, the rain and mud-soaked ground quickly seeping through the layer of pitch waterproofing on my boots. I stopped and, barely thinking, yanked them from my feet, tossing them back to the ground in front of Col and the ha-mazaans. As my bare toes squished into the cold mud, I felt the last of the morning's stupor lift from my mind. In its place came a centered, quiet calm.

I moved forward steadily, the sounds of snorting, impatient horses and the muttering voices of Scoloti men and women, who were now approaching the gate, receding into the background. The walk was long, but it felt even longer as I walked alone, vulnerable to arrows or treachery, but Eri's glittering eyes eventually came into sharp focus, and I was glad for the time to assess her.

She nudged her horse forward as the women pulled at Inara, forcing the mare back up the small rise toward the trees. She lunged and kicked, but the three of them dragged at her relentlessly until each of them wound their ropes around the trunks of trees, leaving her cross-tied on the ridge. I was aware of this, but I did not look away from Eri riding toward me, the unhurried movements of her horse rocking her slender body from side to side in a motion that seemed to mock me with its supple, unworried calm. The rain had eased into a fine mist, though large droplets of water gathered on the edge of her golden axe blade, dripping with every step of the horse.

Eri remained well outside of an arrow's reach from the city walls, making me walk through the mud and slush, but I did not mind. It gave me time to settle myself. To call up every morning of weapons training since my mother had first put a sword in my hand at the age of twelve. I knew this fight would not be like training. This would not be practice for either of us, nor would it be like our Trials. We were not fighting as friends, or even pretend enemies.

Eri did not smile as our eyes met. I wondered if she was going to fight me from the back of her horse, and I couldn't help but stare at the sharp golden pike of her axe. She still had not unslung it from her back. I stopped walking. I did not draw my sword. Wet dripped from my chin and down the front of my tunic. It stung on the tattoo, and I imagined it soaking into the deer, watering it with life. I could almost feel Col's hands on me, brushing blood and ink away. I shook my head to clear the distraction.

"Why do you do this, Eriboea?" I called. "We are your sisters, yet you turned against us. I was your friend, and now you turn against me."

"Yes," she said simply, surprising me. "And you of all my supposed friends cannot judge me for what I do."

I gaped up at her, incredulous. "You take my *rhu-tasiya* and would harm her in order to force my hand. Who among our ha-mazaans would not condemn you for that alone?"

Her mouth twisted a little, and I thought a flash of guilt filtered over her features, but a contemptuous curl of her lip quickly replaced it.

"You condemn me for a belief I do not even share," she said. "And what I do today is more important than your precious mare."

"What do you mean? What do you not believe?" I asked, genuinely taken aback.

Eri looked over her shoulder at Inara. The mare stood rigid between the trees, her head as high as she could make it when ropes pulled from three directions, her legs splayed in every direction. The women had disappeared into the forest, but I was sure they watched from a distance. Waiting.

"I mean, you cling to useless superstition because it is what brings you comfort," Eri said finally, turning back to me. "It is utter foolishness to believe an animal will serve you once it is meat in our belly and its hooves are scales for armor. You know nothing of what happens when you die, other than your body turns to dust."

I answered carefully, wiping my face as the mist gathered on my eyebrows and dripped into my eyes. "I know what happens here. Even if my spirit did not journey with her after, it must do so here. I will not absolve you of your guilt if you harm her. Even if you no longer believe."

"Perhaps," Eri said easily. She still did not dismount, and her horse, the same dark bay that she had taken from the village herd, cocked its hip and shifted its hooves in the wet mud.

"And what do we do today that is so important?" I asked, coming back to her original statement. "Why did you challenge me alone, when we could have met in the coming battle and settled it there?"

"Oh, you intend to fight their battle for them?" she asked, curious and mocking at the same time. "I am here to prevent a war at all and to prove my husband has a right to the throne as strong, or stronger, than any of his brothers."

Husband.

It was chilling to hear my own intentions, my own words spoken back to me, from someone who was now my enemy.

"And I think *you* are here to finally realize you have been living a lie," she went on.

"Am I? I think I am here to protect my people. Because you see yourself as Ishassara of the ha-mazaans and even queen in Gelonia and would remove me as an obstacle." I knew my words were true, but her easy, agreeing nod set my teeth on edge.

"Arpoxais will not win this battle, Eri. He will not take the throne of Gelonia so easily, just because you aid him. Did you know his oldest brother brings an army of his own to fight us all?"

I knew from her shocked expression that she had not.

"And the ha-mazaans will never accept you as queen, even if you defeat me." I regarded her steadily for a long moment. "There is still time to do what is right and return to your sisters, Eri. We have shown mercy to another who went astray. We could—"

I had not intended to offer mercy, and was wondering at my own words, but she laughed.

"When I return to the ha-mazaans, it will be as their queen, Cyra, and it will not be because they choose me. It will be because I made it happen. Because it is my destiny. A destiny they will accept because it is what will save them from certain destruction."

With a nimble swing of her leg over the horse's withers, she dropped to the ground. Her hand reached behind her shoulder. I drew my sword, lifting the shield on my left arm a bit higher.

"You pretend you know what is best for everyone," she continued, moving forward toward me on careful feet, "but I am the one who is doing what will save them. What I was chosen to do. So yes, you are the only thing still standing in my way."

"You save no one, least of all yourself, by choosing power over our people. Over our Ways. This does not need to be your destiny, if that is what you think. If it is not what you really want."

She smiled, but it did not reach her eyes. "What do you know of my destiny?"

"I know what you told Glaukia. About the Oracle. About Theseus. About poisoning the *kimiz*."

Her smile twisted. "Ah. Glaukia. I was not as merciful to her as you were, when we came upon her in the road. You should not have let a traitor live, Cyra. Especially one who betrayed us both," she shook her head, as though she was my mother chiding me for not completing my chores.

"I will not make the same mistake again."

Eri cast a glance at the open gate far behind me, where I knew all the ha-mazaans, and Col, along with a growing number of Scoloti, stood watching.

"I knew I could count on your stubborn sense of honor to leave the others behind," she said.

"Even if you kill me, the ha-mazaans will not let you live, Eri. They know you for a traitor now. They will cut you down without hesitation."

Her smile sharpened. "I *will* rule in my husband's city, Cyra. In *this* city. The flames have already shown me. And the flames also showed me the hands which would pierce me. They belong to no ha-mazaan. Not even you."

She swung the axe as she said the last, and a glistening spray of water arced out from the blade as I blocked it with my sword. It bit into the hard wood of her axe handle just below the blade, but she pulled her weapon away easily, holding it low and ready. The first swing was just a test. Just like our last practice in the mews less than a year ago. Just like every morning together since our first moon-blood.

I could tell the long winter in Arpoxais' settlement had not softened her or made her slow on her feet. Her leanness had hardened with muscle, and some of the girlishness in her cheeks had been replaced by a chiseled, firm resolve, the outcome of surviving in this harsher, less forgiving land. I wondered if she saw the same changes in my face as we circled with low sideways steps, measuring each other. Looking for a weakness.

I swung toward her thigh, but she moved out of reach just enough that it swept by harmlessly. She took advantage of my sword swinging wide by bringing her axe up in a swift jab. I parried it with the shield, feeling her pike stick into the tightly woven wicker and through to the hard leather backing. I tugged my arm backward, pulling Eri off balance slightly as the axe, stuck in the weaving, came with it. But she wrenched it free as my sword swung again, parrying blade on blade with a shriek of cold metal.

After this, there was only the blur of her golden etched axe and my star-forged sword, the ding of metal and the splintering sound of my blade on her leather-wrapped wooden handle, or her blade on my shield. My arms soon grew tired, and my bare feet numb from pushing into the cold mud. The ground around us became slick with it, the last of the slush churned into the dark earth with our lunging steps. We fought on, our fogged breaths coming close enough to mingle together, and our grunts equally filled with fury, and frustration, and eventually, desperation.

We were too equally matched. We always had been.

I had just pushed aside a heavy blow with my splintering shield when Inara screamed from high on the hill. I glanced toward her and saw a figure nearby, black-cloaked and hooded, astride another horse. They held a sword, and one of Inara's ropes. I hesitated, thoughts and fears jumbling into my mind all at once.

I saw too late the blade swing at my chest. I jumped backward, but not fast enough. The deadly sharp edge of the axe sliced deep into my leather belt and the scales of the vest beneath it, forcing the air from my lungs in a strangled cry of pain. I fell back, and my feet slipped on the slick ground. I landed heavily. Eri wrenched the blade from my side and swung the axe again, her face grimacing with the effort. I brought my shield up, and only the fact that I was low enough to deflect the blow to the side saved my arm from being sheared off at the shoulder. The shield disintegrated from the impact, and I tried to wriggle my arm loose from the straps so that I could use both hands for the sword, but there was not enough time.

I barely brought the sword in front of me before her axe swung again, and this time my arm felt the brunt of the impact. Eri now had all the leverage, and I was simply defending myself against the momentum of every downward stroke.

Time slowed.

Every movement became drawn out, every sound heightened. I heard my breath rasping and felt the coldness of the mud seeping through my tunic at the armpits and the nape of my neck. The air smelled of freshly churned soil, of decay and rot and sleeping roots teeming with new life in spring. I felt the sting where the axe had caught my ribs, though the pain was dull now. I listened to Eri's furious screams as she brought the blade down, and some part of me wondered what could have caused such hate where there had once been friendship. All of this my senses took in with an elongated, calm perception, while my leaden arm, also slowed to an impossible, fatal speed, struggled to parry that deadly golden axe.

Two, three times I brought my blade between my chest and her axe, my neck and her axe, my leg and her axe, and each time, though I tried, I could not find an opportunity to get my feet under me again.

It was on the fourth swing that I heard the hoofbeats.

They were close and fast enough that Eri was startled into turning her head toward the sound, and I seized the moment to scramble backward through the mud. Even as I came to my feet, expecting to see Col or the ha-mazaans coming to intervene, Eri turned her back to me completely and crouched, axe ready to fend off a fresh attacker.

But it was not Sagitta, or Alkippe, or Col.

It was Inara.

My heart jolted with a sickening thud when I saw her charcoal head stretched straight over the ground, her ears flat against her neck so that she looked more like a mythical dragon flying over the blackened earth. The three lassoes were still around her neck, the ends flying dangerously between her galloping hooves. The frayed ends of them made them look like snakes lashing into the air. The harsh ropes had dug deep into her flesh, and I wondered if she had broken free by sheer force.

Eri's curved blade, gleaming sharp, was ready to swing at the mare's hurtling body. The image of it buried deep into the mare's chest or shearing her leg in one blow flashed through my mind.

"No!" I screamed, lunging.

I forgot I even held a blade. My reaction was instinctual, primal, like a panther leaping from a tree onto the neck of its prey. I hit Eri's back hard with my body, knocking her to the ground with my weight and falling on top of her, my hands furiously pushing her face into the cold ground.

Inara roared with fury as she sought vengeance with her sharp hooves, so that I was forced to roll aside to keep clear, though the mare was holding back for my sake, I knew. I clawed for the handle of her axe as Eri rolled toward me, out from Inara's deadly striking forelegs. I heaved myself at her again, covering her with my body, for I outweighed her by a stone at least. She fought back, despite Inara rearing above us. My hands were slick and slimy, and when I caught the handle of the axe, it slipped through my fingers as though it had been greased with pig fat. Eri bucked under me, tossing me sideways, and I lost my grasp on the handle. She scrambled away and onto her knees, axe swinging wildly for the horse again.

I whistled shrilly, signaling for Inara to stand down and away from the sharp blade, but the sound of thundering hooves filled my ears again. I rolled onto my back and flipped to my feet, the pain in my ribs burning bright, whistling another desperate, shrill sound even as I expected to see Inara charging straight for Eri's axe again.

But Inara had obeyed, front hooves clawing at the air just out of Eri's reach. The sound of hooves had not been hers. Beyond her were riders, and they did not come from the gates of the city. They came from where Inara had been tied. From the forest. Eri's loyal followers come to lend aid.

I looked around wildly for my sword, but it must have been trampled into the muddy ground. I could not find it.

I swung back to face Eri, thinking she would surely be closing in on me now that the tide had turned in her favor, but she was not. She was facing the oncoming riders with the same crouched stance she had used for Inara. Confusion paralyzed me. When she glanced at me, I saw that confusion echoed on her face. I looked back at the riders, their horses all dark and their cloaks the same. And in the front, I saw the bared teeth of the rider, his mouth a grimace of determination.

Liopoxais.

CHAPTER 38

THE STAR-FORGED DAGGER

whistled the command for Inara to run and then lunged at her as she bolted into a gallop. I caught her mane and leaped, screaming her forward with all the air in my lungs.

But there was not enough time. Spears and swords swirled around us, cutting us off in every direction, forcing Inara to rear to a stop or be pierced through with their lances. Eight men surrounded me, and more circled Eri, who had rushed for her own horse but could not mount in time. The bridles of the men's horses jangled, their shouts clamored my ears, and everything was a whirlwind of confusion and sound as I tried to look for a way out or a weapon to fight them with. Several men snatched at the ropes that still dangled from Inara's neck, wrapping them tightly around the rings on their own saddles.

I registered shouting from a great distance and looked past Liopoxais' black-cloaked men. Ha-mazaans thundered through the gate toward us. Col and his stallion were in front, neck and neck with Alkippe's red roan, the mighty stallion quickly outpacing the smaller horse. Sagitta and Ossy were close behind, and even a few of the Scoloti women that we had been training were urging their horses forward.

They came fast, but they would not be here in time.

Liopoxais circled his horse around Eri on the ground, as the other riders circled me on Inara. Eri followed Liopoxais with her blade in front of her, pivoting on her feet as her breath billowed clouds into the air. Her arms trembled with exhaustion from our fight, but her blue eyes were fierce. I had no weapon other than Inara's hooves and the knife on my arm.

"The axe, woman!" Liopoxais shouted, his voice urgent as he looked at the riders beyond her shoulder. He drew his sword and leveled a slow swing at her as though hesitant to hit her with it. Eri bared her teeth and swung her axe with much less timidity, but he parried easily with the advantage of height. His horse danced another circle around her; she followed him in a low crouch, swiping once at the horse's legs, but Liopoxais guided it safely out of her reach before her swing could connect. I looked back over my shoulder at the others thundering toward us. I glimpsed the white fletching of my arrow and my bow in Col's hands.

Eri bellowed. My eyes snapped back to her.

She threw the axe with all her might, her shout lending force to the throw. The blade buried itself deep into the neck of Lio's horse. It shrieked with pain and buckled forward so that Eri had to leap backward, scattering the men on their horses. Liopoxais leaped free as the horse landed heavily, but he raised his sword and swung it at Eri's neck even as he stumbled forward to find his balance. She jerked back, and the blade caught only in the rope of her braid, severing the length of it. The red plait arced through the air and landed with a wet splat, looking like braided blood beside the horse slowly dying in the mud, the golden axe still buried deep in its throat.

Liopoxais swung his sword again, without finesse or care. Eri ducked back again, weaponless now, and I saw the edge of my muddy blade at the same time she felt it under her boots. She knelt, feigning a stumble, and, thinking she was at a disadvantage, Liopoxais struck at her skull. His sword came down in a flash of bronze against the grey sky, but his eyes widened in surprise as she lifted the hidden blade, the entire length of it coated with chunks of dripping mud, over her head. She had not had time to find the handle, though, and held the sword by the sharpness of the blade.

It bit into the palms of her hands with the weight of the blow, and she cried out in shock and pain. But it was enough to catch Liopoxais off guard and to give herself a chance to regain her feet. She leaped backward, grasping the sword's handle in her bleeding, muddied hands, ready for his next attack.

Another man spurred his horse forward to help but gargled a shocked cry as a ha-mazaan arrow bit through the side of his neck. Liopoxais dragged him mercilessly from the saddle, flinging the man to the ground and dropping his own sword in the mud. He wrenched Eri's axe free from the dying horse's neck, then leaped onto the back of the dead man's horse, tugging its head with brutal force until he faced me. He spurred the horse in my direction, axe held low and face grim with intent. Eri ran after him. As the men surrounding me scrambled aside to let Liopoxais through, another ha-mazaan arrow took one of them in the chest, and I saw the white feathers of my own arrow fly past.

Inara reared as Liopoxais drew close, but the men still clung to her ropes. There was nowhere for us to go. His free hand closed around my braid, fingers digging into my hair, but he did not slow his horse. He yanked me by the hair, even as the muddied blade of my own sword in Eri's hands swung toward me.

Inara reared. Then she shrieked with rage, or pain.

I screamed as well, my voice echoing the fear and pain of the mare, mingling with the furious howl coming from Eri, as Liopoxais dragged me by my hair from Inara's back. Blood surged along Inara's neck.

I flailed a fist at Liopoxais, but even though he was only using one arm, he managed to haul me face down across the horse's withers. Eri raised the sword again.

"*No!*" I screamed, anguished.

Inara echoed my cry with another shrill scream of her own. I tried to push myself up, to see if the mare was fatally injured, to see if the ha-mazaans were closing in, but Liopoxais shoved my head down, his horse spinning in a tight circle so that I couldn't see anything but horse legs and my swinging black braids and Liopoxais' muddy boots. Ha-mazaans shrieked our battle cry, their voices close enough to distinguish Alkippe's roar. Men shouted.

Eri's face was a desperate mask of fear and fury when the horse under me finally turned full circle. I raised my head enough to see her sword swinging down toward my exposed neck. White feathers sprouted suddenly under her raised arm, in the side of her right breast. The dirty blade finished its swing. Then, all was black.

)(

"Look!" someone called, but Col was already looking at the two women fighting. Could not look away. It was at once breathtaking and terrifying. He could not help but admire the clean lines of both of them, the precise movements, the practiced, consistent thrust and parry, swing and block, sometimes too fast for the eye to follow. It was like watching the most wonderfully choreographed battle. Only, it was the woman he loved, and the weapons were real, and the ending was not rehearsed.

"Look, Colaxais. There," Ossy said urgently beside him, and her hand came into his vision, pointing beyond where Cyra struggled in the mud. "Who are they?" she wondered.

Col tore his eyes from the harrowing scene and looked up to the ridge where the women had taken the grey mare. A figure on a horse, cloaked in black, and sword raised. Another figure appeared, and Col watched them cut at the ropes binding the mare to the trees. Each of them clung to the ropes and began pulling, but the mare reared and struck out with her feet. Both of them lost hold of the ropes at the same time.

A ha-mazaan's cry beside him made him jerk his eyes back to Cyra, heart lurching in his chest. It took all of Col's self-control to hold Faelan back when Cyra stumbled backward, falling to the ground with the red-haired woman's axe buried in her side.

He may have cried out. There was a burst of voices all around him, exclamations of horror and disbelief, and his own voice was likely one of them. He was not sure. He could feel a sharp pain in his side that might have been fear, and his breath went out of him the way a hard fall knocks it away. But then Cyra's arm came up to block the next blow, her sword flashing silver in the misty air.

All was not lost.

The red woman swung the axe again and again, ruthless and frenzied as she stood over Cyra's prone body, and each time Col's lungs squeezed a little bit tighter, and the pain in his side worsened. But each time, Cyra managed to block the blow, though she lay prone on her back and the tall woman stood over her.

"Inara!" Ossy called, her voice triumphant.

The mare flew toward the two warriors, ropes flailing in the wind beneath her hungry hooves. Behind her, the two mounted figures rode in pursuit, but they were not swift enough. Col watched, stupefied, as the red-haired woman, facing a different enemy now, lifted her axe high. The grey mare thundered toward her, ears pinned and nostrils drinking in the air. Cyra tossed her sword away and leaped, knocking the woman to the ground barely in time for the axe to swing wide and miss the mare's neck or knees. The two rolled under the horse's hooves, where they struggled in the mud. Beyond them, more riders galloped down the ridge, their horses slipping on the soft earth. All of them were armed. None appeared to be women.

"Forward, ha-mazaans!" Alkippe's voice reverberated through his chest, shaking him from his stupor as she spurred her horse forward.

As one they charged, and he gave Faelan his head, dropping the reins to his neck so that he could take up Cyra's bow and nock an arrow. The bow felt small in his hands, but the string was tight, and the draw had enough tension that his arms strained against it. All around him, ha-mazaans drew their axes and swords, spears and bows as their horses galloped faster. Then, they shrieked a battle cry.

For a moment, Col was back at the crossroads, the day they raided the caravan and he had been so sure a griffin had returned to terrorize the Scoloti lands. Even though he was on their side, plunging into the fray with them, the hair stood on the back of his neck to hear it. He added his shouts to theirs, his voice hoarse with both fury and fear.

They would not reach Cyra in time. Already the riders were upon the two women, and though Cyra mounted her mare, her escape was cut off by men with spears and swords. The red woman was hemmed in as well, and as a rider danced around her, engaging her with sword against axe, Col could see, even from a distance, the grim smile on his brother's face. He felt a moment of stunned anger before Liopoxais suddenly surged forward, the horse rolling to the ground under him, and both disappeared from Col's line of vision behind the riders who turned to face him and the ha-mazaans closing in.

An arrow sliced into a man's neck, and the man fell from the horse's back, disappearing from view. Col loosed his own arrow, but his hands were unaccustomed to the shape of the bow, and it went wide and much farther than he had expected. He drew another from Cyra's quiver and nocked it. He was close enough to see Cyra's terrified face and hear the fury in her scream as Liopoxais reached for her, dragging at her head. At the same time, the red-haired woman slashed at Cyra, but Inara reared and intercepted the blow with her own body.

Col aimed the arrow at Lio, who had already dragged Cyra onto his horse's neck. His breathing stilled, and all sound condensed into one great rushing of wind in his ears. The red woman was still open-mouthed, shouting. Her sword swung downward. The muddy skin of Cyra's neck draped across Lio's horse lay below the blade.

Col shifted slightly at the last instant, loosing the arrow with a soft exhalation of prayer to Tabiti that she would help it find its mark. It pierced the side of Eri's ribs, through her right breast. She dropped the sword, the flat of it connecting with the back of Cyra's head before Liopoxais spurred his horse forward, splitting the riders like a rock parting an oncoming wave. They reformed quickly to face the oncoming horde.

Col did not hesitate. He used his knees to steer Faelen to the side and around his brother's men, racing past them. The clash of metal and the screams of furious women and horses told him the ha-mazaans would take care of his brother's gang quickly enough. He did not look back.

Lio's black cloak billowed behind him as the horse thundered toward the ridge, but the animal labored under the weight of two bodies, and Faelan quickly gained ground. Col sighted another arrow and loosed it. It caught harmlessly in his brother's cloak. His stomach clenched as he saw how close it had come to hitting Cyra. Too dangerous. He flung the bow to the ground and drew his sword, shouting at Faelan for greater speed.

Lio's face was cast in grim lines of determination when he looked back to see Col closing in.

"Lio!" Col bellowed, just as another horse overtook Faelan.

There was a flash of silver and black hooves as Inara fairly flew past them. The mare's neck, stained red with dripping blood, snaked toward his brother's back. Her teeth closed on his shoulder even as he lashed out with the golden axe. She wrenched Liopoxais backward from the saddle, and his own horse lost its balance on the hill, stumbling as it ran. Inara reared up as she dragged at his brother, but even as she tore him from the saddle, she fell heavily, the blade having done its worst.

Cyra fell headfirst from the careening horse and landed in a tumble of churning hooves. Col's heart missed a beat as her body flipped on the rocky ground. But there was not enough time to see if she was injured, or worse. Lio had landed heavily on his back but almost immediately gathered his feet under him, bloodstained axe raised and ready as Col was upon him.

Col did not hesitate. He slashed his sword down as Faelen raced past, but Lio met the blade with the long axe and flung the blow to the side. His sword blade caught in the curved lip of the axe as Faelan tried to stop on the muddy bank and slid sideways. Col's balance shifted, and

Faelan's back shifted out from under him. There was a cry then, like the cry of a wounded lion, and he wasn't sure if it was horse or human, or even himself, but Faelan was falling. He tried to jump clear, to pull his sword free of the axe still pulling back at him. He could not do either.

He fell heavily with the stallion, his head hitting the ground until stars spun in his vision, and then there was a crushing weight, like the entire slate sky was falling, smothering him, forcing the air from his lungs, until all went black.

) (

I opened my eyes to see ground rushing beneath me, mud splashing into my face from hooves pounding dangerously close to my face. I couldn't take a breath with the horse's withers jolting into my stomach with every stride. My head felt wet and heavy, pounding as the blood pooled in my temples. I flailed my arms as Liopoxais' grip loosened on my belt, feeling myself slipping further over the horse's heaving shoulder, but there was nothing to grab except a churning leg. Then, the horse stumbled, and the ground moved toward me with furious speed.

I hit hard. There was no time to tuck my shoulder or even think about rolling. The horse's hooves dug into my arm, my ribs, my legs, flipping me from back to stomach and over again in the rock-strewn mud. I cried out, only nothing sounded because my lungs had no air. My vision dimmed once more, going black around the edges in a slow haze, and only when everything became bright with impossibly white light did the pain come. I wanted to scream. It felt like everything in me had been broken and was still being crushed. As the bright light in my eyes dimmed and the air rushed back into my lungs, I did scream, but it was more of a howl, like an arrow-wounded wildcat.

I heard another scream, and it did not sound like my own. I was on my side, my body curled into itself. I opened my eyes, expecting to see deep black or bright white again, but I saw the red stallion, the long white socks of his front legs flailing in the air as he fell backward. I saw Col fall underneath him, sword spinning away to the ground. I saw Liopoxais. He staggered back as the horse fell, the golden axe in his hands flinging wide.

A sharp pain bloomed in my leg. I thought, as though in a dream, that it must be broken.

I watched, still dazed in a fog, as Liopoxais changed his grip on the axe and began to walk forward, his black cloak raking through the churned mud. Everything grew quiet, without the sound of hooves thundering. I felt a drop of rain on my face through my haze of pain. Another slapped onto my mouth, icy and jolting. It startled me, bringing me back to my senses.

My body was made of multiple detached parts, and none of them wanted to work together. But somehow, I pushed myself to my knees, and then to my feet. I stumbled forward, though no one could have called it running, because my left leg was as useless as my left arm. The bones or muscles were either broken or cut by the horse's hooves. I jolted forward anyway. My right hand slipped the star-forged dagger free just as Liopoxais raised the axe high over his head. Over his brother's head.

Col lay still on the ground below him.

I did not have time to be delicate about it.

I swung wildly, arcing the knife out as I came up on his left side. The blade sunk itself into the side of Liopoxais' neck, and even as he held the axe high above, his eyes turned to me in astonishment, and then shock. Then pain, and horror. I pulled, wrenching him backward, but I had used the last of my strength. He fell, and I fell with him, under him, but his axe did not fall on Col, and that was all that mattered.

I felt rain on my face and cold mud under me, and then I felt nothing.

PART V

ALSANTI

CHAPTER 39

A SACRIFICE

I awoke in a haze of orange light, muted and dim, and heavy furs pressing into my chest with a suffocating weight. I tried to move them aside, but sleep paralyzed my body. My eyelids did not want to open fully. They felt heavy and thick, as though the furs lay over them as well. I could smell the smoke of the hearthfire and hear the ferocious, aggressive crackling of wood. I had not heard that sound in many weeks. Where had Col found dry wood? Compared to the smell of dung fires, it was like blessed roses in the nostrils. I took a deep breath, filling my lungs with the heady scent.

Pain blossomed instantly across my chest and back, along my side, down my left arm with a sharp, stabbing thrust, down to my left shin where it bloomed into a sharp ache, then throbbing up into my head again as I gasped the breath back out with a startled moan. Almost instantly, a hand was on my forehead, on my shoulder. I pried my eyelids apart.

"Shhhh, Cyra. Shhhh."

Tekmessa's voice. Tekmessa's cleanly shaved head, the downward point of the blue triangle on her forehead making the worried crease between her brows seem deep and foreboding.

Memory flooded my body, heavier than the furs pressing me down.

Blood welling along Inara's neck.

Col's motionless body under his horse and a bright gold blade falling toward his exposed neck.

The ha-mazaans rushing into the fray.

All these images fought for supremacy in my mind, and I tried to speak my worries, tried to ask, tried to wrap my tongue around the fear eating at my throat. Nothing would come out, and I simply stared up at

Tekmessa's face, terrified of every possibility my mind was conjuring, unable to decide which was worse.

"Col lives," she answered my wordless plea with a gentle smile. A surge of relief was replaced with a frantic worry. It was not enough. I tried to ask about Inara, but my throat had no sound.

I sighed, or sobbed. It was too strangled to tell. Tekmessa held a wet cloth to my mouth, and the cool water eased some of the parched feeling, but only some of the thickness in my throat. She held another cloth to my face, wiping my brow and the sleep from my eyes so that they did not feel as swollen. I tried to lift my arms, to move the furs aside before they suffocated the shallow breaths I was managing, but I could not find the strength to move my left arm, and my right fumbled feebly beneath them. Tekmessa saw the struggle and peeled the covers away. I immediately regretted it, as cool air rushed over my skin and pressed cold, cruel fingers to every bruise. Which seemed to be my entire body.

"What—" I began, but had to stop to swallow. Tekmessa gave me more water. "The ha-mazaans? Col?" I said.

"Our ha-mazaans are fine. Col recovers from his wounds, as you do," Tekmessa said. "In the king's chambers. Camilla and Ossy tend to him now." She busied herself with something at the bedside. "It has been four days since your fight. Your arm is badly broken, Cyra. And your ribs. You have stitches on your side from where Eri's blade struck you. More on your face. And you have many bruises that will take considerable time to fade."

That must be why my leg was so sore, I thought. Almost more than my arm, which felt numb.

"The other ha-mazaans were not hurt?"

Tekmessa paused. "Most have minor injuries. Prothoe tried to stop a sword with her hand and lost it. She will recover. A few of the Scoloti women—who are far braver than you give them credit for—have some scratches and dents, but considering it was their first battle, and against some of their own men…they will also need some time to heal, but they will be better for this, I think."

I was glad to hear it. I had not wanted anyone to come to harm because of my decision, and felt a pang of guilt for Prothoe's injury, though I knew this would be a reality of my role in leading the ha-mazaans. Still. It gladdened my heart to hear the Scoloti women had

thrown aside their timid ways and fought with bravery. But Tekmessa
had not answered all my questions.

"Inara."

Tekmessa's hands shook above the cup of herbs and water she was
preparing. She did not answer. The pain of her silence, answer enough,
was worse than any of my injuries.

"Tell me."

Her eyes were wet with tears when she turned to me. For all her
gentle ways, I had never seen her look so sad. My face crumpled.

"No. No." It was all I could say. I whispered it like a refrain, trying to
make it true.

"She gave her life for yours, Ishassara. She waits for you at the Gate
now. I am so sorry."

I will take care of you, anyway.

We both cried, then. When I could bring my own tears under control,
shoving away the memory of red blood splashing across her neck, I
sucked in another shallow breath.

"The axe?"

"It is here."

"Arpoxais—"

"Is not your concern right now," Tekmessa said, more sternly than I
had ever heard her speak. I managed to frown at her despite the tugging
I felt along the side of my face.

"There is nothing you can do, Cyra. You will not lead the ha-mazaans
against Col's brother."

"I must—"

"You must rest, Ishassara. And to make sure you do, the door has been
locked. From the outside."

I stared up at her, shock and anger warring within me. She smiled
wryly.

"He knows you well."

Shock won. I gaped at her.

"But we have grown fond of him also, Ishassara," the *zizenti* continued
lightly, rearranging the furs over my legs and stomach, leaving my arms
free. "And so his door is also locked. From the outside."

I closed my eyes, lest my emotions give me away. But Tekmessa was
no fool. She leaned forward over me, and the humor had disappeared
from her round face.

"I can assure you that it is the only way to keep him from trying to crawl to you every time he opens his eyes, Cyra. But his leg is badly damaged. We have needed to restrain him several times during the worst of his fever."

She stared down at me, her dark eyes luminous in the dim firelight. I met them with some discomfort, since she seemed to be looking into my very soul. "I do not think you will be as successful in leaving him behind as you think," she said softly, and her eyes dropped to the center of my chest, lingering for a moment. Then she raised her eyes to mine again, giving me a stern, knowing look.

"You play with Old Magic, Cyra." Her eyes were grave as they searched mine. "There is a reason the horses do not have our own mark on them, for the binding to go both ways. And he has the Old Magic himself, which only makes the binding stronger. Do you know what would have happened if either one of you had been killed? Did he?"

I looked away, but there were only the log rafters and thin haze of smoke floating amongst them to stare at. She waited until I looked back at her.

"Mostly."

"And still you will leave him?"

"It is not *him* I leave. We cannot stay, Tekmessa," I said desperately, though my words were laden with grief. But they were sure. I was sure.

I was also sure she loved someone. "Esten—"

"Will come, if the others accept him. If I ask him. That is not my concern."

"We cannot stay here, Tekmessa," I said again, more insistently. "If we do, we lose our Ways. We lose freedom and choice. We would lose our identity."

I stared up at her, imploring her to see what I had been seeing. Despite how much it hurt, I knew I was right. "We cannot lose who we are. As women, or as ha-mazaans. It is not our destiny to always fight in the wars of men and to let them think their hands, their laws, are what grant us the right to wield a sword. Or to rule. Grant us the right to live out our Ways. That is not who we are."

"No," Tekmessa agreed but held my eyes. "Do you think that is the type of king Colaxais will be?"

My lips curled up slightly against my will. "No," I murmured. "But I think many of his people would see him deposed before they accepted a change to their ways. He is to be their king, and he will serve them with his life. That is what we do, as king or queen. It is not my right to ask him to change who his people are, or give that up. I cannot ask it of him. I will not. Just as he will never ask it of me."

"Of course not," Tekmessa said in a strange voice.

Before I could speak any further, ask her what she meant, she stood, suddenly brisk. I turned my head as much as I could manage, to see her sprinkling something into a small cauldron on the fire. Almost instantly, I smelled the cloying, putrid smoke as cannabis flowers steamed inside the pot, smoke billowing in thick streams down the side and out into the room. They curled white tendrils in the air as they traveled, mesmerizing me.

Tekmessa came back to the side of the bed, looking down at me. She looked older. The last six months had graven their own kind of tattoos along the sides of her mouth. She looked exhausted, and I wondered how much she had slept if she had been helping to tend both Col and me for four days.

"Sleep, Ishassara. The smoke will ease the pain of body and soul. When you wake again, I will bring you food and more news."

Then she was gone, and my eyes were closing, the white tendrils snaking into my mouth and nose and deep into my lungs, unfurling beneath the sleeping tattoo of a deer.

)(

Col eased himself into a sitting position, trying to make every movement as calculated as possible so that nothing jarred his leg. The women had not yet let him see the wound, but he did not need to see it to know it was bad. If he did not value the use of his foot so much, he would have been willing to cut the whole thing off at the knee with a dull axe just to make the pain cease. But he could not lie flat any longer, even if it meant his leg would turn to fire.

He finished the agonizingly slow process of pulling himself backward, inch by inch due to his left arm aching with a fierce intensity even though it had the smallest of bruises, until the stuffed hides could support his back. As he leaned back, grunting softly when the bandages pulled against his shin and a sharp stitch in his side protested every movement, he heard the latch on the door lift. An *outside* latch.

Col scowled, meeting the unrepentant eyes of the red-robed priestess as she glided through the door, and someone, likely Ossy, closed it again behind her with a click of the latch. Again, from the outside.

"You need to let me see her now."

"I hope you're finally ready to eat something," Tekmessa said, completely ignoring his demands, as she had since the moment he had awoken. She held out a small platter with venison, freshly baked bread, and even a few wild strawberries, and then promptly set it on his lap when he refused to touch it. Col's stomach betrayed him with a loud growl. His scowl deepened.

"Camilla will come soon to help with the bandages."

"You cannot hold me hostage. I am the son of a king." He stared at her, trying to make himself appear more regal. Respected. Authoritative. Her eyes were placid, doe-like. Infuriatingly non-compliant.

"Yes," she agreed easily. Maddeningly calm. "Also, our Ishassara has awoken."

The mark on Col's chest jolted. But it was only his heart, pounding a sudden rhythm of relief. An imploring look of entreaty replaced his scowl. The *zizenti* smiled down at him, softening slightly.

"She will be fine, Colaxais. She is sore and stubborn. Some things you both have in common." She raised an accusatory eyebrow, the blue lines on her forehead lifting. She turned away to the fire, dropping something into the already hot cauldron. It hissed, as water does when it meets hot stone. Steam rose, putrid and thick. The odour of a dying skunk. Col wrinkled his nose and made a disgusted sound.

"Unpleasant, yes," the *zizenti* said, turning back to him. "But it helps with the pain. And your appetite," she looked pointedly at the plate in his lap, but he made no move to touch it.

Another sound at the door. The latch lifted, and Camilla, slender as a willow wand and brown as the bark of a pine, entered with an arm full of clean linen. Ossy followed with a copper bowl of steaming water. Col's eyes shifted to the open door.

"You will not even make it out of the bed," Ossy said quellingly, her eyes reprimanding him more than her tone. It reminded Col of his mother, and a flush crept into his face as he felt like a toddler being chastised for stealing rolls from the kitchen.

"You women—" he began and quickly changed tack as three pairs of eyes pinned him to the bed more effectively than a crushed leg. "I meant to say, your ha-mazaans cannot keep me locked here forever. I must speak with my father. And manage my troops." He did not say the thing they already knew.

"Your father awaits our permission to see you," Ossy said, setting the copper bowl down on the edge of the bed. "Which he will have as soon as your leg has been tended. Camilla, close the door, please. The smoke will be lost."

The slender girl scurried to close the heavy door, leaning her full weight against it to push it closed. Col marveled that only a few days ago, this wisp of a girl, for she could not have been older than fourteen or fifteen, had been astride a horse, spear in hand, fighting side by side with the other ha-mazaans against Lio's treachery. And had helped them win. Some of the indigence leaked out of him, then, and he looked back to Ossy, who was frowning intently as she carefully peeled away layers of bandages wound around his lower left leg.

"Are you going to let me see it this time?" he asked quietly, absently raising a strawberry to his mouth. It tasted like spring.

Ossy glanced up at him, and then at Tekmessa. The priestess shrugged.

"The last time we did this, you were in a terrible fever, raving about Cyra and Arpoxais, and...other things. It was not a good time," Ossy said bluntly. "If you feel you must see it, then that is your choice, although it will not make it heal faster. *That* will happen if you listen to us and let us do our work."

Col grunted, then grit his teeth as the bandages stuck to dried blood, pulling at the wound. Ossy stopped and began applying hot compresses on top to loosen them. Tekmessa lent her help with a small, sharp knife similar to Cyra's.

"Is that also forged from pieces of a star?" he pointed at the blade.

"It is," Tekmessa glanced up at him, then pointed to the young girl. "Camilla's mother made it for me."

Col glanced at the girl, who ducked her head in embarrassment at being singled out. "Do you know the secret to making such metal?" he asked, curious. She peeked up at him through dark hair. Her hazelnut eyes were enormous in her fine face. She gave the slightest of nods.

"Yes, Ishassari," she said.

Col was careful to keep his surprise from showing. He was less startled that she knew such a complex, secret craft, and more that she would use that term for him. None of Cyra's ha-mazaans had ever called him that.

Ossy finally pulled the bandages away, and despite how careful she was, they pulled painfully at his wound, making him clamp his lips together again. He looked down at his leg and grimaced anew. The skin gaped in several places between his knee and ankle where the bones had ruptured after being crushed by the weight of the horse, the whole length swollen almost as big as his thigh. The bruises were purple-black, and in some places, yellow-white with the pressure against the skin. His eyes met the light brown ones of Cyra's goddess-mother and the doe-eyed ones of the priestess.

"It is not so bad anymore," Tekmessa said gently. "Not since the leeches finished their work and we set the bone. We collected as many of the shattered pieces of bone from the wounds as we could, which is why they look so bad. The key thing now is to keep the infection down. But your fever has broken, and that is a good sign."

Col nodded, watching and trying not to wince too badly as their hands, gentle and steady, cleaned around the wounds. Tekmessa brought a stone pestle and began crushing something inside of it, adding honey and various herbs. She began to apply it, easing it onto his skin with incredibly gentle movements that barely caused any pain. He could see why Esten loved this woman. They had the same gentle spirit. He observed silently as she carefully smoothed the mixture over a particularly bad-looking split in the skin and finally found the courage to ask what had been fretting in the back of his mind since he first saw the bandages.

"Will I walk again?"

"Do not tense so," Ossy said gently. "It will not improve the wound if you cannot relax."

Col consciously tried to loosen every muscle that had tightened in anticipation of their answer, but he held Ossy's eyes with firm entreaty.

"I think you will," she began. She returned her eyes to winding a new bandage over the poultice. Camilla's slender fingers crawled under his leg to keep the winding tight without lifting his leg.

"But?"

"But you will need help. For a long time. A cane, perhaps," she finished, keeping her eyes down.

Col nodded.

"If I can walk, I can ride."

"Perhaps," she answered noncommittally and frowned disapprovingly as she felt all of his muscles tense once more.

"Faelan—"

"He eats your storehouse dry and sleeps in the padded stall all day," Ossy assured him.

"And...Inara?"

Their grim silence was enough of an answer. Tears burned on his face, and his throat was tight with grief for a long while. He pictured the mare's furious hooves flying after his brother. The vicious axe biting into her throat.

A sacrifice had been made that should never have been required. He wondered if Cyra would ever forgive him.

"Does she know?"

Tekmessa nodded, and Ossy looked troubled. Tekmessa pressed a hand against his shoulder.

"She has only you now."

Her eyes were solemn when he met them, and then they looked to his chest, where the tattoo of the panther curled over his heart. Col nodded, understanding.

Ossy tucked the end of the bandage against his ankle and stood straight, brushing her hands against her woolen tunic with a brisk efficiency.

"Now then," she said, as Camilla gathered the linen and refolded the unused strips. "Are you ready to see your father?"

"Please."

"And you will consider what I told you? Before?" Her eyes darted briefly, almost imperceptibly, to his chest as she picked up the copper pot.

"I will. I have."

The three of them left, but they did not lock the door from the outside this time. Seconds later, it swung wide again. His father pushed against the wooden wheels of the chair to move it forward into the room, and it made a loud rumbling as it moved across the planks of the floorboards. A soldier pulled the door shut behind him, giving them their privacy.

"Father," Col greeted him politely, warily. "I'm sorry—"

"Do not," Targitaos interrupted gruffly, rolling the last few feet to the end of the bed. His own bed. He made a face at the smoking pot over the fire, and then he stared at Col's leg, once more hidden by bandages. "I will need to give you my chair as well as my bed, from the looks of it. But the women say you will eventually walk again."

Col smiled. "So they say. I can be moved to another room, though, Father. These are the king's chambers."

"They are."

Their eyes locked, and Col shifted. "Father—"

"I do not care if you don't want it, Colaxais," Targitaos said. His voice had lost none of its timbre over the years, not even after his accident. "Not only did you receive your mother's blessing, as was her right, you also won the axe. And my firstborn is…" he did not say it.

Col's own grief echoed in the silence. Ossy had told him the news. He could not feel that a victory had been won, even if he did have the axe. And now Inara…

His father went on after a few moments, but more quietly, some of the gruffness leaving him. "Even if Arpoxais attacks the city, many of his men have turned back to you, as did many of Liopoxais' army, for the simple fact that the axe is yours. You have everything you need to be king. It is done."

"No," Col said, just as quietly. He met his father's irritated frown with a sad smile. "It is not done, Father."

"If you are worried about his army—"

"I'm not."

"Then what are you on about?"

Col shifted on the bed again, trying to ease some of the pressure in his leg. They had raised it high with pillows, but he was regretting the decision to not lie down after all. However, he could not face his father and have this discussion flat on his back.

"I must speak with Arpoxais. I would have a message sent to him. For him to come here and meet me."

Targitaos snapped his head back against the chair in disbelief, making a scoffing sound. "He will not be so foolish as to come here after he set traitors against the throne! Against your inheritance. Against *me*."

"He will, because you will assure him safe passage," Col said firmly. "I cannot go to him." He waved a hand to his leg without looking away from his father's face.

"Do you think you can talk him out of attacking you? Because you're injured?" Targitaos shook his head. "You struck his wife with an arrow. I cannot think he is going to listen to anything you have to say."

"He will listen," Col said grimly. "I will have the message sent today, Father."

Targitaos pushed against the wheels of the chair with uncommon agitation, making it spin slightly on the floor. Finally, he nodded, though grudgingly. "I will do as you ask, but I cannot imagine what it will accomplish. Our men will be prepared to fight, if he does advance."

Col nodded.

"And—the women also seem prepared," Targitaos added, his tone uncertain.

"I have no doubt they are the ones preparing the men," Col said wryly. Targitaos was nodding absently, seemingly unaware he was agreeing.

"Yes. Quite remarkable. I never thought—" his father stopped and shook his head. "Nevertheless, whether my son comes to our gates in peace or in battle, we must all be ready. And, Col," the king said, piercing him with blue eyes.

"Yes, Father?"

"I...I am glad we did not lose you along with Liopoxais."

Col nodded, his chest tightening. He reached out a hand, and his father gripped his forearm with tight fingers before turning the chair and heading toward the door. His father called for the door to be opened, and Ossy appeared, stepping out of his way respectfully as he pushed through. She came to the bed as the king left, laying down the small block of wood and the sharp knife he had requested earlier. She aided moving his leg along the pillows to help him lie down again. As she left, she turned to him once more, a questioning look in her eyes. Col nodded his head on the pillow, and she smiled slightly, almost sadly, before closing the door again.

CHAPTER 40

CHOSEN ONES

I dreamed of Inara. She was still dappled, but where the silver dappled through the black, it glowed with the light of the moon. She was free and unharmed, walking beside me. When I put a hand to her neck, she vanished in a wisp of smoke.

When I awoke, the pain in my body had lessened, but not the one in my heart. That one had expanded into the shape of a horse, dappled like shadowed water, and another, less defined bruise that started behind the deer tattoo and spread into my soul.

I could not stand it any longer.

I dragged myself out of the bed, and the pain in my leg blossomed as I stood on it, making me gasp. I looked down at it. Not even a bruise, from what I could see in the dim light of the fire. I could see the bruise leaking down into the fingers of my left hand, though, peeking purple and blue from the ends of the thickly wrapped splints Tekmessa had fashioned.

The pain was intense as I hobbled to the door, fully naked, and tried to pull it open. Still locked from the outside. I limped to the wardrobe and found my tunic, which was far more difficult than anticipated to don with only one working arm. The stitches in my side pulled, along with the cracked ribs, making me hunch like a grandmother with every move. I took up the leather arm guard. I couldn't wear it on my splinted, throbbing arm, but I took the knife out and made my way to the window. I pulled the wool batting away from the inside of the casement, stuffed there to keep the cold at bay. No light filtered through the oiled skin covering. Night. Good. I sliced the sinews lacing the rawhide to the frame and breathed in the fresh, non-skunky air as it wafted cold over my face.

I cried out when the shock of the short jump made the pain in my left shin splinter into a thousand sharp fragments. I went to my knees, another soft mewl escaping my lips, but after a moment, I pushed myself up and limped on. Soon enough, I found the window I was searching for and began cutting through the rawhide at the bottom, which was all I could reach. I had not yet figured out how I was going to climb through it with only one arm to pull me up, when I felt a presence at my back.

I spun, dagger ready to fend off whoever tried to stop me, and immediately staggered sideways as my leg protested. The great shadow came closer, and ears dropped sideways against the lighter shadows in the sky. Faelan. I relaxed, and the stallion came closer still, whuffing his breath onto my chest. The tears came hot and swift as his great head pressed against my collarbone. I leaned my forehead against his, imagining it was grey, and smaller, and forgiving me. After a while, I stepped away, and regarded the stallion, or what I could see of him in the moonless sky, with a considering eye.

It took some time, and I was staggering with pain and exhaustion by the end, but I managed to get the great horse to tuck his leg and let me climb onto his back. I nudged him sideways to the window, and he eyed me sideways with irritated ears as my strange signals confused him. But then the window ledge was within reach of my toes, and the rest of the rawhide parted under my knife. I pushed the wool into the room and used my good arm and leg to pull myself into the casement.

The room was dim; the fire settled into orange coals in the hearth. I oriented myself for a moment before dropping down, being careful to land on my right leg. My arm throbbed to the point of nausea, my ribcage felt like a griffin was trying to scratch its way out, and even my face had begun to burn along the stitches. I ignored it all and crept forward. Behind me, Faelan remained at the window, his nostrils searching for the same one I sought. The one we loved.

Col slept on a grand bed, the king's bed, his left leg raised high on stuffed hides. It was bandaged much like my arm, but it seemed to be his worst wound after I pulled the furs away to inspect the rest of him. I touched the mark on my chest, looking at his leg, and no longer felt the pain in my own leg as an irritation. I understood now that it was not my own pain I felt, and this made me glad. I made my way to the other side of the bed, moving a block of wood and dagger to the floor, and slowly crawled onto the stuffed mattress. It was awkward, with my left arm and his left leg untouchable, but I curled back into his side as best as I could.

His arm settled on me like a heavy ballast, and I did not mind, though he had not awoken. I fell asleep to the sound of his breathing, and one of the pains in my heart eased, if only slightly.

)(

Col woke to the sound of Faelan snorting a long sigh.

He opened his eyes slowly to sunlight filtering into the room much more brightly than he was used to. He turned his head, grateful the air had finally warmed enough that the windows could be opened to the fresh air.

Faelan's head was in his room. Through the window. Looking at him with expectant ears. Wool batting littered the floor, and rawhide flaps gaped into the room around the stallion's neck. Col started, and as he moved his hand, his fingers felt warm skin and soft silk. He turned his head slowly. Cyra's back pressed against his side, her left arm swaddled in splints and bandages, resting awkwardly on her hip as she slept. His heart squeezed with a glorious pain.

He reached his left hand over his chest to tenderly pull her braid from her throat, revealing the long line of stitching along her cheek and jaw. His touch woke her, and she rolled her head, confusion and pain pulling her brows into a raven's bent wings across her forehead. She opened her eyes. Col could not stop the tears from crowding his own eyes as soon as he saw the pain there. The relief that she was okay was immense, but the sorrow for her loss was close behind.

"I'm so sorry." They both said the words at the same time.

Col did cry then, for his brother, for the guilt on her face, and for her grief over Inara. Cyra crawled around until she was curled against his chest, and she wept softly into his skin while they clung to each other. They stayed that way for a long time, Cyra lying against his chest, the weight of her a welcome anchor. Col may have even dozed again; he was not sure. The sound of the latch lifting brought him fully awake.

His eyes met Ossy's as she halted a few steps into the room. Her eyes took in the bed, the horse still poking its head through the window, the wool batting spread across the floor. Her lips pursed in frustration, but when her eyes met Col's again, over Cyra's sleeping head, her expression turned to wry resignation. She left the food and water next to him on the bed, stoked the fire, and when he shook his head at her questioning glance toward the cannabis, she left again, wordlessly. The latch did not close on the other side.

When Cyra awoke again, Col had already spent a blessed eternity feeling her heartbeat against his stomach, her hair itching his tattoo, her warm breath puffing into his skin. He had spent a long time thinking about what Ossy had told him.

Cyra sat up blearily, pushing away from him to cradle her broken arm. She looked down at him with a worried frown, but he smiled gently and pulled her back down by her braid to kiss her lips.

"How did you get through that window with a broken arm?" he asked when she struggled upright again, clutching her ribs with her good arm.

"Faelan," she said. He raised his eyebrows, but she didn't elaborate. The horse was no longer watching him, but he could hear the tearing sound of grass being eaten outside the open window.

"How is your leg?"

"I would like to cut it off with a ha-mazaan axe. Preferably have one of you do it for me."

She nodded. Her eyes went to the plate of food Ossy had brought, and she frowned again.

"They already know the panther has escaped its cage," he said.

Her face set in familiar stubborn lines, and her eyes glinted down at him. "They should not have kept me from you."

"They wanted you to sleep. I was fever-dreaming for many days."

She pursed her lips, her chin still set.

"Strawberry?"

She looked at it with suspicion, and when he held it to her lips, her teeth were cautious on the small berry.

"Delicious," she said, her eyes glowing.

"Like spring," he agreed, eating one and giving her the last.

They ate in silence, bread and meat and cheese, but finally, the words began to come. Cyra recounted her battle with her former friend and stumbled over the part with Inara and Eri's blade. She could not meet his eyes when she told him of how she had brought his brother down, but Col squeezed her hand, his eyes earnest, though his heart was heavy for his lost brother.

"You did what you had to. What was right. And you did it because you love me," he said.

"Yes," she said simply. "Just as you shot Eri for killing Inara. Because you love me."

"I shot her because she was going to kill you. Eri is not the one who claimed Inara's life, Cyra. At least, not the only one."

Her dark moon eyes met his, confused. He told his own version then, and this time, when he had to tell her how his brother's hand had lashed the golden axe at the mare's neck, he was the one to look away from the pain in her eyes.

"She was badly wounded even when she raced after you. She may have yet lived, if not for Lio. I don't know." He looked back at her. "She could run like the wind."

Her face crumpled again, and she gulped back sobs, fighting her grief. Col squeezed her hand again, wishing he could do more.

"Your grief honors her. Do not hold it in."

"And now?" she asked after a long while. "Ossy told me Arpoxais does not attack yet. What is he playing at?" She chewed her lip, a strange expression changing her face. "When I fought Eri, she told me they were bound already. As husband and wife. She told me her prophecy..." Cyra shook her head, the raven wings diving inwards again in puzzlement.

"It was so strange, Col. When she told me about her prophecy and her destiny, there was so much in it that sounded like mine. That she had been chosen to lead our people. That she would one day rule this city. But now she is dead, and...and I don't understand my own destiny any better than I did before. There could not be two chosen ones. And therefore, I do not think either of us were chosen at all. Not in any magical way, at least. But one thing is for certain." Her eyes were grave, and her mouth flattened into a stern line. "I will never allow my hamazaans to put their children, if they have them, through such a curse again. There will be no more Oracles. No more promises of being a chosen one or cauldron visions of what is to come. It only leads to destruction, and confusion, and pain."

Col nodded slowly. "It is good for people to choose freely. To search out their destiny, rather than have it drag them forward like a runaway horse. You are wise, Cyra Ishassara."

She did not smile when she looked down at him. He did not ask her what her eyes hid from him.

They talked until they slept again. Col dreamed of his mother, her light curls blowing in the wind, her green eyes smiling.

I'm sorry, Mother, he said sadly.

She smiled, and the wind blew a curl across the curved bow of her lips.

You will still be a king, as you deserve to be, she said. *And I will always love you.*

Lio stood beside her, and the hardness was gone from his eyes. They were only brothers, and there was no throne to fight over in the dream. But there were also no more words, and when Col woke, he made sure that what he asked of his father had been done.

CHAPTER 41

FAREWELL

"That is an utterly barbaric way to transfer kingship."

"Strange. I would have guessed you and your ha-mazaans would delight in seeing a man's testicles removed. Especially my father's."

"What would possibly have given you that idea?"

"Well…" Col paused, leaning back in the rolling chair and holding his leg aloft as Esten pushed the contraption over a rutted mound across the road.

"Well?" I prodded impatiently, not sure whether to be appalled or irritated.

"I suppose…" he continued with unhurried care, wincing as the chair jolted sideways.

"Because you seemed to want to do that very thing to Col and me when you took us hostage," Esten supplied helpfully and turned an alarming shade of red when I leveled a baleful glare in his direction.

"I wanted no such thing."

"Ossy did," Col said, grinning sideways at me. I sniffed dismissively.

"And the one who questioned me," Esten said, shivering slightly. "Your general."

"Alkippe would have done no such thing," I said sternly, completely unsure if he was wrong. We walked a bit more, and I sent a sly glance to Esten.

"You know…the ha-mazaan's *zizentis* are the ones who would perform such a surgery at home. It is part of their duties. As midwives of life and death."

Esten's face was every bit as chagrined as I had hoped.

"Not that they go around castrating kings, of course," I continued breezily. "Just men who do not wish to be fathers. And some priests of Kubileya. And the odd man who disrespects them, maybe."

While Esten turned from red to white, Col glanced up at me, squinting against the sun behind my head.

"And those who force themselves on women, I would assume."

"We do not need a *zizenti* for that. It is easy enough to remove a man's testicles once he is dead."

"Ah," he said.

"Ah," Esten said, sounding strangled.

"And so your father is okay with this?" I said, getting back to the original conversation. I used my right arm to help Esten push the chair up the slight hill to the rowan tree at the top. It was a very short hill, and a slight slope, but by the time we made it to the top, I felt weak with exhaustion. I had not even used my left arm, but I felt every heartbeat in the bone slowly mending between its splints. Col massaged his own forearm with a small frown, even as I felt the dull ache in my left leg. I concentrated on walking normally as I moved forward to sit on the rock under the tree so that he would not notice me favoring it. "Your father is truly going to go through with something so painful? Humiliating? In front of everyone?"

"It is tradition," Col said, shrugging.

"Does that mean..." I waved a hand at him in the chair. "When you..."

Col hesitated. It was slight, but I noticed. "All kings who wish to pass their throne to an heir before they die must do so, yes. In this way, they father no more who would challenge the throne."

"One would think that is no longer a concern for your father," I said, and then bit my lip, ashamed at myself for being so callous. Col simply shrugged.

"Traditions are strange things, and often they remain only because those with the power to change them have never bothered to do so. Perhaps it will change one day for the Scoloti. Perhaps soon. I am sure there are things in ha-mazaan tradition, in Themiscyra, that you find odd. Archaic."

I nodded absently, looking out over the city. Or what we could see of it, from this far eastern corner where the Tanais river acted as the city wall from the north all the way to south of the timber fortifications. This was the only treed place in all the hemmed-in spaces of the walls, other than the oak in the central courtyard. Beyond the trees, men and women tended their chores in the stubbled grain fields, and the horses and deer grazed happily on new shoots of grass in the warm sunshine.

Col had told me that many would have already left with their wagons and the deer, returning to the summer pastures, if the Kingship ceremony was so soon. I understood why they would stay, but I wished they would go. I wished there would not be as many of them left in the city to look at me with their judgment.

"Esten, may I speak with Col for a while? Privately?"

Esten nodded, sending me and Col a quick glance before he trotted down the hill toward the river. I watched silently from my rock until he was at the water's edge, tucking my knees closer to my chest as I wondered how much Tekmessa had told him.

Col was looking at me curiously.

"Is it hurting?" I asked, stalling, gesturing at his leg.

"It is not so bad."

"Liar."

"It would be better if I could get out of this blasted chair and move a bit," he admitted. "Though on days like today, I am grateful my father lends it to me."

"Yes," I said, looking up at the soft blue expanse of the sky. "Col..."

"Yes, Cyra."

His green eyes glinted down at me on my low seat. They seemed almost amused. I jumped to my feet, uncomfortable being so much lower than him. Especially for something like this. I paced to the rowan tree and put my hand against its trunk, feeling the deep grooves of the bark.

"I still can't believe Arpoxais just accepted a peace deal with you," I said, instead of what I needed to say. I frowned at the tree and picked one of the leaf fronds from overhead, pulling at each separate leaf absently. "Even though he has not left with his army. He has not even hinted that they will attack. I can't even imagine what you said to him, after..."

After shooting his wife, I was going to say, even though Col had assured me her body had been returned to Arpoxais as a gesture of peace directly after our battle.

"I think I was fairly convincing that my proposal would be best. Better than us killing each other, or hundreds of men dying, anyway," Col said easily, watching me with those too-perceptive eyes.

"And he will come as well? To this ceremony where they will castrate your father to transfer the kingship?" I wrinkled my nose, still disturbed at the thought.

"Yes. My brother will be there."

"Col…"

"What is it, Cyra?" his voice was gentle. Loving. Impossibly kind.

I picked another leaf from a branch overhead. The leaves were almost the same color as his eyes, but they were easier to look at right now.

"I don't think I will be coming, Col."

He did not say anything. I picked another leaf.

"I…"

I had not thought it would be this difficult. Yes, I had. I had not thought it would be this *soon*. I thought I would have more time. But it had been more than a month since my fight with Eri. Since I had killed Liopoxais. Two weeks since Col had secretly had himself carried to the gates, without telling me, and met with his brother to discuss some kind of peace treaty. He had kept that treaty as a confidence between him and his brother, and I had respected that decision. But now, his father had called the Kingship ceremony to be held on the next new moon. Six weeks.

"The poor tree is going to be bare well before winter if you shred any more of its leaves, Cyra. And no one will force you to watch the ceremony if you don't want to."

I dropped the last of the leaves into the surprisingly substantial pile at my feet, feeling the sticky green resin under my nails. My palms were sweaty when I wiped my hands on my thighs.

"No, I mean…I mean, I will not be there. Here. I will be…" I waved my hand in a vague swirling motion, toward the river. "With my ha-mazaans."

I could not say the actual words. The tattoo on my chest, long healed, burned and itched under my tunic. I almost touched it but stopped my hand in midair, tugging at my braid instead. Col remained silent, watching me. Making it worse.

"Say something."

"What is it you wish me to say?" he said.

"Do you understand what I am telling you?"

"I don't know." He shifted in the chair.

I clenched my fists and dropped my head back to let out a long, agonized groan.

"You are not making this easy for me, Colaxais."

"Should I?" There was a hint of something almost censorious in his voice that made me glance down at him sharply. His face revealed nothing.

"No." I felt my shoulders slump in defeat and terrible grief. "No," I said again and began to weep.

He reached out a hand and took my uninjured one in his, pulling me closer. I wanted to sit in his lap, crawl into him, but it was not possible with his leg. I kept my face turned away so that I would not have to look in his eyes, though the tears were blinding me anyway. So much crying since I had been in this strange land. It was intolerable.

"Cyra—"

"I cannot stay here, Col," I finally managed, my tears and grief pushing the words out. "I know you would...you would make me your queen. But it is not the right thing. Not right for my ha-mazaans to stay here, amongst these people who cannot support our Ways. I must do what is right by them, Col. I need you to understand."

"I *would* make you my queen, Ishassara Cyra," he said earnestly, squeezing my hand. "Would you not trust me as king?"

"I would," I said, without thinking. "Of course I would. But you are not what would make me a queen."

I looked at him with renewed resolve as I said it, and he shook his head, waving his hand to say that was not his meaning. I went on before he could say anything more.

"My people and your people do not belong together. Our Ways are not the same." I shook my head. "We killed some of your men in the raid. And now we have killed so many more. I killed your brother. I see it when the king looks at me. He does not forget. Neither will the others. It would not work, Col."

"Do you not think it worth trying?"

"I cannot," I said again. "I know you will not ask me to betray the Ways of my people."

"No."

"I love you. I do. But—"

"There is nothing else but love that I want, Cyra," he said, his voice filled with sorrow. And more kindness. It made the tears burn hot on my face. "I made a vow to you already," he said. "Do you not remember?"

I frowned, searching my memories.

"I told you that my love will never be a chain that binds you. If it is your wish to leave me, you are free to go."

"Not my wish, Col," I said, shaking my head. "My duty. But it is not my wish to leave you. It is not even you I leave. It is...it is that I must create a space for my ha-mazaans, where they are free. Where we can all be free."

He smiled sadly, squeezing my hand again. "Must it be so soon?" he said finally.

I had thought he would put up more resistance. Be more troubled. Angry, even. I did not know if I was glad to not argue with him, to not be forced to convince him I was right, and this course was the wisest. I felt insecure for the first time with him, and it made my heart ache in a way I had never experienced before. I wondered if he actually wanted me to go, in some small place in his own heart. If he was relieved.

"Yes," I said, swallowing my newly expanding grief. "It is expected at the ceremony that my people pledge their allegiance to the new king. Is this not so?"

"It is," Col agreed, looking up at me.

"Then we must go before that."

"Where will you go? Will you return to Themiscyra?"

I paused and bit my lip, chewing at it for a long moment before answering slowly. "I do not think I would be a good Defending Queen if I asked what is left of us to die on a long road back home. From what you said of the western lands..."

Col nodded. "You are mighty, but you are not many. West would not be wise. If you go east, you will have my seal to give you safe passage. At least as far as the mountains, where my mother was from. But those mountains bring death on their own, without help from warring men."

We were silent then, our fingers intertwined as we thought our own thoughts. I heard footsteps on the hill. I turned to see Esten trotting back up the trail, his long yellow braid and beard shining brightly, like a dandelion in the spring sun. It seemed so incongruous to the way I felt that I caught myself staring at him like a dumb sheep. He smiled brightly at us, and then quickly caught sight of my wet face and our somber expressions. I turned away, wiping my cheeks. Everything in me felt heavy and dull.

"Come, Esten," Col said easily, waving his friend closer before he could run away again. "We must go back to the Hall. I am famished, and Cyra wishes to feed me freshly roasted lamb from her own knife, and serve me wine to ease my pain, and tell me stories of how great a king I will be."

Two of us stared at him with doubtful incredulity, but Col only smiled. I returned it, somewhat weakly, grateful for this kindness. I helped Esten hold the chair steady on our slow descent, and we walked the rest of the way in silence. I could not guess what Col was feeling, but the way my heart was twisting and tearing was a strong indication that I would not be eating anything that tasted different from ashes for quite some time.

) (

Col scratched the end of the long stick back and forth across the soft dirt, scraping it into long furrows and obscuring what had been there before. He looked up to watch Ossy slip into the great hall.

"Sixteen wagons is a great many," Esten said, dragging Col out of his reverie.

"Aye," Col said. "But it will be done. Even if I have to climb out of this chair and build them myself."

Esten sighed in resignation, pushing his weight against the chair to get it moving, and Col winced as it bumped over the courtyard's dried mud. Now that he knew how uncomfortable the thing was, even with added cushions, he had much more sympathy for his father. Still, it had been useful for both of them. And hopefully, within another few moons, he would not have need of it at all.

"Do you think she will accept them? She seems rather..." Esten hesitated.

"Proud?" Col supplied, smiling wryly.

"Aye."

"She is. And she will. Because they will be for her people. Shelter for the rain and snow. Ways to carry their provisions and their...their wounded. She will do what is best for them."

Esten was silent once more until they reached the carved door of the Hall. "Five weeks, though," he said, shaking his head as he pushed the door open. "And the language on top? It doesn't seem possible."

"I suppose that means we should get to work then, doesn't it?" Col answered, smiling up at his friend.

) (

The mood in the Hall that evening was more jovial than usual, especially from many of the ha-mazaan women. He watched as they laughed and jostled each other playfully, their eyes glinting with joy. He noticed also the curious, wistful look on some of the Scoloti faces as they observed the women, who had become almost legendary overnight after the battle with Liopoxais' band of men.

Many Scoloti men and a few of the ha-mazaan trained women had come to the gates and run toward the battle, but they had arrived well after the ha-mazaans had dispatched every one of Lio's soldiers, or at least the ones his brother had brought with him that day. They had witnessed the women in full combat, and it was nothing like seeing them in training. They had killed every man on the field. Men who had once lived here, in this city. Husbands to these women, nephews and brothers and cousins to these men, dead now. But the dead had been traitors. And they had tried to harm their future king and the woman he would make their queen. Now, the Scoloti viewed the ha-mazaans in their midst with a sort of reverent fear, but, for some, there was still a mistrust that may never fade.

Col watched as Cyra and Ossy spoke with his father, far away at the other end of the table. No doubt the king would be happy with Cyra's decision, although Col had asked her to keep it amongst her ha-mazaans for a little while longer. He needed to speak with some of his people first. He looked for signs of Targitaos' displeasure or thoughts of his dead eldest son when the king looked at Cyra, but he saw nothing that would make him suspect his father was upset with her. However, he knew women were better at detecting these things, so he trusted Cyra was right. Partly. Col was sure the other part was the guilt he wished she did not carry.

Cyra lifted her grey eyes to his, then, meeting his gaze down the long length of the table. She smiled, and it was such a sad smile that Col had trouble not succumbing to guilt himself. But then her eyes slid away, and she spoke something to Aife sitting next to her, and the woman smiled brightly.

Everything was exactly as it might have been if she was his queen. Perfect. Destined.

The only problem being, he had not been able to convince her of that.

) (

When the slim waning crescent of the moon finally rose in the night sky, I stared up at it, praying to Kubileya for more time. She did not answer, except for the breeze running its warm fingers through my hair and the gentle, laughing rustle of the oak leaves over my head.

When I came to Col on our last night together, neither of us spoke very many words. We did not cry. I poured the *zizenti's* potion into the dark earth, and then I made love to him one last time, sitting astride his hips to be careful of his leg and feeling our tattoos come alive under each other's hands.

It reminded me of that first time, in the meadow. It already reminded me of the last time, and it wasn't over yet. Morning came, as it always did, and with it, the crushing realization that there would be no more making memories. Only the memories themselves.

And they would never be enough.

I folded what memories I had around me like a comforting cloak as I made my way outside, trying to keep the chill of grief at bay even as the sun climbed into the sky. The wagons Col had heaped with provisions for our journey rumbled into the courtyard. A golden eagle screamed far above in the summer sun. The space was already filled with people, some tying bundles to their horses, some crying and hugging each other as they said their goodbyes.

Col and I did not say goodbye. He had forbidden it. Instead, he pressed a long kiss onto my forehead as I knelt on the ground before his chair, my hands gripping his. He had already given me all the gifts he could think of. Hand-tooled armor, including a new arm guard that protected the freshly healed break on my arm, and still held the dagger within easy reach. A new carving of Inara that could have been her spirit trapped in wood. It was so beautiful I cried. Silver coils for my braids. A new hilt for my star-forged sword, the ivory pommel carved in the shape of a horse's head. Perfectly straight wands of ash and oak he had been collecting and whittling for some time so that I could make enough arrows to last a lifetime. New bronze arrowheads, though not attached to the shaft yet because he knew how particular I was about my arrows.

Gifts fit for a Defending Queen, he said.

There was little I could offer him in return, for my skills were not with my hands. I had tried to give him my star-forged knife, but he had staunchly refused. I gifted him a pair of golden cuffs, like a pair I had once seen in a dream. They were wide and fine, engraved with eagle and deer and tree and his never-ending knots, and dotted with precious stones. Camilla's brilliant smithing, so I could barely take credit. He allowed me to fit them to his wrists, and when they were snug against his flesh, I thought how well they looked on his strong arms.

Gifts fit for a king.

I asked him to call for Faelan, and he did. The stallion plundered his way through the crowd within moments of Col's whistle, heedless of the goings-on. The tall horse came to stand close to Col, dropping his magnificent head down and snuffling it against his chest. Col looked at me, questioning, as I stood.

I moved my hand to the horse's shoulder and clicked my tongue. Immediately, Faelan tucked his head between his legs and bowed, kneeling on one knee. I smiled at Col's astonished expression.

"So you can mount him while your leg still heals," I explained.

"Thank you," he said, his eyes solemn.

"I must go," I said.

"Yes," he said, and in that moment, I felt all the pain a person could possibly endure and still breathe.

CHAPTER 42

ALSANTI

I t had been one year since my feet last walked the cobblestone bridge of Themiscyra. One year since I had seen our last Sister Queens.

I thought of Hippolyta, and Heracles' blade in her chest, her sunset hair setting one last time, forever, over the deck of the ship. I thought of Antiope's noble face as she stood on the rock that night, Theseus' blade at her neck. Her voice commanding us to fight, knowing it could mean her death. I thought of my mother charging into the fray, axe swinging, her courage as big as her heart.

I only hoped I could serve the ha-mazaans with the same courage. I hoped I had not steered them wrong already and led them to their doom. Led them to lose faith in me and what I believed was best for them when I asked them to leave behind the safety and familiarity Gelonia had provided.

Tonight, at moonrise, I would find out.

There had been many avoidant eyes, awkward pauses in conversation, and general evasion of talk about the future from more ha-mazaans than I would have expected the last few weeks. If they regretted their decision to leave Gelonia, they had not said so with their words, but their actions were beginning to make me suspect it was true. Yet, despite the way my heart burned every morning when I woke up alone or when I turned a corner and expected to see Col's green eyes smiling at me, I still believed we had done the right thing. For all their sidestepping of authentic conversation with me, the women were happier, freer, and more themselves. I only hoped they could see that when it came time to cast their stones, but I would accept their choice either way.

I was not Eri.

The day was warm, stifling even, and I spent much of it alone by the river. I listened to the eagles crying above me and watched one of them spin lazily above the river, fantasizing that Col watched me through its eyes. I swam in the cool current, letting the healing touch of water quench some of the roiling within me, and then lay on the bank in the sun, dozing fitfully, taking solace in the warmth, and in the sounds of the life teeming in the Mother's earth around me. Once, when I raised my head from my folded arms, Inara drifted through the trees in front of me and then disappeared like smoke. I smiled a sad smile.

She was still with me, even if I never felt her run beneath me outside of my dreams.

Her spirit's presence did little to quell the anxiety coursing through my veins as every ounce of insecurity in my leadership flared up in me. All the mistakes I had made over the last year, the lives that had been lost from my decisions. The hearts that had been bruised and broken with goodbyes. All the efforts I had made to find home again, only to have them fall flat, useless, hopeless.

Even where we were now seemed a failure of my own making. A choice gone awry. The wagons Col had given us, thoughtful, extravagant gifts to keep us sheltered from the rain and store our supplies for the oncoming winter, had been more of a hindrance than a help, it seemed. Two had broken their axles without even seeing hard use, which was even more surprising since Col had overseen their construction himself. Several of the horses, and more unexpectedly, quite a few ha-mazaans, had recurring maladies that prevented us from moving any further than this spot. Leya was sick every morning, and again every time she smelled cooking meat or *kimiz*, although this was something I could not be upset with her over since I had given her my blessing gladly before we had left Gelonia to bear a child.

We had only traveled away from Gelonia for a fortnight before coming to a sudden, frustrating halt. Not that there was anywhere specific we were supposed to be before winter. Ossy repeatedly assured me we would be on our way soon enough, but for now, this space by the river, with its wide-open fields and plentiful grasslands, was as good a place as any to stay a while. There was no reason to disagree, but I still felt a restlessness. A need to be farther from the ache that never left my chest, even though I knew I could never outdistance it.

Twilight descended as I made my way back to the encampment. My left leg ached with a relentless torment, as it had every day for the past two weeks. Even worse than before I had left Gelonia, when Col's leg had begun to heal. But I felt the pain gladly, knowing it eased some of Col's. The deer on my chest pinched at me, and I smoothed a hand over it, willing it to slumber until this day was over. Then I smoothed a hand over my stomach and smiled. Even if the ha-mazaans found me unworthy, my life would not be without purpose. And if they did reject my leadership, perhaps only because of the child I carried—I had confessed to them that I followed in my mother's footsteps and would keep the babe even as Defending Queen—maybe I would return to Col after all. If he would even take me back.

The bonfire already glowed orange against the trees when I returned to the camp, sparks rising like stars flung upward into the gathering indigo of the sky. The space was a muted simulacra of its normal cacophony of meal-time chatter and women calling orders out to each other. They still moved about, making preparations for the ritual, but silently, and as I made my way to my tent, their eyes turned away from me, hushed and somber.

Tekmessa came to my tent shortly after I arrived, as though she had been watching for me. She helped me out of my vest and tunic and washed my dusty feet in a wide copper basin. She took the rings from my hands and the silver coils from my braid, laying them aside with my clothes. She broke open one jar of frankincense we had taken from the Achaean galley, and as her hands smoothed the fragrant oil over my skin, I closed my eyes, not wanting her to see the sudden, bright blooming of tears there. I had not realized how much I missed Col's touch on my body until her hands reminded me. I wondered if she missed Esten's touch like this.

If she hated me for the fact that he had not joined us. Had not even asked to follow.

When the *zizenti* finished smoothing the oil over my body, she unplaited my hair, smoothing the waves gently over my shoulders and waist, her hands fussing more than usual. When she stood back, her eyes were inscrutable.

"Are you ready, Ishassara?" she asked, her habitually soft voice giving me comfort.

"I am."

When I followed her out into the night, the air was chilly on my bare flesh, still wet and pungent with oils. My thighs slipped against each other as we walked toward the fire, and my toes felt each thin blade of grass as they speared upward into the soles of my feet. I held my spine straight as an arrow when I walked past the ha-mazaans gathered in the lowering dark, but I felt exposed, vulnerable, and not because of my nakedness. Their eyes followed me with solemn formality. Their hands already held the stones which they would cast, either in my favor or against it.

As the last round nub of moon congealed into place above the north-eastern horizon, I turned to face them. Those closest to me were bathed in the flickering light of the fire behind me and the blinding torches beside me. The rest were mere shadows in the night, their features obscured by the dark. Unknown and hidden, just like their thoughts.

The flesh rose in bumps all along my body, the hairs standing on end even though the oils were still heavy and slick, weighing them down. But the time for doubt, for insecurity, was behind me. I must face the consequences of my own choices.

"Ha-mazaans," I said. I was glad my voice did not waver. "I stand before you as Ishassara. For this purpose, I was tasked by the Sister Queens of the Ha-mazaans and by you. And as Ishassara, I have served you to the best of my ability for a year and a day. You must choose, now. Choose whether I have been found worthy to serve you, guide you, lead you forward. Protect you. To give my life for you and the Ways of the ha-mazaans as Defending Queen. Let Kubileya be your witness, and mine."

Ossy stepped forward from the dancing shadows.

"Cyra, daughter of Melanippe," she said formally. Hearing my mother's name made my heart squeeze painfully, and I worried for a moment I would lose my composure. I fought to keep my face serene, dignified. She moved forward to stand in front of me.

"We have witnessed your service as Ishassara for a year and a day," she said. "We thank you for the defense you have provided to us. We thank you for the sacrifices you have made to protect our Ways. We thank you for the learning you have undertaken to prepare yourself as a worthy Defending Queen. Will you accept our judgment of your actions, now, as Matar Kubileya is our witness and yours?"

"I will."

"And will you allow those who do not recognize you as Defending

Queen to go freely and to decide for themselves whether they will serve another, as Matar Kubileya is their witness and yours?"

"I will."

"Kneel."

I knelt. The ground was hard under my bare knees, even through the animal skin. Ossy moved forward and marked my forehead with something sweet and musky. I could smell the fresh scent of cedar oil on Ossy's arms and the crispness of crushed grass beneath us. I smelled the smoke from the fire and the fragrant oils mixing with my own scent as they sunk into my skin. I almost thought I smelled Col, but it was only sweetgrass and leather and soft musk. I took a deep breath of it anyway, filling myself with the scents and the memory of his shining eyes, letting them add strength to my quaking heart.

"If you would be queen," Ossy said, "you must carry the burdens of those whom you would swear to serve." I felt fingers on my left hand, and she raised it in front of me, palm extended. "Let all who would serve you as queen, who are willing to trust their lives in the hands of Cyra, Daughter of Melanippe, come forward. It is time to cast your lot."

She stepped away. The wind was a gentle caress on my hand as it remained outstretched. Reaching. Waiting. I waited for what felt like an eternity, the bonfire crackling behind me with ferocious hunger. I waited so long I was sure no one would step forward, and I felt the void begin to yawn within me, deep and wide. But it was likely only a few heartbeats before the footsteps came.

"Cyra."

Alkippe's voice. She drew her dagger across her own palm, pressing her stone into the inky darkness of it. She pressed the heavy rock into the palm of my hand, and my fingers clenched around the thick wetness of it.

"With this stone, and the sacred vow of my blood, I place my life in your hands, to do with as you will. I bind with my own blood my promise to serve you as you have served me, to give my life for you, and for the Way of the ha-mazaans, as you have chosen to give yours. My axe and my service are yours. Together, may we bring glory to the Great Mother."

"May we bring glory to the Great Mother," I repeated, my tongue feeling thick and awkward. I placed the rock in front of me, gently, reverently, and extended my hand outwards once more. Alkippe's steps moved behind me to stand at my back. It was not such a long wait for the next ha-mazaan.

"Cyra." Ossy's voice. Another cut palm. "Daughter of my beloved friend. With this stone, I place my heart in your service, as I would have offered to your mother before you." Her stone pressed into my palm, and I gripped it with a fierce desperation, focusing on it to keep the tears from spilling over.

"May my words never lead you astray. And may you know that nothing you have sacrificed has been in vain. Where you lead, I am happy to follow. May our journey together bring glory to the Great Mother."

"May our journey together bring glory to the Great Mother," I repeated, hoarse with emotion.

"Cyra," Sagitta said, stepping forward with glittering eyes. The cut she made was swift. The blood felt hot on my hand when the stone pressed into it. "Sister of my heart," she said. "I pledge all that I have to you. Even the child I carry."

She pressed a hand to her stomach, and I gasped, staring up at her through tears of happiness. "You have shown me what it means to be ha-mazaan, Cyra. And I will be honored to serve at your side, to guard and protect the Defending Queen, and to raise our daughters in our Ways."

When she stepped away, I felt in a daze and had to adjust my knees again on the fur, to give my mind something to center itself again.

But there was a pause in the approaching footsteps, and I waited, wondering why the others held back. My arm trembled with the exhaustion of holding it extended for so long, and I feared my trembling was visible to everyone. Then, soft steps, uneven, slow, and purposeful. A figure loomed into the circle of firelight.

"Cyra."

Everything inside of me halted, jolted to a stop, unfinished thoughts crashing into each other with a violent, excruciating force that stilled my lungs and my heart. When it beat again, it was thunderous in my ears, drowning out every sound.

Except for his voice.

"Carrier of my soul."

I began to shake, deep in my belly.

His eyes glinted down at me, not looking away while he made the cut across his palm. A stone pressed into my hand, but I could not look away from his face. His hand squeezed around my fingers, holding the rock and my arm steady. I wanted to stand and throw myself at him, but I was frozen to the ground, immobile, unable to think clearly. Everywhere on my body was gooseflesh, tiny bubbles of skin vaulting to attention. I was suddenly very aware that I was naked, although this man had seen my body more often than any of the women here.

"With this stone, I cast my lot with yours," he said in my own language, his voice ringing through the night so that all could hear. I heard it in the deepest parts of me.

"With my own blood, I bind myself to serve you. I give you my body, that it may defend and protect you unto death. I give you my mind, that it may serve you with wisdom, with courage, and with honor. I give you my life, and I will honor you as my queen for all my days. I remind you that my heart is yours already. Always. I vow to serve you and the Way of the ha-mazaans faithfully and to protect your soul as though it were my very own, in this life and the next."

He paused, his hand still folded over mine, squeezing.

"May our love bring glory to the Great Mother."

I was supposed to respond, but I could not form my lips around the words. Could not catch my breath deep enough to move it out again. My chest felt like the bonfire had moved to burn within it. There was no movement in front or behind me. Only waiting.

"May...our love bring glory to the Great Mother," I managed huskily.

His fingers squeezed mine gently before letting go, and eventually, I placed the stone on top of the others, the clink of rock on rock grounding me somewhat. But Col did not leave. There was shuffling as many bodies moved, and Tekmessa stepped forward.

I watched in a dumb stupor as she removed Col's tunic, then his loincloth, until he was completely naked. His skin smelled of cedar oil, and when he knelt next to me, shameless in his nakedness, my head turned to him, inhaling his scent. Like leather and soft musk. *How long had he been in the crowd? How had I not noticed? And what was happening?* My mind stumbled stupidly to the broken axles on the wagons, and the sick ha-mazaans, never able to look me in the face. The furtive meetings between him and Ossy before we had left Gelonia.

They had planned this.

"Colaxais, son of Merida," Tekmessa intoned. "Keeper of our

Defending Queen's heart and spirit. One who would have been king in his own right."

Her eyes flicked to me, and a soft twinkle overrode the solemnity there.

"You kneel before us now as a man. By the sacrifice of your inheritance, and of your heart, you have proven yourself worthy to stand beside our queen, and also to protect our Ways. We recognize within you the fire that burns. We see it is of the same Source as that which burns in us. We honor this Light of Kubileya in you."

Ossy stepped forward.

"We thank you for the learning you have done, to be worthy of our Ways, Colaxais. We have witnessed your sacrifice to serve your queen. We have witnessed you serve our people, provide for them a home that is safe from harm and unnecessary bloodshed. We have witnessed you tend to the ever-burning hearthfire as a faithful servant.

"For this, we would honor you with our fealty as our Hearth King, if you would promise to fulfill this task with all the honor due to the Great Mother. Is this an honor you will accept, with a free and open heart, Colaxais son of Merida?"

"I will."

I had been watching Tekmessa and Ossy with increasing shock, but when I turned my eyes, Col's face shone in the night. His hand reached out to take mine, our fingers twining together.

"What have you done?" I whispered. It was all I could think to say. He smiled, green eyes twinkling softly down at me even in the darkness.

"What needed to be done to be with you," he said simply.

One by one, the ha-mazaans, and to my embarrassment, since I was naked, the Scoloti men and women—sixty-four of them in all who had chosen to follow a new way—stepped forward. Esten and Aife and Essri. All the women I had seen in weapons training. Men who had scouted with our ha-mazaans. Even Arnan, with only one hand. They cast their stones for a Defending Queen, or a Hearth King, or for both, which the majority did choose. And when it was over, and they smoothed cloaks over our nakedness, Col finally took my face in his hands and kissed me, his fingers a gentle anchor on my spinning soul.

EPILOGUE

Col watched the clouds float lazily across the sky. He raised a languorous hand, pointing toward one directly above.

"A leaping hare. See the legs, there? And the ears, there?"

His golden cuff flashed blindingly in the bright light, and he lowered his hand again, settling it on Cyra's thigh.

"It could be a jackal," she said, predictably contrary. The seeded end of the stalk of grass she was chewing bobbed in the air in front of the cloud rabbit.

Col chuckled. "It could be, if you are bloodthirsty and vicious like my wife."

An elbow dug sharply into his ribs, but he simply laughed and rolled overtop of her, effectively pinning her hands between the bare skin of their chests. He kissed her, and was about to attempt more, when the screeching laugh of his daughter echoed around them, shortly before her tiny body hit his, knocking him to the side. There was a tumble of legs and arms and laughing, gasping breaths as two sets of hands tickled at her, making her shriek with delight.

Then she was running again, out into the grass toward the horses, her laugh piercing into his heart until he thought it might burst with joy. When he looked back at Cyra, she was watching him with a thoughtful, serious face. He pecked her lips with a kiss and pulled her up to sit next to him.

"Why so serious?" he said, tugging her vest into place.

"I was just remembering something. A dream I once had."

"Was I in it?" he asked blithely, pulling the laces closed.

"You were," she said.

His hands smoothed over her belly before he closed the final laces and obscured her beautiful skin from his view. "Will you give me another, like Ania? I did not know my heart could be so full. I would know how full it can grow."

She frowned at him in feigned irritation, swatting his hand.

"Babes do not just grow like sheaves of rye, ready to be harvested in autumn, you know," she said sternly, but her own eyes went to their daughter, and her face softened.

Col smiled, satisfied his wife would need even less convincing than the queen in her, and lay back to find more shapes in the clouds.

) (

The Oracle had been right, in all ways. But Oracles, as I now know, are simply the Great Mother's version of practical joking, playing Her tricks on unsuspecting, hapless people through cryptic messages and half-truthed prophecies no one can correctly decipher until it is too late. It was certainly too late in my case. If I had known the truth of what she meant about my mother, or my aunts...well, I would not be where I am now, but they would be alive. We all must sacrifice something. Whether by our own choice or someone else's.

When I think of what Inara sacrificed, my heart still aches, but I only have to look at the new foal born of Faelan and the white mare who used to haul the wagons. The grey filly's eyes are young, yet I am sure the constellations spin in them. And I have not seen Inara's spirit in the woods for some time.

And when I think of Eri's prophecy...

Even now, she sits on the throne in Gelonia, next to Col's brother, and the six women still alive who pledged their loyalty to her over me are reportedly living their own destinies between those wooden walls.

When Col told me that she still lived, I could barely believe it. I had been furious when I learned that he, along with Ossy, who said she had prophecies of her own to fulfill when it came to keeping me safe, had hidden the truth from me, so that I would not ruin their perfect plans or further harm myself trying to finish a task left undone. But I cannot be angry now.

Eri found her destiny through her choices, and I through mine, and I regret nothing. She, on the other hand, must regret everything, and for that, I can only feel grief. She betrayed herself and her sisters for the sake of a prophecy she did not, could not, understand.

Whether the Oracle was right about me being the grandmother of so many, I do not know, although Col delights in teasing me about the subject far more often than is safe for his continued wellbeing. I tell him so, but he laughs and tries to kiss me again.

COMING SOON

Releasing in Winter of 2022/2023:

THE LAST HEARTH QUEEN

Discover what happens with those who were left behind in Themiscyra as the adventure continues!
sign up at www.alessandrawoodward.ca for more info.

AUTHOR'S NOTE

Dear Reader,

I hope you enjoyed this story, and that you will forgive the terrible fate of Inara. As an animal lover, this was the most difficult scene I've ever written, but it was important to portray the agency of her character, and also pay homage to the fact that many ancient cultures and religions that predate Christianity had their own concept of the "sacrificial being/god/goddess."

This story was, in essence, an origin story of the Scythian Sarmatians, woven from myth and historical retellings, and a liberal dash of fanciful imagination. Below are some "myths" and records of the Amazons vs the Achaeans, and the Amazons vs the Scythians, which served as my inspiration for how Cyra and Colaxais, two people from separate worlds, may have met and begun a new culture of the Sauromatae ("those who live free").

We know them now as the Sarmatians, one of the most powerful egalitarian cultures of the ancient world.

If you liked this book, please leave a review either on your preferred purchasing platform, or on Goodreads, and sign up for The Woodwardian Newsletter at www.alessandrawoodward.ca, where you can receieve a free downloadable bookplate featuring my own original artwork of a Greek pottery inspired ha-mazaan battle. There are companion novels on the way that will delve into what happened to those who were "left behind," and also the ha-mazaan's role in the Trojan war.

Your feedback is so appreciated, and your company on this journey of exploring the fate of the ha-mazaans is greatly cherished.

Thanks for reading!

~Alessandra Woodward

"Myth" : traditional story, especially one concerning the early history of a people or explaining some natural or social phenomenon, and typically involving supernatural beings or events.
-Oxford Reference Online, https://www.oxfordreference.com/view/ 10.1093/oi/authority.20110803100220460#, accessed 29 August 2020.
(From Herodotus, the Father of History, and the Apollodorus Library)

****

Heracles, Having put in at the harbor of Themiscyra, received a visit from Hippolyte, who inquired why he was come, and promised to give him the belt. But Hera in the likeness of an Amazon went up and down the multitude saying that the strangers who had arrived were carrying off the queen. So the Amazons in arms charged on horseback down on the ship. But when Hercules saw them in arms, he suspected treachery, and killing Hippolyte stripped her of her belt. And after fighting the rest he sailed away and touched at Troy.
—Apollodorus- The Library, 2:5:9

****

Theseus joined Hercules in his expedition against the Amazons and carried off Antiope, or, as some say, Melanippe; but Simonides calls her Hippolyte.
—Apollodorus. Epit. E.1

****

About the Sauromatae, the story is as follows. When the Greeks were at war with the Amazons (whom the Scythians call Oiorpata, a name signifying in our tongue killers of men, (for in Scythian a man is "oior" and to kill is "pata"), the story runs that after their victory on the Thermodon they sailed away carrying in three ships as many Amazons as they had been able to take alive; and out at sea the Amazons attacked the crews and killed them. [2] But they knew nothing about ships, or how to use rudder or sail or oar; and with the men dead, they were at the mercy of waves and winds, until they came to the Cliffs by the Maeotian lake; this place is in the country of the free Scythians. The Amazons landed there, and set out on their journey to the inhabited country, and seizing the first troop of horses they met, they mounted them and raided the Scythian lands.

The Scythians could not understand the business; for they did not recognize the women's speech or their dress or their nation, but wondered where they had come from, and imagined them to be men all of the same age; and they met the Amazons in battle. The result of the fight was that the Scythians got possession of the dead, and so came to learn that their foes were women. [2] Therefore, after deliberation they resolved by no means to slay them as before, but to send their youngest men to them, of a number corresponding (as they guessed) to the number of the women. They directed these youths to camp near the Amazons and to imitate all that they did; if the women pursued them, not to fight, but to flee; and when the pursuit stopped, to return and camp near them. This was the plan of the Scythians, for they desired that children be born of the women. The young men who were sent did as they were directed.

When the Amazons perceived that the youths meant them no harm, they let them be; but every day the two camps drew nearer to each other. Now the young men, like the Amazons, had nothing but their arms and their horses, and lived as did the women, by hunting and plunder.

At midday the Amazons would scatter and go apart from each other singly or in pairs, roaming apart for greater comfort. The Scythians noticed this and did likewise; and as the women wandered alone, a young man laid hold of one of them, and the woman did not resist but let him do his will; [2] and since they did not understand each other's speech and she could not speak to him, she signed with her hand that he should come the next day to the same place and bring another youth with him (showing by signs that there should be two), and she would bring another woman with her. [3] The youth went away and told his comrades; and the next day he came himself with another to the place, where he found the Amazon and another with her awaiting them. When the rest of the young men learned of this, they had intercourse with the rest of the Amazons.

Presently they joined their camps and lived together, each man having for his wife the woman with whom he had had intercourse at first. Now the men could not learn the women's language, but the women mastered the speech of the men; [2] and when they understood each other, the men said to the Amazons, "We have parents and possessions; therefore, let us no longer live as we do, but return to our people and be with them; and we will still have you, and no others, for our wives." To this the women replied: [3] "We could not live with your women; for we and they do not have the same customs. We shoot the bow and throw the javelin and ride, but have never learned women's work; and your women do none of the things of which we speak, but stay in their wagons and do women's work, and do not go out hunting or anywhere else. [4] So we could never agree with them. If you want to keep us for wives and to have the name of fair men, go to your parents and let them give you the allotted share of their possessions, and after that let us go and live by ourselves." The young men agreed and did this.

So when they had been given the allotted share of possessions that fell to them, and returned to the Amazons, the women said to them: [2] "We are worried and frightened how we are to live in this country after depriving you of your fathers and doing a lot of harm to your land. [3] Since you propose to have us for wives, do this with us: come, let us leave this country and live across the Tanaïs river."

To this too the youths agreed; and crossing the Tanaïs, they went a three days' journey east from the river, and a three days' journey north from lake Maeetis; and when they came to the region in which they now live, they settled there. [2] Ever since then the women of the Sauromatae have followed their ancient ways; they ride out hunting, with their men or without them; they go to war, and dress the same as the men.

—Herodotus, with an English translation by A. D. Godley. Cambridge. Harvard University Press. 1920.

The Scythians say ... A man whose name was Targitaüs appeared in this country ... and he had three sons: Lipoxaïs, Arpoxaïs, and Colaxaïs, youngest of the three. [3] In the time of their rule (the story goes) certain implements—namely, a plough, a yoke, a sword, and a flask, all of gold—fell down from the sky into Scythia. The eldest of them, seeing these, approached them meaning to take them; but the gold began to burn as he neared, and he stopped. [4] Then the second approached, and the gold did as before. When these two had been driven back by the burning gold, the youngest brother approached and the burning stopped, and he took the gold to his own house. In view of this, the elder brothers agreed to give all the royal power to the youngest.

—Herodotus, with an English translation by A. D. Godley. Cambridge.   Harvard   University   Press.   1920. http://www.perseus.tufts.edu/hopper/ text?doc=Perseus:text:1999.01.0126:book=4 accessed August 20 2020

ACKNOWLEDGEMENTS

No woman is an island, and no book can be birthed into the world without the aid of midwives to the creative process. Without the encouraging, tangible support of family and friends, especially the hamazaans who surround me, this book would never have been possible. While I hope that my expressions of thanks have already reached the ears and hearts of those who have my utmost appreciation, I am sure my memory falls short and my words are not enough to relay the difference so many have made in making this book a reality.

I would like to thank my mother, Isabel, for always encouraging me to pursue anything and everything creative, for supporting me in times of struggle and joy, and for consistently modeling the dedication and often torturous hard work necessary to see anything worthwhile through to the end. Thank you for providing a home, and minding me and my animals with so much love—especially when I get lost in that other world where imagination roams freely.

Thank you to my sisters, Coralie and Paula, whose adventurous, independent, horse-loving spirits have always been an inspiration of strength and capability.

Thank you to my "other parents", the ones I have been blessed to adopt as family: Theresa and Tim Noot, and Doug and Ellie Hagey, who have each provided me with home and loving support in so many ways. I spent many hours writing under roofs that were not my own, but they will always feel like home to me because of your generosity, your guidance, and your love.

Thank you to Kyla and Holly, who are the most enthusiastic, supportive cheerleaders anyone could wish for, and the best of friends. Words cannot convey my appreciation for your heartfelt support of birthing this book and watching it grow up. Many thanks to Robin, alpha and beta reader, blurb-writer, reality-checker, first developmental editor—this story would not be what it is without your invaluable input. Ellie, Sacha, Buffy, Lisbet, Kathy, Tao, Nicole, Angela, Samantha, Liisa—who bravely waded in when the waters were still murky, and helped the river of the story flow swift, smooth, and clear. Thank you.

Many thanks to developmental editor Jacquelin Cangro, for all the invaluable advice, the supportive encouragement, the way you hugged yourself when speaking of the hero in this story, and the perspective you gave for the themes nested within the plot. Thank you to my copyeditor and proofreader, Iulia Marin, who polished the manuscript into a shining jewel. Thank you to the talented Lena Yang, designer extraordinaire, who made the cover shine more brightly than I could have hoped. This book had an amazing team of women who excel in their craft, and it would not be what it is without your special touches.

To the friends and patrons who supported this writing journey, or my many, often meandering paths before this manuscript began: Amanda, Suzanne, Wanda, Gibson, Buffy, and so many more. Co-workers and colleagues, friends and sisters, coaches and confidants. You have added joy, encouragement, support, loyalty, accountability, and friendship to my life, and those things are irreplaceable.

Thank you to Adrienne Mayor, for the extensive and exhaustive research on the ancient Amazons and their historical and archaeological ties to the Scythian culture; your work infused my manuscript with life, and further bolstered in me the fierce belief in the power of women.

Thank you to all the women who have gone before, who forged the paths, burned down the established order of things, fought for justice, died for the rights of all, and made it possible to live freely, as ha-mazaan, which simply means in whatever capacity one chooses.

Finally, thank you to Mr Holtz, who, in my ninth grade English class, graciously accepted my writing assignment more than nine weeks after its due date, and more than a thousand words over limit, and returned it to me with the following note:

"A+. You are going to be a writer someday!"

Those simple words ignited a spark inside of me, a flame of hope and desire that, though it sometimes sputtered in the harsh winds of life, of doubt, of time, never went out.

Thank you, thank you, thank you.

~Alessandra Woodward

ABOUT THE AUTHOR

Alessandra Woodward is an Author, Intuitive Coach, and Creatrix. She currently lives and writes from the traditional and un-ceded territory of the Syilx peoples, in the Okanagan Valley of British Columbia, with a rescue horse named Piglet, a fierce Chihuahua named Zoë, a Maremma shieldbeast named Stormcloud, and various other well-loved rescue critters.

Sign up for her newsletter at www.alessandrawoodward.ca to get the inside scoop, and updates about new releases.

CPSIA information can be obtained
at www.ICGtesting.com
Printed in the USA
BVHW031435110921
616352BV00003B/10

9 781777 597900